Born in the Midlands city of Worcester, Susan Daniel has spent a career in education after attending Edge Hill College and obtaining a Bachelor of Education degree from the University of Liverpool and subsequently a Master of Education degree from the University of Birmingham. She continues to live in Worcestershire with her businessman husband. In retirement, with her children grown, she has been able to indulge her love of writing and *Tangled Web* is her first novel for which she has written a sequel. Susan says she enjoys all the opportunities that the freedom of retirement has given, from spending time with family and friends to keeping fit, participating in outdoor and social activities, travel and discovery as well as the quiet pleasure of her garden.

To my parents,

whose ambition, fortitude and care shaped who I am.

Susan Daniel

TANGLED WEB

AUSTIN MACAULEY PUBLISHERS™
LONDON * CAMBRIDGE * NEW YORK * SHARJAH

Copyright © Susan Daniel 2024

The right of Susan Daniel to be identified as author of this work has been asserted by the author in accordance with sections 77 and 78 of the Copyright, Designs and Patents Act 1988.

All rights reserved. No part of this publication may be reproduced, stored in a retrieval system, or transmitted in any form or by any means, electronic, mechanical, photocopying, recording, or otherwise, without the prior permission of the publishers.

Any person who commits any unauthorised act in relation to this publication may be liable to criminal prosecution and civil claims for damages.

This is a work of fiction. Names, characters, businesses, places, events, locales, and incidents are either the products of the author's imagination or used in a fictitious manner. Any resemblance to actual persons, living or dead, or actual events is purely coincidental.

A CIP catalogue record for this title is available from the British Library.

ISBN 9781035820702 (Paperback)
ISBN 9781035820719 (Hardback)
ISBN 9781035820726 (ePub e-book)

www.austinmacauley.com

First Published 2024
Austin Macauley Publishers Ltd®
1 Canada Square
Canary Wharf
London
E14 5AA

When a lifelong friend, Sue (Rosie) Wrennall, asked me about any unfulfilled youthful ambitions, it was easy to respond that I would have liked to write a novel. Her belief that it was not too late and her challenge inspired me. It was her encouragement and suggestion of a working title *Tangled Web* that put me on the road to enjoy and complete the story and for this I am truly grateful. Other friends persuaded me to seek publication. It was their confidence, reassurance and interest that gave me the courage and I thank Pat Jones and Jane Horkan. However, the driving force for me to pursue publication has been my granddaughter Erica Levett and I thank her for her enthusiasm and faith in me.

My husband and family have always been my rock allowing me to fulfil dreams and supporting any venture.

Finally, I thank my publisher for firstly taking the time to read the whole work and approve publication and then guiding me through the process with consideration for my inexperience.

Table of Contents

Chapter 1: The Lost Child — 11

Chapter 2: Take It as You Find It — 29

Chapter 3: The Loss of Innocence — 43

Chapter 4: Founding Father — 59

Chapter 5: Heads I Win, Tails You Lose — 72

Chapter 6: Love Is Where You Find It — 87

Chapter 7: Nowhere to Be Found — 99

Chapter 8: Seek and Ye Shall Find — 113

Chapter 9: Paradise Lost — 123

Chapter 10: Making Up for Lost Time — 141

Chapter 11: Better to Have Loved and Lost Than Never Loved at All — 154

Chapter 12: Finding Your Feet — 171

Chapter 13: All is Not Lost — 182

Chapter 14: Finders Keepers, Losers Weepers — 194

Chapter 15: Win Some, Lose Some — 212

Chapter 16: Find the Lady — 226

Chapter 17: Losing Your Nerve   238

Chapter 18: He Who Hesitates Is Lost   251

Chapter 19: Finding Hidden Depths   264

Chapter 20: Loss of Face   278

Chapter 21: Take Your Pleasure Where You Find It   293

Chapter 22: Long Lost Friends   306

Chapter 23: Losing the Plot   317

Chapter 24: Losing Balance   330

Chapter 25: Finding Answers   343

Chapter 1
The Lost Child

Sweetest love I do not go,
for weariness of thee.
Nor in the hope the world can show
A fitter love for me;

Song: Sweetest love, I do not go: John Donne

2005: Gillian

Gillian had been on holiday once when she was a little girl and the three of them had visited an empty beach with the sand hard packed from the tide and Gillian had drawn in that sand, words and pictures as only a child can, tracing her fingers through the soft sand until the images got larger and larger, running forward in increasing wildness and excitement, her parents at the far corner of the beach, towels spread on the rocks and a picnic basket waiting to be opened, watching their daughter, as she careered freely forward to fresh sand for her imprint. The tide turned and they called her back. At the edge of the beach, eating her paste sandwich, her heart broke as she watched the waves gradually, but relentlessly, wash away her childhood fantasy. She never forgot that hurt.

The little girl grew into a restrained young woman who joined her parents watching from their safe retreat by the rocky outcrop, sheltered from the winds of change and secure in daily routines that obscured any vision of the distant horizon. Deep down she knew she had chosen a path of avoidance and steadily built her own refuge. While other girls dreamed of palaces, Gillian built a castle that had been almost impregnable.

As womanhood progressed, she retreated into the tower that held her aloof from the dangers and disappointments of the swirling society below. Even in marriage, she guarded her heart. It was a conundrum that the more she strove for security in her life, the more she felt vulnerable. It had become easy to build a fortress against the world she feared which had imprisoned the free spirit of the child she had left on the beach.

The red brick house that was her stronghold was set back from the leafy avenue. It had a waist-high wall at the front embellished with a traditional stonework cap and a small wrought iron gate giving access to the front door. The avenue featured the tolerant and hardy plane trees planted at the time of build but now big and bold absorbing the sunlight with roots kicking at the pavement. From the gate, a little path reached to the front door before branching round the study window to the sheltered side passage. The front garden spilled onto the slabs brushing against any protuberances and making the path narrow and forbidding.

Gillian liked the feeling that she was safe inside the strong walls and could look out over the path and the wall beyond from her desk in the study, watching the infrequent passer-by as she ploughed through the annual examination papers.

In the little square of garden between the path and wall grew a hybrid tea rose called Fragrant Cloud, a gift of love, that she watched daily through the summer months and periodically escaped from her self-inflicted imprisonment to dead head with personal satisfaction, the secateurs clipping the green straight stem to discard the unwanted limp petals ready for new growth.

The rose, a vibrant shade of pink, seemed to repel the black spot that plagued the rose bed at the rear of the house. This rose was pure and exquisitely formed and unlike many modern roses its scent was powerful enough to seep into the study through its open window. For Gillian, it was a glimpse of summer as she struggled to focus her attention on the writing in front of her.

Gillian, now in her middle age, had acquired a discipline to guard her against unwanted feelings. Her years of self-reliance as an only child had made her solitary and strong. She had a quiet resilience to the turmoil that life had occasionally presented, although she had forged her way through avoidance rather than conflict. She had never been brave and never set out to conquer the world, preferring to remain hidden in the undergrowth and observe others through fronds that guarded her sanctuary.

The rose that Steve had bought her from Bill's nursery was a vindication of her outlook. It stood proud and beautiful and hardy and disease free. Gillian felt all of these things. She was fundamentally proud of her achievements after her humble beginning and she knew that when she discarded the drab teacher's attire, if she so desired, she could display physical beauty; although it was more that she felt there was an inner sanctuary that radiated from her soul as she had nobly rebuffed selfish greed, despite Abigail's assertions to the contrary, and she, like the rose, had been hardy: a survivor who would not be subsumed by the stress she had so often felt.

The rose flourished facing her from the outdoor space while Gillian toiled inside. It stood serenely in the sunshine and in a gentle breeze the leaves would flutter as if they trembled with the anxiety that Gillian tried to keep well hidden. Gillian believed she had achieved a good life so it was inexplicable that she so often felt incomplete or empty. That was a betrayal of everyone and everything she knew. It confused her.

Gillian had taught in the same comprehensive school for three decades and was confident that she had been a good teacher. Her examination classes had profited from her expertise and sheer hard work. Never had she been slack in marking work, never had she been unprepared for a lesson and never had she been dishonest with a student about their expectations and how they could achieve their hopes. She had been a consummate professional and that was her identity even in a world that had changed substantially from the beginning of her career. Gillian always persevered.

She had begun marking GCSE examination papers to alleviate their finances and now five years later it was the expected norm. The scripts would arrive from each of her allotted schools and sat behind her on the floor of the study in thick piles encroaching on her space as she sat hunched over the cluttered desk by the window.

At first she had found the marking difficult as she tried to interpret the guidelines which had at times seemed conflicting or produced what she felt had been inaccurate results but once she combined the experience of her thirty years in the classroom she found the criteria indeed supported her views and she aspired to her usual perfection, so that she consistently earned 'A' grades for her marking standard from the board.

She could be proud of this too, although there was only Steve to tell and he was pleased for her rather than impressed. Steve had never been critical of her and in fact as far as her teaching career was concerned, he had accepted any highs and lows with equal measure. School for him was a distant memory that he was only too pleased to forget. Gillian's life there was a life apart from his.

The money earned from the workload of the summer examination marking had been absorbed into the family income becoming an acceptable and useful addition rather than a perk to be squandered. Sometimes she would feel defeated by the parcels of scripts that arrived for her attention on top of her school day, but gradually, day by day, evening by evening and week by week the scripts would be marked and returned to the board leaving a clear carpet once more and a mild satisfaction of achievement.

Each year she planned to withdraw from the load but the extra income when sometimes Steve's earnings were so precarious discouraged her. Throwing in the towel became unthinkable. She thought she was being strong. Sometimes she'd hear the sound of voices through the window, laughter and distant wild shouting and screams from children playing in the sunshine. At times like this, the resentment could flare through her and she tried not to listen but occasionally could not resist the lure of joy in the air. She was honest enough to know it was not just the effort and time of the marking that took her away from the outside world but it was the noise of childish voices that hurt.

May and June and the beginning of July, those weeks of high summer, were lost to her for yet another year and sometimes with a heavy heart she consciously blocked out the sounds of life. She had a schedule to keep. The rose that bloomed in front of her window was her summer.

Gillian was a lady of mature years, as she liked to describe herself at fifty-three years old. Born in 1952, her early life had a simplicity which at the time had often felt harsh but now looking back felt charmed. Summer days were warm and winter days cold. All had been certain. For her, there had been no fears of global warming, no panics about future careers or getting on housing ladders, no travel to foreign fields as some of her grammar school friends experienced, her childhood and youth had been spent in the little house on the edge of town with her loving parents. She had been cocooned in their sedentary life and the routines of school. It had made her feel safe.

That safety had come at a cost. She saw the world through her observations of others and through her books. As a child when she was very young, she had relished the characters in her books as friends and saw how it was only circumstance that had intervened in their difficult lives to deliver them a promise of 'happy ever after'. She truly believed that fate would deliver her into a fulfilled life and destiny had marked her out for a special future. She had to be patient and wait. In the books she read it was all too clear that the heroine needed fortitude and imagination. She had adored The Secret Garden and how Mary and Dickon had brought not only the garden but Colin to life.

As she grew a little older, she marvelled at the audacity of Jo in Little Women and the spirit of Polyanna or Anne of Green Gables, or the resilience of Heidi and the nerve of Katy in What Katy Did and What Katy Did Next. These girls became her friends. They were her champions and her yardstick. Much later in her teenage years, she grasped the emotion of Cathy in Wuthering Heights, feeling an inner passion and exuberance so different from her own life. She agonised with Maggie Tulliver, wishing she had a brother like Tom even with his faults and rejection, feeling the romantic attachment of Stephen Guest, although willing Maggie to take Philip Wakem as a suitor, a sensible option while on another confusing level to her immature mind desiring the passion encountered with Stephen.

She knew she was no Maggie, with her free spirit and mourned her as if she had been a sister. There was no daring in Gillian. Later still, she used the values of Jane Austen heroines to strengthen her resolve. Sometimes she wondered if she were more suited to a nineteenth century life when rules of society would shield her from decisions.

Gillian had led a controlled life. Routine dominated her early life. Her parents had been older when she had been born, her mother almost forty and her father a year or two older. They moved to the little house when Gillian was five which allowed her mother to work part time in an insurance office to help pay the mortgage. Her parents came from humble beginnings and stressed the importance of work to reap rewards. They worked and Gillian worked. It was built in to their routines.

It was only when Gillian went to the Grammar School that she glimpsed other lives, girls who had professional fathers and not one who worked on the factory floor, girls who went to France for holidays, and girls who lived in large detached houses on the other side of town. She hid away from their glare learning the art of concealment. She travelled through school behind a veil of industry and application. It was the only way to survive.

Predictably she attended teacher training college and maintained her demeanour. When contemplating Robert Frost's poem, 'The Road Not Taken', she realised that back then there had been no choice in the road for her, rather she had stayed rooted at the crossroads. It had been a safe option. Her parents were delighted, she had a secure income and she continued to live in the little house on the edge of town.

She sighed, momentarily distracted by her musing and with a little shake of the head concentrated on her task. The exam paper on her desk was neatly written. She had already marked most of the paper. The Marion Richardson style of handwriting was thankfully easy to read even if childlike in substance. She cast her practised eye back over its contents and noted the candidate had chosen to write a response to a task on something or someone he or she treasured. She prepared herself for the tedium based on the degree of insight from the rest of the paper.

The creative writing could be vital for this candidate who was definitely from the other responses border line in ability. Conscious of the importance she must concentrate and give a fair assessment. Later this evening she could unwind with a glass of that new wine as she listened to Steve recount his exploits of the day.

She began to read:

When I was 15, I decided I wanted to know about my mum. One day when Dad was at work and I was bored so I looked in his bedroom for clues. She had left when I was a toddler. I think I remember her a bit but I might have just thought I did from the photograph on the mantelpiece. I always wanted to know why she had gone but I did not want to upset my dad so I thought there might be something in his bedroom. My dad never talked about her. He said I was enough for him and we were a team and we did not need anyone else. It made me sad. Sometimes Auntie Vera would mention her but always in a whisper and then she would look at me.

This definitely had possibilities and Gillian was already intrigued which was a good sign. She had read too many essays where candidates had found valuable booty or described a well-loved grand parent or friend. This had potential.

Dad wasn't great at doing housework and there was washing on the floor and lots of clutter on the bedside table and chest of drawers. There was a magazine on his bed with a woman in a red bikini on the front. There was dust around too and there was a coffee stain on the carpet by the bed.

Gillian smiled, acknowledging that this paragraph was good. It was clear with some descriptive detail. Gillian took up her red biro to credit the candidate with appropriate notes in the margin of the script.

Gillian drew a breath and read of the frustration as the candidate listed the myriad items from the various drawers. She sighed as she found the section boring, although it did convey the life of the man involved. Gillian willed the boy to recapture the earlier style. She inevitably felt a responsibility in her assessment. While examination marking was tedious in the main, Gillian had learnt from the kaleidoscope of life presented through essays, sometimes too personal for their teachers. A stranger was someone they could address and sometimes rant at the world and sometimes divulge deep dark fears.

Gillian dreaded reading of abuse or criminal activity and the responsibility of passing her findings to the examination hierarchy. A greater fear was in reading of fantastical stories and rather than alert her seniors dismiss cries for help. Somehow the students unfolded themselves to her even in the most simplistic writing. She often felt privileged to be the reader.

The wardrobe was stuffed full. It was the last place to look but apart from old clothes that should have been taken to the charity shop years ago there was nothing much, more magazines with naked women, an old sewing box, a small broken lamp, a picture of a wood in spring with bluebells and then underneath the picture there was a shoe box.

Again, this was a better piece of description. The candidate had built some dramatic tension. Her red pen highlighted the fact and she was eager to continue.

I expected nothing but I opened the lid and looked inside. There were papers, a little notebook, a couple of rolls of film and a couple of old photographs. I peered at them but they were faded and unclear.

Gillian's red pen circled the vocabulary.

One showed a girl of about four in an old-fashioned dress sitting on a swing and the other the same girl holding a doll. At the bottom of the box was a letter. I opened it.

This candidate at times could engage the reader. She wondered what he would have been like to teach as she instinctively recognised potential. He had his own voice, although kept to a safe, careful delivery and with the right encouragement she was convinced he could develop his writing further. Gillian's great asset as a teacher was the urge she always felt to push her students. With this candidate, Gillian began to feel pleased that she should be able to find enough evidence to award marks for the essay that would help to secure an overall 'C' grade.

Gillian read on concentrating on the discovery. The idea of a letter was appealing; perhaps it was a love letter maybe from war-torn lovers. Gillian could never resist romance and her heart beat a little faster. Indeed the candidate had reproduced an extract which did set her heart racing because the words took on a familiarity and a memory bubbled inside her. She reached for a tendril of hair that she began to twist round her finger.

The candidate revealed the content of the letter and she could not suppress a little gasp as the candidate imparted the plea of the letter writer to forgive. Gillian felt hot and her chest tightened as she reread the words that the candidate had reproduced so accurately. Her finger gripped the lock of hair more tightly and it began to pull against her scalp.

As she read Gillian left her role as examiner and was suddenly transported to a different time, a time of her life that she had not thought of for years, a time that had been suppressed into her sub-conscious when she had written a letter. The boy had quoted phrases that had clearly made an impact. Gillian paused and felt a slight nausea. The words resonated as though they had been written yesterday. In her heart she knew they had been written thirty-five years before.

It was like finding a ghost of her past. She felt her muscles tense and her brain battle against the nuances of the discovery. She took several deep breaths and smoothed her hair, arguing that this was unlikely to be the same letter. It was a coincidence and she must squash the awful fear that had stolen into her stomach. She was tired and ready for a rest. It had been a long day. How could a candidate of just sixteen be in possession of the letter from so many years ago?

Within a few minutes she had managed to quell the misgiving and continue with the task in hand. She was once more in control and had taken on the mantle of examiner. It had just been a reminder, a quirk and nothing more. She had suppressed the episode and was determined that the memory would not disrupt her. The essay yielded nothing more about the letter or its writer or his family. It had momentarily taken her breath away but still she feared its portent. She did not want more knowledge of the writer because she found she already knew.

There was little chance of identifying the candidate from his examination number even if she could establish the school from the centre number and right at that moment she wanted distance between them.

It was important for each candidate to be anonymous as far as the marker was concerned and she was glad of it. Gillian pushed the paper into the pile and tried to focus on the remaining papers from this centre. Before doing so she took a quick break to go outside in the fresh late afternoon air pausing merely to clip a beautiful bloom of the rose to bring inside and place in a thin vase on her desk. She needed its essence.

Later that evening she sat glass in hand, face poised, as she listened to Steve recount his efforts to complete the renovation of the run down terraced house he and Simon had bought several months previously. Steve described himself as a property developer and certainly over the years, multiple properties had passed through his hands.

As they drove around the town, he would proudly point out the flats and small houses he had bought and sold, always with a profit to vindicate the initial purchase. Gillian who had another handle on their finances never liked to remind him of the spending required to achieve the said profit. There was enough to worry about without adding the burden of a recalcitrant husband to the mix. He was happy and occupied. She could live with that.

"Michael is going to fit the new kitchen next week. I got a good deal there. I was lucky to get those show units at rock bottom price. It's really going to sell the place. These days everyone wants a smart, modern kitchen even in a small house. Some of those people who live in Rashwood hardly have two pennies to rub together and yet they have fancy stuff. Michael will be able to make it fit. He's a great workman. I know he takes time but it will be well done and it will sell quickly I just know it.

"It's a pity I could not do it myself but the Kings are good customers and I can't let them down. Anyway, we are lucky that Michael was free so we do not have any delays. When it does sell, maybe we could take the trip to Italy we talked about. You look tired. Take a break. You are working too hard. I can't believe how much time you spend on all that stuff."

It had been a difficult day and she felt angry and sad. Her equilibrium had been shattered and in response her thoughts directed any venom at Steve, although she tried to allow his comments to drift over her as she sipped the ruby liquid and as they did, she could not help editing them in her mind with increasingly barbed comments arising from her emotion. Her finger twisted her hair as she listened. She said little but as usual thought much and as each thought popped maliciously into her head, she felt the rise of her blood pressure.

The kitchen might have been cheap but how much will it cost to get a master carpenter to fit them? Michael is not cheap. The thought answered her anger as well as raising her esteem.

Our kitchen is old. It needs updating. You are like a cobbler who does not see the holes in his own children's shoes. She was tired but as she formed the thought, she grudgingly recalled the kitchen Steve had installed at her father's house and for an instant yearned to be back there until Steve prompted another bitter response.

Lucky people at Rashwood! Half of them are on benefits amounting to more than I earn. Maybe they can afford it. She would never utter this but it was satisfying to acknowledge her own feelings of abuse.

What trip? The one I've wanted for the last five years. This thought prompted her eyes to water perhaps from the regret of the hard pulling of her hair as her temper rose at the injustice.

How can we do that? It won't be sold for weeks and weeks, well after my summer break. Gillian looked down to stop the glare she might have given her husband. Sometimes he was an impossible dreamer.

Of course I'm tired. Teaching and marking to pay the mortgage. It was not true but this thought made her feel empowered.

Steve smiled at her and took another gulp of his lager. She felt crabby. She began to release the lock of hair.

'You're not listening. I know you're tired but this is important to us and you ask me to share things with you. I need you on board, Gill. We're a team.'

Team, Gillian thought, was this a man's expression to move away from difficult issues? She thought of the candidate whose father had pushed him away with the word team. There's no 'I' in team. That was the saying. It was popular at school, too. Certainly in the home team she thought there was no Gillian and maybe the exam boy, too felt excluded at home.

After all, there had to be a team captain who often selected the team and decided on style of play. Gillian thought of teams she knew. Premier League teams with star players taking the glory and the wages to match, officious super charged managers who despite their assertions could be sacked in an instant by the board if found wanting, the hopeful young players promoted to the bench before being cast into obscurity after being brought on the pitch in a crucial moment only to fail in that ten minute window of opportunity. She remembered other teams.

At school the clique of the netball and hockey teams with their high-handed dismissiveness of anyone who did not measure up. That was funny too. Gillian had been rather good at games but her lack of height betrayed her as the rather more well-endowed girls stole the limelight. *I wonder where they are now* she thought. Gillian no longer wanted the team. She had played in defence for years and years, she had bowed to the style of play in her parent's team, on marriage she had fielded the penetration into her life from the precious ex-wife and the son with the ego of Colossus, and she had held fast against the onslaught of classes of frustrated teenagers, and headed away attacks from the insufferable heads of year or department, and faced the derision from the stands of the parents of power and finally she had taken the penalties from the husband of self-delusion.

Gillian could not hold back the tide of emotion flowing over her. She wanted to be calm and reasonable but underneath there was a wave of passion that she could not dispel. The turbulence of her thoughts was still hidden by her composed exterior.

"Another glass of wine? No school tomorrow so maybe it would do you good to unwind and we can make a night of it." With twinkling eyes, he sought her acquiescence.

She shook away her thoughts and looked at him realising with a jolt that she had been cruel in her contemplation and here was a wonderful man. Steve was her solid foundation. He poured her another glass; bending over her and reaching with his spare hand to brush significantly across her breast. Gillian as ever was lost. She had reasserted her equilibrium from a simple touch of affection.

She awoke at two o' clock and remembered the evening before. She had luxuriated in Steve's embrace, and as his demands reached a pinnacle, she had allowed herself to become abandoned in an emotional zenith. She had been so near her climax when somehow she was gripped by a rationale which forfeited her delight. Steve absorbed in his own passion was unaffected and left her, pushing himself to the side, caressing her hand and then her thigh uttering a guttural thank you before slipping into a position for sleep.

Gillian settled into the familiar groove of his body and urged herself into sleep aided by the wine. Now in the early hours she was awake and emotional.

She had deliberately avoided ruminating about the boy but now in the deep dark she silently allowed memories to invade her peace.

It was such a long time ago and buried, she had thought to disappear without trace but the awakening had been unexpected and disconcerting. In bed she tried not to tremble as she was overcome with sensation. Steve was slumped on his side of the bed. She must be still. She must not disturb him as she was disturbed.

It was morning break in spring of her Upper Sixth when she found Diana in the toilets throwing up.

"I'll get someone."

"No don't. You mustn't."

"But you're not well."

Diana emerged pale from the cubicle, "I'm fine really. All better now."

Gillian was not convinced and gave her a sympathetic glance.

"Look," Diana reached out her arm as if to restrain. "I've been a bit silly and I don't want Mum to know. They were out last night and I sort of raided the drinks cabinet. This is my punishment and I'm much better now."

Certainly Diana's colour was returning and her voice had gained strength. Gillian remembered Diana's mother, a lady of some authority and standing, definitely not a modern woman in any respect or given to levity, someone who could pierce through any story of excuse and cast an attitude of disapproval that was unlikely to be forgotten.

"But won't she realise when she notices the missing booze?" Gillian's logical brain prompted the question.

"No it's ok. They had a party at the weekend and really they don't know how much was drunk so as long as you don't say anything…." Diana implored, fixing her dark blue eyes on Gillian.

Gillian had been flattered to hold the secret. Diana was nice and generally friendly but Gillian was usually beneath her notice. She had admired Diana, a girl who had charm and panache. Diana was usually the centre of attention and other girls shimmered from her brilliance. Her portrayal of Titania in Midsummer Night's Dream had been stunning. She had taken on the ethereal quality of the role in the blend of her movement and voice. It had been a truly commanding performance.

Diana was a leading lady at school while Gillian had a walk-on part. Gillian came from the wrong side of town and Gillian was always conscious of her nonprofessional parents. The request for discretion was of no consequence to her and it seemed to matter hugely to Diana.

"Of course, I won't say anything if you don't want but do take care. There's an awful bug going around and you don't want to be ill with A levels round the corner."

"I'm sure it's the alcohol. I was getting stressed and mixed the drink. You won't say anything to the other girls either," Diana was insistent.

"Not if you don't want. Honestly, I was only bothered about you. I'll forget all about it." Gillian basked in the knowledge. Discretion would be easy. She did not mix with Diana's set and she rarely volunteered information in conversations. She had always kept a lid on her personal life.

The bell was ringing and Diana obviously relieved, asked what lesson Gillian had next, making a witty detrimental comment about the teacher concerned as though they were best buddies.

Gillian genuinely forgot about the encounter. She had so much to do and worried about the examinations to come. She knew she needed to prepare well. There were no brothers or sisters at home to disturb or help her or even aspire to and her parents had had no formal education which might assist their daughter so it was up to Gillian to set the standard. It was not the same for the Diana's of this world.

Her next encounter with Diana was about a month later. They had exchanged pleasantries in between and nodded or smiled in corridors as they journeyed to their prospective classes. Gillian had a free period and as was allowed went into the sunshine to read her revision notes. She would find a quiet corner so she could concentrate. Gillian had been a retiring girl, so she knew where she might find her solitude. If she skirted the PE store and nipped through to the back of the gym there was a narrow strip of grass along the hedge which lined the back road.

There were no benches there and strictly speaking, she should not be there, but Gillian loved its privacy and the small enclosed space between building and bramble gave her protection. The grass was longer here, too and as she lay down it gave off a summer fragrance.

All she had to do was make sure there were no tell-tale grass stains on her school dress and not doze so that she missed her next lesson. The school, even for sixth formers, took a dim view of tardiness or unnecessary absence but she had lots of time that day as the free period adjoined the lunch break. She had spread her books and files on the grass and curled her body so she could access them easily. Soon she was both in tune with the day and thankfully also her task.

A small noise caught her attention. Damn, she thought, I am really getting this at last. Fearing discovery, she tried to shrink into the shadow of the hedge near her chosen spot. She could see no-one but there it was again like a muffled breath and a muted cry. It was definitely human. Gillian peered out from her nest of grasses. There was someone at the far end of the gym wall.

Whoever it was, leaned against the wall as if needing its support. She watched and saw the heaving shoulders and the arms that alternately hugged the leaning figure or obscured the face. It was clear this girl was distressed. She could not from this point with the sun in her eyes identify the person but she knew it would have to be a sixth-former. Gillian could not continue her study so tentatively got to her feet and quietly made her way to the girl. It was Diana.

"Hello. Can I help?"

Diana was startled, so absorbed had she been in her own misery.

"Oh gosh, it's you."

"I'm sure it's not as bad as all that. It can be sorted." Gillian was at a complete loss.

"You don't understand. It's too late. I'm lost," Diana's eyes looked momentarily wild as they glistened with tears. "Please leave me alone. I don't want anybody," and a sob erupted suddenly spilling a sliver of spit from her mouth.

Gillian was astonished. Never before had she seen anyone so distressed, well maybe in films when there was always exaggeration, but at school or home it was restraint at all times and, especially someone of the calibre of Diana. It was like witnessing a sleek yacht in peril in a maelstrom. This was serious, she could tell. If only she could walk away and leave her alone.

"Look I've been revising over there. It's quite private. Let's sit down. I brought my lunch out so we can eat and I have water. It will make you feel better." Gillian did not want the intrusion but she could see the despair in Diana's face and her natural compassion wanted to provide a life line and help her out of her misery. Diana had seemed hunted and vulnerable. Gillian was kind.

Reluctantly Diana acquiesced. Gillian knelt down and Diana sat elegantly beside her.

"You don't need to say anything. Sometimes, life seems impossible, doesn't it? I can listen if you want but it's your call."

"I'm pregnant."

Cocooned in her bed with Steve breathing steadily beside her Gillian recalled the shock she had felt at the time and her ineffectual responses. Diana talked steadily while Gillian floundered. Gillian had no experience to draw on, and as she listened she realised how naïve and innocent she really was. Her older-self reflected on how different things had become for the modern teenager. Indeed 'history was another country'. The swinging sixties were not swinging for many.

There was the music, the beat to which they all danced, the songs of unrequited love and desire, the apparent arrogance of the boys, which probably hid their feelings of inadequacy, through their group dynamics and chat up lines and most girls who lived in mortal fear of pregnancy as much as from the sexual act itself. Gillian had been in awe that someone she knew had actually done it. Gillian had never been to parties or rather the kind of parties that some of the other girls attended.

Boys were completely outside her radar and even at seventeen she had a very haphazard notion of what went on between the sexes. Her understanding was that in the real-world marriage was a precursor to any intimacy. Her personal experience was sadly lacking and, although she had attended to conversations with other girls on the subject there had never been enough detail to imbue her with understanding or any confidence in relationships so she had kept aloof and unattainable. Diana however, had not had any restrictions and had seemed impervious to any recrimination or responsibility. To know that Diana was no longer a virgin had aroused shock in Gillian who had determined to preserve hers at all costs until the time was right.

"What are you going to do?" Gillian dreaded the answer.

"I tried to get rid of it—you know the scalding bath and gin. It doesn't work. You found me in the toilets the next morning."

A stunned Gillian could only gape at the disclosure but then asked what she thought was an obvious question.

"Will the father stand by you?"

Diana looked horrified and then almost amused.

"Don't be ridiculous. There's no way I would want to harness myself to him. It was just fun. You know. I've been so unlucky."

Gillian's hackles rose and she swallowed a mouthful of her water. Gillian had no answer. Her world was different. She was torn between condemning the boy for being so cavalier and condemning Diana for not at least acknowledging her part in this catastrophe. To Gillian it was a catastrophe. To have a baby was a life defining event. A baby required love and care, a tender unselfish commitment, a safe haven in which to grow and develop, a family to nurture and teach it the ways of the world and more than anything a parent to protect it.

"At least, I don't think I look pregnant, do I?"

Gillian nodded. "I think I can get through the exams without anyone knowing. Thank goodness there's no PE. That would be too hard. I know I will have to tell Mum and get organised. It's been so helpful talking it through with you. I feel so much better. Don't forget Mum's word," and she giggled. "Did you say you had some lunch to spare? I seem to get ravenous."

Suddenly, Gillian had gone cold and she pulled the bed covers over her and stared at the ceiling. There had been no 'talking through' as far as she remembered. Diana had been oblivious to her lack of response. Steve turned and flung his arm over her and she used it like a lifeline clinging to it to escape the past.

After Diana's confidence, the next few weeks were spent revising and then doing the exams. She would look for Diana but their exam timetable didn't coincide much. Gillian was stunned at how unperturbed Diana seemed and one day she had the opportunity to ask her how she was. Diana said she was well, seeming pleased to have Gillian's interest, and said she was forgetting about it until it mattered. Gillian could not help but admire the girl and promised to keep quiet. She hoped that when the time came for the birth, she would be permitted to see and even cuddle the baby. There had never been any experience of babies in her young life and she dreamed of one day having a family of her own.

Gillian kissed Steve's arm feeling the light hairs brush across her lips. She studied his face, the muscles relaxed in slumber and his mouth slightly open fishlike as he took in air and emitted the occasional snore. Even after all these years, she felt jealous of Diana.

Diana had contacted her at the end of the exams and all these years later she realised had used her. Diana had told her mother. Gillian could only imagine the exchange but the upshot was never in doubt as far as Diana and her mother were concerned. Diana would go away, a treat after the exertions of exams, and then at a discreet unit would give birth and return home alone and unencumbered.

Until her departure, Gillian was chosen as a suitable companion, invited to spend time with Diana as she eased more into her obvious pregnancy. Diana's mother and Diana banked on her discretion, after all she had said nothing so far and she did not hang about with Diana's usual set. In those few weeks they talked about anything and everything. Gillian was surprised by Diana's love of poetry and her powers of recitation. Gillian began to get a grasp of the conventions of the society in which Diana lived. She felt sympathetic and pleased that her own background which at times seemed remote had in fact more freedom of expression.

Gillian learnt a lot from Diana. She had wondered what Diana had gained from the time they had spent together that summer and now thought she had been merely some sort of agreeable companion. Gillian acknowledged it had been an unequal relationship. When Diana departed for London, they had corresponded. For Gillian it had been a glimpse of another life. She had found Diana confusing, sensitive and imaginative and fun but at the turn of a switch brutal and cold and calculating. Diana's mother cast a shadow over the house. Gillian had often cowered in her presence. Gillian had liked Diana.

Gillian thought back and wondered why she had done it. It was such a stupid thing to do and none of her business. What repercussions might there have been and even had been? The letter had resurfaced or was it a coincidence, some awful black comedy at her expense? The birth seemed to have gone easily and the arrangements for the disposal of the infant made. Diana was allowed to visit the foster mother who had the care of the baby until adoption was completed.

Gillian who had lived the whole experience with Diana felt nothing but compassion. The baby, who Diana named Louise, captured Gillian's heart. She hated feeling a willing conspirator and yearned to rescue Louise from the uncertain future. Diana returned home and after meeting briefly with Gillian she resumed her old friendships leaving Gillian confused and within weeks sidelined. True, Gillian was busy at college and Diana had got a job arranged by her parents in London but the letters dwindled into nothing.

Gillian understood. Diana would not want to be reminded. Gillian had been expendable. Louise, however, shouldn't be and when Diana had said she had declined to leave any mementos or personal letter to go with the adoption papers; Gillian felt compelled to write the heartfelt letter. Louise would need reassurance. Louise would need to know she was loved. Diana should have written.

Gillian could not bear such an omission. It had been one of the few impulsive actions of Gillian's life and now in the early hours dark outside with only the glimmers of street lights and the digital clock counting down life's minutes and

Steve's bulk breathing beside her she felt tingles of panic at what she had done mixed with a deep yearning for the baby who had been wasted from a moment of fun. She thrust her fist in her mouth to smother the inner scream for her own childless state.

The following morning when she sat at her desk to resume her marking she saw the rose so recently picked had drooped in the vase, its head had bowed limply and forlornly and two fallen petals were curled on the surface below instantly reminding Gillian of teardrops and once again she experienced a rush of unwanted emotion.

Chapter 2
Take It as You Find It

*While better men than we go out and start their working lives
At grubbing weeds from gravel paths with broken dinner-knives.*
The Glory of the Garden: Rudyard Kipling

2001-2007: Jake and Jim

Jake, the student who had caused Gillian such consternation, spent the rest of the morning pulling up the carrots and picking the peas. The carrots were small and slid easily out of the soil. Their amber colour glowed through their foliage. He hunted down the pea pods relishing the task and occasionally splitting a pod open to taste the sweet contents. He took his time as the day opened up before him.

The other kids had gone into town to celebrate but Jake had slouched away saying he might join them later. They shouted after him but he had merely shrugged his shoulders. Somehow, he did not feel like a raucous ramble through the town square. He wanted to savour the moment. His GCSE results were better than expected which gave him satisfaction, although he knew he was no academic.

In the early days of secondary school, he had been feted for his football talents and secretly he had harboured hopes of a signing from a professional club. As the years slipped by, he realised he was a useful amateur and should have put more effort into his school books than his football training. He had no regrets but he did not see the point of downing cans to prove a point of success. Maybe, he was just odd.

Mr Woodhouse three doors down had got him interested in gardening. Sometimes he would chat with Ken, Jake's dad, as they sat over a pint in the pub garden when Jake had been little and played with his ball. Mr Woodhouse was a widower who later started talking to him as he practised his football moves in the street. Mr Woodhouse knew a thing or two about football. He had been groundsman at the City and had met lots of the players. By the time Jake knew him he had retired and scraped by on a limited pension. Mr Woodhouse said he would not change a thing. He had been a decent footballer in his time but an ankle injury had scuppered his chances.

"Them were the days when the balls were hard and men were fierce," he would say. Mr Woodhouse did not have much time for the 'mamby pamby' footballers of the modern era.

Jake had been twelve when Mr Woodhouse took him in hand.

Jake had so wanted the boots. Of course his dad could not be expected to get them. It was stupid to ask. One day, Mr Woodhouse caught him looking at them in the sport shop window in town. "What are you after then, young Jake?"

Jake turned with a practised dismissive air. "Nothing. Just looking."

"I know, you young lads of today have a hankering after the new kit but you know there'll be another better kit tomorrow and another even better kit the tomorrow after that. It's what's inside the kit that counts, lad."

Jake had walked back with Mr Woodhouse who told him more stories of past players. Jake knew if he had opportunity he wouldn't squander it like some of these players had. The day was cold and Jake without a big coat had shivered slightly.

"Hey lad it's a bit parky out 'ere. Let's go and have a cuppa. It'll warm us up a bit."

Jake had never been into Mr Woodhouse's house before but Dad was at work and his house was cold and unwelcoming. "Thanks Mr Woodhouse. I'd like that."

The little semi-detached house was a replica of the house Jake and his dad occupied but it could not have been more different. Mr Woodhouse hung up his anorak on the hooks in the hallway and bustled into the front room to turn on the electric fire. Jake hung around in the hall way before following the old man into the cosy kitchen where he filled the electric kettle and took a flowery teapot from the shelf. Everything was tidy and clean. The surfaces only supported essential items and there was a plant on the windowsill in a bright red pot. Mr Woodhouse seemed to guess his thoughts.

"Ida used to keep everything spotless you know, always grumbling about my dirty boots traipsing mud round the place so I think I owe it to her to try to keep it up. Mind you it's not easy and you really appreciate what a woman did after she's gone."

Jake looked away. Mr Woodhouse looked sad. Jake wished he could remember his mum. Did she keep the house smart and tidy?

Mr Woodhouse reached for two mugs from the wall cupboard.

"If Ida had been here, she'd have insisted on a cup and saucer but me, I like a good big mug. Anyhow, I broke most of them in the first six months after she died. She was a good woman but could be a bit pernickety, you know."

Jake didn't know but he nodded.

"Here we are lad. Now get this down you. You look frozzen. Aye and I've got some chocolate digestives 'ere. We need spoiling on a grey day like this."

Jake followed him into the front room. Mr Woodhouse sat on a big armed chair on the opposite side to the modest television in the corner by the window. Jake perched on the sofa and as he relaxed began to lean back into the squishy covers. Looking out of the window Jake realised that Mr Woodhouse could see not only the street but the patch of wasteland beyond where the lads generally played their football.

Jake's own house only looked out onto the parked cars and the last house on the opposite side. The yellow lines in front of Mr Woodhouse's home meant he had a clear view. Mr Woodhouse caught Jake's scrutiny.

"I've watched you many a time. You're good son I'll give you that. Best of the bunch, I'd say."

Jake stared back at Mr Woodhouse. There had been little praise given in his lifetime. Football had been an accepted skill from a young age that had made him popular with the older boys when they needed him to help turn a match but otherwise they left him alone and his dad was generally too busy to watch him play. Football had been an escape as well as a means of expression.

"That fair tall lad, he thinks he's something, doesn't he?"

Jake realised he was talking about Carl.

"Dirty player. Uses his muscle and little else. Bit of a bully I'd say. Watch him. You have the march on him and he's not the type to like it."

Carl was the king pin in the group and the others followed his lead. Jake realised that none of them would really challenge that. It had got annoying sometimes as Jake wanted to take the ball forward but the bulk of Carl demanded he pass.

Jake did not know what to say, so said nothing and took another digestive from the plate.

There was a bookshelf under the window crammed full of books. There were few books in his house, although there were newspapers and some magazines that his dad furtively took up to his bedroom. Jake's teachers had kept urging him to read more. Occasionally he would bring a book home from the school library but often took it back unfinished, as he had spent his time playing with the lads and the librarian had wanted it back. He never renewed it as he did not want to admit he had not read it in the time allowed.

"I like my football," Mr Woodhouse said, "but by god, it's changed. Watch the odd match on the box you know but rather watch you lot and do me garden."

"Dad doesn't have time to do the garden and with his bad back I have to keep it tidy," Jake volunteered.

"I know you do, lad. Seen you cutting the grass with that old mower and a bit of digging at the front."

"Dad says keep the front straight and not worry about the back." Jake somehow felt he had to justify things. Mr Woodhouse looked at him with a perception that was rather unnerving, although it also aroused Jake's curiosity. At twelve he was beginning to want a diversion from his current existence.

"I'll show you my garden in a bit if you like. Be nice to see what you think and the weather seems a bit brighter now."

The sun had begun to seep through the low clouds and the wind had dropped when they went outside. Again, Jake could not help comparing it with the wilderness at home. Here was a small lawn edged with shrubs against the fence, a fence not broken and leaning but upright and freshly painted with creosote.

A little greenhouse was on the other side and beyond that a cold frame in which were plants that Jake couldn't identify. Beyond the lawn was another flower bed and then there was a low wall dissecting the garden. A path skirted the lawn with a washing line draped above it. Mr Woodhouse led him beyond the wall to a patch of vegetables. To Jake, there seemed every vegetable he could think of but at the time he was easily impressed.

"Here I'll cut you a cauli and get you a few carrots and you can have them with your Sunday roast."

Jake did not like to say they rarely had a Sunday roast. Sundays were a late lie in and if he was lucky a fry up before his dad would head off to his local. Jake might go to the park to see who was around or if any of the local boys were up for a kick-about he would go to the waste ground opposite Mr Woodhouse. Dad usually stayed out until late afternoon and then full of beer collapse on the settee to sleep it off. Jake would try to get on top of his homework.

"Thanks Mr Woodhouse. Great having stuff straight from the garden. I'd better be off now. Dad will wonder where I am."

Jake hated lying but he did not want to hurt the old man's feelings.

"Come and see me again if you like. Kettle always on."

His dad was not home when he got there. The house was cold. There were newspapers and the chip papers from the night before strewn on the floor by the couch. The racing pages were visible and Dad's pen-circles were around the names of runners for the Lucky 15 he placed every Saturday. Sometimes, Jake and his dad watched the racing on the television but more often his dad was down at Corals on Baxter Street.

Somehow, Jake wanted the order he had just left and made an instant decision that it would be up to him, his dad was a lost cause in that respect. By the time his dad returned he had tidied away the debris, washed up the mugs and dishes left over from the last couple of days, put the burnt pan to soak and cleaned what surfaces he could find. He felt good when he had finished. Dad was in a great mood too. He had a win and his 10 pence lucky had yielded fifty quid. They had a Chinese for tea. Jake was happy.

Jake and Mr Woodhouse became an unlikely pair. For the next few years Mr Woodhouse would chat to him about his football and show him the wonder of the garden. Jake learnt when to sow seeds, the best fertilisers to use, how to prune and how to take cuttings. He began to apply the lessons to the garden at home and tore down the undergrowth making way for new growth.

At first, his results were inconsistent but the pride he felt when he picked the runner beans, the lettuce, radishes and spring onions was even as good as scoring the winning goal. He began to grow courgettes and peas and peppers. His dad would sit on the chair at the back porch watching him.

"You're a wonder you are son. Don't know where you get the green fingers from. Can't be me."

Jake wondered if it was his mother.

"Did Mum garden?" Jake casually asked him one day.

"No she liked sunbathing but never saw her garden. I did a bit until my back went."

On a clear April day when Jake was fifteen after a day helping Mr Woodhouse who was finding the exertion of digging more and more onerous they sat together at the kitchen table sharing their customary mug of tea and digestive and Jake plucked up the courage to ask.

"Did you know my mum?" Jake ventured. He waited for an answer. He tried to keep his tone casual but underneath he was nervous. Jake had grown noticeably since first visiting Mr Woodhouse. He was what Mr Woodhouse would call a 'strapping lad' which had begun to earn him admiring looks from some of the girls, in fact he realised, he had pulling power as far as the opposite sex was concerned. He was not sure why he held back but there was a sort of unfinished business in his head that made him hesitant to form a relationship.

"Not very well. Saw her out and about you know and passed the time of day. She seemed very nice, pretty too, no wonder your dad wanted the two of you."

It seemed a strange thing to say. Of course he would want his wife and his son when he was born.

"There was a bit of gossip at first when you and your mum first showed up. Your dad didn't seem to be the settling down type but it was clearly a happy house. It was a shock when she left."

Jake sat frozen. Mr Woodhouse did not realise anything was amiss and continued.

"You were a bonny baby. All the women fussed over you. I remember when you and your mum came to live with Ken. He smartened himself up pretty sharpish. He obviously thought the world of you both. To be honest after his mother died he rather let himself go. She was the sort of woman who fussed, he would not have had to do a thing when she was alive and then she died suddenly when he was only twenty. He went off the rails a bit, you know drinking a bit hard and too much spent at the bookies but he was a decent chap at heart and your mum and you brought the sparkle back."

Jake had been studying the vase of daffodils on the kitchen table. Their trumpet flowers seemed to shriek and scream at him. 'Ask him' they seemed to shout nodding their heads in agreement. He thought how remarkable they were, standing strong and straight on slender stalks and vibrant with their golden corolla robustly ready to repel the early storms of the year. Jake felt feeble and frightened but these noble blooms gave him courage.

"Another cup me lad? You've worked hard today. I dunno what I'd do without you these days. I used to be able to work at the ground and then come home and dig the whole patch. I'm getting old. Be my turn to push up daisies before too long. Wonder how many more springs I'll get to see."

"Don't say that!" Jake almost shouted. His eyes were wet.

"Nay lad. Don't you get yourself all in a tizz. We all have to go sometime, that's nature and I've had my three score and ten. Didn't mean to upset you. Didn't know you cared." Mr Woodhouse winked. "Here, have another digestive."

Jim Woodhouse had been taken aback by the reaction and, while it perturbed him, he also felt gratified. Jake had begun to mean a lot in his life. He had no children with Ida and as the pragmatist he was he had expected to see out his days with independence and self-preservation but Jake had become a natural fixture. There was no expectation but they had gravitated to each other. Jake had filled a void for Jim that he had not even known had existed until that moment.

Jake did not ask Mr Woodhouse any more or for that matter his dad. When he thought of his dad, he would curl his tongue round the word wondering if he had been duped all these years and desperately clinging on to the hope that Mr Woodhouse was mistaken. Jake argued with himself. His dad had been a bit wayward and probably met his mum, she became pregnant and had the baby, him, and his dad later had them live with him. Yes, that was it.

Jake would sigh with relief and then at some odd moment when he was unprepared the notion that his dad was not really his dad came back to taunt him. At these times, he physically felt the lurch of his stomach and the tight feeling across his chest. It took all his strength to take a step away from the inner demon. He became hesitant in using the word dad. What had been so normal and natural became strange and surreal. His dad did not seem to notice, or if he did, put it down to growing up into his teenage time.

Dad took to asking him what he was going to do when he left school. His dad kidded him about staying on and going to university but they both knew that was an unlikely scenario so Jake would retort with wild ideas like brain surgeon or nuclear scientist. His dad worked in a factory. It was a good job and he had been recently made a foreman. He had responsibilities and position and yet remained one of the men, debating with the others about the latest government gaff or the disastrous run of a particular team and whether the manager should be sacked or the players get a rollicking, or playing dominoes with his particular mates or even having a quiet pint. His dad talked to Jake a lot, recounting the idiocies he witnessed and asking Jake his opinion.

Jake felt a quiet pride and understood that his dad saw him as growing up and they were a team: that is until he felt the undercurrent suck him down into the deep waters of doubt. His dad thought he was a bit moody, a typical teenager, quite normal with brief interludes of rebellion so he congratulated himself on his parenting skills, giving his son some space as well as building a close relationship. Jake meanwhile, felt guilt and fear and worry and anger. It all came together, mingling in his sub-conscious. He could not explain even to himself and sought refuge when he could in the garden.

The day he found the letter had been an odd frustrating day. He finished helping Mr Woodhouse. Mr Woodhouse had told him to call him Jim but somehow it didn't seem right. Mr Woodhouse had an appointment in town he said. He had been rather quiet that morning and there had not been the customary cuppa and digestive. Jake would have liked a kick around but Carl who had left school and the others had gone on some jaunt to the city.

Then Flick, the little dog from number 10, had gone missing, so Jake helped to look in the alleyway at the back and then the park. George, the little boy cried a lot but soon cheered up when he saw Flick trotting down the road towards him wanting some dinner.

Jake went home, did himself some toast and scraped some meat paste on the top. He was about to go and hoe the vegetable patch when he had another of those sobering moments. Unable to summon any energy, he sat for a while trying to subdue the emotion he felt. Where was his mum? Why had she left? Who was his dad? He felt lost. He wanted resolution but concurrently dreaded the outcome.

He never went into his dad's room. He was not banned. There just wasn't a need and there was a sort of unwritten code that Jake did not invade his dad's private space and his dad did not invade his. Of course, it was a bit different when he was younger but only because his dad came into his room and not the other way round.

The conviction grew that he might find something about his mum. His conscience kicked in and told him to ask and this was sneaky, it was underhand, it was wrong, but the temptation was strong and before he knew it he was outside the door. He decided a quick look would not hurt, he would not spend long and besides which his dad would be back soon. He did not know what he thought he might find but just maybe he could find the truth.

Jake was so nervous, he almost pitched forward over the tattered rug on to the bed side table, bringing down all the paraphernalia there but averted the fall by grabbing side of the bed. He was aware of the magazines strewn over the bed, the kind Carl would leer over and pass round to the other lads. It felt seedy and he did not want to feel like that about his dad but at the same time he was, in a way, glad his dad was still interested.

All these conflicting thoughts and emotions were difficult to handle. He got on with his task. The general untidiness meant he could be fairly free in rummaging so he set about looking in drawers. There were some odd finds like a screwdriver and hammer, some old condoms, a pack of cards, a bow tie to name but a few but nothing relevant to his mission. Then when he was about to scurry downstairs, he found the shoe box and inside the photos and amongst other papers, a notebook and a couple of rolls of super-eight, he discovered the letter. He did not recognise the child on the photographs and picked up the letter.

My dearest daughter,

It has been such a short time that I have known you but you have stolen my heart. You are the most precious and beautiful gift and my heart is breaking that I am not permitted to care for you and love you as I would wish. I am desolate that I must say farewell to you my darling and I want you to know that I do so in the knowledge that you will go to a good home where there are people to care for you as you deserve. This is all beyond my control and I can only hope that when you read this you will have enjoyed a wonderful happy childhood and can forgive.

I will think of you every day of my life. Be happy my darling.
Mum x

Jake read the letter twice before he could appreciate its contents. Who was mum and who was the child? What did it mean to his dad? He sat for a while and then glanced at the bedside clock. His dad would be back anytime so he slipped the letter back in the box and returned it to the bottom of the wardrobe. Somehow, he knew it was significant. He would return another day.

He was not able to do that for a while. His dad slipped at work and twisted his ankle meaning that he had to stay at home for a few days and then it was a new term and back to school, an important year as GCSE beckoned. When he did manage it, he found that the papers were mostly invoices and bank statements, the notebook contained a sort of diary of transactions in shorthand that he did not understand and the rolls of film portrayed indistinct images of people. He studied the photographs but could not recognise the girl or the location in which they were taken. All he knew was that, they were taken a long time ago and Dad had kept them. The most intriguing thing was the letter and he read that so often, puzzling over it, meaning that he almost knew it by heart. He wondered when it had been written. Who had it been written to and why? Did the box belong to his dad or did he dare to hope that this was a clue to his mother.

He knew, because his dad told him, she had had a falling out with her mother but this letter did not seem to allude to that because they had parted ways when she was older not long before she met his dad. It was funny, how he could recite the letter but never remember even easy quotations from his English books. He somehow could not ask his dad but the ache he felt kept gnawing away at him. He found the only escape came from physical work and spent even more time in the garden and playing football.

The seasons slid by as Jake wrestled with his studies. October, the 'season of mists and mellow fruitfulness' gave way to November when the cold, dark, long nights enveloped the homes and forced residents to cluster around fires even with central heating. Dampness seeped through collars and trainers. Clouds brought mist and rain. People scurried to shelter. December abruptly brought icy mornings and slippery journeys to school or work, but to make up for this there was a sparkle in the shops and the streets were invaded by appetising smells and laughter of revellers as they spilled into the streets. November seemed a long hard month while in contrast December flew to the festivities.

Jake continued to visit Mr Woodbridge and help him with his garden. Mr Woodhouse had lots of old gardening books and introduced him to old fashioned ways. To Jake it seemed that this had been a more patient era. Roses were painstakingly budded on to briars and seeds tended carefully in the greenhouse before being planted out in neat rows using a dibber.

Jake thought about how people now wanted immediate growth and floral displays offered by the garden centre. They wanted ground cover so that weeds were repressed rather than have the trouble of laborious weeding. They chose plants that would give an exotic feel around their garden furniture and barbecues. The garden was an outdoor space to demonstrate status and entertain. Mr Woodhouse was a traditionalist. He did things the proper way, the old-fashioned way and quietly nurtured his plants. He grew vegetables to eat and flowers to bring colour and pick to adorn vases. Jake learnt much from Mr Woodhouse.

Mr Woodhouse appreciated Jake's efforts, although sometimes he would find the rise of impatience in his gullet when Jake hacked at the hedge or the bushes instead of pruning them with more deliberation and finesse but Jake's efforts were improving and Mr Woodhouse knew his garden would be a source of frustration and despair if he did not have Jake to help him. He offered to pay Jake but he refused. Their relationship was formed from mutual respect, the increasingly frail old man and the increasingly sturdy boy.

Jake tried hard in his mocks and at his career interview he ventured to suggest that he would like a career outdoors preferably with plants. It was arranged that he should go to Larkhill Garden Centre for a work experience week. Mr Woodhouse was very interested.

"That will be a great idea. Of course, I don't go there meself. The prices are too fancy for me."

"Maybe I can get some freebies," responded Jake.

His dad would drop him off on his way to work and then pick him up on his way home. It all worked perfectly. Jake was set to work and found himself shifting boxes, shifting containers, shifting bags of fertiliser of every description, shifting gravel and stone and the nearest he got to the plants was when he was entrusted with a hosepipe to water the shrubs.

Jake was not lazy and he was a strong lad so he willingly followed his instructions but underneath he was disappointed. His report from Larkhill was positive and they indicated that there was every chance of a job at the end of school maybe with day release to go on a horticultural course. His dad was delighted.

"Never thought you'd just walk into a job like that," he said. "I can give you a lift every day and you get twenty percent off as well. We could have a regular treat at their café too."

Dad thought it was exactly what Jake wanted, but Mr Woodhouse was not so sure.

"Doesn't sound much of a place," he muttered when Jake described his week as they were sowing the carrot seeds. "Thought you would be full of new-fangled ideas but sounds like you had a free work-out at the gym."

Jake reasoned if he could get on the horticultural course it would all be worthwhile but Mr Woodhouse had another idea.

"Why don't you and me have a little trip out to see Bill. He has a nursery out at Rainwick, thriving in its time but he's knocking on a bit now and might like some help. He's not as old as me o' course but I know his lad isn't interested and he is not ready to retire yet. He really knows his plants and might appreciate the help as well as let you go to college. What do you think?"

Jake agreed and one May Saturday they caught the two buses over to Rainwick. The place was certainly run down and the sheds were dilapidated in sharp contrast to the ordered slick operation of Larkshill but Jake liked Bill from the start. He liked his friendly approach and the enthusiasm with which he spoke of his plants. By now Jake's practiced eye could see his plants were strong. There was no forced growth here.

Mr Woodhouse explained and after a few questions Bill said he would love some help but he could not afford to employ Jake full time. He could maybe manage three days a week. They would all think about it and Jake would contact the college.

To his dad's disappointment and Jake's relief he started work at Bill's nursery and enrolled for the two-day course at the college. The course was much more intense than the day release and Jake scraped the qualifications he needed for it. Bill was easy going and cheerful and Jake benefitted from his plant experience. He had time to help Mr Woodhouse too, although owing to his lack of work hours his pay was not great. He began to have ideas for improving the business too.

Mr Woodhouse became his sounding board as he would bring his enthusiasm to his door.

"I was thinking we could do that old garage up that's there and have a pop-up shop for people to hire. There are a lot of people doing crafts and paintings and the like so they could use it to sell things and it would attract more footfall at the nursery."

Mr Woodhouse smiled at the word 'footfall'.

"We need to advertise the business, you know get a website and maybe that new network Facebook."

Mr Woodhouse wondered if Bill wanted the intrusion.

The years unfolded and it became clear that Mr Woodhouse relied on Jake's visits and Bill rather reluctantly began to look forward to semi-retirement. Business had certainly been better with Jake at the nursery but nothing went on forever. Bill hated the increasing irritation of paperwork associated with running a business. He found Health and Safety a burden, although used it like a flag, if he wanted to rebuff a suggestion for the business he did not like.

Bill had been the master of his territory for most of his working life and could not relinquish that with ease. Bill's son Simon who still lived at the nursery and helped out when he could, believed selling was a sensible option or at least trying to get planning permission for some of the land and maybe do something themselves. Simon who was into property development thought they could achieve a good sale price. The land was becoming more and more valuable and maybe even more so if there could be planning permission for houses. It was all an exciting proposition for Simon who had been showing increased interest but it became a deep worry for Jake. His time with Bill had however yielded horticultural qualifications to use when needed.

One bleak January day, at the beginning of 2007, almost two years after leaving school; Jake left the nursery early and called in on Mr Woodhouse. The old man was dozing by the fire and Jake realised he had not had lunch probably because of the effort required. Mr Woodhouse, now in his mid-seventies was thin and his hand shook as he picked up the tea Jake had made him. It was a worry. He made Mr Woodhouse some cheese on toast and said he'd pop back later.

Jim Woodhouse heard Jake close the door and switched on the television. He flicked through the channels before settling on a popular quiz programme. He thought of Jake and how lucky he had been to have his help. He loved his garden and he could rely on Jake to get it up to scratch. He thought of Ida and the years they had enjoyed. There was pain in his heart when he thought of her. She was always young in his mind, never aged and ill with the terrible cancer that had beaten her. He missed her and wanted to hold her and for her to laugh and call him a daft beggar.

He heard the click of the latch on the back door. It was very soft but deliberate and Mr Woodhouse roused himself to welcome Jake. The dark figure paused in the doorway. Mr Woodhouse cried out,

"Who the hell are you?" He could not see his face and then he heard the whisper of another person.

"Get out. Get out," Jim Woodhouse cried.

"Stay there old man. No need to panic. Just a quick visit."

Jim Woodhouse grasped the plate and flung it at the figure. He got up and unsteadily advanced on the intruder, finding what strength he could in his fury. There was little else he would remember.

Voices swam in and out of his consciousness. He seemed to be reaching out into a void, his arms flailing wanting to clutch someone but there was only empty space. Then Ida was stroking his hand, reassuring him, a soft voice allowing him to drift into oblivion. Suddenly, he woke, felt young and strong and there was his beautiful Ida, indistinct in form but enveloping him in sensations of devotion.

   The pain briefly forced her away from his side and then at Ida's touch the pain receded, and Ida was there again beside him with her gentle touch and encouraging him to rest. He slipped in and out of consciousness. Beneath his eyelids he saw Ida with a boy, both smiling at him and he reached his arms to form a trinity with them embellished by the illuminating light. He had felt complete.

Chapter 3
The Loss of Innocence

E'er felt such rage, resentment, and despair,
As thou, sad virgin! For thy ravished hair."

The Rape of the Lock by Alexander Pope

1924-1943: Ida

Ida Woodhouse, formerly Brindell and born in spring 1924, had lived with her mum, dad and two elder sisters in the little hamlet of Stonebrook, not two miles from the town of Marketborough. She was a happy child petted by her siblings and feted by her parents. She was full of laughter and her dad could make her giggle uncontrollably when he tickled her armpits after he got back from his shift at the mine. She had fair curls that bounced in the sunlight and after the long hours down the pit he delighted in the little girl. She had a favourite rag doll that she used as a companion in the absence of any girls of her own age. The doll became the repository of all her childish secrets and her co-conspirator in any games and the odd piece of mischief. As she grew from infancy to childhood it was her mother who began to exercise discipline. She would berate her for not coming promptly when she was called, not eating up all her supper, leaving her woolly scarf on the floor instead of reaching for the hook on the wall where it should go and countless other misdemeanours.

Her mother worried that all the fuss the others gave Ida, could turn Ida's head and make things difficult later on. After all, it was a hard life and expectations were low. Gradually Ida understood that she gave her mother continual displeasure and not to expect anything less and her behaviour would respond accordingly. Her mother had started her censures with good intentions but soon found an inevitability of constant disapproval regarding her youngest child.

It became a wedge that continued throughout their lives gradually driving them further and further apart. Ida responded by donning emotional armour when she was around her mum. The irony was that they were closer in disposition than any of the other family members. They each suffered from the loss of connection.

Stonebrook had been a thriving little community at the turn of the century but that was with the security of the Victorian notions of landownership and service. The Brindells occupied a small cottage with a four-acre smallholding on which they kept pigs, chickens, a couple of goats, a mare and a house cow. They grew vegetables to eat and sometimes sell and collected apples, plums and pears from the fruit trees on the edge of the acreage. Mrs Brindell and the eldest daughter Daisy did the bulk of the work.

The cottage was rented from Major Dalrymple who owned the majority of land thereabouts and strictly speaking it was a tied cottage for agricultural workers. Fred had worked on the estate before the Great War and after he returned he found his position had gone to one of the Catling boys so he reported to the mine a mile down the road. He would cycle there and back come rain or shine.

At first, Molly his wife, worried that the Major would see them out, but he had not the spirit of before the war and let it go. Major Dalrymple had lost sons at Somme and Ypres. It had broken him. He sat absorbed in his dire thoughts, drinking tots of whisky to banish the pain. The estate fell into neglect. After a time, Molly Brindell began to breathe easy, especially when her middle daughter took up a position of lady's maid at the manor.

Ida was immune to the deprivations of the depression. Her father brought home a steady if meagre wage, there was food on the table and she had the countryside in which to roam. Her little school was pleasant enough and she attended to the lessons so that she kept out of trouble. There was latitude if any of them did not get to school any day as everyone understood that boys particularly were needed in the fields at crucial times of year so as long as they had good general attendance there was no trouble.

Ida skipped along the lanes happy in her own company dreaming of a bright future in which she would be adored by a handsome husband who would work hard to take care of her and provide a neat little house in a pretty setting and there would be happy handsome children playing in the country garden. She was a typical girl of the era waiting for that wonderful moment when she would embrace her destiny. She had no doubt that her day dream would come true. By the age of fifteen she had shelved childlike characteristics.

She was taller than her mother and had a comely figure so that her simple work clothes draped engagingly over her curves. She coaxed her hair into attractive curls or fashionable pleats which framed an amiable face. People warmed to her open smiles which could easily turn into a gentle giggle or full laughter. Daisy was courting steadily and there were expectations of marriage which meant that Ida increasingly took on her role of helpmate to her busy mother. While her mother was still stern there was peace between them and mutual appreciation. Ida waited for her time.

"It's war, then," her dad announced gloomily. "Knew it. Hoped it wouldn't but can't stop the blighter."

His wife had lived with his moods the last year as he was inevitably reliving his experiences in the Great War.

"Will you have to go again?" She nervously ventured.

"No, not me. They'll need the mines. I'll have dirty work alright," and with that he plodded out of the kitchen perhaps she thought to seek solace in the open air. She knew he would be remembering mates lost like Charlie and George and others that she did not know. There had been Alf too who had come home with his nerves shot and one fine day in desperation strangled his wife before taking himself to the train tracks. It had been an ugly business which had sickened the community.

There was tacit agreement that no-one spoke of Alf or Edna ever again. They were buried and gone as they all hoped the war had gone. Fred had been called up in 1917, so to his mind he had not seen a lot of action but what he had witnessed had changed him from a cheeky youth to an embittered man. There were times when he became his old self like when he was with their Ida and she would catch the laughter from the two but in between he closed himself off and she felt their marriage had lost something because of it.

They had got engaged when the call up came and hastily married after the war was over grabbing the life that had been spared. Three daughters had been born quickly and now they were almost grown and another bloody war about to start.

The war advanced upon them, not dramatically but gradually, and irrevocably. Fred joined the home guard so with work at the mine and his duties it was up to the women to keep the smallholding productive and comply with the increasing demands from the Ministry. Then, Daisy announced she was getting a job in the munition factory that had opened up on the edge of town. Her mother could not blame her. Wages were good and she needed the company at her age and she had been courting Mick from the factory for a couple of years. He had failed his medical so avoided the call up to his bitter regret.

Daisy was a solid dependable girl who deserved some happiness. Major Dalrymple had died the previous summer leaving the estate to a cousin. His only daughter had married and disappeared to Yorkshire. His heir the Honourable Lionel Dalrymple was needed for the war effort down in London so he mothballed the manor house, keeping on a skeleton staff and dividing the home farm into manageable chunks for the remaining estate workers to tenant and provide much needed food.

The 1930s had seen the estate dwindle so any new tenant would be hard pressed to resurrect the forsaken fields and besides which most of the fit younger workers would be called up to fight resulting in a bigger load for women, children and the old. Doris was invited to travel to London with the party. She had become a valued employee and after listening to some misgivings from her parents accepted what she thought of as a challenge and the satisfaction of being part of it. Ida and her mother metaphorically and at times literally put their shoulders to the plough.

Ida was getting impatient. At fifteen a war had loomed into her consciousness. She did not know what to expect and hopes and dreams were alternatively aroused and dashed. It was her job to deliver any excess fruit and vegetables to the market. She would load the cart and drive the old mare down the rutted lanes until she emerged into the leafy suburbs of the town. She looked forward to these excursions and sold the produce easily helped by her winning ways. They began to sell jams and chutneys and then with some entrepreneurial spirit made pies and cakes to aid the women whose work at the factories made it difficult for them to bake. Ingredients were in short supply. Molly found she could make extra with a bit of clever management and established a barter system for her produce to get some extra sugar and flour. It was no lie to say the family prospered. By seventeen Ida was ripe for change.

While his female family thrived, Fred Bindell dwindled. At first, he would complain about anything and everything.

"How the hell can we produce the coal, if they won't give us the labour?"

"Them French shouldn't be in charge. Look at my war and now our boys are being hounded down at Dunkirk."

"It's all very well for those fat cats. They don't have to exist on rations."

"This war will be the death of our way of life. You mark my words."

"That copper's been searching the barns. What does he hope to find? He wants to get the real criminals instead of harassing good people trying to do their best for their kids."

And then Fred became more personal.

"What you want to put the shoes where I can't get them."

"Where's me tea woman? I need a good meal when I get home after the shift I've had."

"Nag, nag, nag. I'm the man round here and don't you forget it."

"You want to smarten yourself up. What on earth do you do all day? You look a real mess."

Molly gritted her teeth, hurt after her hard day digging and planting. Much of their four acres was given over to growing stuff except for the little reserved for the few livestock. She helped the neighbours too. She knew Fred worked hard and mines were tough, unforgiving places but it was the war that had sent him into this petty meanness. Even Ida would occasionally get it in the neck, although Molly more and more relied on her younger daughter to pacify him.

The atmosphere at home contributed to Ida's impatience. Her sisters had moved on with their lives and her parents were living separate lives. In the middle of this she thought she would physically burst if she could not find her *raison d'etre*.

Then Dave did burst on to her scene.

Dave worked for the military, requisitioning goods. According to him he was a crucial cog in the supply chain. He had joined up at the outset of war and sustained an injury to his leg at Dunkirk. He used his time away from the front well by becoming indispensable first to his unit and then to the regiment in sourcing their requirements. His mother had a shop in Lowton, a town in the next county and he had been brought up on commerce. For him it was a win-win, as he was able to be the heroic soldier injured in the line of duty, able to continue serving his country in the armed forces and never encounter another battle even though his injury had healed. He relied on the charm offensive and his quick mathematical brain could negotiate costs and quantities often to the detriment of the seller who because of his charm rarely realised they were being short changed. Dave travelled around to secure his booty.

The week he noticed Ida, had been trying. He was deflated by the way the war was going and the increasing difficulty in getting provisions. There was just not enough food to go around and the soldiers in the local barracks seemed to consume huge quantities. He took himself off for a lunchtime pint and sat outside the small market square hotel in the late autumn sunshine. He was pondering his options generally watching the market traders pack away, musing at their limited lives when he noticed Ida.

A shaft of sunlight marked her out and Dave felt a tug in his groin. He realised, he had not enjoyed female company for a while and even though his girl at home wrote and waited, a man needed to squeeze flesh and taste the scent of a woman. He wanted someone on his arm, someone to spoil and someone who would admire him as he deserved to be admired, someone in fact like Ida.

He did not follow up his desires that day but the girl stayed in his thoughts and he found himself looking for her and timing any appointments so he was in the vicinity when she was at market. He bought apples from her and took one delicious bite as he stood over her, feasting on her loveliness.

"What's the name of this apple? It tastes real good."

"Yes, it's a great apple, so white and sweet. Trouble is it has such a brief season. Picked too early it can be bitter and it does not last at all. I love the blush on the skin too which sometimes bleeds into the white flesh beneath. I'm sorry, I do not know the name."

"Irresistible," he said.

Ida found herself blushing.

Dave would saunter off conscious of the girl's eyes following. He seems nice she thought, but not really my type letting her eyes drift towards Roger who was already taken by Angela. Now he was a hunk and she thought of Angela in his strong arms. Ida looked forward to selling any surplus produce from the smallholding.

Her family had profited from the better war prices and any extra from the small market stall meant that in relative terms they prospered. The war was not being fought on their patch as yet, although they had been horrified by the reports of the Blitz in London and waited anxiously for news of Doris. Ida felt the pulse of nature in her veins.

The routine began. On market days when in town he would buy fruit for his lunch and engage her in conversation as much as he could. She began to look for him and was disappointed when he was not there.

Dave judged the moment to perfection. He was feeling good having just secured a profitable delivery which would please the captain. For Ida it had been a miserable day and by lunchtime the rain had seeped into her core.

"You must be cold standing here all day." Dave had surprised her coming from behind.

"Oh. Hello. I get used to it. It goes with the job but I am ready to get home I must confess." She wiped her hand across her damp face and brushed her hair back under the scarf. Dave saw the enticing glisten of a raindrop on the corner of her sweet mouth. He inadvertently licked his lips in response.

"If you've time, let me get you a drink at the White Hart over there. It's warm and cosy inside. They do nice food too if you're hungry."

Ida had never been in the White Hart. Actually, she'd never been in any public house or hotel or inn or anywhere she suddenly realised. She was tempted and she reasoned that she was old enough having just turned eighteen on Valentine's Day earlier in the year and her mother would not be expecting her for another hour or two.

She was still reluctant. "I don't know if I should," she faltered.

"It's up to you. I thought you looked as if you could do with a bit of cheer. Perhaps another time if you have to get back." Dave made as if to turn away having noticed temptation light up her eyes.

Ida had a moment to decide and in a rush as she imagined the experience being closed on her she agreed.

"Great. I will go and get us a table and you come in when you've finished up here." He marched away turning up his collar as he retreated from her.

Ida would have liked him to say that he would help her but she was glad he had taken the trouble to ask her for a drink.

There really wasn't much to pack away and taking courage in both hands she made her way to the front door of the hotel. Self-consciously she put her hand on the open door and glanced inside. To her relief, she spied Dave in the corner of the snug. He was downing a pint and stood up to signal his presence. Unsure what to drink, she opted for a port and lemon having been permitted to have a glass at Christmas and she thought it sounded sophisticated enough. He asked if she wanted food but she decided that her mother would be suspicious if she got home without an appetite.

The drink filled her consciousness so that she felt a glow seep into her face, aware that Dave was studying her responses. For Dave, her inherent shyness cast a spell and his determination to get to know her grew.

He ventured to suggest they meet socially and asked her to the dance at the public hall. Ida knew her sister usually went with Mick so she agreed. He said he could pick her up and take her home afterwards which gave Ida some apprehension, nervous about her mother, but her sisters had broken free and this was her turn. Arrangements were made.

It took all the rest of the week to decide what to wear, not that there was much choice, and to build her nerve. She had told her mother who had not seemed surprised or worried. Anticipation grew. She wished her sisters were there to ask about things like what she should do if he wanted to hold her hand or put his arm around her when they were not dancing or worse try to kiss her in the dark or in the car.

As the youngest daughter, she had retained a childish innocence regarding the world at large. She almost wished she had not said yes, but only almost, and never completely, secretly excited at the prospect. On the morning of the dance she took special care in washing her hair, rinsing it in vinegar water to make it shine.

Dave was on time and came to the door. He was not bashful.

"Good evening, Mrs Brindell," and he extended his hand. "You have a fine place here. Maybe, you might be interested in selling some of your produce to the military—if you have any to spare of course?"

Mrs Brindell eyed the young man and reserved judgement.

"Always ready to help the forces," she said in a non-committal way. She was wary of strangers, especially if they seemed to represent authority and even more if they conveyed a confident air that denoted power.

"I'll look after Ida I promise and bring her home by eleven." He stood firm at the kitchen door. "That is if you are happy for her to be out until then. The dance usually finishes at ten thirty."

Mrs Brindell remembered fleetingly the times she had danced in the arms of her husband. It gave her a sharp pang and she turned away from his gaze. Her daughter deserved the attention.

"Eleven o'clock will be fine. Not a moment later."

"Bye Mum," and she was gone.

Ida had a wonderful time. For the whole evening she had Dave by her side. The thrum of the music invigorated her and the chatter of voices uplifted her. True to his word Dave brought her home before eleven. He had briefly held her hand as he guided her to his car, particularly in the black-out, and only held her close when they danced and did not try to kiss her. She wished he had.

The tunes remained in her head as she lay in bed and worked the land and she would hum and sing as she worked 'Taking a Chance on Love' and 'Zing went the strings of my heart.' She knew what it felt like to be on cloud nine.

They arranged to go again and then to the cinema to see In Which We Serve with John Mills and Ida, moved by the story and absorbed into the sacrifice, felt tears prick her eyes and, on giving a little sigh, had been comforted by Dave's arm and she leaned into his shoulder.

Afterwards, he told her about Dunkirk. She knew of the event but in terms of heroism and fortitude and felt wonder as Dave told her how his leg was smashed in his efforts to escape and he was lucky that another soldier had dragged him on to the vessel. He described the noise of the shelling intermingled with screams of pain and shouts of rage and the torment of the waves inviting and repelling the frantic servicemen.

"There were heroes that day but most of us were scared witless."

Ida wanted to smother him with affection and take away the pain of remembering. She squeezed his hand and he lifted his head, took her into his arms and kissed her. He had kissed her before but this kiss had a yearning and passion that obliterated her being. That night became a turning point when Ida felt she had come of age. Dave had shown a vulnerability that aroused a devotion and compassion in her that lifted the relationship in her mind to the interdependency that heralded a merging of souls. She trusted her instinct.

Daisy was married. It was a simple affair. Ida recognised the quiet dedication Daisy and Mick gave to each other and the undercurrent of desire as they looked at each other. Ida was entranced. She had never thought of Daisy as romantic and had smiled at Mick's clumsy advances towards her sister but the wedding day showed real warmth and tenderness. Ida thought of Dave and his confidences about Dunkirk believing in their combined destiny. At Daisy's wedding Ida's feelings were cemented.

Autumn crumbled into winter. She had been aware of far-away battles at El Alamein and Stalingrad but tucked away in her little corner of the universe she did not foresee any battle closer to home.

Dave was worried. He could not shift the feelings. He had never before felt at a loss. He had experienced many feelings but they were always explainable. Feelings of physical attraction were basic desires of mankind, revulsions were prompted by an ugly encounter, admirations were prompted by striving for something more, joys were from self-satisfaction, pride was from endeavour and success but this feeling was insidious. It seemed to reach into his core and twist his gut, ever so slightly but constantly revisiting him in his quiet moments. Perhaps he needed a break. He decided to ask for leave to visit his mother. It had been a long time.

Ida understood his visit home. She encouraged it and asked about his widowed mother and the little shop she ran. She waved him off and longed for his return. Dave knew his mother would lay out the red carpet. He was her only son and the townspeople would soon be informed of the return of the prodigal. Not that Dave had ever left home deliberately it was just the demands of war.

There was a feast waiting for him and Dave's heart soared. Sheila who helped in the shop and had kept a correspondence with Dave had made a huge steak and kidney pie in spite of war shortages and apple crumble to welcome him home. She would prove her suitability as a wife. He had dated her a few times before the war and his mother encouraged the friendship. Dave felt comfortable and untroubled basking in the adoration of the two women. He felt revived. He was at ease.

Ida was waiting for him on his return.

He felt the familiar tightening in his solar plexus and grasped her outstretched hand. She wanted to know all about the visit.

"How is your mother?" Ida wanted to feel she belonged.

"Is she managing alright?" Ida wanted him to recognise her concern and encourage him to share.

"Did she spoil you?" Ida needed personal details.

"Did you meet up with any old friends?" Ida worried that he had a life separate from her.

The questions came thick and fast and Dave began to feel cornered. Her persistence meant that Ida learnt about the shop and the various customers and neighbours. Her heart missed a beat when he mentioned Sheila and, although she brushed away any doubt her intuition told her to be warned. Dave was back now and she would make the most of it. She was certain that they were both ready to take the relationship to another level and glowed at the prospect.

They resumed the habit of the dance or cinema as the winter eased into early spring. Ida loved the white snowdrops poking out of the ground defying the bleak wind and occasional dusting of snow. Nature was reasserting itself. Ida felt buoyant. She would be a year older, she had a steady boyfriend who was a man of the world to take her beyond her small universe and her future was certain.

The night Ida lost her virginity had not begun well. It was a harsh February day a week before her birthday. There was a merciless cold wind that curtailed anyone venturing outside. She was to get the bus into town to meet Dave at the venue. It had been increasingly difficult for him, he said, to use the vehicle to ferry her back and forth. There was an air of determination in the war effort and small shoots of optimism.

Dave had seemed preoccupied since his return from his visit home and he confessed he thought he might be sent back to the front. Ida wanted to protect him. She wanted to provide a shield for him and watched him intently, holding on to him before any harm could befall him. She was swept along with a sense of urgency, a sense that today was essential and tomorrow was peripheral.

The atmosphere at the dance hall was electric. There were some new soldiers there and the local girls competed for their attention. Ida had always marvelled at the spunk of these girls as they would chassis towards their prey. In the toilets she might linger to listen to them discussing the merits and demerits of each new applicant for their affection. Nina included Ida and smiled at her innocence. Ida was quite aware that Nina had done more than sample the wares on offer and was in awe of her worldliness. There was no doubt in Ida's mind that she was destined for one man and one man only.

The exit was slow. There was a crush at the doors as coats were retrieved and farewells executed in the porch before venturing into the cold. Ida and Dave elbowed their way through but the delay had resulted in Ida missing her bus. Ida knew she could stay with Daisy. She had done so before but that was when Daisy was in local digs and now Daisy, since marriage, lived several streets away. It could not be helped. She knew her mother would not worry so she turned up her collar ready for the walk. Dave realised he should escort her. He was tired and he would have double the distance, there and back.

"Listen darling, why don't you come back to mine? It's round the corner. We'd be warm and dry in a jiffy." Dave leaned close and nibbled her ear so she squirmed and giggled.

Ida had never been to his lodging. She was curious. They had dated for almost a year and she was comfortable in his presence.

"I'm not coming on to you. I think it would be sensible. You'll get soaked before you're half way to Daisy's and you'll have to wake them up and think of all the fuss. Besides it would be fun sneaking back with my lovely girl. I'll always look after you." Again, he bent his head towards her cheek.

Ida did not need much convincing. She recalled the excitement of venturing into the White Hart and felt a familiar exhilaration of the prospect of an illicit night with him. He had been trustworthy and now he was looking after her.

The room was shabbier than she expected but it was of reasonable size. The bed loomed invitingly by the wall. Dave put on a small lamp and checked the blackout curtain. The glow of the bulb cast a magical aura over the covers hiding any defects. There was a bathroom a couple of doors down. Dave removed her coat and hung it over the back of the chair.

"You are so beautiful Ida." He touched her cheek with his hand and she winced slightly at his caress.

He backed away slightly.

"Why don't you take your dress off and slip into bed? I promise I won't look."

He turned and she did as she was told, the fire of her body hitting the cool sheets.

"I can sleep on the floor here." He raised his eyes to her, a smile playing on his lips and he tilted his head to one side. Otherwise he stood still paused in his assessment. The girl in his bed had aroused his lust. He had invited the situation and it had become a test. He felt randy and knew his physical needs were overpowering any sense of caution. The hesitation gave Ida a chance to respond. He was glad he had waited.

Ida stared out from her nest. She reached her arms and at her signal he slid in beside her, folding her into him. She felt the maleness of him. She felt tender and yielded to his embrace feeling his finger under her slip working at her brassiere fixings. When it was released, she felt a sudden surge of liberation. His hands moved under her slip squeezing her breasts and touching her nipples and then drifting down to work their way under her panties. Ida held her breath unsure and delighted. She lay still until he guided her response. She allowed him access to her body and soul and with a wild wind raging outside she surrendered to him in absolute trust.

The next day was bright. The bitter wind had abated and the rain had washed the ground to create a shimmer from the thin sunshine. Ida felt alive. She reflected on the experience, which to tell the truth, was not the ecstasy she had been led to believe. It had been incomplete somehow and even at the back of her consciousness, vulgar, but all that was pushed aside as she reasserted her will for escape.

He had been forceful in his assault, separating her legs and using his fingers to prepare the entrance; she had squealed with discomfort and then Dave breathing heavily mounted her slight body, crushing any further protest and whispering words of reassurance before a final grunt exhaled from his mouth and leaving her body he roughly pushed her aside. She had felt sore and soiled, the penetration had hurt, but she also felt whole so when he muttered how wonderful it had been; she had been reassured and even more in love with him. Dave slept little, conscious of what had happened and reluctant to acknowledge the insidious feelings that had returned in the still dark night.

They went to Daisy's house. Mick opened the door and told them Daisy was sick. Dave decided he should go leaving Ida. He promised they would meet as usual the following week. Mick and Daisy would take Ida home. It soon became clear the cause of Daisy's sickness and diverted, no-one at home pried into Ida's activities.

There were repeat performances over the next month except with the difference that Ida was more willing and bold.

Dave made another trip home. She hoped he would take her but this was never suggested. The war will not go on forever she thought and then they could make plans.

He told Ida he was being reassigned on a blustery day in the middle of March. The majority of his work would be in another county, nearer to his home. He promised to write and come when he could. Ida had clung to him.

By the end of April she was scared. Dave had vanished and, although she had received a couple of brief letters, he was not the writing type he had told her, she had little evidence of what he was up to or who he was with. She thought of confiding in Daisy but Daisy and Mick were flushed with expectation and somehow, her predicament would not fit, so in the end she told Nina.

Nina produced a large handkerchief and told her to dry her tears. In her no-nonsense way Nina said she was not the first girl to be taken advantage of and it all could be dealt with and no-one would be the wiser. Ida wanted to say she had not been taken advantage of and she had been a willing participant but the words stuck in her throat. There was no time to lose, according to Nina and she proceeded to make arrangements.

Ida was surprised that she was to report to a house in Lavender Road, a smart residential area, where a Mrs Thomas would take care of her. Nina would lend her the money if needed and she could pay it back a bit at a time so no-one would notice. Dave had left her circle and she knew time was passing so she allowed Nina to make decisions. Later, when Dave returned she would be more careful taking advice from her experienced friend. It never occurred to her that their relationship was over.

Looking back in later life Ida could hardly remember events. She had been gripped by fear and full of anguish about the sin she was about to commit. Not only was it against her Christian principles but it was a product of the love she and Dave shared. Guilt stole into her soul.

Mrs Thomas had been quick and efficient. The pain had been excruciating and the subsequent cramps debilitating. Nina met her afterwards and took her to her little bedsit, feeding her with tea and toast and encouraging her to sleep. Ida wondered how many other girls had been ministered to in this way. She returned home, as expected, two days later having had a little break with her friends as her mother believed.

Leaving Nina on the bus home, she sat as still as she could, frozen on the outside, withered on the inside, and looked out of the window. She could not be mistaken. She took a long second look, allowed as the bus stopped at the junction. It was certainly Dave and he had his arms round someone. She was a pretty girl and she caught them laughing, before the girl planted a kiss on his lips. Ida wanted to die.

Daisy was visiting. Molly loved the visits as she would catch up on news from the town.

"Hey, Ida. Mick saw that chap you used to knock around with. Dave was it. He was getting pints in at the Crown, celebrating, he was with the lads from the base, as he had got himself engaged. It seems he's going to settle back at his mother's and will be taking over the shop after the war. All been planned for years apparently. Had a bit of a break from Sheila, I think her name is, but he said it was only because of the war. He was in good form Mick says, and Sheila had come to say hello. Funny, I thought you two were still together. I can't keep up with your love life."

Ida disappeared up to her room.

Her room at the rear of the cottage was no more than a box room with whitewashed stone walls and housed a small truckle bed no more than a foot off the floor that was hard and narrow plus a chest of drawers and a narrow wardrobe. There was a small window which let in a meagre amount of light, especially on this dismal April day.

A few days earlier, before her visit to Mrs Thomas, Ida had installed a jug of daffodils to cheer the room and now she seized them in her fist and threw them from the window to scatter haphazardly onto the thorn bushes below before she shut the casement firmly and sank on to the low unforgiving bed.

She covered her face with her hands allowing tears to course through her fingers. Her foolishness overwhelmed her and anger rose through her body, wishing she could have confronted Dave and even his fiancée. She wanted to shout at him and hit him with the news of the baby wanting it still to be alive in her body. Eventually, all emotion subsided. She sat empty of passion and empty of hope.

It was several days later when she was smitten by sudden overwhelming cramp in the early hours. She felt the dampness seep from her body even though she had worn additional sanitary layers. The cramp subsided and then came back more fiercely forcing her to clench her fists and bring her knees to her chest to try to alleviate the pain. An hour later, her sheets were sodden with a mixture of blood and perspiration. She felt weak and sick and was slipping in and out of consciousness. Crying out brought her mother to her bedside.

"Good grief. What's to do?" Molly saw the stricken girl and was frightened.

"Fred, Fred. Get up. We need Dr Lewis."

She expected Fred to grumble and protest but he was taken aback when he saw his darling daughter in the mess of the bed, a pale face shining with sweat and creased with exhaustion gazed pleadingly. All Ida wanted was relief. She knew this was the end.

Fred was lucky. The doctor was able to come straightaway having visited an elderly patient nearby. Fred was banned from the room as Dr Lewis rolled up his sleeves and with Molly's help tried to stem the blood flow.

"Hospital for you, I think."

Ida had been given an injection and drifted away from the turmoil around her.

She awoke several hours later. A man in a white coat stood over her.

"Ah back with us I see. You've had a bit of an ordeal but all sorted and you'll be released later. A silly girl I think." The doctor had critical grey eyes beneath a balding pate and rose menacingly above her.

"Thank you," Ida murmured and drifted into semi-consciousness.

Lying closed in with the curtains she recognised her mother's voice and tried to focus.

"Yer dad doesn't know what it is. No point in upsetting him." Ida nodded and closed her eyes in shame.

She wanted the comfort of her childhood. Even when her mother scalded she had always been fair.

Then her mother leaned over and in a whisper uttered a word that pierced her heart like a dagger.

"Slut!" Ida kept her eyes closed and closed her heart.

She was discharged into her parent's care, given painkillers and a warning not to visit them again. The doctor referred to his notes.

"No children for you now. You understand," and he emphasised, "There will be no babies." Ida hardly understood but she did understand that she would never ever take a husband.

At home, Ida was aware of the spring continuing to unfold, the daffodils that her mother plucked to provide sunshine in the house, the pussy willows, the feel of which had enchanted Ida as a girl, the catkins that danced in the soft breeze and the offspring of the livestock strongly represented by the lambs in the adjacent fields. The wheels of life turned and in late summer, Daisy gave birth to a son. A boy in the family was a blessing. Fred, for once, had something to provide him with hope.

Even as summer delivered heat and light Ida had pulled her winter cloak around her. She would not let go as she mourned the demise of all she held dear. She threw her rag doll on the fire in the hearth and watched it burn. Inside she was numb. She had been forsaken. Her identity had been stolen. She would not emerge from her winter blast for ten bitter years. Only then, when a young man called Jim Woodhouse came to the cottage would she be forced out of her collapse.

Chapter 4
Founding Father

That time of year thou mayst in me behold
When yellow leaves, or none, or few, do hang
Upon those boughs which shake against the cold,
Bare ruin'd choirs, where late the sweet birds sang.

Sonnet 73: William Shakespeare

2007-2008: Jake and Jim

Jake had found Jim Woodhouse unconscious in a pool of blood at the doorway to his lounge. The television flickered and jangled in the corner bringing a macabre and menacing atmosphere to the scene of crime.

The police refused to let Jake go to the hospital with Mr Woodhouse. There were questions to answer they said. Jake was incandescent with rage. He kicked the gate where he was standing and it flung back against the hedge almost striking a female police officer standing taking notes.

"No need to get violent," said the sergeant in charge. "You need to calm down if we are to get anywhere. Mr Woodhouse is in good hands. It looks very serious and you need to answer questions."

Jake did not like the look that was cast in his direction by the officer.

"I don't know anything except I wish I had been there. I would have given them what for."

Jake suddenly seemed to realise and turned and muttered a "Sorry" to the uniformed woman.

It was soon established that Jake lived nearby and the sergeant permitted him to return home saying he would be along shortly to take a statement. There was quite a crowd gathered under the street lamp as near as they were allowed to the property and he caught some comments.

"Looks like he was bludgeoned to death."

"No he's not dead yet. Hanging on by a thread, the medic said."

"Terrible shock. Never had anything like that happen here before."

"I heard he had a stash of cash."

"Must have been what they were after. No point coming to us we haven't got a sou."

As Jake left for home Colin, Carl's father, tried to detain him wanting to know what he had seen. The woman from number 24 whose name he did not know pushed to the front to hear Jake's response but Jake could not say a word. He was too shocked. He was churning inside and now outwardly shaking. The cold evening air crept round his neck to shroud his face so that he felt he could not breathe, although he saw his breath coming out of his mouth in short, sharp bursts like the emissions of a little toy steam train.

"Get home lad and we'll be there soon," advised the sergeant.

It was almost three quarters an hour later that there was a knock on the door and Jake opened it to a plain clothes officer. At the same time his dad appeared, having been to the Swan for a pint or two after work.

"What on earth's going on?" His dad had seen the clutch of neighbours on the street and the police vehicles with activity from uniformed and white suited forensic police officers.

"It's Mr Woodhouse," and Jake could get no further.

"It seems there has been a very nasty assault." The plain clothes officer informed Ken Lewis scrutinising his reaction.

"Not Jim." Ken looked at Jake and the policeman in turn for confirmation.

"Can we go inside sir? We need to get a complete picture. Maybe, a cup of sweet tea would help," he said studying Jake.

With mugs of tea in support Sergeant Wilkes asked Jake to describe exactly what he had found. He listened quietly without interruption. There was something soothing about the CID officer. He sat very still, absorbed and appreciative. Jake's dad on the other hand could not suppress the occasional interruption as though it were all too much to bear such as a comment "Never" or an emphatic "Sure you did the right thing" or "My god" or "Bloody hell" but managed to resist his more natural F word expletive, and then he would emit the occasional cough or stirred his tea loudly at some crucial moment. The policeman remained unperturbed but alert.

"Well Jake, you've had a nasty shock. Thanks for telling me. I am sure it will help us to catch the intruder. Now I need you to make a formal statement at the station. You understand Jake. So shall we say ten o'clock, tomorrow?"

Jake, 'horrified at the idea of going through it again,' blurted his reluctance but the detective waved away his protestation and said it was necessary and straightforward and made his way out of the door. His dad and Jake could not look at each other.

Jake wanted to go to the hospital but they decided a telephone call should be made. The hospital gave them no information at all. Jake was not a relative and it did no good for him to explain that Mr Woodhouse did not have relatives, or at least any that were close. Jake decided he should go. His dad would stay home.

The hospital was not far on his bike. It was located at the edge of a quiet residential area of the town where the swathe of lights dominated, a constant reminder of human misery and need. Jake located the pedestrian entrance to A&E and made his way through the woebegone public to the desk at the end. The man said he would find out what he could but returned saying he was not permitted to give any information as it was a police matter. Jake pleaded to see the old man but that was flatly denied. The only comfort in the exchange was that it established that Mr Woodhouse was alive.

Jake called Bill the next morning to explain his absence and reported to the police station.

He was escorted into a side room and asked if he would mind having his fingerprints and DNA taken. "Only for elimination."

Jake could not refuse.

It was an even different policeman and woman who met Jake and showed him into the interview room. Jake agreed to a recording and recounted events. He described returning to the house at about 6.30pm. He could not be sure of the time but the news was coming to an end on the television. He went round the back because he knew he could let himself in if Mr Woodhouse did not hear his knock.

Instinctively, he knew straightaway that something was amiss and shouted for him. The kitchen was not how he had left it earlier. Drawers were slightly open and cupboard doors ajar. He was aghast to see the body of Mr Woodhouse slumped across the door of the front room. There was blood oozing from the side of his head forming a sticky puddle. He could not be entirely sure of the sequence of events. He knew he fetched a towel from the kitchen for the blood. He tried to check if he was breathing but failed to find a pulse. He was frightened to move him so, hovering over him, would intermittently speak to Mr Woodhouse urging him to stir and of course, at some point he telephoned for an ambulance. It all took such a long time to his mind but in actual fact the paramedics and police arrived within ten minutes of his call and at this point, redundant, he removed himself to the garden. In the dark, Jake had felt bereft.

The police retraced some of his account squeezing him of every last detail he might remember. Jake found it exhausting and confusing, wondering if he had imagined some details and his memory was playing tricks. What was absolutely clear though, was the sight of Mr Woodhouse awkward and pathetic as if he was a child's discarded broken toy soldier after a vicious battle.

Then the interview turned to the relationship between Jake and Mr Woodhouse. At first, they wanted information like how long had Jake known Mr Woodhouse, when did he start helping him with his garden, how often he visited him, what times of day, and then the questions seemed more insidious seeking out why Jake visited so much, why wasn't he out with his friends reminding him that he had dropped away from his football which he had said he enjoyed.

Jake felt ill at ease and began to feel a more threatening timbre to the questions. They seemed to be searching him out, pressing small buttons to respond, grasping at small insignificant comments making them larger and at times, even shameful.

"Did you go upstairs at all, Jake?" The female officer asked the question in a flat monotone but the question was undoubtedly loaded.

Jake could not remember going upstairs and confidently said, "No." He was tired and getting slightly agitated. Surely, they should be out searching for the culprit and he wanted to know how Mr Woodhouse was. There was a definite undercurrent in the tight little airless room. Jake twisted his neck, clammy against his polo shirt.

"Can you tell me how Mr Woodhouse is?" He used the moment to redirect the interview trying to maintain a calm that he had been losing in the heat of the grilling.

The policeman shuffled his papers. "He is still alive you will be relieved to hear but it is touch and go. We hope he will wake up to give us information that will nail the perpetrator and if he doesn't…"

There was a long pregnant pause, "well," he paused again, "it will likely be a murder charge." The policeman stared forcefully at Jake.

Jake felt his eyes water, betraying his weakness and it seemed to him betraying his guilt.

"Can you explain why your fingerprints were found upstairs at the house?"

Jake could not think. He could not marshal his thoughts. There were alarm bells in his head that stopped him thinking clearly. He could not remember going upstairs. He did not even use the bathroom but would nip home if he needed. He could not explain. He was trapped. He could only deny going upstairs wildly wondering if he had forgotten an occasion when he had. His self-doubt was troubling and he felt his hand involuntarily shake on the table, the friction causing a diverting sound.

The police woman took up the interview.

"Tell me about you, Jake. You live with your father three doors down from Mr Woodhouse. You are not in full time work?" She looked enquiringly at Jake evoking a softer inviting manner even though Jake was not fooled about the inference.

"I've just finished my college course and I have been hoping that Bill, Mr Cartwright, would give me more hours and we can build the business," Jake tried to show a positive constructive attitude. He had been caught off guard and he wanted to regain some control.

"Struggling is it? The nursery?" The policewoman looked intently at him and Jake sighed as he realised his answers would always be found wanting.

"No it's fine. It's been doing a lot better lately." Jake felt it was somehow important to defend the nursery and Bill.

"But you've had no extra hours as yet? How does that make you feel, Jake?" Again, the gentle nature of the question disguised any intended menace. Jake was not without the gumption to recognise the tactics.

"I don't feel anything. It's just the way it is." He shrugged his shoulders trying to stress the unimportance.

The woman gave him a long sympathetic look. "Yes, but it must have been frustrating. You seem to have a good work ethic, doing other gardens too like Mr Woodhouse. How much did he pay you, Jake?"

"Nothing. There was no need." He responded quickly and then he caught the look that was exchanged between the two officers.

Jake was again floundering. He felt he did not have the right answer. True he had helped people from time to time. He enjoyed it. There were people who came to the nursery and would hesitate about buying plants because the planting would be too much for them but they enjoyed looking so sometimes if they were regulars he would offer to come and plant the shrubs or roses or bulbs for them, like Mr and Mrs Frazer, since his stroke at the age of fifty-eight he had lost his balance and his wife was plagued with arthritis or Miss Thompson who had been a teacher for forty years and now at the grand old age of ninety needed a strong pair of hands sometimes. "All part of the service," he would say and, reassured that it would not cost them, they would give him a small tip for his trouble. Mr Woodhouse had somehow taught him the value of neighbourliness. He had thought that now that he had qualifications, he could offer a gardening service for the better off customers which would go hand in hand with his nursery work.

Jake was not without ambition but he was not greedy. He had learnt during his young life that asking for the new expensive up to the minute trainers was in fact profitless in the long term. Mr Woodhouse had shown him that. Maybe, Jake had been too content with his life. The other lads were always after things. Carl had got himself an old sports car, flashy and noisily emitting fumes as it roared down the road driven by Carl, usually with a shrieking girl at his side. Carl thought he was impressive. Jake had thought he was stupid.

"How much did Mr Woodhouse pay you, Jake?" The question was an attack and the arrow found its target.

"Nothing." The truth seemed inadequate. Jake had been paid substantially for any work. How could he explain the benefit of having someone like Mr Woodhouse taking an interest in him?

Penny the policewoman knew all about the lads from this side of town. She had patrolled round there for the last three years and knew their calibre. They would deny anything but eventually she would get the truth. Admittedly she had not come across Jake before.

"So you are telling us that you worked on the garden for nothing." She implied many things. Jake wanted to defend himself from the implication that he was lying or at best a simpleton and at worst a schemer.

"We were friends. He needed me." It was the truth.

"He needed you, did he? How did he need you, Jake?" The policeman interjected. The echo of the word 'need' rang in Jake's head and he felt disloyal. He coughed before he could respond.

"He couldn't manage things like he used to that's all." It was imperative that he convince the officers that the regard he had for Mr Woodhouse was genuine and there was no ulterior motive.

"So out of the goodness of your heart you helped him?" The statement was an insult.

A line seemed to be drawn by the statement and Jake felt bile rise in his throat.

The male policeman took up the challenge.

"Can you explain why your fingerprints were found upstairs in the house?" Jake was caught off guard. He could not explain. He remained silent.

Eventually, at about one o'clock he was allowed to go with the warning that they might need to talk with him again so it was a good idea not to leave the area. Jake realised he was being given more than just friendly advice.

He left hurriedly and breathing heavily. Instead of going home he decided to make his way to the nursery even though Bill had said take the day off for the shock. He needed the comfort of Bill, his plants and the solace of the soil through his fingertips.

Bill was all for going down to the police station when he heard but Jake wanted it left so the two of them pottered, keeping busy and distracted but achieving little. They could get no real news of Mr Woodhouse, except that he was in a critical condition. All they could do was to wait.

When he went home, Jake saw the cordon at Mr Woodhouse's place. Neighbours, trying to glean any information they could, seemed deliberately to stray to that end of the street. Jake's dad was home when he got there and they shared beans on toast as a comfort of normality. His dad refrained from his usual beer and they watched an episode of Prime Suspect which left Jake even more troubled. His dad had had a few run ins with the police in his wilder days and, while he was a model citizen these days, it still left him a bit raw when he thought about it.

Sergeant Wilkes appeared at their front door the following evening. Jake had liked the detective from the start and did not have the same nervous tension in his presence. He was somehow reassuring unlike the two interrogators at the station.

"I thought I would call in for a chat," he said.

When settled again with a cup of tea in hand, the sergeant explained that there had been a lot of talk and he wanted to make sure he was up to speed and there were no loose ends. He told them that Mr Woodhouse was still in a critical condition but stable and he would let them know of any change. He had not regained consciousness.

The detective was very amiable and both father and son relaxed in his company. He was one of those men that seemed trustworthy, with old fashioned principles and courtesy, which put anyone at their ease. He mentioned other people in their area but in a friendly conversational way that encouraged a sharing of confidences. There was no aggression only genuine interest. He talked about Jake's football mates. Most of them played in the Sunday League but somehow Jake never got involved. He thought it was owing to the heavy drinking after a match. His dad at times had shown him what drink could do to a man and Jake had formed the habit of good exercise and good nutrition from Mr Woodhouse.

The detective seemed to soak up all that they told him like a sponge. Jake's dad had lived in the house since he was a nipper and was a fount of all knowledge. Only Jim Woodhouse had lived in the street longer. At times, Jake sat back and listened as his dad would regale the detective with some incidents of the past.

Sergeant Wilkes did not seem to be in any hurry. The sergeant wanted to know about Mr Woodhouse's family. Jake could not remember his wife but felt he knew her from talks with him and the photographs in the front room. It was her choice of furnishings in the house. He knew she loved yellow and loved spring flowers, particularly daffodils.

Mr Woodhouse had said once in a nostalgic and sentimental mood how he had watched as she emerged from a frozen winter when she had been lost from life and he had nurtured her like a delicate flower to emerge in sweet spring as if she had been a bright yellow crocus from the iced ground and later she had become radiant as a daffodil blazing into his lonely life. Jake had been impressed with the sentiments, hoping he would be lucky too.

Jake was becoming aware of the power of love as well as its fortitude and also its anguish. His dad was able to tell Sergeant Wilkes that as far as he knew Jim Woodhouse had no siblings but Ida had had two sisters and several nieces and nephews. He did not know where they all lived.

This led the conversation naturally to Jake's mum who had been friends with Ida for a while. Apparently, Ida would take Jake to give his mum a break and Jackie, his mum, would chat with Ida for hours on end. The policeman asked about Jackie. There was a flutter in Jake's stomach. His dad said, she had been unhappy for a while and one day left and did not return.

Sergeant Wilkes sympathised, "That must have been very difficult."

"It was, I suppose; but I had Jake to see to. Ida was wonderful then, she organised me, looking after the boy and sorting out nursery for him. I don't know what I'd have done without her."

"Do you know where she went or where she is now?" Jake held his breath.

"No. She got in touch with Ida though. Told her to tell me not to worry and it was for the best. Maybe, she had found someone else. I don't know and I couldn't blame her. She was an attractive girl. At first, I wanted to go after her of course, in a blind impulsive way but Ida sat me down and gave me a bit of a lecture really. She said I had to step up to the plate and be a good dad to Jake. She was there to help me and maybe Jackie needed some personal space and would come home one day.

"I think they kept in touch. Trouble was, she never came home and Ida got ill and died so I was on my own. I could have done better by Jake but I did my best." Ken did not mention the cash that had been sent each year at Christmas and on Jake's birthday. He had worried about the source of the money so put it away in a separate building society account. He did not want any trouble and Jake was none the wiser.

The policeman watched both of them carefully. He said he had spent a long time with them and needed to get off to do some police work. He was very polite and thanked them for their hospitality saying he would of course, keep them informed about Jim Woodhouse and then silently seemed to slide out of the house leaving not so much as an empty space behind.

Two days later, Mr Woodhouse regained consciousness. He was, as the doctor said, almost 'out of the woods' and two days after that, Jake was allowed to see him.

Jake was shocked at what he saw. It was a small ward and Mr Woodhouse had been assigned a corner bed. He seemed shrivelled within the sheets and shut within himself. Jake paused by the bedside, awkward and embarrassed. There was a drip into his arm and where the skin was exposed were dark ugly plum coloured bruises shifting into a raw red tinge. His face though, was clear of injury but a padded dressing had been applied to the side of his head.

Jake stood there wondering if he should stay or go. He felt self-conscious, a big strapping boy, muscular from the physical work he had done and bronzed from the outdoor life he led, full of energy and health, with easy movements of a sportsman. Mr Woodhouse shifted in his bed and his eyelids fluttered open. Suddenly, there seemed a transformation in the corpse lying there as he smiled broadly and the skin at the edge of his eyes crinkled giving life and humour to the prostrate form.

"Well, you're a sight for sore eyes, to be sure," and Jim Woodhouse tried to push himself up in the bed.

"Here I'll give you a hand."

"Always there for me aren't you Jake. Well, I got myself in a pretty mess this time," Jake blinked as he felt emotion well up inside.

There were lots of get-well cards on the table and windowsill as well as a bowl of fruit.

"The directors at the club sent the fruit. Nice to know I'm not forgotten," The two of them grinned meaningfully at each other both pleased to have the repartee of their relationship restored.

Jake had not brought anything. He was a bit ashamed.

"Get yourself a chair lad and we can have a good catch up. Can't offer you a tea and digestive though. Tea's rubbish anyway. Always stewed and lukewarm."

Jake was relieved that Mr Woodhouse had regained his critical voice. They chatted peacefully and naturally. Jake was gratified that they still had a comfortable relationship. He did not tell him about the police interviews. Mr Woodhouse told him he had not seen the intruders clearly and it was likely he had fallen and knocked his head on the doorway so even if they were caught they probably would only get a reprimand. However, Mr Woodhouse did have his suspicions and said he would tell Jake when he was up and running again. The police had asked him about Jake of course, but he was soon ruled out of the equation.

Jake wondered why the police had not told him he was no longer under suspicion. It was certainly a relief but he also felt annoyed and even tarnished. He thought of the words that were used for the intruders that could darken or lighten their responsibility for what had happened, like 'perpetrators', 'burglars', 'assailants', 'attackers', 'trespassers', 'robbers', 'thieves' but Jake thought the word that seemed to fit most in this case was 'scum'.

Mr Woodhouse was not very happy that a social worker was to arrange help for him. She was a pert little body but he did not want strangers poking their noses into his business. He realised he was getting on and living on his own added to his vulnerability and he could not do the things he used to do.

He resisted a full-scale onslaught of home help, especially reckoning up his monetary contribution after he had to declare the extent of his savings. His needs were simple and inexpensive and besides which he had other ideas for any money he had accumulated over the years. However, as it turned out he liked Barbara, the home help, who would come and do his laundry each Monday.

He smiled, as it had always been Ida's insistence that washing was done on a Monday and he remembered when she lived at the cottage, seeing the steam clouds out the back if it was cold, and the sheets soaking in the tub before being attacked by the old mangle in the scullery, aided and abetted by a determined Ida. Ida with her arms soaped to her elbows, Ida singing in the back yard, Ida reaching for the clothes line. There were so many photographs of Ida in his memory. She was still with him, always.

Barbara would clean the bathroom which was a definite bonus. He hated doing it and wondered how women managed to achieve a sparkle when his efforts could not. She would do some shopping too and it was easy to slide into a life greased by her ministrations.

Jake continued to visit and kept the garden up to scratch. Things moved into another year.

It was too much for Mr Woodhouse to get to the nursery on two buses so Bill would pop in and see him. In fact, Mr Woodhouse had lots of visitors. What had happened had seemed to shake up the community as much as shake up Jim Woodhouse. Former players dropped in and most brought a bottle of Scotch or a few cans, neighbours asked if he wanted any errands doing and other friends from over the years visited or even took him out for an hour or two. Jake joked to Mr Woodhouse that he had a better social life than him.

Jake had decided that he needed to move forward too. He enrolled at night school for bookkeeping and with Bill's approval set up a small gardening business from the nursery. There was a considerable demand and Jake soon used up all his spare hours and more, licking people's gardens into shape and being paid for the privilege. He was able to promote the nursery too, so everyone benefitted. He managed to get a van for his tools which also gave him independence. He would see the old gang from time to time but he found they had little in common. He was no longer scrubbing along. He had a clear future and was proud.

Bill's son Simon was becoming more interested in the nursery. He had never wanted to be a plantsman, shying away from what he and his sisters called his dad's hobby but he saw potential in its location. Everywhere there was a demand for houses and Simon recognised an opportunity. His dad had enjoyed his life. It was the turn of the next generation to enjoy theirs. He had been in the army and then after he was demobbed he had done this and that ending up in security. His father did not know exactly what he did but guessed it was fitting alarms.

Simon always built up any position he had. His father knew he had not the innate intelligence for MI5 or GCHQ at Cheltenham but he would be honest and trustworthy so would be an asset in providing security packages for private homes and businesses. The job had seemed flexible and allowed Simon the time to follow a different passion. Bill had been with him at the auction when he had bought the first cottage and had been relieved when it had turned out well.

In fact, since Simon had returned home father and son had learnt to respect each other. They were different in outlook but either would defend the other to the hilt. Simon could be relied on to help in the nursery with heavy work that Bill found tough and Bill encouraged his son with his plans for property, even helping him out from time to time or lending him funds to help a project along. They bickered and cast insults at each other but these banters were an act as privately they looked out for each other as best they could.

Simon had teamed up with a chap to buy and renovate houses. It seemed to be successful and certainly kept Simon out of mischief. Simon always seemed to have repressed energy. Bill was pleased to see him busy, in fact anything to keep him off his own back as far as his precious nursery was concerned. Simon had not the patience for his father's way of life.

In the spring sunshine Bill discussed things with Jim.

"I've loved that nursery, you know. First bought the land cheap from the estate when it was all split up when National Trust took over the house. It was scrubland and I got it for a song really, although at the time the wife thought I was mad. Best days of my life clearing and planting it and it's hard to give it up. I can't blame the lad really, for seeing the potential. I am finding it difficult to let him have his head and walk away. It's been my life, Jim."

Jim did know. In the last few years there had been so many endings, his dear wife Ida and his marriage, the job as greenkeeper, his physical ability to do things but yet there were other things that focussed his mind, things that gave him purpose and above all hope. He knew he was old, he was now nearer eighty than seventy, but he had been lucky. He had not fallen on the wayside like some he knew.

Malcolm's wife had dementia and now Malcolm was trapped in an ever-decreasing circle from where there was no release. Jim thought he still had opportunity and decided that now was as good a time as ever to seize it.

"Yes, it's difficult to let go."

He hesitated but only briefly and outlined an idea that he had had for a while. Bill was surprised and heartened. "Are you sure? It would want looking into properly. I have no idea about value or anything."

"Oh yes, all signed up good and proper with a solicitor. I've already spoken with someone and we would involve your Simon and Jake. It would be no good if they weren't on board."

The two men decided to have one of the beers Jim had been given.

Chapter 5
Heads I Win, Tails You Lose

That time is past,
And all its aching joys are now no more,
And all its dizzy raptures.

Tintern Abbey: William Wordsworth

2005-2006: Gillian

Gillian was furious. "How dare they?" She muttered to herself as she made her way to her car a couple of weeks after marking the exam paper that had given her a few sleepless nights. It had been another full-on week of marking and she was tired because she had been burning the midnight oil in order to keep up with her schedule which was making her feel particularly irritable.

None of the answer papers since had presented her with any unease like the discomfort that had arisen from that candidate. She had been sorely troubled and even noted down the centre number to locate the school but the possibility of finding anything further frightened her even more. She deposited her bag of folders on the back seat and eased herself into the driving seat. She was justifiably upset. She watched other teachers load their cars and wave greetings before driving off. Somehow, she could not move and crouched into her seat hoping no-one would come over and talk. She did not trust herself with any response.

Eventually, she steered the car away from the school, away from her persecutions. It had all been so underhand and unexpected. She had been given no warning and now it was too late for any alteration. She had effectively been passed over and rejected for younger models. She seethed. She imagined Shane, Fiona and Rebekah, with a k, meeting for a gin and tonic at the Stag Hotel bar with Frank the head of department after the Thursday department meetings and making their little suggestions.

Frank was a good sort but sometimes, Gillian thought, he was entirely out of his depth and more and more he was becoming a mere figurehead seeing out his time before the promise of retirement by the sea. When Rebekah, with a k, had been appointed second in department after only two years at the chalk face, things in Gillian's opinion began to unravel. Rebekah with a k had redesigned the year eight curriculum first and then in the wake of her apparent success tackled year nine.

No longer did the students aspire to Wordsworth or grapple with a full Shakespeare play or a meaty Dickens' novel; they were encouraged to believe in levels of performance contained in rap, media or Roald Dahl and, heaven forbid, JK Rowling. There was nothing wrong with any of these and they had their place in the curriculum but it exasperated Gillian to lose her beloved classics.

Gillian was not narrow-minded at all, although argued that at thirteen the students should be challenged and guided through the study of the literary canon by an experienced teacher. Of course, they still met the classics but only briefly through extracts, the heart had gone out of the subject, and Gillian longed for the wide ranging discussions of her former teaching years when passages had been used to illuminate the whole rather than the PowerPoint presentations which seemed to have the power to entertain and keep the class busy but not the power of real understanding.

The houses gave way to the countryside resplendent in its summer glory. The horse chestnut trees lined this particular section of the route and unfailingly transported Gillian away from the ordeal of the classroom. The verges were lush and the hedges laden with green foliage. The trees reached over her in a canopy adorned by their pale cream or blush blossoms. Sometimes, if she had time, she would pull into the little layby and drink in every aspect so that for a few precious moments there was a mystical sensation of 'the inward eye that is the bliss of solitude'.

Gillian loved all the seasons but this section of her journey home was a delight, delicious to taste and potent in its power during high summer, so Gillian understood that word no longer current in our language, 'rapture.' Inevitably, Gillian would feel a greater purpose and a dominance that would sweep away any trivia from her mind, albeit in a temporary trance. Dearly she would have loved to stop today, but time was always her dominating factor and she merely allowed the allure to nudge her gently out of the tightness of her mind gradually surrendering to serenity in her soul.

Gillian, driving now more easily, realised that she had been stuck in her ways and maybe she could have been a bit more open to change. She had resorted to her natural default position of head down, get on and do not rock the boat. She could have volunteered for the group looking at raising literacy standards or the group investigating the effect of modern culture in the classroom or any number of groups that had emerged over the last few years, reporting and redesigning well known and well-beloved schemes of work. If she had been more active, then maybe she would not have been passed over.

By the time she turned into Primrose Crescent she was feeling calmer, although her anger had not dissipated and somehow, rose again, as she entered the house physically weighed down with bulging book bags.

Steve was home before her. He was sprawled on the settee, a half-drunk mug of coffee on the side table and gently snoring in a late afternoon nap. The curtains were drawn against the sunshine which gave the room a gloomy look. Gillian felt impatience rise and she felt her body clench. She bustled into the kitchen clearing away the debris of breakfast that had been hastily abandoned that morning, storing cereal in the cupboard, loading the dishwasher and wiping surfaces. None of it was hard and it helped her get rid of pent up anger but somehow it also redirected her passion ready to take on any unfortunate victim. Steve now awake, sauntered in.

"You're late. What's for tea? I'm starving." His words were not delivered with any venom but rather in a conversational tone of observation but they riled Gillian even more and she felt the impact. It took all of Gillian's control not to fling the glass she was handling at the man. As ever, Steve just did not seem to notice her agitation and he carried on regardless leaning against the cupboard by the door.

"We got the fireplace sorted today. Terrible job. The old one wouldn't budge at all and we had to smash it out in the end. This is when I really appreciate having someone like Simon around. He's strong. Must be all his army training. Once we got that antique out, we could brick up ready for the new electric fire. We're hoping to get the wall plastered in a couple of days. Wondered if you might be up for doing a couple of hours at the weekend, cleaning? Bit of dust from today and you've always had the magic touch. I know, you have your marking load and I hate asking but it would be great if you could spare me a little time. I told Simon we'd get it done alright. He's off to see a mate this weekend."

Steve did not wait for a response. He knew she would silently demur and then come up trumps at the weekend. It was typical of Gillian to under-promise and over-deliver. She had paused in her action and her fingers had strayed to her hair which she twisted in her fingers. He was instinctively wary and looking at the clock on the wall commented.

"Ah news is on. We are late tonight." And he left to switch on the television in the lounge.

Gillian had kept her back to him, not ready to let him see her discomfort. She would no doubt say something derogatory and in her emotional state it could end up in an almighty row which would send her completely out of kilter. She hated any upset. Sometimes, her school life invaded every crevice of her life outside and left her no time to expand herself. She stopped herself reaching for the remnants of the wine from a couple of nights ago admonishing herself for her weakness.

Somehow, if Steve offered her a glass of comfort it would be a sign of closeness and reassurance whereas to help herself to a glass would be a sign of desperation and weakness. She must sort something out for tea.

Steve had returned. "If you've not started, why don't I go out for fish and chips or we can ring Benedicto's and see if there's a table? I was going to suggest we go there for your birthday but there's no reason why we cannot go twice or somewhere else." Steve then added in a conciliatory tone, "Of course, you've probably got lots to do so your choice. Thought it might help and be nice." He was again wary of her response.

Gillian looked at him. Yes, she had loads of work before the term came to an end and the annual examination marking to complete but then what the hell. There had been so few occasions when she had been impulsive.

"Let's try and get a table," she said. Steve was slightly taken aback but in a pleasant way. Rarely did they go out on a week day in term time. Gillian had been governed by schedules and over the years he had adapted.

The day had been horrible. She had been given her timetable for the following year at morning break and could only tackle Frank and Rebekah with a k after school as she had lessons. Frank as usual floundered and said all responsibility for timetabling had fallen on Rebekah's shoulders that year and what a brick she had been taking on that duty and sorting it out in record time.

Gillian knew something about the perils of timetabling, having done it for a few years under the previous head of department and replied that it would have been nice to have had prior discussion to have any preferences noted. Rebekah smiled in her sweet saccharin way and explained that there were additional constraints this year as it had been agreed that Shane and Fiona needed sixth form teaching experience. Gillian still had her Upper Sixth but as she had enjoyed sixth form experience for many years it was only fair that she temporarily step down in the Lower Sixth. Gillian did not know how to explain that she did not mind stepping down if it was fair but the rest of her timetable was rubbish. She had been allotted two year-nines, neither of which top sets and she had had no input into the year nine schemes of work, so would have to get up to speed over the summer. She had also been given a bottom set in year ten and was being given the year seven special needs group.

She mused at the word 'given' as though it was some sort of prize or gift when it was anything but. She was an examiner and had maintained high standards with the very best students over the years so the whole thing was insulting her intelligence. It was clear to Gillian that Rebekah had cherry picked and Gillian was left with the damaged fallen fruit.

"You are so wonderful with struggling students, Gill," Rebekah wheedled. "Look how you motivated Liz Pullen's set the year before last. They deserve someone with your expertise and experience." Only Steve affectionately called her Gill and Rebekah had invaded her space yet again.

Gillian knew she was being manipulated, although at the time she had been proud of the relative success of Liz and co. Liz had been a particularly troublesome and defiant teenager who scared most teachers but somehow Gillian's perseverance and high expectations had won her trust and gradually Liz and Jade and Beth and what was that other girl's name, ah yes Dawn, had improved beyond recognition to get middle of the road grades. Gillian enjoyed a certain celebrity status for a few weeks in the aftermath as all their other subject grades were weak. It was smart of Rebekah to bring it up.

The meeting had come to an uneasy end. There was nothing to be done as the deputy head had sewn up the school timetable and it would have been a major upheaval to change it. Gillian was not about to raise her head above the parapet.

Steve interrupted her thoughts. "Table booked for eight, so you've time for a nice hot soak if you like and I'll bring you a cup of tea up, or even something stronger."

"Tea would be perfect," she murmured.

"I might even scrub your back for you," and he winked. "Now get a move on woman."

Steve really did have the knack of deflecting her thoughts.

The bubbles in the bath skirted her nipples and swallowed her stomach in the heady aroma. She had pampered herself with the expensive bubble bath hardly used that Steve had bought her for Christmas. Gillian was not one to waste anything but somehow, tonight, it did not seem like an indulgence but a necessity. Steve had set her special mug on the shelf near enough to reach but far enough away to be safe and sat on the toilet seat gazing at her. His fingers traced the edge of the bubble line and gently pushed under the water line, feeling the curves of his wife. Gillian closed her eyes better to relish his touch.

"A promise for later," he said teasingly.

Gillian chose the emerald dress. She had last worn it for a ruby wedding celebration of their neighbours in March when she had wanted to shine. Normally she was discreet in her clothes with the majority of her purchases being school appropriate but this dress had beguiled her. It was close fitting but the soft silky fabric seemed to float over her body. She felt feminine, sensuous and desirable, feelings that had often been deliberately suppressed in her busy life. With slight apprehension for being too risqué, she descended downstairs.

"Wow. Maybe, we should stay in after all."

Gillian laughed. It was good. Steve had booked a taxi so they could both enjoy the wine. It had been so long since they had been out like this and at first they both seemed a bit shy. As usual, it was Steve who opened the conversation. Only half way through the renovation, he already had his eye on future investments. It seemed Simon was keen to carry the partnership forward. Gillian listened to the familiar spiel, acknowledging in a practised way, before venturing to mention her concerns over a divine Tiramisu.

Give Steve his due, he listened, although it was apparent he could not see what the fuss was about. She had always complained about her marking load and that would be a bonus. He had every confidence that she would, as he put it 'beat the little buggers into submission' and it was a job. She should learn the art of leaving the job at the school gate. Gillian felt little hard pebbles in her stomach.

"I know all that but, I feel so abused by it all." Her hand strayed to a tendril of hair which she twisted in her fingers.

"If that is the way you feel, why don't you quit? Give in your notice. It's not worth suffering like this." Steve reached over and gently removed her finger from the twist of hair and looked steadily at her.

The pebbles in her stomach had become bigger.

"I can't. We need the income. It's impossible you know that." Gillian knew she was being assertive, using her teacher voice, as Steve would say.

"Actually, I don't know that at all. We could manage you know and maybe you need to break away. You could help me with my business and with you on the case we could do well and you've often joked about supply teaching with all its advantages so you needn't shut the door completely. You might find a better job, something more interesting." There was a masculine control in his voice that was appealing.

Whether it was the wine, the intimacy of the restaurant, the little candle fluttering between them, Gillian opened her heart to the prospect.

Her voice took on a more tremulous quality and wanting reassurance. "But what about my pension? I had all those years part time when I looked after Dad so, although I've been in the classroom thirty years, I don't have that many pensionable years. Long term it's not a good idea." Gillian took another mouthful of Tiramisu, biting back her dismay.

"Gill, love, we have to get to retirement first. Is it worth a further five or so years of stress and depression? I doubt it. Simon tells me about his dad sometimes. He's got a nursery. According to Simon, it's not profitable at all and his mum and dad live very hand to mouth. Maybe, that's what makes Simon ambitious. Anyway, the one thing he always says is that his dad's hobby is his job and vice versa and he is as happy as Larry tending his plants and gossiping with his customers. Sometimes, I think that a man like that has all the riches of the world."

"I don't know. It's all so hard." Gillian had spent a lifetime being careful and sensible. She had been weighed down with responsibility in one way or another. She thought it was not wise to open the floodgate and took deep calming breaths as she recognised her own entrapment.

"Think about it. I hate to see you so careworn most days and I know, it's partly my fault."

"No, you work hard."

Gillian reacted quickly, moved by his remark and loving him for his support.

"Yes, but I'm doing what I enjoy. I know, I should provide for you much more, but you know how it has been with Alex and Abigail. But that is much better now, they are all sorted." He tailed off, noting her face. Gillian did not want their evening hijacked by his ex-wife. Abigail had a tendency to emerge into their lives just when least expected. Steve had never managed to shake her off completely and sometimes, Gillian could not help wonder how hard he had tried. Tonight, neither of them wanted the invasion.

"Maybe, we could sit down together and think of ideas and do some sums." Gillian felt lightened and it was the easiest solution to defer any decision as well as keeping the prospect alive.

"I want you to be happy, Gill." It was a gentle, sincere statement that stole into her heart.

"I am," she returned with the warmth of love.

Gillian sank for a few minutes into a reverie of possibilities. Steve lived in the moment. Gillian lived in anything but, fearful of making wrong decisions, always assessing and reassessing and often inactive. Had she squandered her life? Had she squandered her opportunities? How can one ever know? Backwards was not an option. Gillian had been filled with doubt but she emerged from the evening with a little glimmer of optimism.

They did talk about the options, although it was difficult as each came from a different perspective. Gillian hugged the possibilities and explored feasibility by taking more of an interest in Steve's projects. It was an escape in her consciousness, if not in reality.

As it happened, choices would soon be made for them.

The autumn term closed in on Gillian. She worked hard to bring her classes in line and found she enjoyed the repartee with the personalities of these lower groups. The marking load was indeed easier to handle, mainly because of smaller classes rather than more limited responses. Steve meanwhile, had completed the house and having sold it made a worthwhile profit. Steve and Simon discussed the future over a pint. Simon was anxious to keep his funds in reserve as he had his eye on the bigger picture, reckoning his dad was ready to relinquish the nursery land. He felt he could make a killing.

Steve on the other hand had identified another small property, ripe for renovation. For the moment, they agreed to go their separate ways. Simon had been particularly busy with security work, the firm having a contract to increase security on a property on the outskirts of Midchester. He had said little to Steve, as it was occupied by Steve's ex-wife and her new husband.

Steve always needed a creative challenge over and above his day job and he was perennially bullish about his prospects. Simon had proved to be a good partner and Steve thought they were getting to the point that a more official partnership might have to be negotiated. He would mention this to Antony, his accountant at their annual meeting next spring. His son, Alex had been more settled in his job with Corneille, which meant Steve's resources were not plundered as they had so often been in the past by either Alex or Abigail, and indeed, Abigail seemed too busy in her social sphere now to have any time for Steve. It had taken him until his mid-fifties but he now felt success was round the corner, in more ways than one. If only his wife had the same belief, not only in him but in herself.

The news broke at the October full staff meeting. There had of course, been rumours but the extent of the financial difficulty was on a scale no-one had imagined. True, Gillian had seen class sizes shrinking but until more recently taking the examination classes and top sets to boot Gillian had not been fully aware of the shrinkage. She had thought that investments were being made in smaller classes for the less academic. This, she reasoned, had been a deliberate decision to improve standards but the figures were stark. The new school over the river, where there was a posh housing development, had been proving increasingly attractive to families in their area, despite the journey across town, and their old rival, Forest Hill, had seen a shift in popularity since the new head.

Gillian realised their school had been coasting. In fact, as the figures were presented on the inevitable PowerPoint, she saw a wanton disregard for trends from the management team and to boot reckless spending on inessentials, including, in her view, expensive support and secretarial staff. The room was hushed when Mike put the question to the management panel, grouped together on the stage as though they were the solution to the problem and not the cause.

"What does this mean for the future?"

The head nodded sagely and replied, "Of course, there will need to be cuts. In the present climate, we cannot avoid it. My team has worked tirelessly to avoid such measures but we will need to reduce staffing levels at the end of this year." There was a whispered response in the hall as staff digested the impact.

Doreen raised her hand, "You are presumably considering redundancies. Have you a figure in mind?"

"We are still looking at options of course, but we will have to look at our surplus. We would invite anyone thinking of, say, early retirement to approach us and of course, anyone else who might wish to avail themselves of a generous redundancy package to speak with us in the strictest confidence."

Eyes seemed to travel to the more age senior members of staff, curious for possible change and perhaps hopeful of filling dead men's shoes.

"I think, we will close the meeting there and we will work towards a development plan which we will unfold next term. Good night, ladies and gentlemen. Have a safe journey home." And with that he picked up his papers and strode out of the room followed by his entourage shuffling and nodding to each other towards the exit, as though following Black Rod out of the Commons' chamber.

"Well, what do you make of that?" Deidre addressed the little group which included Gillian.

"It's been on the cards for the last few years and only now do they wake up and smell the coffee," was one response and the others nodded in agreement.

"I bet none of them will volunteer. Too cushy."

"I wonder if Frank will consider it," Gillian pondered.

"Doubt it," Deidre responded. "The twins are only in their first year at uni and I heard on the grapevine, he is thinking of stepping down in two or three years when Rebekah will step neatly into his shoes."

Gillian shuddered at the thought of Rebekah being head of department. Maybe, in two- or three-years' time she would feel secure enough financially to leave with him.

The caretaker had begun collecting chairs so the group disbanded to take the news to their separate homes.

Over the weeks that followed it soon became clear that a plan was developing helped by the input of key members of staff. Rebekah with a k naturally featured in the steering group. Frank declared he had no intention of vacating his chair as he put it and sat resolutely in it allowing the storm to swirl about him. Further inconclusive proposals were put forward in January and letters were sent out in February. Gillian was handed hers on Valentine's Day.

Steve was upbeat when she told him.

"Look Gill, maybe it's for the good. You've been fretting and you can still do your exam marking. We can work together. It looks like a decent package."

Gillian could not banish the hurt after all her loyal years of service. She said nothing but felt everything.

The meetings were painful but aided by her union rep she negotiated her way through hoping that the axe would not fall on her head even though the charge had been made. Other staff members looked at her with varying degrees of sympathy. There was tension in the air.

By the beginning of May, the list of redundancies was determined, giving those involved a brief opportunity to enter the jobs market for September. Gillian said her goodbyes to her Upper Sixth, who were very sweet and brought her chocolates and wine as well as a signed by them all copy of the poems of Wordsworth. The year gradually closed down.

Once more, as the summer term progressed Gillian marvelled at the horse chestnut trees and how nature was continually resurrected and replenished. She was sad that she would have no reason to travel this way again. No longer would she have the awe-inspiring journey, she would have to forge another path. Time was taking her away. Time was her mistress. Time was determining her fate.

By August 2006, Steve was on a new project. This time a pair of houses, built originally in the 1930s, with the benefit of large gardens. He urged Gillian to be involved, suggesting she research interior and exterior designs so she would spend happy hours browsing magazines, comparing prices and quality in DIY stores and investigating hard landscaping possibilities at garden centres. She suspected he was directing her against any backlash of feelings from her school departure and he could quite easily have sourced everything a lot more efficiently without her help. It did keep her busy and roused her interest.

On one occasion, near the end of September she had taken refuge in a homeware store café. It was crowded and after purchasing a latte she only just managed to bag a vacant table. She put the brochures on the table to peruse as she drank.

"Mind if I sit here?" The girl scraped a chair away from the table and pulled the pushchair into position next to it. Gillian looked up.

"Hey, Miss, didn't expect to see you here," Liz Pullen plonked herself down on the chair and as she did so waved at a waitress with a tray laden with a Coca-Cola can, orange juice, biscuits and a huge cream doughnut, plus a generous supply of paper serviettes. Gillian moved her brochures back into her bag.

"Thought you'd be at school, Miss. Not skiving are you?" She chuckled in that hoarse throaty way she had.

"No, I left in the summer."

"Well, we all thought you would be there forever."

Actually, Gillian admitted inwardly that she did too but said something to the effect that she needed a change and was working with her husband biting her lip before offering too much information.

Liz was much more interested in her own doings. "Well, we thought you were the best teacher. You believed in us not like some I could mention," and she proceeded to give an accurate, if not kind appraisal of some of Gillian's colleagues. Liz Pullen's gang had been merciless at the time and Gillian was caught between agreement of the ineptitude of some members of staff or to defending their honour but in the end, sat back amused at how perspicacious a girl such as Liz could be.

"Pity you are not teaching anymore. You should do private lessons. I used to do a bit of cleaning for this lady and she had three kids and they all had extra lessons. I thought it was a waste of time really, and cost a bomb but she was dead set on them all going to university." Gillian had never thought about this, having been much more used to ploughing her furrow in mainstream education. Liz seemed to bubble with life, in all her actions and words, eating her doughnut with cream escaping from the corners of her mouth as she talked and also feeding biscuits and juice to the little girl.

Gillian asked about the toddler. "This is Carly, named after Carl her dad," and Liz's eyes travelled to her stomach. Gillian had already noticed a bulge. "I know, should have been more careful but I've got a flat and Carl gets work on the building and with my benefits things aren't bad. 'Course he doesn't live with me, you know I can't risk that." Liz winked conspiratorially at Gillian.

There was no sense of holding back with any figure of authority. Liz was blunt and forthright. It was what had made her frightening at school. Gillian was glad she had not been intimidated. She liked Liz and enjoyed her company, although longer would be physically exhausting.

Gillian having drunk her latte and seeing the increasing smears from the chocolate biscuit on Carly and the table thought this might be a good time to depart.

"I need to be somewhere. Nice to see how well you're doing and all the best," and then in an impulsive moment she reached into her bag and extracted a fiver. "Here, buy something nice for the little one." Gillian smiled as she handed over the note.

"Thanks, Miss. Hey I might get something educational, like a book." They both laughed.

Gillian's meeting with Liz had got her thinking. Maybe, she could keep her teaching hand in and earn something for herself as well as help Steve. She had been working up to contacting local schools for some supply work but now she had experienced the fresh air outside the classroom she had been more and more reluctant. Indecision had forever been her curse. As was customary, she would ponder on it and talk to Steve.

She had parked her car on the edge of the car park. Unaccountably by the time she got there Gillian felt tears rush into her eyes. The contentment she had felt when she had sat alone with her coffee and selection of brochures had from her encounter with Liz been replaced by uncertainty and disquiet.

Gillian sat in the driving seat willing composure. She stared at the people bustling into the shopping outlets. Some strode purposefully and others, mainly women, sauntered along the pedestrian way. The bright store lights penetrated into the recesses pulling in customers with their eager faces wanting to be hypnotised into purchases to make a difference to their lives.

The homeware store she had visited had been vast. There were sections for every conceivable lifestyle choice. Duvets and bed linen, fancy lighting, kitchen ware, knickknacks for every room and occasion had been grouped in enticing displays to convince even the most sceptical that this would transform a dull life. Gillian knew the ploys, but she too had been sucked into the belief. It was as though there was a commercial conspiracy keeping the masses happy.

She thought of Liz, a girl of no more than eighteen with a child and another on the way. It was this that had really upset Gillian's equilibrium. Gillian found Liz entertaining but she could not approve of her lifestyle, an opinion that made her feel pompous rather than virtuous.

Liz showed no regret for her state. She took her situation as a fact of life and faced any consequences manoeuvring through the benefit system to gain as much advantage as possible. There seemed no emotion or moral compass in her attitude but there she was, granted what Gillian had wanted most throughout her life. Gillian did not actually blame Liz, but it reflected her own inadequacies and she felt angry and bitter and forlorn.

When she had been eighteen, she knew few boys and had very little chance of knowing any more or knowing them well. It had been a statement of her life really. She could remember the yearnings she had felt but always accompanied by alarm that suppressed any action on her part. She avoided gatherings because she did not know how she was expected to behave. She understood that girls, on no account must lead boys on. That would make them responsible for any misunderstandings and gain a bad reputation.

The question was how could she successfully have a nice boyfriend if she was not polite and interested which in turn could be construed as flirting. It had all been a conundrum. She had known so very little and, although her mum was approachable and kind, it was a topic she avoided. It was easier to stay put and look for fate to play a part. Her ignorance essentially made her incapable of a relationship even if there had been the opportunity as Diana and the other girls had so easily taken.

Gillian had been awkward and shy. She dreamed of romance but shielded herself from it. Now at fifty-four, her heart was torn for the cruelty of the past. College had offered her a few dates but her awkwardness had defied anything meaningful. She had chosen a college in the vicinity of home, so, sheltered there rather than being exposed to the uncertainties of relationships. She was neat, careful and perfect.

As a goldfish in a glass bowl, she swam in circles looking out at the world beyond, admired as an ornament but condemned to a solitary life. Then teaching had led to her being marooned in a classroom, adrift from real life, creating another world within the four walls with her students and her literature for company.

Gillian had kept everything immaculate. Her tidy, purposeful classroom with its evocative wall displays set a scene of inquiry both for herself and her students. She made it a haven, a sanctuary away from the prying eyes of the world. At least, that was how it had been at the beginning of her career. She resisted identifying with the mentality of Jean Brodie but now conceded that she had used her students to assuage a hunger. She had faith but that faith could not extend to Immaculate Conception.

Gillian had remained barren. What had begun at eighteen as a preservation of her honour had become by the time she was forty a fortress of fear. She had built the edifice brick by brick and stone by stone, as a protection for her own cowardice. It needed a strong man to break down the portcullis and claim the virgin inside.

Gradually, over those years Gillian found expectations turn to hope and then that hope turn to cold resignation. Eventually, the drawbridge had been lowered for the princely invasion in a rare moment of desperate surrender by Gillian.

Gillian grieved. Steve could not offer comfort for this. He had his son. Gillian felt alone, spurned by the world. It was no consolation that Steve too had his cross to bear. Alex had been a complete disappointment. Gillian knew the efforts that Steve had made with Alex but Alex had inflicted wounds to her husband that had left deep and lasting scars. Gillian had at first tried to appreciate the difficulties for Alex. She had thought he was being loyal to Abigail. She now thought he was a misfit. She loved Steve for not abandoning his son but she hated him too for the way he allowed his son the freedom to ruin things for them.

The Millennium episode still burnt fiercely. Alex was more than baggage for them to carry. He had been a judgement of sin that required an eternal penance. It had been hard.

Chapter 6
Love Is Where You Find It

Love bade me welcome: yet my soul drew back
Guiltie of dust and sinne

Love: George Herbert

1990-1993: Ida and Jackie

Sergeant Wilkes was awaiting news of promotion. He had sat his exams and was quietly confident that an inspectorate was in the offing. It was also possible that a position might become available at the neighbouring county or even at his current station. As he lived near the border of the two counties, he would not have to uproot his family. He could manage a commute and anyway he was out of office so much it hardly mattered which part of the county was his home base. He looked forward to new challenges.

The spate of burglaries in the area had perturbed him, especially as there had seemed a vicious streak in them and the victims came from the more vulnerable in society. The usual suspects had proved elusive and Tom Wilkes was convinced it was a new operator on the streets. Others at the station had had someone in mind but Tom was unconvinced and held off any arrest, sure that the evidence would not stack up. Sometimes, that meant he was not that popular at the station; his careful painstaking ways were to them slow and plodding and he knew behind his back he was referred to as PC Plod. He did not mind, especially as he climbed the career ladder. It was good to have a nickname and persona that allowed him to operate in his own methodical way and even be underestimated by some. He understood that there was circumstantial evidence against Jake but he believed he was a good judge of character and Jake really did not seem to be the type.

In fact, he found he liked the lad, although none of that was going to influence him in his investigation. It had been a shame he had been called away when Jake was interviewed, although reading the notes and listening to the recording, it had been more like an interrogation. Penny and Graham had really set about him. They had wanted to charge him and wrap the case up but Tom knew a good brief would soon see through the case. You could not fault their keenness Tom thought, but their gung-ho approach while seeming effective, did not dig out the truth of the matter. Their assumption about the finger prints was a case in point.

Jake's prints were found on objects upstairs, things that he might have touched downstairs and then were transported by Jim Woodhouse upstairs, like a couple of books and a mug. There were no prints on door handles for example. Tom Wilkes was always glad to have Penny and Graham at his back for any drugs raid or tricky arrests but intelligence was not their forte. Tom was glad he had persuaded them against the arrest, as on waking up Jim Woodhouse was able to exonerate Jake. It would have been a waste of time and resources. What did get Tom's juices flowing however, was Jake's missing Mum. Now that was intriguing.

****

Ida Woodhouse had taken to the new occupants, three doors down, especially the little boy, Jake. He was a darling. When they arrived, it was winter and he would be all snuggled up in his push chair with big blue smiling eyes popping out to view the world. Ida loved children, although there had been none for her to dote on during her lifetime. She would watch them play on the waste ground over the road and then attempt to get to know them giving them sweets and cake. She became a familiar figure and many a child would gather in the hope that Ida would feed them a treat.

Parents too, felt she was keeping an eye on their offspring and relaxed in the knowledge. Ida was a well-liked popular character who had lived there forever. Ida would take walks in the park where she would gaze longingly at the watching mums and dads as they pushed their small children on the swings or stand, arms wide, to catch them on their way down from the slide.

Sometimes, she would visit the outlets for baby and toddler clothing picking up the cute clothes to inspect and fingering the soft fabrics. She would tell shop assistants who asked that she was looking for gifts for a grandchild and occasionally bought something which she tucked away in the drawer under the bed in the spare room. If Jim was out at a match and she knew she would not be disturbed, she would steal into the room and lovingly go through her purchases, lying them on the bed for inspection before reluctantly storing them back again under the duvet covers of her life.

Jackie did not seem to have any friends not being local and would be pleased to chat as they emerged from the local shop. It did not take long before Ida would invite Jackie and Jake round for tea and her special fruit cake.

Ida learnt that Jackie had left home under a cloud. Ida could understand the dynamics of family life, especially when a young girl made a bid for freedom. She hoped that her influence might heal the rift.

"Mum was good at first, when I had Jake. She was shocked, you know, and called me all the names under the sun but she said we would work something out." Ida lapped up any confidence.

Ida wondered if she should have given her mum, Molly, a chance but deep down she knew she had been doomed whatever option she had taken. She admired Jackie for her determination in keeping Jake, although conceding to herself that times were different. Even though Ida had managed to suppress her memories there were moments when they would lurch at her, raw and rancid. At those times she curled within herself fending off the demons that seemed to attack her very core.

Of course, for Ida there was the survival of the war years and for her and her family even more the treacherous post-war years. The small town and surrounding area had largely escaped the cruelties of bombing occurring in their larger counterparts. Newspapers kept them informed and there had been personal losses in local families. There was one memorable night, when a crippled enemy plane had eventually nose-dived into a wheat field. After the bodies had been removed some of the locals took souvenirs and it became a favourite playground for local boys until eventually the farmer tired of shooing them away from his precious crop, managed to get the wreck removed and serve its war purpose as scrap metal. After the war, men back from the front claimed jobs and both Ida and Daisy became unemployed. Daisy was glad and devoted her time and efforts to her husband and growing family. Ida was no longer needed part time on the estate so cast her eye around for work in the town. The town was growing. Houses were being erected nearer and nearer their little smallholding which meant that they had a ready market for their produce from the newcomers but somehow Ida felt this invasion of people more threatening. She had wanted to stay in her closet.

"It was Mum that said I should call him Jake. She said it would give him a sense of belonging. I didn't really like the name at first but Mum was being so helpful I just could not refuse. Mum lined up the vicar too for the christening. She did the church flowers and always organised a craft store for the fete so I suppose he felt obliged. I'm not sure what she told the neighbours and the rest but something about me being taken advantage of and being left to pick up the pieces. Looking back, I think she enjoyed the sympathy. She always liked being the centre of things, especially if she was being charitable, you know."

Ida did know. In her time she had met lots of women who held themselves up as paragons. Meredith Pugh, Jackie's mother was right on cue for that. She began to get a picture of the lady in question.

"I was so lucky to meet Ken. He didn't ask questions and took me and Jake in. I don't know what would have happened to me otherwise. I couldn't go home," Jackie said this as a statement of fact.

Bit by bit, Ida learnt how Meredith had controlled her daughter in little insidious ways. She would come home from school and find a new dress laid out on the bed that her mother had bought for her. There were other gifts too but all a projection of what Meredith wanted in a daughter. She would alternately offer Jackie a small glass of sherry at Christmas but then ban cider or wine for her birthday.

Meredith kept Jackie's bedroom immaculate. Her things were tidied away for her every day and her bed was made with the new duvet cover that Meredith had seen at BHS. All this, Ida gleaned from the girl as she sat in the kitchen having tea, or walked in the park, or played with little Jake in the front room.

Ida thought how family can really influence and curtail a person. Her own mother was not naturally unkind but Ida had felt her displeasure and avoided any conflict. Molly was always delighted to be with Daisy and the children, her cheeks would glow, her eyes would sparkle and her mouth would relax into a smile and even embrace laughter.

On the infrequent occasions when Doris and her new husband appeared from London, Molly would clean the cottage from top to bottom. She would get out all the best china as though it were for everyday use and fuss over Derick who had a job in the civil service. Ida had been part of the fixtures and fittings.

"What about your old friends?" Ida asked one day.

"Oh, there are none I would want to see. I had to move away for Jake's sake you see. I have a new life now." Ida did not really know. It was strange how as a child family was a dominating feature and then on adulthood some people would cut ties completely. Ida had been close to her family but they had drifted apart. It was never intended but Ida was wise enough to know that when the baby had been ripped out of her body her belief in others had been ripped out of her soul. She wondered what had happened to force Jackie away. She knew it would be personal and absolute.

"Will you visit your mum, do you think? I'm sure she would like to see how bonny Jake is now he is growing," Ida adopted an encouraging tone. They were watching Jake toddle between the chair and the settee. Ida watched Jackie close down.

"I want a fresh start. I know, you might not understand but it is for the best, believe me," and Jackie would gaze out of the window deep in thought as she looked out over the waste ground opposite the house.

"None of my business," Ida tried to reassure her. She wanted to give the girl a hug but held back, although was determined to give Jackie the security that clearly the girl was lacking. Ida trod carefully and gradually earned her trust.

Ida noticed how Jackie kept away from other mums and resisted any attempt that was made to take Jake to playgroup. Sometimes, Ida thought Jackie seemed like a little fluttering bird protective of its young, always watchful and wary. Ida wondered what had happened to make her so guarded at her age. Ida knew it must have been something serious. It was not just Meredith. Something had happened to Jackie before she came there.

Jackie was making Ida reflect. She had tried to banish Dave from her thoughts and truth to tell she could not picture him now. There were certain things about him she remembered like the little flick of his hair on his forehead or when they were intimate the mole on his left shoulder blade but he was never whole in her mind.

She did have one recurring image of him, his back to her, arms round a girl with short brown hair in a dark red coat but it was unclear and every time she tried to concentrate and capture the moment it would disintegrate before her eyes leaving her frustrated. The picture of him might have left her, but the feelings she had endured at his betrayal never did.

Jim Woodhouse had given her a different and better perspective on love. He had sauntered up to the smallholding to buy fresh spring vegetables one day in

May 1954. Molly served him. Ida continued with her chores but there was something about him that made her take a second look from her position at the kitchen sink. He noticed and winked.

Jim had become a regular customer and passed the time of day. He was a strange combination of youth and vigour yet the worldliness more fitting to an older man. He was twenty-two years old. Ida was thirty vastly older so she was drawn into his easy manner with no thought of anything more. Jim was there on the dreadful day that changed everything.

"I love your garden," said Jackie. "Everything is perfect. Ken is not really a gardener."

"Not without a lot of hard work you know. It was a mess when we came here and there was builders' rubble everywhere. Jim barrowed everything away and would dig it over in every spare minute. He was very strong then. He could do the physical work easily and we planned it all out so I could have my flowers and there would be a separate section for vegetables. I missed being able to pick things in season when I moved into town before we came back out here. Jim understood that. He bought this house, especially."

Jim had told Ida he had a surprise for her when he brought her to the house. They had been married three years and still lived in a flat in the centre of town, easy distance for Jim to get to the ground and Ida had got a job in a local chemist. Ida had pined for the countryside but that had gone from her hands. After her father's stroke everything changed.

Jim had been there. He had been calm, organising an ambulance and ferrying Molly and Ida to the hospital. It was serious and the two women sat waiting in the corridor. Her father had lost his speech and only made guttural sounds as they sat by his bed, his face was contorted and his right arm, always muscular from his work at the mine, now lay immobile. There was limited use in his other arm and he lay there in his bodily prison.

Molly, on leaving the ward was inconsolable. Ida suddenly realised the bond that had existed between her mum and dad and the interdependency of the couple. That cord had been cut and Molly's tough exterior had been breached. Ida became the source of stability. Jim had made himself useful.

Ida's father had died the following week. He was just fifty-five years old.

"What about your dad?" Ida asked Jackie when they were walking in the park.

"Dad was lovely but I think he gave up years ago. He wanted a quiet life I suppose and spent more and more time at the office probably avoiding Mum. Mum was the powerhouse. He said her kitchen was the engine room where she was chief engineer. Trouble was, he was never the captain. He was content to let her bring me up as long as he was left to his own devices. I think it might have been different if they had had a boy, but Mum chose a girl."

Jackie remained silent about what she had seen when she saw him at work that day. At home, he was nice and retiring and helpful. Unusually for a man of his generation he would clean and occasionally cook. Sometimes, it seemed to Jackie that her parents had swapped roles except that her quiet unassuming father went to the office and his tyrannical wife stayed at home.

Ida was puzzled. She had heard in the news that there were medical advances that could possibly lead to choosing the gender of a baby but she did not think it was available even in 1991, never mind when Jackie was born.

Jackie must have realised and confided, "I found out I was adopted when I was sixteen".

Ida wondered if that was why she was so reserved and said nothing, allowing Jackie to tell her if she wanted.

"I had a job in a craft shop. Mum had organised it. She knew the owner. Mum supplied her with some of her creations. One day, I wasn't well and went home early to find Mum clearing out her craft cupboard in the back room. There was a folder on the chair and I picked it up so I could sit down. It slipped out of my hand and the contents spilled on the floor. Mum was so angry and told me it was private. Something about the way she was, made me want to know what was so private."

Ida urged her on with the story.

"When she went out to do the church flowers, I had a look. I found my birth certificate and there was a letter with it that had been written by my birth mum."

Ida looked steadily at Jackie.

"When I left for good, I took the certificate and letter. It's in the wardrobe at home. I put it in a shoe box that Pauline had given me before she died."

Pauline had told her to guard the contents of the box with her life and trust no-one but she said to Ida about her own letter, "I trust you. I want you to read the letter and see what you think." Maybe, Ida would help her decide what to do.

Ida was more than flattered. The confidence put their relationship on another level. Ida felt protective of Jackie. She did read the letter in due course and gave her opinion that her biological mother must have been very distressed at having to give her up.

"Do you really think it's genuine?" Jackie was eager.

"Genuine. What do you mean? There is so much love here and regret and she has promised to think of you every day." Ida had been transported back to her own tragedy and understood the intensity of feeling. She had nothing but compassion for the woman who had been given no choice but to give up her baby.

"When I confronted Mum, she said she had found out about the girl, my mother. It seems strange saying this. Mum had a knack of finding out people's secrets you know. She sort of used her church connections and her craft circle connections to know things, so I believed her when she told me that I was certainly not wanted and the letter was just to impress the lady from the adoption agency. She said she only kept the letter in case."

'In case of what?' Ida thought. Meredith Pugh, for all her Christian ways, at times seemed rather unprincipled if it suited her. Ida did not need any convincing about strength of feeling in the letter. Her loss was with her every day and somewhere out there was a woman heartbroken by the loss of her daughter.

Jackie looked unconvinced, but said nothing. She wondered if it would be possible to find this woman. The letter gave her promise.

That night, Ida could not sleep. Too many memories collided with her present thoughts. She slipped out of bed and when Jim stirred reassured him that she wanted a drink.

She had had no intention of ever marrying. What could she give a man? She had felt defiled and ashamed. It was better to do the best she could on her own, but Jim Woodhouse punctured her resolve. His quiet determined manner gradually eroded any restraint. At first, she had thought he was being helpful and friendly to a family in trouble but then she realised he was singling her out.

Eventually, they shared a drink at a local inn and against her better judgement she unfolded in his presence. He encouraged her to talk and she told him of her hurt, although could not bring herself to confess her real sin. Jim told her about his National Service, part of which was spent in Korea. There were bitter moments, initially in training at the hands of regular soldiers and then in Korea in the aftermath of the civil war. He touched on some heart-breaking scenes of despair and loss, not wanting to upset Ida unduly but wanting her to understand his passion. He admired the resilience and fortitude of the Korean people even though they had suffered dreadfully.

He told her of kindnesses from villagers who would share what they had even though it was so little. He told her he had coped with the initial bullying of National Service better than most. He was fit from his football and his ability in that field drew some admiration which offered him some protection but others were not so fortunate and one of his mates took his own life to extricate himself from the tyranny.

Ida poured another cup of tea and clutched her dressing gown tighter. Jim was a very special man. He had not told her much about Korea but he had witnessed bad things she knew that had tainted his outlook. He had told her that she had been able to banish the blues and give him hope. He was not interested in the shallow girls he had seen around the town. It was Ida, with her quiet mysterious manner, that had captured his heart. When she yielded to his embrace, she had felt safe and when she responded to his kiss she had felt the flame of life.

She had no intention to marry but he wore her down. She was now on her own. Her mother had moved in with Daisy and the new management at the estate had declared their intention to sell parcels of land, some even for housing developments. Ida had been told her days there were numbered.

Jim's persistence was hard to resist and she was only human. His love was delicious and enticing. She needed an escape from her past. She wanted a future. She had felt weak.

Ida poured yet another cup of tea from the pot. Sleep was out of the question. She returned to her reverie.

It had been a simple wedding two years after the death of her father. Ida had tried to tell Jim as far as she could that there was unlikely to be children. He waved away her worries assuming she was concerned about the age difference. He said he loved her. She was his special woman. On the day she felt the censure of her mother, her disapproving glances well known to Ida from her childhood, and there was an audible huff in the quiet church when procreation was mentioned by the vicar but when Jim squeezed her hand her spirits lifted and she vowed she would do her utmost to make him the best wife she could possibly be. If only she had had the courage to tell him, then maybe they might have adopted but she had known that in those days her age would have counted against that and as usual, she felt damned.

Ida was glad to return to the warmth of her bed and lie as close as possible to her husband.

Autumn descended on them. Jackie had been there for almost a year and to each woman for different reasons it had seemed forever. Jackie encouraged Ida to cut her hair. It was pale now rather than the gold of her youth and Jackie persuaded her to visit the new hairdresser on the High Street. She was very nervous but Gareth after removing the pins and letting the tendrils fall had been full of compliments handling the curls and pulling them into different shapes around her face. Ida began to enjoy herself and readily agreed to the proposed new style which included the merest of highlights to bring shape and depth. Two hours later feeling pampered and cosseted she emerged into the busy street catching her reflection in the shop windows. She strode purposefully and crowned the occasion by purchasing the dress she had seen in the window of Debenhams.

Jim on return from the ground, had been quite taken aback. He hesitated, wanting the old familiar Ida but her radiant smile reminded him of the young woman he had fallen in love with all those years ago. After all these years of marriage, he did not know how to tell her and muttered something about liking her new look and then overthinking it and reassuring her he had liked how she was before and popped out to inspect his vegetables in the garden.

He had been concerned for a while that Ida would eventually be badly hurt, when inevitably Jackie and Jake moved out of her orbit, although the present joy that Ida was experiencing must be worth the risk. He would just have to be there for her when she needed.

Ida had grown more and more fond of Jackie. She liked her thoughtfulness and the way she cared for Jake. She would be mindful of him but let him explore. She was not a restrictive parent like some of the mothers she saw about with their timetables and strict regimes for play, food and sleep. Jackie was relaxed with Jake. She did not mind if he got dirty and would laugh as she told him soil was not for eating, supplying him with a biscuit instead. There was no preciousness in her ways and she was always happy to include Ida.

Jake began to call Ida, 'Nana.' At first, she thought he could not get his childish tongue around Ida but Jackie seemed to encourage the word and Ida was transported every time. She knew Jim worried that she was getting too close but she did not, could not, care. The word sealed the bond.

The local children had always gathered on the waste ground opposite, particularly as the nights drew in and they could not roam further afield. Sometimes, there might be a little cluster of girls sharing their secrets but more often, it was the boys having a kick about. It was a scene that Ida was aware of every day of her life.

"Funny they've never built on that," Jackie remarked one day.

Ida agreed and said she hoped they never would. The cottage had been gone a long time. She had watched it fall into a ruin, brick by fallen brick, as her life had been while she had been living there. Some days it was painful.

Molly only visited them once, declaring it brought back bad memories to see the place. Ida thought it rather brought back good memories that hurt her much more. Daisy and Co came rarely because of their mother and Doris seemed to live on another planet so while she was living across the street from the old family home there was no-one with whom to share the memories.

Jim had announced his surprise three years into their marriage. He brought her in the little Austin 10 to see the semi-detached house. She was interested of course, but there was also a churning inside at she looked out at the crumbling cottage opposite and the fields beyond. She was surprised he had the keys and let her in to explore. In truth it was a little paradise.

There was a decent sized kitchen with a door that led out to a small plot for a garden. There was a modern electric oven, a refrigerator and even a neat washing machine. Upstairs there was a bathroom and separate toilet. The large front bedroom had a bay window identical to the front room below. "It's very grand," she had said.

"Yes, and it's all ours," he was bursting with pride. "I wanted to do something special for you. When I had the chance, I knew you would love it."

Ida had been aghast but the love in his face quashed any retort and she pushed herself into his arms so he would not see the stricken look on her face.

She had been worried about the cost but he told her he had savings and his inheritance. He had calculated that the mortgage could be paid. He was earning more from being groundsman and her job at the shop could go for luxuries unless of course, she had to give it up for any reason. Ida squirmed inside.

Jim and Ida had lived there over thirty years when Jackie turned up. No-one else in the road had lived there that long and from the beginning. No-one she now knew, had any memory of the girl who had lived in the cottage that had been completely obliterated leaving rough grass to cover any remains.

Jake was a sturdy chap who was easy to spoil. Ida bought him presents, nothing too ostentatious but little gifts to enjoy the thrill as he opened a box or tore at wrapping paper. She sometimes treated Jackie too but usually in a more practical way—taking her to lunch at the garden centre or offering to look after Jake while she had some personal time. Jackie seemed content with Ken. At weekends Ida would watch the little family, Ken, Jackie and Jake, leave in Ken's Ford Fiesta for a day out together. There might be a little pang of jealousy before she turned to suggest something she and Jim could do. Ida and Jackie kept weekends for their families.

Two years after she had appeared Jackie left one dark day in January. Jake was left behind. Only Ida knew the reason.

****

Sergeant Wilkes examined the records. Ken had reported his wife missing the next day. He had naturally been interviewed but he had been at work and the little boy had been with a neighbour. There was evidence that her departure was hasty as most of her clothes had been left but basic items were taken. A considerable amount of money had been withdrawn from the joint account but there were no further activities on the account. There was a CCTV image of her at the train station but then it seemed the trail went cold. Tom wondered if the case had been abandoned because the officers believed she had left legitimately of her own accord. Maybe, they were of the opinion that there was trouble in the marriage. Ken Lewis seemed a decent bloke, a few silly actions when he was younger resulting in police cautions but nothing serious and nothing nasty. There was a report that Jackie had walked out on her parents so it seemed she had a habit of running away. She came from a good home. The Pughs were not well off, but they were certainly comfortable and the baby had been welcomed into their home. It seemed that the flaw may rest with Jackie herself. The case remained on file but as there was no real cause for concern the file had lain in the police archives gathering dust.

Tom Wilkes still wondered.

Chapter 7
Nowhere to Be Found

A wounded deer leaps highest,
I've heard the hunter tell;
'Tis but the ecstasy of death,
And then the brake is still.

A Wounded Deer Leaps Highest: Emily Dickenson

1992-1993: Jackie and Diana

The girl on the doorstep looked familiar but Diana really could not place her. Assuming she had arrived early to set up for the garden party she directed her to the rear garden. The girl looked uncertain and hesitated.

"Really, I have not got time today. I'm sure you can find your way round," and Diana shut the door in the girl's startled face.

What is the matter these days thought Diana. She remembered the parties she had attended in the seventies when staff really did know their place and consequently how to behave. These days relying on agency staff was so unpredictable. Some of them were far too friendly and 'in your face' and others retreated to a silly side-line gossip instead of replenishing the guests' glasses or handing round *hor d'oeuvres*. This girl looked as if she was completely devoid of any training, so Diana concluded she had not been around at any of her previous gatherings. It must be one of those faces so typical of the bland current generation.

It was becoming a testing day. Tony had telephoned to say he had missed the earlier train. It was always so much more comforting if he was around as she could direct him to organise the bar staff and make sure the gardeners had cleared up properly. She liked to oversee the way seats were arranged so that guests could circulate as well as take their rest in small groups. The florist had been late this morning with the flowers which was a complete nuisance as she had banked on being there when she set up the displays before she had her manicure. Helen was generally reliable so with a sigh Diana had crossed her fingers.

The day had started brightly too but then the benign white clouds had gradually turned darker and by eleven o'clock there were clouds of charcoal threatening to dampen her day completely. Diana was on edge. This garden party was important. She needed to impress Clive, Tony's current boss, or Tony could be passed over for promotion. By now she knew a lot about the machinations of city politics.

She glanced out of the window. That girl was standing there on the edge of the patio doing absolutely nothing and goodness the girl caught her eye and waved. Diana turned abruptly away from view. She would give Melanie from the caterers a piece of her mind.

Diana looked at the clock. It was midday already and her nerves were in shreds. She needed to relax and headed for the drinks cabinet in the dining room. She would take a bottle to her dressing room where no-one would dare to disturb her for half an hour. She deserved a break.

In the garden, there was intense activity. Marcus, the co-ordinator, was shouting instructions and urging the troops under his command. Seeing the clouds and having checked the weather forecast predicting the possibility of late summer showers he had taken the precaution of erecting two gazebos at either end of the lawn and utilising the spacious conservatory at the rear of the property. He had supervised a number of functions for Mrs Carstairs from intimate soirees to impressive anniversary celebrations.

Diana Carstairs liked to flaunt her position. Antony Carstairs was a big wig in the city so Marcus was always mindful of important guests who might aid the growth of business. Diana clearly relished spending his money. Marcus was a fixer sparing his clients the stress of planning the event, the logistics of arrangements and the final stage, the delivery of the enterprise. Diana Carstairs had given him good business, although she was no push over and he had to work hard for his rewards. Marcus knew he was only as good as his last event so was constantly under threat from his exacting clients.

He had been engaged in checking the menu with the caterer in their preparation tent at the rear of the shrubbery. Melanie was the best but standards could easily slip if there was not constant vigilance. Marcus liked to establish his control over all departments. At times he would be curt and abrupt with staff and at others avuncular and teasing. It was important to keep them on their toes.

He emerged from the shrubbery and cast his expert eye over the expanse of lawn exercising a mental check list over proceedings. He noticed the girl by the patio. She did not fit in to his preparations at all. He strode over to confront her.

"What are you meant to be doing?"

She was startled. Her poise momentarily left her but she gathered her wits for the rebuff. She was here and she was going to see it through. There was nothing to lose.

"Nothing, I am just waiting," the girl answered quietly and politely. She had a demure, rather old-fashioned quality about her.

Marcus appraised her, questions automatically downloaded into his brain. Had she come with any of the contractors, was she an interloper or press, was she family, was she a guest who had arrived far too early, was she a trouble maker? People like Antony Carstairs could attract admirers and critics in equal number. Marcus had a sense of foreboding pass over him like the low grey cloud that had suddenly obscured the sunshine.

"May I ask who you are?" Marcus was always polite at first. He always trod carefully.

"My name is Jackie Lewis," she said. "I came to see Diana Carstairs and she told me to come round here. I am waiting for her." She answered clearly and firmly with a slightly dismissive air as though she was justifying her position in case of eviction.

The girl stood resolutely almost statue like as his staff circled round giving finishing touches to the tables beyond.

Marcus was puzzled. Diana Carstairs always hated to be disturbed a couple of hours or so before a party. Officially, she was getting herself ready for the grand entrance, although he knew Grace, her beautician, was not due for another half hour. He knew she would be locked away in her boudoir as he liked to call it fortifying herself with Dutch courage. Appearances were everything to Diana Carstairs. It was getting more and more challenging for her to fulfil her obligations. Marcus understood.

"I don't think she will be down for a while. Perhaps you should come back another day when things are not so hectic," Marcus tried to encourage her gently to depart of her own free will and gave an appealing, quizzical look.

Marcus caught her eye as she raised her head to face him and for an instant recognised the deep emotion lodged there. He wondered if he was about to have a weeping girl on his hands. That would not do at all.

"I'll tell you what. I could do with a break. I have been on the go since six this morning and everything seems to be progressing nicely so why don't I get you a coffee and you can tell me. I look after things for Diana. I can probably sort it out for you unless you want to come back some other time." He had made a decision that the girl would be much more likely to respond to a friendly and solicitous approach. He liked to think he was a good judge of character.

"No, I can't come back. It's taken me two hours to get here and I do not think I will have the courage another day."

The admission made Marcus raise his eyebrows. Oh dear, Marcus thought, this does not bode well. She is someone who has some sort of grudge. It was inevitable that city men picked up their share of trouble, after all power, position and wealth brought jealousy and inevitably some people could be hurt and suffer and want to confront the person responsible, although to his mind the girl did not seem that sort and even less did she seem to be a spurned lover who wanted to inform the wife to get recompense or revenge.

Marcus could smile at the thought. Antony Carstairs was no gigolo. His lack of height and muscle meant he blended into backgrounds. He was a clever accountant Marcus knew but he also knew that he was a trusted employee of the mightier men and never major general. Antony was no risk taker and Marcus could never see him jeopardising his position for a romp in a hotel room, no matter how pretty the girl was and this girl was certainly pretty.

Marcus escorted her to a little table out of general view. Instinctively, he knew discretion was required. He signalled to Luke to bring coffees and snacks.

Jackie was grateful to sit down. Like Marcus, it had been an early start and her courage seemed to evaporate in harmony with the receding miles. She had forced herself to complete her journey. It seemed vital to know once and for all.

"I hope the weather is going to hold. I think it will," Marcus knew the art of seducing someone with innocuous conversation. Jackie studied the impressive garden which from this viewpoint made her feel small and insignificant. She gritted her teeth knowing that if she missed this opportunity she probably would not venture here again.

"Do you know Diana well?" He ventured while pouring the coffee.

"I have never met her before today," the girl volunteered. She so wanted to unburden herself to this nice stranger but knew discretion was vital in her mission.

Ah Marcus deduced from her comments that she was there to cause some ruction before the party. Obviously she had some beef with Mr Carstairs and maybe expected him to be here too or maybe she wanted to embarrass his wife. Marcus was confident of deflecting any difficulty and in turn earning even more brownie points from his client. Marcus had always taken trouble to avail himself of as much background detail as possible on his clients. It was always worth the trouble and sometimes extra business could be generated from his discretion.

"I did not know there was a party today. I don't want to make any trouble," The girl volunteered.

"Jackie, maybe you should tell me what it's all about and then I can give Diana a message." Marcus changed his opinion yet again and now he was more than intrigued.

Jackie considered. "I don't know you and it's very private. My friend rang to find out when I could see her and the lady who answered said she would definitely be here this morning. She said she was going away tomorrow so if it was really important, I might manage to have a quick word this morning but must get here before eleven if I wanted a word with her on her own but I have been waiting for ages and I can't go home without finding out," Jackie gave a deep sigh and squeezed her eyes shut trying to stem tears.

"Finding out what, Jackie?" Marcus leaned forward and almost took her hand sympathetically but at the last minute drew back.

Jackie who had been on the verge of breaking down composed herself. "She would want to see me when she knows who I am. She sent me a letter."

Marcus was at a loss. He wanted to get rid of Jackie before he lost any more time but at the same time beneath his irritation he was beginning to feel sorry for the girl.

"Look, sit here and have another cup of coffee if you like and I will see what I can do. Are you sure you can't tell me? I am very discreet and I do know the family very well." Marcus wondered why he felt so protective towards her. He was usually distant when his business was involved, he could even be ruthless, although he believed he was always fair. This girl did not fit into any category and he was getting really interested in her reason for being there.

Jackie shook her head quite deliberately and gave him a small smile. "I will see you in a bit," uttering this he departed leaving Jackie to ponder. She reached into her bag and checked the letter was there safe and sound.

Ida had been just the right person to tell. She was an excellent listener and would give an honest opinion even if unpalatable to the recipient. She was a lot older but this seemed to give her wisdom rather than make her narrow minded and staid. Together, they had sat down and applied for her adoption file. As she had been adopted prior to the 1976 Act, she had to agree to counselling sessions, which at first horrified her but Ida thought it was a good idea and encouraged her to continue with the application. Ida thought that judging by the letter, her birth mother would be delighted to find she had a grandson. It would be a sort of consolation for the years that she had missed with Jackie.

However, Ida did issue her with warnings. Circumstances change over the years so beware of your expectations. It was impossible to know what she might have told her family even if she had told them anything. If there were additional children, there might be resentment. Her mother might have fallen on hard times or might have health issues. Ida said it was very important to know why she wanted to know about and even meet her birth mother. She again suggested she visit Meredith and discuss it with her. After all, Meredith had provided her with a home and security. Ida was wise enough not to say provided her with love.

As it happened, everything went smoothly and armed with all she had learnt from Ida and her counselling sessions she determined to seek out her birth mother. It proved a lot easier than she thought. She now knew her mother's maiden name but it was likely she had married. It was Ida, on her visit to the hairdresser, perusing society pages, who had picked up a photograph of Diana Carstairs who looked incredibly like an older Jackie; although on closer inspection, Ida determined that Jackie had a softer face.

As if to confirm her first thought, Diana had been photographed with her parents James and Eunice Duggard who had apparently joined their daughter and son-in-law Antony Carstairs at the charity ball to raise funds for Save the Children. Ida asked Gareth if she could buy the magazine from him but Gareth looking at the date said it would be discarded soon anyway, so it was fine to take it.

Of course, it was sensible to check as much information as possible. The article attached to the photograph encouraged them both that here was a generous woman and they felt convinced that her participation in various fund-raising events for children's charities indicated someone who had a desire perhaps to make up for past events. Both women for their own separate reasons wanted to believe in a happy ending. A visit to the records office of the town where Diana

Carstairs' was born and grew up to verify the parentage seemed just a formality and a nice day out.

"I've had a word with Diana and she can spare you five minutes," Marcus indicated that she follow him to the house. Jackie rose from the chair clutching her handbag more tightly and strode deliberately behind him. Underneath her nerves were frayed but outwardly she was calm. This was a moment to lay one ghost to rest. There was something unreal about the event and she felt strange and unsettled, but above all she wanted at the very least a conversation with her real mother and this was it.

Antony was tired. There had been so many delays that morning and he had to tell Diana that Clive might not after all be able to make it. Considering the whole shebang was really in his honour and costing a fortune it was a bitter blow and he knew Diana would be furious. These days his wife's temper was unpredictable, probably because she was picking up the vibes from him that his position at the company was precarious to say the least. He had for some time felt he was on a precipice, for months, even years if he was honest.

The job gave big rewards and because of this he had been desperate not to lose it. The children's boarding school fees were astronomical and the upkeep of this house a burden he could do without. The tide seemed to have turned when he had refused to incorporate the amended figures into the accounts a couple of years ago and then there had been other occasions when he had been asked to compromise, maybe forget a transaction and this duplicity had given him sleepless nights.

He had generally found another way that would accommodate his bosses and yet salve his conscience. He hated deception of any kind and fought against it as far as he was able. He strode into the house with what authority he could muster and almost collided with Marcus who was ushering some woman into the sitting room.

"Ah, how are things Marcus? All on target? Will we get away with the weather, do you think?" Antony was awkward in company and resorted to affable politeness.

There was no recognition from Antony for Jackie which was a relief for Marcus. It was natural for them all to file into the living room where Diana was waiting poised before the beautiful Edwardian fireplace above which the family portrait reigned supreme.

"Thank goodness you are here at last," Diana ignored Marcus and Jackie. "It has been such a dreadful morning and I am quite worn out." She did not relinquish her station allowing Antony to move to her side.

Antony was used to Diana's complaints and knew how to calm her. "Well, I am here now and it looks like everything is splendid. Marcus has it all in hand so no need to fret," he then looked enquiringly at Marcus and Jackie.

"I've brought Jackie as you asked," Marcus pushed the girl forward with an encouraging smile.

Diana appraised the girl again. There was something disconcerting about her. She was a reminder in the way she stood somehow, or the way she held her head at a slight angle. The girl stood inside the door nervously fingering her bag. In the grandeur of the room she looked insignificant, although there was a quiet presence about her that seemed almost threatening. She would have been quite attractive too if she had made an effort but her simple cotton dress evoked a lifestyle of need and anxiety.

Diana prepared herself for the application for money. She would refuse of course, making it clear that she did extensive charitable work and suggest she apply to one of those organisations.

"As I said, I am not really available today but Marcus has persuaded me to give you a few minutes so can we deal with whatever it is?" Diana as a consummate actress portrayed gracious charm.

All eyes were trained on Jackie. "I rather hoped to have a few minutes with you on your own," Jackie made her voice strong and steady, although she knew she was blushing.

Marcus was the first to withdraw and then Antony left significantly saying he would be back in exactly five minutes in support of his wife.

"You have my undivided attention. Now what do you want from me?" Diana enunciated each word deliberately and purposefully. The situation was unusual and something unnerved even her. The older woman and the younger girl faced each other across the room as if assessing each other before a fencing match.

Diana inexplicably felt the force of her opponent and prepared for an onslaught and yet instinctively she recognised a kindred spirit as though she had been unmasked. It made her feel uncomfortable and she resorted to her natural ability to perform.

"I do not want anything from you but I would like to know something." Jackie raised her head and looked Diana in the eye, "I believe you are my mother."

Diana clutched the mantelpiece before she remembered herself and consciously drew herself up to her full height. She could be imposing but the girl had resolution and continued in a more conciliatory tone which left Diana bewildered and afraid.

"I know, this might come as a shock, me appearing like this, but the lady on the telephone said to pop round this morning and you were sure to be here. I am not here to make a fuss or anything. I wanted to know and meet you, maybe get to know you. I really do not want anything so please do not think I want money or anything. I thought you would want to meet me, especially after reading your letter, the one I found with my adoption papers and I wanted to tell you about your grandson." Jackie realised she was jabbering.

"Stop," Diana's mouth was dry and the word came out like the short sharp stab of an assassin's knife.

Jackie knew at that instant that she was to be abandoned again.

"What letter?" Diana suddenly took control of herself and Jackie handed her the letter she had cherished. Diana looked at it and smiled. Her face seemed to relax a little.

"I did not write this. I am sorry my dear but you have made a mistake." Her voice had softened as she was confident of dismissing the girl without trouble.

"But I have my birth details and I have checked very carefully. I am sorry. I should have been more sensitive but I so wanted to see you and the letter gave me confidence you see."

"Well, I cannot be your mother. I would know, wouldn't I? This letter proves it. I did not write it."

At that moment Antony returned. Five minutes had elapsed. He looked at Diana quizzically. "This girl, Jackie is it, is trying to claim I am her mother which is obviously quite ridiculous. She has a letter she says I wrote when she was adopted. Here, Tony." She handed him the paper. "I obviously did not write this." Diana rose above the situation determined to delay or better still scotch the assertion. Today was too important and she could not deal with any of it then or maybe ever. She did not allow herself to think beyond the obvious and that was to create a shield against any outside invasion. It was to Diana a matter of survival. She had made a life and she dare not allow anything to dismantle it.

Antony scrutinised the letter. This had not been written by his wife he was absolutely certain. Diana had always had an untidy scrawl that had irritated his ordered mind but this letter had exquisite handwriting.

"I can categorically say, my wife did not write this letter. It seems you have had a wasted journey. I will get someone to show you out." Antony sounded cruel but that was his inability to converse easily and he wanted a line drawn then and there, before the afternoon's proceedings got underway. He wanted to extricate his wife from a potentially embarrassing situation and he was aware of how easily false rumours could circulate.

He took his wife's hand. "Shall we go and inspect the garden?" He added to Diana who nodded and both left Jackie alone clutching her precious letter.

Marcus popped his head round the door. "All sorted?" He asked cheerfully but one look told him it was anything but.

Marcus sat Jackie down. She looked at him imploringly. "Tell me," he said.

Jackie told him, occasionally stumbling as her throat contracted with emotion. Marcus had had his share of rejection. His own family had not been able to accept his leanings as they called them and, although he was now settled with his partner Paul and managed to keep in touch with his parents and sister, there was still the distance of disapproval. At forty, Marcus recalled the distress of his youth and how the cornerstone of his life had been shattered. He had managed to acquire self-belief and self-reliance through the steady support of Paul and the success of his business but underneath he had never quite lost the fragility of his youth.

After speaking to the sympathetic Marcus, Jackie was able to collect her thoughts and feelings and take her departure. Marcus with his natural courtesy escorted her to the door. Guests were starting to arrive which meant that progress down the front drive was somewhat slow. Jackie admired his complete composure as Marcus greeted guests.

This was a whole new world for Jackie, that is, until she noticed Clive Corneille arriving in his chauffeur-driven black Jaguar. Diana and Antony almost immediately materialised to welcome Clive as he emerged from the motor.

"So pleased you were able to come after all," Antony reached out his hand while Diana smiled broadly and went round to greet his wife.

"Unfortunately, it is only a flying visit but we did not want to disappoint," Clive with his black hair and dressed in a black silk casual shirt pecked at Diana's cheeks in greeting and then jerked his head to survey the scene as if he was a crow looking for its next meal. Clive, as was his habit, held back as the ladies made their way to the garden to check out the scene. Antony interposed as the host, "Come and I will organise a drink. Some Veuve Clicquot, perhaps or are you ready for a scotch after the week we've had?"

Clive had noticed Jackie who had turned quickly back to Marcus and with some urgency said, "I need to go to catch my train. Thanks for being so nice."

She almost ran down the driveway. Before she had reached the gates, Clive had excused himself to Antony and doubled back to his driver. He whispered to him. Having received instruction the driver turned the car round and negotiated his route through the incoming vehicles to the gate and the road beyond.

Marcus made a decision.

Jackie made it to the train station without mishap. She was relieved to get away not just because of the rejection but because of the spectre from her past. It seemed so long ago to her young mind and the last year or so had made her as secure as she had ever known.

Ken was a good partner, affectionate and kind, allowing her the freedom of spirit she relished. She imagined their life together and maybe more children which she knew would delight Ken as well as her friend Ida. She had become too relaxed. She had forgotten to be careful in her enthusiasm to find her birth mother. She had imagined she could live a normal life and not keep looking over her shoulder.

There was some time to wait for her train so she joined the queue for beverages, busy as the London train was due in five minutes. There was a light tap on her shoulder.

"Don't turn round," he whispered, "It's Marcus. I saw you were followed and clocked by whom. I am a sucker for a damsel in distress."

Jackie felt weak but Marcus momentarily pushed up against her in support.

"Listen carefully. This is what we are going to do. Trust me."

Jackie purchased her tea swiftly followed by Marcus. She went to the far end of the platform as if to board the next train. Amongst the crowd she looked inconspicuous. The passengers gathered as if on their marks to board and claim a coveted seat. Marcus had identified his quarry. Allowing him sight of Jackie boarding the train he quickly positioned himself in front of the man seeming in his agitation to board to spill his drink accidentally on the man's jacket.

The distraction allowed Jackie the opportunity to disembark further up the train and slip into the old-fashioned waiting room out of sight. Marcus was profuse in his apologies, delaying the man and obscuring his view at the same time, but doors were being slammed shut and the whistle was about to go. The man now impatient brushed him aside and leapt on to the departing train.

Through the window, Marcus saw a satisfied smile of relief on his face but it was Marcus who enjoyed the real smile of satisfaction.

There was another ten minutes until Jackie's train. Somehow, Marcus was just the person in whom to confide. He had seen life in all its many guises and his connections with the great and the good allowed him more than a glimpse of how power worked. He knew, for example, to avoid Clive Corneille and somehow, his events and hospitality company had always been engaged elsewhere if there were any enquiry from Clive.

Marcus wanted to be able to sleep at night. He knew that not all clients and guests were squeaky clean but there was no point in inviting danger and Clive was danger with a capital D. He was aware too, that Clive used all his good works and his associations with leaders in business and politics to protect his reputation and deflect any suspicions against him. In fact, he had only recently heard at a prestigious cocktail party he had organised for a government minister; a whispered conversation that Clive Corneille would be Sir Clive in the not too distant future. He was glad he had helped Jackie.

"I have been so careful, especially having Jake, and now he will find me. I will have to leave again."

"Not necessarily," reassured Marcus. "You've been happy and comfortable for two years, you tell me. He does not know about your son or that you have a husband and a home. His man has gone on a wild goose chase to London. No-one here knows who you are except me and perhaps Diana but she could not wait to get rid of you."

Jackie's face fell.

"I know you wanted fairy tales but you now know what she's like and you can build a good secure future together with Ken. You really have the best cover in being a wife and mother in a nice respectable area of a small town and Clive will have too many other things to bother him. After all, what happened was some years ago and it's only now that by a fluke he recognised you today. In his position he won't want trouble. He knows you could tell a tale or two but have not in those years so he probably wanted to find out where you live so he could keep an eye on you and maybe exert a little pressure." Marcus had a knack of reassurance, a trait that had been useful in his career.

"I suppose you are right. It freaked me when I saw him but I did not think he had clocked me." Jackie had begun to relax. It had been one of the most testing days of her life.

"Well, you will not be in the same circles so worry not. Here this is my card. Keep it safe and if you need help then get in touch, although I honestly doubt you will."

The train had pulled into the station. Jackie gave Marcus a brief kiss on his cheek. "Thank you so much," and she left him on the platform.

Marcus had abandoned his post for more than half an hour so made haste to return. He parked the van discreetly at the rear and slipped into the garden where he blended into the scene. It was his job after all to get things done but not to be noticed.

Diana was thankful that the party had gone well. The rain had not descended on the scene. The garden had looked magnificent. The food had been delicious. The drink had flowed. The girl had not caused trouble; that was no obvious trouble. Underneath, Diana had been troubled. She had left the misery of that year firmly behind but now recollections stealthily pushed through the curtains that she had so deliberately drawn across the unfortunate episode. She had felt disquiet throughout the afternoon. She had not written the letter so could not be held responsible.

The trouble was she recognised the hand and this made her feel entirely responsible. She felt the finger of guilt stirring her emotions.

"That went very well, didn't it?" Antony interrupted. "Clive stayed longer than I thought. You were brilliant, Diana. He was charmed by you. It will make such a difference to my career at the company. Shall we have a sundowner to celebrate?" he tucked her arm in his leading her to the patio.

Tomorrow they would visit the children at their boarding school before jetting off to Venice for a well-deserved September break confident that school fees could be paid for the foreseeable future. Neither realised how short that foreseeable future would be.

Clive driving to his country home also reflected on the afternoon. It had been a nuisance not locating the girl but he was not unduly worried. He fleetingly wondered if she had been a relation of Diana Carstairs noting certain physical similarities but thought that was unlikely judging by her hasty departure. One departure, however, would take place soon and as he thought about Antony he chuckled. Antony had been a good servant and a good front man. He had been scrupulous and honest, therefore an excellent person to represent the company. He had no imagination and his practical capabilities were staggeringly poor so it had been relatively easy to use the company as a cover for other dealings. It was time to cut Antony loose. There were younger clever men around who had a wider range of skills. Antony had served his purpose.

Jackie returned to the warmth of Ida's embrace. Ida held her hand while she recounted what had happened with Diana. There was little to say but Ida reminded her that she had a son and husband who loved her. There was a future to grasp and a past to leave behind. Jackie had not told Ida at this point about the other past she wanted to leave behind.

That point was reached a few months later when it was announced that Clive Corneille had made a substantial investment into the football club. Jim heard the news first and then it was emblazoned in the local newspaper. Jim did not like his beloved football club invaded by city men and he had not liked what he had heard about Mr Corneille and the changes he would undoubtedly want to make. He even thought his own job might be in jeopardy. Clive Corneille was a ruthless operator who did get results but at a cost, never to Clive of course, but there were always casualties with a man like that.

The newspaper lay on the kitchen table with a prominent photograph of the new investor. Jackie on her pre-Christmas visit stared at the headline 'Massive Financial Christmas Bonus for Borough Football Club'. Jackie was horrified. He would be here at the club. He would be here in the town. There was no escape if she stayed.

Chapter 8
Seek and Ye Shall Find

Here lies a most beautiful lady,
Light of step and heart was she;
I think she was the most beautiful lady
That ever was in the west country.
But beauty vanishes; beauty passes;
However, rare—rare it be;
And when I crumble, who will remember
This lady of the west country.

An Epitaph: Walter de la Mare

1993-1994: Ida and Jackie

There are moments of total clarity in a person's life, although they may be brief and not at the time needed or desired and so it was for Ida Woodhouse, born Ida Brindell, the youngest of three girls who had lived most of her entire life within a tight couple of acres. Restricted in geographical location, restricted by the time in which she was born, restricted by her childlessness but not restricted by a vista of life only given to a privileged few.

She saw her mother, curtailed by her father's mental suffering after the Great War, loving her family in the only way she knew, providing for them, admonishing if she thought it was warranted, repressing her own passions to accommodate the demands of her husband and daughters and overall the demands of the society of the time. She would have been aware of deeper feelings and desires which she would seek to vanquish in the other perpetual war for women in the mid-twentieth century, the fight for respectability and worth.

Born into Edwardian Britain, her expectations had been gradually demolished and somehow, Molly was not able to adapt to more liberal ways. Ida saw in her mind how the years had schooled Molly to be reduced from a young passionate girl she inevitably had been, when at the tender age of seventeen she had grasped Fred's hand in marriage to the apparent mean-spirited woman of middle age.

Molly could approve of Daisy and her brood feeling comfortable in their midst and showing glimpses of her early self in the banter with her grandchildren and she could approve of Doris in her smart London dwelling, someone she rarely saw in adulthood, only once did Molly venture to the capital and was intimidated by the experience. But Doris was someone to mention in conversation, to have in a locker ready to bring out on occasions when she needed the reassurance of a successful offspring to counter her own inadequacies.

Ida knew she had been a bitter disappointment to Molly. It was not in her marriage to Jim, although her mother pitied him and because of this he was never comfortable in her presence believing Molly wanted someone better for her youngest daughter. The regret was more profound. Ida had been the essence of Molly. Ida was to provide Molly with her escape. Ida had been her touchstone. After Ida's fall from grace, Molly could not banish the resentment she felt. After Molly's death, Ida bore that burden alone.

Her father she knew had believed he was tough and strong but he had found that he was not invincible. The brief excursion into the war had bruised his soul. There had been no balm capable of healing this, only brief moments when he could escape perhaps with Ida as a young innocent child or Molly in the ardour of their lovemaking but gradually, after his years setting his strength, physical and mental, in combat with the dirty malevolent pit, deep underground like a mole burying ever deeper and darker he was overwhelmed.

He had been a man born for the open air with the expectancy of a healthy life on the estate farm as enjoyed by his forefathers and so his spirit had been crushed to be eventually unequivocally broken by another war. It had been a dismal end and Ida was grateful that he had gone quickly after his stroke. He had become an empty shell of a man, exploded by the detonator of circumstance.

Ida knew in her heart, it would soon be her turn. She hoped to see the spring. She had watched Jim planting the bulbs. He had planted dozens that autumn and earlier than normal too. She was aware that he wanted to provide her with the joy of another spring and both of them knew time was not on their side.

She thought of how lives ran in parallel rods. Born to endure the conditions of one's birth and travel with a steady persistent rhythm to an end, the route would have to be negotiated carefully. There would be the occasional cross roads or the experience of a brittle break in the rod maybe even causing a change of angle to reposition to be in parallel to another life as had happened with Dave and Jim.

There were strangers, people who she would never meet but who would follow the same paths and meet similar occurrences, maybe at different times to her, but still a line of life parallel to her own. Other women would be faced with cancers, some would survive but many would not. Ida knew she would be one of the latter.

There were other parallels too. The lives of her sisters, born of the same parents and a close parallel in their childhood, had become distant parallels. In adulthood it was as if their lives were paths on either side of a valley. They would see each other from time to time as from a distance looking over the river of life below but they were always separate. She thought of Dave and his wife Sheila and wondered if they still had the shop and the cosy life he went back to after the war. She wondered if he thought of her at all or had she been obliterated from his consciousness. She conceded that he would not have been aware of the pregnancy but it was also anguish that he had turned his back on her. While he marched forward she had slumped into oblivion.

These were parallel lines that for a brief period had run close but then took opposite directions inevitably taking each further and further away from the other. She had given her heart to Dave and once given it could not be returned. Until Jim she did not know she could grow another heart.

She thought of Jackie and her mothers. She was convinced that Diana Carstairs was Jackie's birth mother. Two women, Meredith and Diana presented another parallel, one giving birth and rejecting the child twice and one wanting to possess the child utterly and completely, sucking the life blood from the girl. Ida was impatient with them. Ida grieved her own loss.

She had been grateful to Jim. She knew she had been doubtful and wary. She had been inhibited and allowed her past hurts to invade their space. She always kept just a little in reserve. He had been a constant in her life and now before it was too late, she so desperately wanted to give him the bliss he deserved. He had been a shaft of sunlight which had pierced through into her dark soul. She had nothing to give him in return.

That morning the old feelings had returned. It was good for him to go to work but she needed his reassurance and she realised his forgiveness. As he was leaving she asked him, "Have I let you down, Jim?"

He knew what she meant. Ida could never tell him of the reason. Her shame was too great.

"Never. We're good together you and me." Jim had no regrets about his marriage, just a fear of being without her. He was not a man who had the words to express his feelings and bridge the gap. They had given each other genuine love, although they had lived in tandem each nervous to open Pandora's Box. There was an urgency in Ida to put things right.

"But you could have had someone who would have given you much more." Ida's innate guilt needed the challenge.

"I married you, didn't I?" Jim could only answer in this obvious way. He had not the means to convince his wife of exactly what she meant to him. It hurt him as much as her.

It had been a wrong time to ask. Jim was in a hurry. He had a meeting with the new chairman Clive Corneille, which was important and he wanted to get back to her as quickly as possible. It was difficult for Jim keeping his job going and caring for his wife. Jim had given her a quick reassuring smile and left oblivious to her inner turmoil, promising to get back as quickly as possible. She let him go, scared that she would damage their union with bitter words if she succumbed and she needed the time left to her to be full of goodness. These demons she always faced alone.

She understood that they both were needy. They both had fears. Jim had three things in his life that made him content, Ida, his garden and his life in football. It was like three sides of a triangle or three legs of a stool. She knew he would be incomplete when she was gone and would totter for a while but she also had faith that he would find support in the other two strands of his life. She wished there had been a son or daughter to fill the empty space.

Jackie and Jake had filled an empty space within Ida. Jim had kept his distance so had not been completely aware of Ida's emotional investment in them. For Ida, the couple of years with Jackie and her son had given her purpose and joy. It had been clear how Jackie had relied on her. Somehow, even though they were vastly different in age there was a gentle harmony between them and each traded their love and needs with the other.

Ida missed her friend. She had left almost a year ago taking Ida's blessing with her and depending on Ida to support her precious son in her absence. She would telephone Ida regularly when Ida would give her an update on the progress of Jake and how Ken was managing. It would not have been fair for Ken to have knowledge of the whole situation. Ida tried to give him hope and the promise that Jackie would return.

Ida had not been able to confess her current situation to Jackie but confidently expected Jackie to return home soon if as expected that awful man Clive Corneille moved on to hunt down a new financial quarry. She knew Jackie had changed her name, taking her birth name, Louise Duggard, and had been helped by someone she had met when she had confronted Diana Carstairs. She did not know where she was living but she had work and accommodation. She knew life would go on without her.

Ida had met Clive Corneille at a function to introduce him to staff at the club. Jim hated these events and clearly distrusted Clive Corneille's motives with his investment. There was a champagne reception and then a buffet meal with whole salmon, turkey, ham, cheeses and salads as well as free wines and beers. Jim grumbled it was all a waste of money, especially as season ticket holders had had a twenty percent increase in price. It seemed Clive wanted to extend the hospitality aspect of the club.

"All that pompous prick wants to do is to smarmy up to his mates. He'll bleed the club. You mark my words," Jim pronounced as they were getting ready. He rarely wore a tie and was fidgeting with it as he checked in the mirror.

"You said he would not stay long so he can't do too much damage, can he?" Ida responded. She wanted the man gone so Jackie would return and reunite the little family. She would listen to Jim's complaints to glean knowledge to pass on to Jackie.

"A man like that leaves damage behind him wherever he goes. You'll see what I mean when you meet him." Ida was already aware of the damage Clive Corneille caused to her friend and in turn others.

Ida had been very nervous about the event, especially knowing what she did about Clive Corneille but she thought he would inevitably dismiss her as a woman of little consequence. It had crossed her mind that Diana Carstairs might be there, an idea that gave her more palpitations. As it happened, Diana was not there and Clive had been anything but impressive. He shook hands and murmured an appreciation to Jim for the excellence of the pitch and they were dismissed.

Ida studied him at every opportunity and found that Jim had summed him up perfectly. There was little to admire in his demeanour. His tone was condescending and even patronising to those around him. He treated the waiting staff with disdain and his hollow laugh seemed to echo round the function room. There had been edginess to the whole proceedings.

While Ida dismissed him as someone not worth knowing she acknowledged how his sharp eyes scrutinised everyone present and she was sure he was assessing any value they might be to him as demonstrated by the lackeys he had in attendance. Clive Corneille was sure of himself and his own requirements.

For Ida, what should have been an evening to be relished, was one that brought a sour taste in her mouth. She loved Jim even more for being Jim and when they returned home each in their own melancholy they found comfort in the physical expression of their love. Both parties celebrated the pleasure that the other gave ridding themselves of any contamination from the evening by their tender intimate touches.

There had been trust in the way each surrendered to exquisite feelings of desire. That night, the couple were complete in their physical climax laughing as they drew back to relish the wonder of their union. This was the final time they would make love so absolutely. Within a fortnight, Ida knew she had cancer.

Ida had lived to see the spring flowers, first the snowdrops suddenly pushing their way through the damp carpet of fallen leaves left in the corner of the garden under the magnolia tree. Ida thought, the white purity of their flowers were like priceless pearls adorning the throat of a young bride, virtuous and innocent full of hope. Then hot on their heels the crocus emerged as if arriving at a party in their celebratory colours. Ida could almost see them grouped as dancers in their satin colours like giggling girls excited to have arrived. Ida was much weaker when the daffodils and tulips lifted their heads. The small garden was ablaze with their colours. The tulips reached towards heaven as goblets offering restorative wine while the yellow daffodil trumpets gave a call to arms. For Ida soon it would indeed be the 'twinkling of an eye, at the last trumpet for the trumpet shall sound and the dead shall be raised incorruptible and we shall be changed.'

Ida had not been particularly religious but she believed in destiny and some greater purpose. She clung on to this.

Jim found Ida one bright day in late March. He had spent an hour or so in the garden, catching the sunshine while he could. Ida had settled into her armchair for a snooze. She was surrounded by vases of various sizes all boasting daffodils that had been picked for her pleasure by Jim. A small bunch nodded towards her on her side table, while a more substantial bunch stood regally on the mantelpiece, a large jug dominated the surface of the coffee table and then a welcoming arrangement stood on the windowsill of the bay window. This vase would be later removed and the curtains drawn; but Jim left all the other blooms until, in time, each flower head had darkened their edges to shades of dusky brown and the petals had shrivelled into thin tissue paper that drooped as if in mourning and were waiting for a resurrection from Van Gogh's paint brush.

Jim coped as well as he could in his stalwart fashion taking refuge in his garden when the power of emotion sought to render him incapable. People were kind. There were cards to read and display. One or two people brought food to eat. He had some visitors. There had been an awkward brief visit from Clive Corneille himself with another director reassuring him to take time off and his job was safe and Clive leaving a generous cheque for cancer research.

The club offered their facilities for the wake too and even though Jim thought the room would be too big he accepted as one less thing for him to do. He also did not want an invasion of people into their very private and special home space.

As it happened, the central pews of the small church were full with those who had appreciated his beautiful wife. Jim wryly wondered if some were attracted by the wake at the club. Even the hairdresser who had seemed to transform Ida's features in the last couple of years, although of course, no-one could transform Ida in Jim's eyes, turned up. Clive Corneille found time to attend and sat conspicuously near the front. He had arranged for a small article to be put in the local newspaper to underline as it were his benevolence. There was to be a fund-raising event at the club for cancer research.

Jim hated being thrust into the spotlight. Daisy, Mick and family came of course. As Ida's sister, she stood in line with Jim accepting the condolences of the congregation as they filed out of the church, intermittently dabbing her eyes as she did so. Jim knew that Daisy was a good woman who had taken in her mother and her offspring were doing well. She had been loved by her sister, particularly when they were young with Daisy indulging Ida as only a big sister can, but in adulthood Daisy had never seemed to understand Ida and they saw less and less of each other. Maybe, Jim thought if they had had children there might have been more common ground. Doris did not make her way from London. She sent an impressive wreath.

Ida's coffin had been festooned with spring flowers. Jim wore his dark grey suit, bought especially for the club function the previous year. He put a daffodil in his lapel. They sang 'For the beauty of the earth' and 'Immortal, invisible God only wise.' Jim was not a public speaker so the vicar read a tribute. Jim kept the real Ida in his heart.

There was one particular mourner who arrived moments after the service had begun and departed moments before the end. She slipped silently to a side pew behind a pillar by the door. She kept her head low but close observation found grief clearly evident. She would not attend the wake. A dark car was discreetly parked outside to aid her swift exit.

During the time of Ida's short illness notable events had been happening elsewhere in other parallel lives.

Jackie had been biding her time in hiding but with the aid of Marcus she was beginning to find her own talents. Burying herself in his office, trading as Louise Duggard, her birth name, she began to immerse herself in other people's lives. He had an interesting and diverse client list and while he operated as front man and chief organiser, she was able to support him by smoothing his dealings with suppliers and much later clients. She found that all the unwilling work she had done for Meredith in organising her craft and church events was paying dividends. Jackie, no Louise, had found a niche. She could be tactful and firm and was ultra-efficient. Over the years that followed, she gained personal satisfaction as well as success. Her earlier inhibitions began to evaporate.

When she first left, she had fully expected to return within months to claim her son and if the damage was not too great her husband but Clive Corneille would have to leave first. She waited with a mixture of patience and eager anticipation.

Discreetly, Ida and Louise had met and discussed events. Ida had been able to tell Louise about the evening at the club and her report encouraged Louise even more to wait in the wings ready for her grand entrance. One day towards Christmas they met at a small hostelry a few miles out of town. Ida would never have ventured so far before meeting her neighbour and certainly would not have gone to any public house. She had never gone with Jim even on a summer evening to sit outside and drink so it had at first been unimaginable to go on her own to meet a friend. Louise had given her confidence and self-belief.

As she travelled on the bus watching the last of autumn colours unfurl majestically before her she let her mind drift back to that other time when she had dared to enter the White Hart. The blend of trepidation and excitement for the young naïve girl she had been then she now felt had led her into Dave's arms. Even all these years later, her stomach clenched and a desperate fear took hold of her body. She still harboured the guilt not only for her actions at the time but in her marriage to Jim. It had been easy to marry Jim.

She did not know if it was her perennial hurt that had meant there was no exhilaration in her feelings for him or that it was Jim, dependable and kind man that he was, that dampened any exuberance. She had not realised that her feelings over the years had deepened and strengthened. If only she had been more liberated and honest. She had allowed her life to happen rather than determine it.

Had she been any different to Molly, her mother? There had been wasted opportunities when she should have brought life to the relationship but she had so easily slipped into an easy contentment. It was hard to challenge norms, especially after she had been traumatised in her youth. Life was so short and it was only with hindsight that she felt there was more than the absence of children missing from the relationship. Jim was a good dependable man who had been loyal and caring. She recognised his faults too.

At times, she had been jealous of his other love, the football club, which could raise his passion as she never could and command his attention and time, leaving her waiting at home but she also knew she had never exerted herself to make demands. He provided her with a home which she commanded. It had become a structure on which to build their marriage that is until Louise had stolen into her life and shown her other things. She began to recapture the girl before Dave, having her hair fashionably dressed for one thing. If there had been time, she would have forced Jim take notice. She knew she had wasted her years.

"You look pale. Are you okay?" Louise showed concern when she disembarked from the bus.

"I'm a bit tired that's all and I will be right as rain after being with you."

Ida knew this was to be their last meeting and it was important for it to be meaningful and good. She would make an effort. Louise must not be aware of her lack of time.

Ida told Louise about her son and how happy he had seemed at the local school which he had started in September. He was such a happy soul and had lots of friends it seemed. It would be wrong to disrupt the child. Ida knew the pain that Louise felt but both were assured of his safety and determined to protect him as far as they could. Louise was getting on her feet in her new job but she was living in a bedsit in the city so even if there was not the matter of their safety it would be unkind to take Jake away from his home.

That as Ida had anticipated was the last time they met. Ida became too tired. Louise rang and they promised to meet but it never happened. Ida could not admit her defeat and could not admit that this was yet another failure in her life. She would leave so much unfinished when the time came.

For Jim, the years after Ida left him would roll by punctuated by the seasons exemplified in his garden. He was not one to socialise but he was not entirely reclusive. His visitors tailed off after the funeral which satisfied Jim and he returned to work, needing the occupation and the break from the empty house. He would have an occasional pint, particularly on summer evenings. The person whose company he enjoyed from time to time was Ken.

Both had empty hearts from missing wives but each man had a pragmatism that allowed their banter to leave personal grief behind and discuss current issues. Neither of them had been interested in technological advances or the doings of the royals but they held opinions on Mike Tyson and OJ Simpson and the like, Bosnia where Jim's friend Bill's son Simon had been serving, the fall of the Soviet Union, South Africa and the release of Nelson Mandela, the scandal for the American President, the price of beer and more importantly and relevantly the fortunes of their own football team.

Over time, Jim recognised how Ken had done his best with young Jake and when Jake was young the two men would sometimes sit in the early evening sun in the Beer Garden watching Jake play on the grass after consuming his pop and crisps. When Jake was older, they could enjoy an occasional pint in the warm snug. Ken was a regular but Jim's attendance was much less frequent. Over time, they found respect for each other and Jim from a distance followed Jake's progress with interest.

Chapter 9
Paradise Lost

I like people quite well
At a little distance
I like to see them passing and passing
And going their own way,
Especially if I see their aloneness alive in them.

People: D. H. Lawrence

1992-1994: Diana and Antony

It had come to pass that Clive had dispensed with Antony's services shortly after the garden party. Antony had arrived back from Venice and made sure he was in the office early. Even Antony discerned the atmosphere from the other early arrivals. Greetings were awkward and abrupt and there were no ingratiating enquiries into his short holiday. In fact, even Marcella, someone who could be relied on to suck up to anyone senior, positioned herself to avoid any dialogue with Antony.

His office was on the fifth floor and looked out over a panoramic London scene. It represented his success and demonstrated importance to the world at large. The office appealed to his vanity and it never failed to give him a thrill of ownership as he walked through the door.

The box had been placed in front of his desk. The corner of a photograph frame was awkwardly poking out of the top. His desk was clear. For an instant he wondered if there was to be some redecoration or rearrangement of offices and he had missed the memo. The books had been removed from the shelves and there were no boxed files to be seen. With a jolt, he realised the computer had been removed. He was processing all this when there was a gentle tap on the door behind him.

"Mr Gordon asks that you see him," Antony looked round and saw Bronwyn and faces from the open office beyond looking curiously in his direction. Why George Gordon he thought, his brain stumbling through the conundrum. He had very little to do with George who dealt with staffing.

Antony raised his head in good public schoolboy fashion. "Thank you Bronwyn. Please tell him I will be with him in ten minutes." Instinctively, Antony knew he needed ten minutes to organise his thoughts.

When it came, the axe fell cleanly. Antony would collect his personal possessions under scrutiny. He was reminded of his legal obligations in not divulging any company information or working for any direct competitor within a time period and he was informed of his severance pay. He was out of the door by ten that morning.

Diana took the news well. She argued that a man like Antony with his capabilities would soon be in a position of worth. It was a temporary setback. However, a man like Clive Corneille had a mean streak. He was a controller and had tentacles into the city institutions. A word here, a word there and doors could be opened or shut. Antony dwindled as the rebuffs mounted.

At Christmas, it was time to take stock, particularly financially. Their money was finite until Antony could find another position and that could take a long time. Boarding school fees had been a considerable expense but they could manage for the next term at least. Their eldest child, Kirsten, eighteen the following January, would be at university the following September so after the summer apart from her expectations of support there would be no crippling fees. Their second daughter, sixteen-year-old Samantha, was no academic and willingly agreed to leave school after GCSEs and look for a college course or suitable job which left Phillip, their youngest, as a problem. It was imperative that he continue his education but their reserves were well depleted and they each feared the indignity of withdrawing him from school. The strain began to tell.

It had been customary to hold a Christmas Eve party, a way of demonstrating their status and their benevolence. There would be a raffle and an auction to raise money for local charities. This year was difficult. Antony wanted to forego it. Diana felt they should go ahead. The costs were considerable and the tension between the couple mounted. In the end, Antony found the courage to veto any plans and Diana seethed.

"It's alright for you when you were out all day, but me, I have to live amongst these people. There's an expectation. Couldn't we, please, Tony?" She wheedled and then added, "It's like telling everyone we're broke and shouting it from the rooftops too."

Antony had steeled himself and replied coolly, "Diana, we are broke really, certainly in the terms of this community. We can hang on a bit longer but unless there's a miracle, not indefinitely."

"You're selfish. I hate you. My mother said you were spineless. What have you done to me?" She raged, not really attacking him so much as life in general. Diana never held back if it made her feel better to explode.

"Your mother had granite for a heart so I don't think I care what she thinks. She's the most self-centred arrogant woman I know, and god knows I've met a few." Antony had never been that forthright.

Diana was shocked not so much by the sentiment but the tone of the statement. She was after all these years seeing a new side to her husband. It was rather satisfying but she retorted, "How dare you! You made enough fuss of her when we first got together." Diana shook her head to emphasise the point.

That had been true to a certain extent. He had been enamoured with Diana and only sought to please. He refrained from more barbed insults, although he dearly wanted to let out his frustration about her family emanating from the time he had fallen for her. There had been intense pressure from her toxic family. He was sorely tempted to give his wife some unpalatable truths but at this point in time he needed her co-operation and his ruthless business brain clicked into gear.

Her father had been distant and authoritative, gruff in manner and conceited in his position of bank manager. Antony quickly assessed the man's shortcomings in financial matters. He was old school and delegated any responsibility for real banking, leaving him free to govern his minions and customers from his grand office in the style of a petty dictator. It was almost a grace and favour role. Antony's quick brain could undo his father-in-law at a whim but of course, Diana was the goddess to whom Antony aspired, so Antony put up with her father's facile opinions. Diana's mother was all about position. She was impressed with his first at Oxford and his other qualifications. She had been in awe of some of his connections in the city, names she had read about in national newspapers.

It was a far cry from Midchester, the town in which she exerted her influence. She would sit upright and stiff, corsets exercising an iron will over her thick set body, pursing her lips to demonstrate her superiority. Antony, who had felt the warm flesh of Diana failed to imagine how her remote parents could ever have come together to produce such a delightful creature except through artificial insemination as a bull to a cow.

Diana's two elder brothers had flown the nest at their earliest opportunity and as far as they could fly. One was in America in some giant commercial bank and another in the Middle East as part of a syndicate to build a fortune from oil. Diana had had to live in their shadow, deprived of a meaningful career and exposed to the constant accolades for her brothers from her parents. A much younger sister, maybe an accidental addition to the family, could never satisfy them no matter how hard she tried and at times Antony had seen how hard she tried.

The lack of the Christmas party had sealed their positions of authority. To make matters worse for Diana, there had been a cocktail party at the Grange but they had been left off the guest list. It was no mistaking the snub and Diana wept bitterly. She drank the champagne left from the summer until oblivion took away the hurt.

Diana could not escape the guilt of the punishment. It was all a retribution for denying her daughter and she drank to deaden her shame. Meanwhile, Antony wrestled with his sums in his study. Kirsten, as the sensible eldest daughter, did her best to bring Christmas cheer to the house. The three children horrified by the situation combined in a way that should have made any parent proud but neither parent noticed.

On Boxing Day, it was decided they should move. Diana bitterly resented giving up her beautiful house and was horrified to learn the extent of mortgage on it, all very well when Antony had been bringing city wages to the pot but now it had become a millstone. Diana took to her bed as much as she was allowed.

January slipped darkly by with more angst for the couple. Antony brooded. He was well aware of the ramifications of debt and the court procedures that would be enacted against them. He knew it was better to seize the initiative and he would have to push his wife into action. They had an outwardly successful marriage. They each knew the value of a united front particularly in the corporate world and over the years they had carried this into their personal lives generally avoiding any difficult issues. In private, Antony would pander to Diana's prima donna displays and Diana would applaud his brilliance to give him confidence. Habits had been formed that drew a veil over deeper personal feelings. The marriage had worked but that was when there was a well-regulated script.

"Diana, we need to talk and act." He brought his boardroom voice to the bedroom as she curled into a ball on the bed.

"I'm not ready." She listened to the rain pounding against the window in a similar rhythm to her heart-rate.

"If we do not take control, it will be far worse. I will not be able to work if there are court cases against me. Phillip will have to leave and you know how people are. If we sort it out, then we can rise again." Antony had a logical even tone that had a reassurance above the threat.

Diana's natural self-preservation kicked in. "Most women would get a divorce."

"That is an option for you of course, but there would not be much of a settlement. Now if you had thought about it last year you might have been sitting pretty." The words registered with both of them and seemed to complete the picture. For a minute or two, they both kept their counsel, Diana lifting her body into a seated position and Antony perching on the dressing table chair watching his wife intently.

"Why? Why? Why?" Diana suddenly exploded thumping her arms onto the pillow and then with resignation a few minutes later, she said, "Well, looks like there's no choice. You'd better call the estate agents and put things in motion but I am not staying in this town to be laughed at behind my back. No, we will not be beaten. I won't let it happen." Antony nodded and wiped the lens of his glasses ready to refocus.

"We can go wherever you want. In a new place I can set up as an independent accountant. I can leave the city behind and even be a country gentleman." Antony had talents and this statement emphasised possibilities.

"Can you imagine me in that role? Honestly, Antony I didn't marry you for this?" Diana was not sure what she meant when she said this but she wanted a different role. She was beginning to realise that her active life had in fact been rather empty. She had muddled success with achievement.

"What did you marry me for then, Diana?" Antony had been mentally strong over the last few months and he needed to know if he would now need to harbour emotional strength. Antony hated confrontation but he also did not avoid confronting problems even emotional, personal ones.

She looked at him with venom. "Oh and why did you marry me then? You saw someone to get you where you wanted to be. You've used me, Tony. I've slaved for you. It's not easy entertaining all your people. You've climbed the ladder through me. I've greased the pole and you are the big city man." Diana was using her new energy as justification and berated her stricken husband. She was unreasonable but she felt ugly and frightened and lashed out. He understood.

"Well, I'm not any more, am I?" He retained his composure that turned her passion.

"What the hell did you do? You don't get the sack for nothing." Antony had shielded Diana from much of his working life which had been a mistake and increased her shock and lack of understanding. Her father had schooled her not to question financial and business affairs, but Diana, Antony realised, needed to know, however unpalatable, and be a part of it. When they had first met, he had been impressed with how astute she had been and yet he had kept her in ignorance. They should have talked more. They should have shared.

"You do in my line of work, believe me? I'm honestly glad to get out of it." It was a relief to be frank.

Diana tried to process his comment. Their whole married life had been directed towards Antony's advancement in the business world. He had done well but now it was all spiralling out of control. Diana's natural default position was to close down. At home, Antony had always taken his lead from Diana. Now it was him that needed to exercise control.

He put the house on the market and dealt as far as he could with the debts. In this respect he could be cold blooded and decisive ignoring his wife until he had determined a solution. The next step was to tackle his wife. They had avoided each other since their last exchange, even occupying separate rooms and Antony had been prepared for eventual legal separation and divorce.

Diana had missed Antony. She saw a new side to him. She saw a calculating man and one who had determination and strength. This was a completely different experience. Previously, when he was at home he had been at her beck and call, soothing her tantrums as necessary and allowing her free rein in domestic decisions. He admired her too and she had basked in that admiration. She was a deft operator in the social scene which had made up for his inadequacies in that sphere. He had expertise in the boardroom while she had expertise in the wider world. He thought they had been good together but this seemed a parting of the ways. He had always been convinced she was out of his class.

They sat down together to discuss the next stage. Diana had listened quietly to his assessment which perturbed him. There was no assault. For Diana the bitterness of their situation had been in her loneliness. She had come to realise she had no friends, that is she had no real genuine friends. She had had an army of acquaintances but there was no person to whom she could turn in her weakness. There was no-one in whom she could share a confidence. She recalled Gillian from school.

It had not seemed to matter when Antony held his position but her new isolation plagued her. She realised she had small time friends who clung to her coat tails. She hated her vulnerability. Antony had been a stalwart partner. She discovered she wanted his respect and more importantly his love. He had been her friend and she wanted mutual friendship. It had taken time and a crisis but Diana hoped it was not too late.

"Let's look at houses near where I grew up. It's a pleasant enough place and the school will be near enough for Phillip to attend as a day student. That will save us something and I have contacts there so we can soon build up a client list. In fact, I've been getting rather tired of the neighbourhood here. I had thought Felicity and Martin would call but I have not seen hide or hair of them and as for Roger and Daphne it beggars belief how they slighted us at Christmas.

"I hate them all. I have not had any invitations in the last three months. I know, I have pretended we have other commitments but it really is too bad of people after all we have done for them. Yes, I agree a clean break is what we need."

Antony was surprised and relieved to have her fighting spirit directed at the future and not him. It had been unexpected and for an instant put him on the back foot. She had found her voice, the one that exerted charm over her audience. That night they shared a bedroom.

To settle in Midchester had an appeal. The only downside would have been the presence of her parents but they had suddenly upped sticks three years previously when her father retired and settled in France. Both of them wrote about their days in the sun living in a grand French chateau. Having visited Antony thought it was more like a large rather neglected country house than a castle but he was happy to have them at arms' length so agreed with their fantasy boasts. The place was cold and needed the summer sun. Antony and Diana confined their visits to summer and Antony had more than once pleaded that his work prevented his attendance.

Diana and Antony had met in the South of France. Diana had been employed as an *au pair*, although as far as he could tell when he arrived at the villa she used as many as she could of the staff there to relieve her of these duties. She was such an entertaining and bewitching girl that he was under her thrall from their first encounter. He had arrived, hot and flustered in quite unsuitable clothes for the heat. His handkerchief barely soaked up his perspiration as he was ushered in to meet the industrialist for whom he was working. It had been totally unexpected to be plucked from the drab office he inhabited and flown to the radiance of this stunning location. It was felt that Antony, in his diligent way, had a grasp of the particular figures needed for the latest coup. The laughter from the patio centred upon a stunning girl lounging on a sunbed. Antony stood transfixed as though arriving for a film shoot as a privileged onlooker. The girl was oblivious to him.

Antony had fulfilled his obligations, which led to a successful financial outcome and invited to stay on for the celebratory dinner. He had been completely at sea in the company of Diana, who he now knew was employed as an *au pair*. Geoffrey, a friend of the industrialist, seemed to be her chosen companion. He was a smooth operator probably about ten years older but with the grooming of a younger man. Geoffrey expertly flattered and teased and seduced under Antony's watchful eye. Antony was no match for a tour de force like Geoffrey and could never presume even to show his interest in a girl who was so out of his league.

Diana was anything but stupid. She enjoyed herself that was true but she was by then not a naïve schoolgirl. She had had a hard lesson in that respect. She shuddered as she remembered. She saw Geoffrey for who he was, a player, a fun companion but not dependable. She relished her place in the society in which she found herself tasting the experience and liking the power that it brought but she knew she was an employee, someone to be included if entertaining and amenable. She wanted so much more. She wanted to belong as an equal. Her mother had instilled in her the need for position. She was prepared to work hard and make strategic choices. Unknown to Antony he began to figure in her plans.

The celebratory dinner was very grand. Antony had begun to regret agreeing to stay on. He had not the capability of conversing in polite society. His range of topics was limited and his serious demeanour was often off putting for companions. He was he had to admit, uninteresting in character and therefore boring in company. He was anxious about who he might have to engage with at the dinner table. Antony who was never late for any appointment reported in good time, trying his best to saunter on to the balcony where champagne was being served.

"Ah here you are, Antony. Come and help yourself to a glass," welcomed his genial host. "This young man has made me a lot of money with his sharp brain," his host's generous compliment gave Antony more confidence even with the embarrassment of the attention.

He tried to articulate but while his brain was sharp and incisive as far as numbers were concerned he lacked any sharpness in repartee. He was not a drinker and the fizzy liquid combined with the occasion dulled his brain.

"Hello you." Diana had noticed his discomfort and grasped her opportunity. "These events are nice but such hard work, aren't they? A girl is expected to smile all the time and laugh even at the most boring jokes. Will you be my protector please? I cannot spend another minute listening to Geoffrey recount his exploits on the golf course. He really is not very good you know but he has to be indulged. Oh god he is coming over, take my arm and we can look at the view," and Diana skilfully steered Antony to a spot on the edge by the balustrade.

The view was indeed magnificent but what was even more magnificent was the touch of the sensational girl at his side. On glancing back, Antony noticed that Geoffrey had been waylaid.

"Now I want to hear all about you. You are so quiet, such a mysterious man," Diana gave him the full attention of her mascaraed eyes and formed her lips into an appreciative bow. Antony was lost in the embrace of her look.

"I hope you don't mind but I arranged for us to sit together at dinner. I so wanted to get to know you before you leave tomorrow. I really wish you did not have to go. We could have had fun together," and she let her tongue hesitate very slightly over the word 'fun.'

Antony was captivated. He had never experienced anything like it and was transported beyond his humdrum life of facts and figures to a world of elegance combined with sensual pleasure. He was both enthralled and afraid. Diana manoeuvred the conversation to be encouraging and complimentary as well as gently seductive and Antony was swept along. He ate little as his stomach had contracted as his chest had expanded and he was conscious of a new and intense feeling in his groin.

Diana knew better than to exploit the opportunity too soon. At the end of the evening she took Antony for a walk in the garden. They could see the light of the moon and the lights of the promenade below shimmer on the water. The flickering movement reflected the quivering heart of Antony.

"Will you meet me when I am back in London?" Diana asked.

"Yes, of course." He was mesmerised.

"I know you probably like me here where everything is lovely and romantic. I will probably be a disappointment in London."

Diana had observed characters throughout her life, using her findings initially to apply to any dramatic presentations, especially at school and then since her sixth form problem she had been more discerning about the males of the species. She would not fall into any trap but was quite willing to lay her own traps.

How could this wonderful girl ever be a disappointment, Antony thought? "You would never ever be a disappointment. It is me that is always a disappointment." It was not a good line but somehow Diana encouraged the confidence. He swallowed the spit that had collected on his tongue feeling even more inadequate.

With this, Diana turned and locked her arms round his neck in reassurance and kissed him full on the mouth, gently but firmly. He clung on to her as his spirit slipped its anchor. He had no idea where the voyage would take him but he did not care.

Diana did not seduce him that night, although she was sorely tempted. She played her cards more deftly and at the end of her contract sought him out in London.

He had not been completely innocent regarding women but Diana presented him with hitherto unknown gratification. She would take his arm possessively, she would charm his colleagues at functions, she would attract admiring glances when they were at expensive restaurants and she bedded him with sufficient reserve to give him a sense of mastery.

Six months later to the delight of her mother they married.

Now almost twenty years later, they would reinvent themselves.

The house had sold within weeks enabling the majority of debts to be paid. The difficulty was in finding a new residence. Both of them despaired at the properties on offer for their budget even though they were moving out of their Cotswold idyll where property prices were astronomical.

It was fortunate that Antony still had connections to offer a substantial mortgage if he required even though he had no regular income. A decision had to be made. It was decided to take a twelve-month lease on a small but chic flat which Diana called apartment, in the centre of town with views across the patchwork of roofs and even a glimpse of the river. They argued that it would be a good place for Antony to establish himself and they could enjoy the amenities on offer. This would afford them time to look at the housing market.

In addition to the master bedroom, there were two smaller bedrooms for Phillip who was to become a day student and Samantha who was to attend the local college that September to take a beautician course. Kirsten would have to share with Samantha or use the sofa bed when on holiday from university. It was as they saw it a temporary arrangement. By the beginning of May, they had wiped away their old life and embarked on a new experience. In the close flat they came together.

These months proved to be the happiest that Diana had ever known.

The couple availed themselves of the cafes and bars and restaurants in the town centre as well as attending the local theatre and joining a bridge club and a walking group. Diana felt free for the first time in her life. Her parents having moved to France no longer had a hold over her activities and she no longer had to impress the business fraternity. She found the people she met interesting and sincere, unlike the seemingly shallow people who had governed her life before.

The friendly community was thriving and an accountant who had worked for major city investors and knew the intricacies of tax laws was an absolute godsend and so Antony began to build a successful practice. Diana was once more in her element.

There was one perpetual nagging notion that marred these days. It had begun after the garden party. While she had managed to send Jackie packing from the house she had not managed to send her packing from her head and even her heart. Diana no longer driven by the forces of her previous life found a new self, softer and more patient. On her walks she discussed matters of the day as well as personal experiences and she found attentive and receptive listeners. She found herself opening up describing something of her previous life.

No-one judged her, although there were opinions about the society from which she had escaped. She began to see how acquaintances could become friends something she had not understood before. She realised she had squandered one important early opportunity for a good friend.

She thought of Gillian more and more. She knew it was Gillian who had written the letter. How could anyone mistake that beautiful italic script? Diana pondered. She had so easily dismissed Gillian after she had served her purpose and yet Gillian had kept her secret and supported her. Gillian had clearly cared too. The shame that crept into Diana's being was painful. She found she could not shut down unwanted feelings like she had done in her previous life.

A year later in March 1994, the day of Ida's demise was the day coincidentally that Diana made a resolution. Ida's watchful eye had been closing in eternal slumber. Diana's clouded eyes had been opening to reveal a new perspective. She decided she would actively try to find Gillian and she would try to track down her daughter.

The compulsion to do so had been getting stronger over the preceding months. Maybe, it was because she had so decidedly broken away from her past, maybe it was because she liked the new gentler, compassionate Diana, maybe it was just curiosity or maybe it was all part of wanting something better, something more fulfilling and complete, something that would soothe the conscience which she now had. She thought that reparations would bring peace of mind but first she would have to be honest with Antony.

That evening, the same evening that Jim was coming to terms with the fact that he would never hold Ida again, Diana broached the subject of her past. Somehow, and very unusually for her, Diana was petrified.

They sat at the small corner table, enjoying the last of the wine, replete after their meal at Benedicto's. It was a small intimate Italian restaurant that they had discovered down a side street. It was somewhere they gravitated to, especially when they wanted good food without fuss. It was a place to unwind. So used to the bright restaurants of their past life where they would be on show it had become soothing dining at the little eatery. Here, they could relax and blend into the rustic setting. Diana wondered how many others might have embarked on difficult conversations in this very spot.

"You seem distracted," Antony cut into her thoughts and gave her an opening. She did not want to discuss this at the flat where the children might burst in upon them and Antony would always be a gentleman in public. Much better she thought to tell him here and now.

"There is something I want to discuss."

Antony prepared himself for the usual topics, the children and their behaviour, a proposed holiday, a house that was a possibility for them but he was unprepared for what she told him.

"Remember when that girl came to the house?"

Antony was at first perplexed.

"The day of the garden party for Clive, it makes me mad just thinking about it. He had already decided you were going. What a two-faced pig. I hope he gets his come-uppance. One day, someone will bring him down. Wish I could be there when it happens." Diana realised she was getting waylaid.

"That's the way things operate, you know that Diana, and things are good for us now aren't they? You don't want to get wound up about it. He's not worth talking about so don't let's waste time. We should look forward. Things are going really well you know. I may have to turn work away soon.

"I was thinking we could take Phillip to the cricket, for the test in June. He hasn't been to Lords. A boy of his age should go and the third day is always interesting. It should be a good match and might even decide the series after Trent Bridge so might be in for a treat. The New Zealand team are not the likes of Australia of course, but England has been struggling and after losing the series in the Caribbean they need to come out fighting. Illingworth will be bound to make a few changes. You used to like it at Lords. What do you think? We can lord it up for a day," and he laughed at his own joke.

"Sounds like a good idea. Will you get tickets? Maybe, we could order one of their delicious hampers." And she noticed his smile of satisfaction. "But Clive was not really on my mind. It was something else. Something I should have faced years ago." Diana suddenly felt sick.

"Whatever it is, it can't be that bad," Antony reassured, noticing his wife's stricken look. Since the last meltdown on leaving the country house, Diana had been much more in control.

The little restaurant was hot. The noise throughout the evening had been stifling but with the departure of the birthday party and the gradual departure of other diners conversations became muted and in the resulting stillness there was a sense of foreboding.

"Let's have a coffee and maybe a liqueur," Antony urged. It was unsettling to see Diana this way. The thought passed through his mind that now he was more on his feet she would be asking for a divorce but things had been so much better in recent months, in fact at times for him it had been wonderful, which was something he had not thought possible when he had been a city man.

Diana nodded and he placed the order.

"The girl who came to the house and said she was my daughter. Well, I think she might have been."

Antony could not respond.

"Tony," Diana used the personal name.

The waiter brought their coffees and Grand Marnier commenting as he did that he hoped they had enjoyed their meal and it had been a busy evening so he hoped they did not feel he had neglected them. In fact, as regular customers they would often chat for a few minutes but now they wanted anything but. Their natural good manners allowed him a few minutes until he was called away by another customer. At least, it gave Antony a moment to process what she said and recall the scene.

"I had a baby when I was eighteen. My mother made me give her up. I thought I had put it all behind me. I called her Louise." It was not how she intended to tell him but it was a simple and honest account. She waited for his reaction, a nervous tension causing her mouth to dry.

"But you showed me a letter and said it was impossible for the girl to be yours." Antony recalled the scene as best he could, peering at her through narrowed eyes.

"I know. I know. It was such a difficult day. It was a shock and then the name was wrong and I wanted the day to go well for you. I wanted Clive to be impressed. I wanted her to go." Diana knew she sounded selfish and heartless as the explanation tumbled out of her mouth. All her normal composure had deserted her and then she recoiled at his response.

"Don't you dare blame me!" He hissed. "You've always done your own thing. What about the letter? You gave it me to read. You did not write it did you?" It was unlike Antony to be so sharp and condemnatory.

"No, I did not write it and I did not know it existed. Believe me, Tony. At the time I could not accept it and it was later, gradually that I realised." She tried hard to reason with him and dreaded an alternative consequence.

"What did you realise?" His voice was hard and sharp like a flint. She recoiled in her chair as though she had been slapped and then grasping the strength she had left she pleaded.

"Please understand. It was another life, another time, another me. I recognised the writing. It was a girl I knew."

"So who knew about this child?" He had the tone of a prosecutor in a courtroom drama except that his voice was small and shrill which made it even more unforgiving.

"We kept it quiet. My mother arranged everything." Diana had never felt so inadequate. She had not expected Antony to be so mean. He had always been generous and kind.

"Oh she would." Antony could not resist interrupting and swallowed most of the Grand Marnier in his anger.

"The girl was someone at school who found out and became a friend for a while. She must have written the letter. I was asked if I wanted to write anything to go with her papers but my mother said I must not so I didn't."

Diana felt the answer was pathetic. It made her reconsider her actions and she saw how feeble and self-centred she had been. She felt exposed in a way she had never felt before. Her naked conscience condemned her as no-one else could, not even Antony, and she succumbed to the pain of his questions.

"And what then about this girl who wrote the letter?" Antony knew he was being hostile but somehow he could not help it.

"Her name was Gillian. She was a nice girl but we lost touch." Again, Diana felt the fury in his look which she interpreted as disgust.

"So why tell me now. Why now when things are good. Is it pay-back for my failure? You want to get your own back. Is that it?" Antony almost slurred his words as his own failings surfaced which gave Diana courage.

"No Tony. It's because things are so good. I feel good. I want to make things right I suppose. I want to help her if she needs and I want to find Gillian. I know, I have been selfish and thoughtless. I don't want to hurt you." Diana tried to understand the shock and tried to appreciate his feelings of betrayal for not having faced it before but she was at a loss to understand his spite. Antony had never been vindictive.

"I think it's time to go," and he rose from the table indicating to the waiter that he would settle up quickly. Diana grabbed her things while he paid and followed him out of the door, trotting behind him along the quiet streets to the flat they called home.

There was no more discussion that night. Samantha had a couple of friends round and they were watching a film. Phillip had taken himself off to bed. The film was almost over and until then Diana retreated to the kitchen while Antony picked up the newspaper he had already read earlier in the day and retreated behind it as he sat in the vacant armchair.

The small flat gave them little scope for avoidance of the other. In bed later Diana tried to reach out to him but he answered with his back. Each of them lay as immobile as possible and neither of them slept.

The truth of the matter was that Antony was insanely jealous. He had known that before him there would have been previous liaisons in Diana's life but he had been able to put them aside as inconsequential and trivial but this included a baby. He thought of his own children and the feelings he had towards them. They were an extension of him and Diana, a sharing, and his mind was blown apart that a life had been produced between Diana and another man. What kind of claims might either have on Diana? Where would he be left if she did locate her daughter? His perfect world had suddenly disintegrated.

Gradually, they slipped back into a routine but the revelation was a sore over which they applied a plaster of normality. Diana had let something cut into her marriage and while there was no gash there was a wound that stubbornly refused to heal. Any search for her daughter Diana put on hold.

In the end, months later it was the Christmas walk that year that ripped off the plaster and brought healing air. It was one of those bright December days, when the air was clean and cold. The sun was low in the sky and that sky was a rich blue blanket. Dressed for the season the group set out for the chosen pub where a lunch awaited. The route took them along quiet country lanes circumnavigating a popular fishing lake and back to the village where cars had been parked. Antony fell in with Michael, a local vet, who was considering retirement. Antony had been giving him some financial advice.

"I suppose I am frightened of change," Michael admitted.

"We all are I think but sometimes it can be for the better. Look at us. We were both so driven that there never would have been any opportunity for walks like this. We were on a merry go round and the more I earned the more I seemed to have to spend and the more we tried to satisfy other people the meaner and nastier they got." Antony relished leaving the city and enjoyed the vindication of what had happened.

"You're right, of course. When I was first introduced to Graham, I was worried that everything would change but do you know it did change but for the better. Graham started coming to the practice to help out and Margaret says he and I are so bonded she sometimes feels left out even though she's his mother and I did not know him until he was ten." The two men were in an easy step that encouraged conversation even on a more personal basis.

Antony thought about this. "You had no doubts about taking him in?" Antony had heard that Margaret had had a son by another man when she had lived briefly in Australia. He had stayed with the father who had died in a motorcycle accident and the boy had been shipped to England to live with his mother and her new husband Michael.

"Oh, of course I did. I had no idea what he would be like and how he would probably resent me but you know with a bit of give and take it could not have been better. The worst thing I think was being reminded that Margaret had this relationship before me. Selfish, hey?" Antony glanced at Michael's relaxed countenance and swallowed his pride.

"It's good that things have worked out so well and you are anything but selfish, I think." Antony began to think deliberately and carefully on what had been banished from his mind for some months.

"I was selfish for a while when we first got the news of Alan's death. Margaret was in a state and I am ashamed I did not help her much." Michael made Antony feel shabby.

"Graham will be with us for Christmas. He always makes sure he spends it with us even though he's thirty and we probably bore him silly. Our own kids seem to have their own plans that do not include us. We're hoping he will introduce us to his new girlfriend soon and Margaret can get excited about a wedding." Michael a good few years older than Antony seemed to have an acceptance that allowed him to experience the best in life. Antony felt regret but kept the conversation light while he re-examined his attitude.

Antony spoke about his children and plans for Christmas in a non-committal way but he was thinking and thinking hard. He wondered if Diana's toughness had evolved through her experiences. He had never liked her mother and now this latest revelation had meant he liked her even less. His own mother had been soft and gentle and some would say weak giving way to the dominant males in her life. He had loved his mother very much and instinctively knew she could never be as callous as Diana's parent. He watched as Diana was talking animatedly with a couple of the other walkers. They were laughing, probably sharing a joke and for a moment she glanced back at him walking behind and each smiled as their eyes locked.

Antony felt unburdened by releasing his resentment. He loved Diana with a depth and passion that amazed him sometimes even though she could be infuriating. He knew his life would be empty without her. They would look together for the girl and the friend. Diana was his wife.

Chapter 10
Making Up for Lost Time

A thing of beauty is a joy for ever:
Its loveliness increases; it will never
Pass into nothingness; but still will keep
A bower quiet for us, and a sleep
Full of sweet dreams, and health, and quiet breathing

Endymion: John Keats

1988-1994: Gillian and Steve

Gillian's mother had died in the final throes of winter in 1988 and left Gillian and her father to soldier on.

In later life, when Gillian recalled these years with her father, it had been perpetual winter. She could feel the cold in her fingers until the fire blazed in the hearth, she could taste the home-made vegetable soup, thick and hot which bubbled in the big, black pot on the stove, she remembered how she would snuggle into the thick long dressing gown, her feet in soft fluffy slippers drinking Horlicks before bed and her father nodding into sleep in his big armchair swathed in the plaid rug.

They both missed her mother. Gillian was still at home as she approached the age of thirty-six that June and now with the responsibility of her father it had become even more unlikely to strike out on her own. They carried on the routine that her mother had created and subsequently set in stone. All seemed to centre upon meals.

After roast on Sundays, there would be cold meat on Monday and if there was enough meat to be minced there would be shepherds' pie on Tuesday. Wednesday and Thursday might be chops or liver or a stew that could stretch for two days. There was always fish on Friday and Saturday might have some variation, although the lack of inspiration meant that more often than not it would be sausage and mash. The week began again on Sunday.

Her father relied on consistency and routine to support his advancing years, although Gillian would have loved to experiment more and try some of the foreign dishes that her colleagues spoke of cooking at their homes but she did not have the rebellious attitude necessary to challenge the regime. Her mother had always ruled the kitchen and her father needed Gillian to do so in the same way when his wife had gone.

Gillian recalled her bedroom in her parents' house. Her single bed seemed narrow in retrospect as had been her life. The chilled air because there was no central heating meant she would clutch a hot water bottle until she fell asleep and annoyingly kick it out hours later because it was glacial against her skin. Her window overlooking the street had metal frames which allowed little penetrating puffs of draught. The window itself was often filmy from moisture or even decorated with flimsy frost designs which Gillian would trace with her fingertips. Her wardrobe was stuffed to capacity as were the dressing table drawers. There was never enough space for the fashion-conscious Gillian. The floor to ceiling bookcase dominated the corner. It was laden with her precious books, her escape from the mundane and the reality. She had used the little box room as a study for her school work and an overflow for her personal possessions. No-one ever came to stay so there was no need for it to be set aside as a guest room. Gillian would laugh at the very term 'guest.' A guest was someone to be feted and welcomed into their midst. Her parents had been private people with simple pleasures that were not for sharing. They relied on routine. Of course, as Gillian looked further back the habits had only been formed over a period of time to cope with middle age and the onset of old age. Gillian could remember, but not well, a time when attitudes were looser. She had a vision of them cavorting round the living room to an Elvis song or later the new Beatles hit and drinking the champagne her father had won in a raffle. They used to play cards and scrabble, heatedly arguing over suspect words and laughing in victory.

Gillian had known that in Diana's predicament things would have been handled so differently but then Gillian was never likely to get into that predicament. At almost thirty-six when her mother died and left with the care of her father that was even less likely.

School had been accommodating in her loss. She had taken a week off, the first real absence on her record. She had always been careful with her health and tried to keep reasonably fit so attendance was natural for her unlike some of the others she could mention who would stay at home for the merest reason. She often observed that these malingerers did not seem to suffer any ill will because of their ill health whereas Gillian's absence for her mother's death and funeral was duly noted by all and sundry.

"Where were you Miss? We had to have Mr Owen."

"I know you've had a difficult time but have you managed to get the predicted grades entered up?"

"We wanted you to run your eye over the year ten scheme of work. We need to get it circulated ready for September."

"Are you ready to put the order in for next year's texts?"

Gillian in her neat and methodical way had generally been the person to do any administration that required attention to detail. It was felt that others did not have the degree of concentration and efficiency. Gillian had never resented this as it gave her a certain kudos which was hard won in a school like hers but in private she rather envied those members of staff who were not so dedicated and still seemed to reap rewards. Sometimes, life seemed unfair.

After Gillian had been called away from school on several occasions to attend to her father, the head called her into his office.

"Do sit down Gillian." He studied her choosing his words carefully.

"I have been made aware of your change in circumstance. It is difficult for you and the school sympathises."

Gillian wondered why he did not sympathise and how the school sympathised. She had not particularly noticed. She felt an upsurge of emotion at his words but in her practised way suppressed any signs of betrayal.

"You have been a valued member of staff." It seemed strange to Gillian to say 'have been' and not 'are.' "We must make sure that all our students have the best education and we have noticed you have been missing lessons recently."

Gillian had begun to apologise but he interrupted.

"Family is always of prime importance and we wish to make a proposal for you to consider. There is no pressure and it does not reflect anything else than our regard for your welfare."

Gillian remembered being at a loss. Should she be flattered or worried?

"If you wish, we can make arrangements for you to step down to a part time role. This may make it easier for you to manage your domestic circumstances." The headmaster waited for her approval.

"But there are my examination groups?" Gillian in shock dearly wanted the status quo.

"I know, you will be concerned not to, as it were, abandon any of your examination students but Kate has for a long time wanted to increase her hours, especially, in confidence, after her recent divorce and it might suit both of you. You could drop hours and have time at home and she could have a full-time role." It seemed that she had been discussed in the circles of power.

Gillian had been taken aback. It was as if another cornerstone was being removed from her life.

"Now no need to say anything today. Go away and think about it. We would have to know in say a month." The head signalled the end of the interview by standing and Gillian backed out of the door and she was swallowed into the corridor beyond.

It had seemed inevitable that she would accept. Her father needed the company. He was obviously at a loss since his wife had died. They could manage financially. There would be her father's pension and even though her salary would be reduced there was no mortgage to pay and expenses were light in the little house. It would mean she would not have the funds for luxuries unless she drew on her savings so her penchant for fashion could not be indulged. At school, she had become distracted and in her sadness for the loss of her mother wanted the escape.

It was a year after her mother died and she had been working part time for six months when she met Steve. She had called him on a recommendation of a colleague to look at some kitchen cupboards that were coming adrift. He came promptly and looked at the cupboards in question. He showed her how they had become damp over time and had warped. They could not really be repaired or rather it would be more cost effective to replace them. Steve discussed things with her father. It was not in Gillian's expertise and she made them cups of tea.

Steve offered to price new units and made one or two suggestions about rearrangements. He did not try to push them and indeed, told them he was busy for the next few weeks. He said they should get other estimates for any work but he was happy to sort it out if they could wait and the price was acceptable.

Gillian really liked him. She liked his easy manner. She liked the way he discussed things with her father. She liked the way he did not push for work. She felt she could trust him in the house and her colleague had sung his praises.

Gillian took her father to MFI on her next day off and they both gushed at the displays of the modern kitchens on display, opening cupboards to find hidden gems such as a dishwasher or microwave. They both realised that their existing kitchen was not only old fashioned but impractical. Gillian remembered running her fingers over the shiny surfaces, noting special storage places and extra preparation sinks as well as the way appliances were discreetly hidden. She had imagined developing her culinary skills in such a kitchen and maybe there would be a little wine rack to help her efforts.

Her father agreed that improvements had to be made and got out his building society book to aid his calculations. Gillian had some savings too, more than her father but she had wanted them to invest in a place of her own one day. If her father eventually had to go into a nursing home, the house would need to be sold to pay for it. They discussed it and her father was insistent that it was his house and he should spend his money. He became animated for the first time since his loss.

They asked Steve to come back and give advice. He seemed so appreciative of their circumstances that Gillian could have cried with relief. Steve was a skilled carpenter and promised to come up with some plans. She trusted him right from the start.

She found out about Abigail his wife and his son Alex from Gail the colleague who had recommended him. Gillian was not disappointed. She was rather relieved to know he was out of reach and the pattern of life would go on as usual.

The kitchen exceeded all expectations. Gillian found her spirits lifted and would sing along to the radio while she was baking. Steve would call in occasionally and enjoy a cup of tea. Her father loved these visits and she would leave them alone to discuss the things men do. Steve gradually became an asset in every respect. She felt she had someone to call on if she needed practical help and from time to time he did the general jobs like re-felting the shed. He was a good person to ask about other workman too. He seemed to know so many useful people.

Gillian had turned forty when things changed. Her father had suddenly seemed to age markedly and his faculties diminished. The doctor said it was to be expected and these little turns were TIA's and he was prescribed blood thinner tablets. He became very slow in his movement and he did not have his former bodily control.

Gillian was grateful for the distraction of Steve's visits who now seemed more like a friend. Somehow, over the years her circumstances and her natural reserve deterred any other real friendships and of course, she did not have a place of her own in which to entertain. Any old school or college friends had become acquaintances as they had married and put their energies into their growing families.

The day when Ida slipped her mortal coil was the day it all came to a head. It was almost as if Ida was orchestrating events forcing Diana to confront her feelings for her missing daughter and causing the other player in the history to confront her spinsterhood.

It had been a hard week. March was always a month when the demands of school were greater. All the coursework had to be assessed and moderated and examinations loomed ahead requiring completion of set texts and regular exam practice essays.

Although part time, she still continued her administrative duties which ate into her unpaid time. She had not the heart to withdraw. This week, whether it was because Gillian was more preoccupied than usual or there had been deterioration in his condition, her father had become difficult and demanding. That morning he had not made it to the bathroom and after she had helped him change into fresh clothing he spilled his morning coffee over himself and the new cream rug. In the afternoon he had again failed to make the toilet, but this time soiled his underwear. Gillian had been exasperated but tried to hold her patience as she cleaned her father and scraped faeces from the clothing before putting it to soak. She had felt reduced. In her forties her youth had finally left her.

Her father, fresh now, settled into his chair and fell asleep tired after his ordeal. In the kitchen Gillian cried and that was how Steve found her. She did try to rally but his kind face prompted more tears. He scooped her up and held her tightly in his arms brushing her hair with his lips in reassuring tenderness. She tried to break away but it was as if a key had been turned in her hitherto locked heart.

They kissed. It had been sublime and Gillian had clutched his jacket smelling the masculine odour which had thrilled her body as he adjusted his hold to squeeze more tightly.

Suddenly, Gillian in panic thrust her hands and pushed at his shoulders. He stepped back and she was crushed.

"This is wrong. You have a wife," she had been aghast, horrified that she had been so weak in allowing his embrace.

"I did have a wife."

Gillian hardly heard the words let alone understood them.

"We can't. I think you should go." She must be strong and authoritative, leaving no room for misunderstanding. Her hand strayed to her hair.

"Gillian, listen to me, Abigail and I, we are separated. We have applied for a divorce." Steve reached for her and managed to take her hand before it had twisted the lock of hair. She looked at his strong workman hands that held her pale ringless fingers. Without moving away she looked at his face drawn to it like a magnet.

"You still live together," she hesitated, "as husband and wife."

"That is only because it has been convenient, we have not been husband and wife. We do not sleep together Gillian. Abigail and I lead separate lives. We have done for years. I have not got the funds to get my own place and keep them too but Alex was eighteen this year and it's time we made a break. I guess I was lazy and I really wanted you but you were out of reach."

He had moved as if to hold her again. She turned away not wanting to communicate her desire.

"My father?" They heard movement in the adjacent sitting room.

"Can I come back later when we can talk?" She nodded before she could change her mind.

"Yes, alright," and she pushed him towards the door. "He usually goes to bed about nine. Maybe, afterwards?"

"I will wait in the car at the back until I see the outside light go on." He left blowing her a kiss which made her heart thump and then he was gone like a figment of her imagination and her father was calling her.

That night changed her life forever.

Steve returned and somehow, talk did not seem so important. In the intervening hours Gillian had realised something more fundamental. She prepared deliberately choosing her undergarments and anointing her skin. It was time and she wanted it to be Steve whatever the outcome. She waited with delicious anticipation, hurrying her father to bed as much as possible.

When he arrived, she brought him into the living room. He had never been there at night before. She had brought extra cushions from upstairs. The table lamp was positioned to cast a glow towards the shadowy corners of the room. The intentions had been made clear and Steve responded.

Taken into his arms again she felt his hardness. He took a moment to look quizzically at her before devouring her. His fingers roamed her body and found her hidden places and she clung to him seeking guidance through the storm. He became more urgent and for her there was a kaleidoscope of feelings. There was joy and desire and the thrill of expectation but all mingled with intermittent fear and embarrassment and even shame. It was a heady cocktail of emotion.

Steve sensing her confusion, whispered, "I love you Gill, I won't hurt you. We can stop whenever you say." And he had paused in his pursuit looking deeply into her eyes. "I want it to be you." She had replied.

Afterwards, they lay spent on the soft rug, her head resting on his bare chest and his hand still cupping her breast. Neither of them wanted to break the spell.

"It's late. I had better go." Eventually, he shook himself free.

Gillian plummeted to earth. "Of course, you need to get back." She could not help herself. She wanted to scream not to go but to stay here with her but she curled once more inside herself and prepared to let him go.

"I meant what I said, Gill. I love you. I think I fell in love with you the first second I saw you. I never thought we would ever be like this. I thought you did not have that sort of feeling for me. Please say there is a chance. I don't want this to be the end. Please say it can be the beginning." Now dressed, he wrapped his arms around her urging her to believe in him. She did not care, only wanting his closeness and signalled acquisition by snuggling deeper into the embrace.

"We should have talked. That would have been sensible but I don't care Steve. I don't want it to end either." She was too scared right then to say how she felt. The word 'love' was too beautiful, too fundamental, too daunting to utter. She had been on a tight rein far too long for that.

They parted with the promise to see each other the following night and so their relationship began. Steve did find a flat but agreed that Abigail could keep the house for the time being. He felt he still had a duty of care. Alex had gone to university. All this took time and for form's sake they did not make their relationship known. It suited them to exist in this semi-clandestine way, especially as her father became more frail and dependent. Sometimes, she would catch her father looking at her in a questioning way but mostly he wanted his physical needs met and she was happy to oblige. She had Steve waiting for her and supporting her. Neither of them realised that this state of affairs would go on for nearly two solid years.

Her father died near Christmas in 1995, after a fall that briefly rendered him unconscious. He was kept in hospital and died two days later. Gillian was bereft. It was as if the play that she had been an audience for had suddenly come to the end of its run, the curtains had been brought down and even the theatre closed.

Steve tried hard to appreciate the way she felt but all he could really see was the release of a very heavy burden for which she should be relieved. He had not the mettle to shake Gillian out of her doldrums. These weeks had been the most turbulent in their relationship.

"I don't know what you want me to say or do," he was exasperated and the tone of his voice betrayed his impatience.

"If you don't know by now, you never will," would come back the retort.

"You're impossible," he challenged her and she thought she would drive him away but she felt desperate. She could not explain herself. There was no firm ground on which to stand.

"You don't care. You are only interested in one thing. Sometimes, I hate you." The accusation hung in the air. Gillian wanted to take it back, she hardly recognised this woman who was berating and not caring for this wonderful man. It was almost that in her misery she wanted to drive him away.

"I can't stay here when you are like this. I'm going to work." He would depart but always returned ready to take more.

This scene was played out in different words but the same attitude over the course of the winter until exhausted by her despair and fighting to keep feelings at bay in public, particularly school, she reluctantly but determinedly tackled Steve.

She had cooked a Bolognese for him and they ate in the kitchen that she still loved all these years later. Steve certainly was good at his job. The kitchen was sturdy in its foundations yet refined in presentation. They largely ate in silence as had become their custom recently and, although they still made physical contact there was an emotional gulf between them.

"I am going to ask for a full-time position at school. I need the income, especially now I don't have my father's pension. I need to work as well. I need to get on with my life."

She argued that she was alone and should be independent in all aspects of her life. She did not want to drift interminably. She needed to heal and this meant moving forward and not being sucked into the past. It was hard for her as her disposition was more suited to inertia.

Steve did not speak. He did not want another row and he did not know where this was going.

"I want to know about us, Steve." Gillian's voice quivered as she dreaded the response to the question.

Again, he was too uncertain of her mood to make a comment. It seemed uncaring to Gillian.

"I thought when we were free it would be wonderful. We would be together but it is worse. I am asking myself if it was just a fling. How do you feel Steve? I need to know." She seemed to be giving him an ultimatum. That was not her intention.

"Maybe, you should think about your feelings first, Gill. Mine have not changed and never will." His voice was measured and warm.

"But you seem to hate me and don't want to be with me." She felt tears well up and felt she was losing the battle. Gillian did not understand.

"It's not me who hates you. You seem to hate yourself." He caressed her cheek and wiped the tear that had leaked from her eye. In response she moved closer.

Still, there was a chasm between them but it was noticeably narrower and not as deep.

"What can I do?" She implored. Her hand strayed to her hair, taking a lock to twist nervously.

"I don't know. I am not one for analysis. I'm a simple workman, Gill. I guess I see things as they are and don't ask too many questions. Yes, we should be happy. No we are not happy, either of us. I never know how you will react these days. I wonder if you wish I was someone else. Maybe, you need time away from me I don't know." He was trying to be sensible and helpful but it was not what she needed.

"Are you finishing with me?" Gillian could hardly get the words out.

"No, Gill. Are you finishing with me?" There was a stubborn set to his jaw as though he was preparing for a punch.

"I want you back, Steve. I want you to love me and want me like I want you. I am scared, Steve." She had crumpled before him and felt diminished as well as raw from capitulation.

"Why would I want anyone else Gill, when I have the most infuriating woman in the world?" He smiled in that cheeky endearing way that was all him. Gillian lashed at him, frantically then playfully and then passionately. Their future together had been sealed.

They married the following summer. They combined resources, the proceeds of the sale of her house and his flat after the mortgage had been paid and they bought an impressive house on the outskirts of town. Even with all their capital they needed a mortgage and at their ages the repayments were high but Gillian would be working full time and they both wanted a special start in their married life so they signed on the dotted line. They would update the property in due course.

It was a simple wedding. Gillian had no family to speak of but did ask a couple of cousins and a couple of her colleagues. Steve invited an array of people. There were his two brothers and their families, an ageing aunt and her daughter, a couple of work friends and old school friends. It became a jolly party and they feasted afterwards at the new swish hotel where they later spent their wedding night. She wore a simple cream silk dress and carried a small bouquet of gardenias which had been replicated in buttonholes.

Steve wanted Alex to be his best man but he in his usual fashion made a scene and told his father where he could stick it. While Gillian was relieved he probably would not be at the wedding Steve was badly hurt. His friend from school willingly stepped into the role. It was left for Alex to decide if he would join them or not. Gillian from her teaching experience felt Alex needed to grow up a bit and not always feel he was the centre of attention for his father. Steve had indulged the boy and it had become clear to Gillian that Abigail used her son to wheedle as much out of Steve as possible. Gillian thought Steve needed to extract himself but the dye had been well cast before she came on the scene and she did not want to spoil their present happiness with past mistakes. Alex was old enough to be completely independent.

Alex did attend the ceremony but not the reception. He slipped into the Registry Office at the last minute and acknowledged his relatives who were already in position at the front. Steve waiting for Gillian raised his hand wishing Alex had dressed more appropriately but to have him there at all was a bonus even if he slouched in jeans and t-shirt with the rude slogan. To anyone paying attention to Alex instead of the bride and groom during the ceremony they would have noticed a smirk on the boy's face and when the appeal was made for any objections he moved his chair noisily and then looked apologetically at the registrar.

The problem for Gillian was in who might give her away. Her cousin was a possibility but she rarely saw him and somehow, it did not seem right. She did not want to reveal this lack of a trusted male to her colleagues either so they would convey the deficiency to other staff members. She hated anyone feeling sorry for her. In the end, Steve proposed they ask his elder brother. He had given away two daughters and was well used to public speaking in his role of sales manager. He was a nice man too and like Steve kind and careful not to offend. Steve and his brother Mike said they were going to be family anyway so it was fitting.

Mike and his wife Jenny spent the night before the wedding with Gillian at the new house while Steve stayed with his friend. It proved to be eye opening for Gillian. Jenny had brought champagne and insisted that Gillian pamper herself while she prepared the meal. The three of them sat round the table consuming the delicious casserole and champagne. It was a frivolous evening and Jenny asked what Gillian had seen in Steve.

Jenny had said she was delighted he had found someone like Gillian in his life. Gillian reflected and gave her answer. She said she knew she had a kindred spirit, another half of herself, someone to both lean on and in turn support, and someone she could both laugh and cry with as they grew old together and then she added cheekily someone who was good in bed. Mike and Jenny laughed with her and Mike said he had taught his little brother everything he knew and they laughed some more.

"I wish I had met him years ago and we could have had a lifetime together and raised a family. Sometimes, I am so jealous of Abigail." It was the drink talking but as it often did it brought out the truth.

"You have met him now," Jenny replied. "You know when he was married to Abigail he was not happy. We all thought it was the wrong decision to marry but Abigail is the sort of woman to steamroller a man into a relationship. Then, when Alex came along Steve was stuck. He would never abandon a child. You have given us back our brother. We've all noticed the difference in him and frankly we all could not be more delighted."

Gillian felt the tears leave her eyes and Mike said, "Hey girls, this is a celebration. Let's open another bottle and let the party start."

A party indeed it was. Although Gillian had played down the occasion in her head, on the day itself she was ecstatic. That night cradled in Steve's strong arms she thought of the love that consumed her just as on the night in March so long ago when they had first made love. There was one other feeling that was common to the conclusion of each of those fateful nights and almost surpassed the feeling of love and that feeling was one she had never really felt before and Gillian relished it. It was the feeling of triumph.

Chapter 11
Better to Have Loved and Lost Than Never Loved at All

*They flash upon that inward eye
Which is the bliss of solitude,
And then my heart with pleasure fills,
And dances with the daffodils.*

Daffodils: William Wordsworth

2007: Inspector Tom Wilkes

Tom Wilkes had been made Inspector in April 2007. There was a small difference in salary, a large difference in responsibility and a new desk. He was fortunate that a position had come up at his station. His colleagues welcomed the promotion too. Tom was well liked and respected as well as having waited patiently for the promotion which they thought was well deserved so, although there was some banter, there had also been genuine warmth as they clapped the announcement even though behind his back they still affectionately referred to him as PC Plod.

Coinciding with the time of his appointment there had been good news on the burglary front. Tom Wilkes had hated to see the fear and despair in the elderly victims' faces. They often had not the resilience to rise from the trauma and those who lived on their own would become even more isolated as they became more and more wary of newcomers. He realised that the air of distrust had been even more destructive than the actual theft.

A number of stolen items had turned up, having been sold on and it had been basic police work to trace the source of the sales. Carl Brewer and Wayne Platt were clearly not master criminals having left a trail of clues. Tom remembered

Carl from his brief investigation into the first burglary at the house of Jim Woodhouse which could have ended so differently.

Carl who had lived nearby had been interviewed of course, and had fingered Jake rather clumsily Tom thought. It seemed that Carl had got himself into a bit of bother with a girl who had been after him for funds for a baby and to make matters worse there was another kid on the way. Tom wondered not for the first time, why youngsters could not do things the old-fashioned way, courting first and then marriage and then children but everything seemed back to front these days. He was not judgemental. He just thought it would lead to less trouble. It was always tough having children, especially on the pocket so while Tom inwardly criticised he also sympathised with the predicaments with which they were often ill-equipped to deal. The lads had been charged and pleaded guilty with reports submitted about their previous good characters and promises for future conduct so the matter was wrapped up quickly and they received suspended sentences which was in Tom's view a nominal slap on the knuckles.

Tom did not want either of the youths to be imprisoned and through that be introduced to other more hardened and street wise criminals but he did want a more severe punishment to deter them from future temptation. He occasionally felt another old-fashioned remedy would have sorted them out, a short spell in a physically harsh young offenders' institution but there were none of them around anymore. He had come across Colin Brewer Carl's father who had faced the courts for handling stolen goods and again he felt that his lack of punishment would have encouraged young Carl not to think enough about his life choices.

Tom Wilkes volunteered to return the bracelet to Jim Woodhouse. He had liked Jim and it was a good opportunity to check up on the old man. It was clear he had fallen and not been assaulted but it was Carl and Wayne who had been responsible. Apparently, at the time Jim Woodhouse had suggested that Carl might be involved but there had been no evidence and there had been the conviction by others that it had been Jake.

Tom drew up in his motor still impressed with the neat garden which boasted the occupation of a proud and attentive person. He knocked on the door which to his surprise was opened by Jake.

"Who is it?" A quavering voice came from within.

"It's Sergeant Wilkes from the police," Jake replied, standing aside to allow Tom to enter. Tom did not correct him.

"Hello there, Mr Woodhouse. Don't get up. I have good news."

"Jake has just boiled the kettle for tea. Can I tempt you?" Jim asked.

Tom had not intended to spend long on the errand but he was tempted and nodded. He was a bit surprised when Jake returned from the kitchen with a pretty floral china pot of tea, matching jug of milk and sugar bowl and three mugs.

Jake seeing his look said, "Mr Woodhouse has me well trained."

Tom dug into his pocket and took out the little package.

"I believe this is yours," he said to Jim, handing it over to Jim who examined it thoughtfully.

The package opened by Jim revealed a simple gold chain bracelet with three small charms. There was a small daffodil with minute golden petals, a silver heart and a drop pearl. Jim fingered the bracelet. His eyes became watery. He could not focus.

He had lost Ida well over ten years ago in March 1994, but memories would steal into his mind like a familiar ghost as they did that day. He had bought the bracelet for their first wedding anniversary and added to it since. The daffodil had been bought for her fortieth birthday. He had seen the little flower in a jeweller's window, the kind of place he normally would never have dared enter. It stood on the High Street and he had gathered all his courage to venture inside. There were no prices on window items which to Jim seemed a bit careless, but in 1964, the jeweller traded on name and reputation meaning only the wealthy would frequent the shop. There was the idea of exclusivity for all concerned. Jim had spent a whole week's wages on the item. It had been worth every penny to see the delight on Ida's face. The other two charms had been chosen for their Silver and Pearl wedding anniversaries, both expensive in his view but not so much that it cost him a whole week's wages.

Ida treasured the bracelet and wore it for special occasions. This was the most precious thing to be taken. They had taken what cash they could find amounting to about two hundred pounds but Ida's rings had been safe where he kept them in a little pouch tucked into his pillowcase, not to secure them against theft but for him to have their reassuring presence nightly while he slept.

Jim roused himself. "Thank you," he whispered.

"You need a chocolate digestive," Jake interposed. Somehow, Jake and Mr Woodhouse seemed to have changed roles. Jake did not know how it had happened but he felt protective of Jim Woodhouse and Jim depended on Jake.

The detective observed the two of them. Jake was watchful and alert. He looked full of health and fitness, not big but robust, quiet in manner but with an underlying energy and power. There was something of a sportsman about him in the way he moved. He was obviously strong in his muscular arms. He was clearly at ease in Jim Woodhouse's home.

Jim on the other hand portrayed a man who had been fit and able in his prime but age was gradually eroding his strength. His skin had the pale looseness of the elderly and his eyes had a liquid quality under their drooping eyelids.

However, there was wholesomeness in the scene before him and it was clear that there was a meeting of minds. While there might be signs of age about his person it was clear that Jim had a sharp mind, resolute and determined. As the conversation progressed, Tom could see how Jim had been a mentor for Jake but now the student was emerging as a thoughtful and assured young man. It was a joy to be in their presence and he stayed much longer than intended.

"How's your dad, Jake?"

"He's good Sergeant Wilkes. I think he's a bit lonely now I am so busy at the nursery and with the gardening business."

"Actually, it's Inspector Wilkes now. Never any news then, about your mum?" Tom trod carefully.

"No and I think it eats away at him." Jake glanced at Jim Woodhouse who added, "Always tough to lose a wife whatever the circumstances."

"Funny though," continued Jake. "I sort of feel she's there all the time watching me. I often have a weird feeling that there's someone, a woman, out there. Sometimes, I think I'm going mad but it's a real powerful feeling and I never even knew her really." In the reassuring presence of these two men Jake felt his tongue loosen. He would never normally admit to personal feelings.

"And you have no idea where she went? There was no letter," Tom Wilkes had never rid himself of the thought that her disappearance was the key to something much more. He feared the worst and hoped she would not turn up in a body bag. Jake was a lad who deserved better.

"No, she vanished." Jake rarely mentioned his mum so the conversation aroused a mixture of feelings but most of all he was gratified that a police officer was interested. He wanted his mum found.

Jim felt he had to interpose. "She kept in touch with Ida and always wanted to know about Jake. Ida told me before she died that she had been frightened of someone. There was something that had happened and she had to escape before it brought trouble on her family. I told the police this but by then they weren't so interested. Ida asked me to keep an eye on Jake."

"And I thought you liked me for my football and gardening skills," Jake joked.

"What footballing skills! And as for gardening I taught you all you know. No I needed a slave to do the donkey work that's all." They both chuckled.

"I found a box with some things of hers when I was at school. There was a letter there possibly from her mum. It wasn't the mum she had been brought up with though. I think she had been adopted. I have always meant to follow it up but I have been busy and I don't know where to start."

Jake remembered the impact of the letter which had been immense for a boy of fifteen. He had fantasised about what it might mean and thought there might have been dark secrets in his family. It had taken a while to let the worries go and since leaving school he had not wanted to disturb his life so had pushed any thoughts to the back of his head. The conversation today made him realise he had only put the desire for his mum on hold.

"Could I have a look do you think?" Tom's juices flowed. There was no major case on so he had time to investigate.

"Well, Dad doesn't know I saw the box. It was in his bedroom you see." Tom did see.

"Do you think he still has it?" Now he was drawn in, he was relishing the challenge.

"Oh yes, Dad isn't the type to have a sort out. He's probably forgotten it's there altogether. It was at the bottom of the wardrobe. I suppose I could come clean and get it. I don't think he'd mind." Jake had never admitted to his dad he had seen the box. It had all been too tawdry but if it meant it could lead to discovering his mum there was no contest.

"Tell you what. Why don't I come round later in the week and see your dad? It might be nothing but sometimes a pair of fresh eyes…" Tom Wilkes knew how people often needed an encouraging word rather than a threat.

It was agreed that Inspector Wilkes would call on Thursday evening. Jake would make sure they were both in.

It had been a strange visit all round and both Jim and Jake felt that rather than a closure of a chapter, a new book had been opened at a significant page.

Ken was surprised and gratified by the visit of Inspector Wilkes. He was not upset to learn that Jake had been poking around. He was not that kind of man. He was pleased that the disappearance of his wife all those years ago had not been completely forgotten. He readily agreed that Tom Wilkes could take the box for a while. As Jake had predicted he had completely forgotten it was there.

After the visit Ken sat contemplating what he had become. He admitted he should have had a clear out long ago. He should have moved forward but he had stood still and without Jake there had been little purpose in his life. Jackie had brought life to the house and when she left it became a place for Ken to eat and sleep but not really a home until Jake as he had grown had brought substance to the dwelling bringing life to the garden and even making the main rooms clean and cosy while Ken's own bedroom had remained a mess.

That evening after the departure of the Inspector Ken and Jake took themselves off to the local where Ken at last filled Jake in on what he knew about his mother.

"The darts team had got through to the quarter final of the county cup and I went in support. We had a mini coach to take us all, team and supporters. I think Jim might have been there as well but I am not sure. It was quite cold but we were fired up so we really did not feel it. We were excited at getting this far, you know all lads together and we had a great chance we thought.

"When we arrived, I clocked a girl with a baby sitting in the little garden at the front. I presumed she was waiting for someone. Then after a while the pub became too hot for me and I slipped outside. She was still there and I could see she was shivering. She really did not have the clothing to keep her warm. Of course, I won't deny she was pretty so I asked her if she was ok. She said she was fine and would be going home soon so I went back in to see the darts.

"Somehow, I could not concentrate and after a little while went out again. She wasn't there which both pleased and disappointed me and then I heard a little cry. It was you. They had taken themselves round the side, hiding, I suppose. She was terribly nervous when I approached her."

Ken stopped to take a swig of his beer. "Go on," Jake encouraged.

"She needed a lot of convincing that I was not going to hurt her and I could not get anything from her at first. It was when I made a fuss of you that she began to relax a bit. She said she could not go home and she had been staying with a girlfriend. I assumed there had been some violence by her bloke but she said not.

"Anyway, the girlfriend had died in some awful circumstances she said and she had to leave the flat and had been hoping for a job at the pub but clearly she had no-where else to go. I know, it sounds ridiculous but right then and there I knew I had a warm safe house and I would bring her there." Ken glanced at Jake to check.

"So she came, then?" Jake adopted an even tone of voice, although inside his stomach was tight.

"No, not that night, and not for a couple of weeks. She needed to trust me you see. I was a bit flush at that time and there was a little bed and breakfast not far from the pub and I took her there. I paid the woman for a week and arranged to see her the next day. I saw her every day and took her to collect her things and after a couple of weeks we agreed that it would be better to live with me. I asked her to marry me too and as soon as we could we tied the knot and I brought her home. Best thing I ever did."

Jake looked at his dad with new admiration wondering what would have happened to him if Ken had not been there. His thoughts about his mum were confused and at that moment underlined with anger and disappointment. His own beginnings had been so desperate.

Jake had to ask. It was the best and only opportunity. "Do you know who my real father was?" He could have bitten off his tongue as soon as he had spoken, he meant biological father, but too late he saw the hurt on Ken's face.

"No she would not say. She told me it did not matter and he was a very brief encounter and she wanted me to be your dad. She wanted to put the past completely behind her. I respected that. I thought she would tell me if she wanted to in her own time and I didn't want anything to spoil things then so I let things be. We hadn't known each other long. You know we were happy. We had a good relationship. We would take you in the car for days out at weekends and we had fun. I did not see it coming when she left. I am glad I had you."

It was the most Ken had said to Jake in all their years together and the sincerity of the speech filled Jake with emotion.

"I'm glad you had me too," Jake said trying to make up for his previous gaffe.

Jake thought another pint would be welcome. Ken was not Jake's biological father but he had been a real father. Jake knew he loved his dad.

Back at the station Inspector Wilkes examined the shoe box. In gloved hands he pulled each item from it to examine and lay on the sheet on his desk. He wondered why she had not taken the letter at least. That must have sentimental value and would have been easy to remove.

As usual, he was slow and methodical, pausing to read and study before progressing to the following object. He looked at the other items retrieved from the box. It took him a few minutes to realise their importance. In fact, he knew they were dynamite. He would need to tread carefully so as not to detonate them in the wrong way. This was a time for methodical reasoning and absolute care.

A week later, Tom Wilkes joined a group of off-duty police officers to attend a football match. Tom rarely attended these shindigs but his wife had persuaded him that it would be a good idea after his recent promotion. Tom enjoyed his sport too. The party had been invited by the Chairman Clive Corneille, a man who seemed to divide supporters rather than unite them. Until the previous week, Tom had merely acknowledged the suspicions of duplicity about Clive Corneille but after noting the contents of the box he was beginning to know better.

When Clive Corneille had first invested in the club, there were expectations of a short stay and indeed, he had given signals that he would be selling his shares. That seemed to be his modus operandi, invest and sell quickly to extract the profits. At first, Tom had only seen him in this way and been irritated that he might endanger the club with his financial antics but recently he had learnt a lot more. He had not of course, been privy to investigations that had led to a belief from the Met that Clive Corneille had been and probably still was a big player in serious fraud and dubious criminal activities in the city.

He had been a slippery character and somehow, had evaded the arm of the law. He still maintained connections in high places, people who feared public knowledge of their affairs would reap disaster on them and their families, and he could be ruthless in sacrificing anyone in his network if needed. It seemed that it had suited Corneille to remain in the provinces while there was too much heat in the city, neatly being separated from speculation and closing down trails of evidence.

Tom knew that the contents of that shoe box could negate that strategy and have dire consequences for Clive Corneille. He had passed his findings on and Tom was given the job to observe and keep tabs on the man. It was to be a waiting game.

The party had been allotted a hospitality box all courtesy of the club. There was the usual lavish spread of food and drink. It was a way of keeping good will between the club and the force, especially when the boys in blue had to deal with any nasty fall out on match days. It was a raucous band of brothers who gathered eager for the afternoon out and to witness a crucial match. Tom could play his part, he could drink and jest with the best of them, his dry wit a welcome addition to the more fruity and coarse humour of some of his colleagues. He realised too that public relations was a vital component in modern policing which depended so much more on cooperation than it had done when he first joined the force. After all, the football club had always been very supportive of police charities.

Today however, there was a little more than obvious interest. Of course, he knew Clive Corneille in his position at the club and had even spoken to him once or twice but in the light of his discoveries in that shoe box his interest was piqued and he had a job to do.

Clive liked to grace each of the hospitality boxes during the afternoon. There was a sort of royal approval in the gesture. He would enter, circulate, encouraging the merrymaking and taking any plaudits for his role in management. By the time Tom met him he was a consummate operator. He would shake hands, clap people on the shoulder, call staff to replenish drinks and with ladies smile and tease to divert them from the usual masculinity of the game. Tom actually thought that Clive seemed old fashioned in this respect and out of touch as he worked his way round the box. Rachel and Clare were excellent footballers and belonged to an up and coming women's team that could give most men a run for their money. He overheard a snippet of Clive's flattery and winked at the girls.

Clive had been well briefed, congratulating Tom on his recent promotion. "We will probably run into each other more now. I like to be involved in law and order matters so I sit on a number of committees locally, particularly with youngsters. They need guidance these days and the club is involved in lots of positive initiatives."

Tom agreed, "Yes, our generation has to set an example and we have a lot to answer for," Tom kept his thoughts well hidden. "But it is unlikely we will see much of each other in the near future anyway as I am part of the serious crime unit and I do not suppose you figure in that."

Clive laughed, "No way, always a model citizen, me, your honour," and he smoothly moved on to the next officer.

The encounter, if anything, had made Tom more determined. He knew it was going to be important to find Jackie who not only could be the key to the investigation but to protect her when the nature of the investigation was revealed.

It was a good tight match with the home team winning on a penalty given in the dying minutes. Ken and Jake had also attended the game and shouted and cheered from their stand seat. The crucial match had been televised so Jim was able to view it at home. They were all to meet later for a drink which in this case would be a celebration.

The Swan was crowded but they were lucky to find a corner seat recently vacated. Jim could not stand for long these days. Ken sorted the drinks. The new barmaid was not the usual young student earning through part time work. She was an attractive dark-haired woman of middle years. It was clear she had experience in pub work. She was quick in service and sharp in manner but with that jocular edge that played her audience. Ken had been visiting the hostelry a lot more since she had arrived as it must be said did others. There was competition for her attention.

The crowd was thinning out and from their corner view the three could observe. Jim and Jake joked about Ken being all too eager to get the pints and linger to converse with Kathy. Then all three discussed the match and somehow, strayed on to relationships probably because Jake could not resist ribbing his dad when he volunteered to do the honours in getting in the second pint.

Three generations of men all concluded that women were a necessity in life but getting the right woman was a matter of luck. Jake had taken out a few girls and enjoyed the experience but, and this was a big but, as soon as any began to show signs of attachment he backed away. Unbeknown to him this was getting him a reputation with the local girls of 'love 'em and leave 'em', which encouraged some in their pursuit of him while others who wanted a deeper relationship were wary. Jake was young and as in all things was determined to make a success of a marriage if he ever found the right girl. He looked at Jim for guidance in this respect. The experience of Ken had left deep marks on the lad.

Ken had gravitated to Kathy at the bar. There at the other side of the bar was another lesson in the fortunes and decisions of life. Carl Brewer looked older than his years, a big boned man with a beer belly already taking possession of his frame. Carl was a couple of years older than Jake. He was coarse in his manner and his language, the occasional expletive drifting through the bar. Kathy would frown in his direction marking his card in the expert way she had before returning to her conversation with Ken. Jake clenched his fists. He would have liked to go over and teach Carl a lesson he would not forget and Jim noticing his intense gaze reached out a hand to pat away the tension and said softly.

"He's got himself two kids. He's no role model for them but don't let him wind you up. He's finding life isn't as sweet as he thought. Colin his dad isn't much better but he stopped me the other day and said he was sorry for things. I was tempted to say a few things to him but what good would it do? The lad has created his own chains. The law saw fit to excuse him but you know sometimes fate has a way of eventually turning the tables. Colin told me that his missus is leading him a dog's life. He has two kids now, a criminal record and a female who has the measure of him. Let him have his five minutes in the pub. I told you once, that you were the better player. Now prove it in the way you get on with life and feel sorry for him, not angry."

"Where did you learn to be so accommodating?" Jake sat back in his seat.

"Different times, different views, different expectations. I grew up in the war and what I saw of human nature in Korea puts a whole lot of things in perspective. I saw the good and the bad. Things no young man should see. Things you do and experience when you are young never really leaves you so you have to learn from it. Don't let it define you. Don't begrudge things. Be your own person. Carl is weak really underneath all that bluster. He is blown with the wind of the day."

Jake wanted to assure Jim Woodhouse but did not have the words. "You're remarkable, he said.

"No. I am an ordinary bloke who has made lots of mistakes." The company had relaxed him as much as the beer and he felt reflective.

"I can't see any. You've always got an answer." Jake took a gulp of his beer. He liked it when Jim opened up to him. It made him feel privileged.

"Well, I should have paid more attention to Ida for a start. I married her and then took her for granted. I should have made more fuss. I took a nice easy life and I think there were times she struggled. You know after she died I cleared out her things and I found a whole drawer full of baby and children's clothes. I never talked to her about it all when she was alive. I did not know she was harbouring these feelings. I was her husband and she had secrets. Why? She could not talk to me.

"I should have forced things, you know, got her to go to a doctor to see why there were no children. She adored you, Jake. I wish I had shared that with her at least when you were little but no I ignored it. I kept out of the way at the club or in the garden. Glad you can put up with a selfish old man now. You know Ida would have been thrilled. I was worried a bit at the time and shut you out. It scared me when I heard you call her 'nana.'"

Jake was learning a lot in the last few weeks and he felt better for it.

"Did I? I can't remember but I do have a vague memory of someone, a nice lady who gave me cake and took me to the swings but I thought that would have been my mum." Jake thought hard trying to resurrect any memory. There had always been a need in him for affection of a different kind and had wondered if that was what made him seem remote.

Little did the three of them, drinking and talking that night after the match, know that the powers that be were currently hot on the case and investigations were gathering momentum in finding Jake's mum.

Tom Wilkes made an appointment to visit Mr and Mrs Pugh. They lived in a collection of bungalows in Lowton some twenty miles away from Marketborough. It was a neat area that flanked a small pretty church. Nearby was a primary school, presumably attended by Jackie, and a short row of shops including a small supermarket, a hairdresser, a chemist, a Post Office which he estimated would be well used by the local population of pensioners and a café. It was a quiet attractive location but would only appeal to those who sought refuge and peace as would appeal in their senior years. Tom felt there was a sad air from the obvious lack of life and vitality.

Meredith greeted him at the door of the little bungalow and ushered him inside. Her husband appeared from the kitchen clutching a tea towel. Tom explained that their daughter's disappearance had been left open and they had been asked to wind things up if possible. It was not strictly the truth but it served its purpose.

At first, Meredith Pugh expressed surprise after all these years and even grumbled that not enough effort had been put into finding her daughter before. Tom in his usual quiet conciliatory manner asked about the adoption and how the child had settled into the family. It seemed that the adoption had been arranged through her church connections, "We were not blessed with children," said Meredith, "and the vicar knew there was an empty space in our home." She had looked suitably forlorn.

Meredith did most of the talking while her husband looked anxiously by. She described a little girl who had wanted for nothing and implied that this had been a mistake on their part to spoil her so absolutely. There was nothing in what Meredith said to ring alarm bells that Jackie had been ill-treated but Tom's experience told him that this had not been a happy home. There was no spontaneity or warmth in either the surroundings or the way the couple spoke. Everything was well ordered and precise. Tom could not fault them at all but he felt how their responses were almost scripted for an effect. At times Meredith would gush or simper in the manner of a bad actress, "We tried so hard with Jackie and brought her baby boy into our home but she really did not want to know. At first, she relied on me a lot with the baby."

"It must have been a shock to find she was pregnant?" Tom sympathised.

"Yes, indeed, we were horrified, weren't we, George? We prayed very hard about what was to be done. Of course, we could never support abortion, heaven forbid, and we did discuss adoption but we ruled that out as we knew we were being given this chance. We talked with the vicar of course, and saw our duty. We could bring the child up in a good Christian home. Jackie had benefitted from us and we would do the same again."

Meredith looked saintly with her hands clasped on her lap and almost beamed at Tom. It was the kind of face that might urge a lesser mortal to slap.

"That was very commendable and forgiving," said Tom and Meredith gave him a thin watery smile.

"Did you know anything about the father of the child?" At this Meredith's voice became suitably angry and condemning.

"Some wild fly by night who took advantage. Jackie was ashamed and would not speak of him and frankly we did not want to know. She was weak Inspector, probably as her mum before her. The morals of society are despicable. I am sure you agree, Inspector."

Tom formed the impression that given the chance, Meredith would have given him a full lecture on the subject so intervened quickly.

"Have you any idea why she left?" Meredith looked at her husband who was fidgeting with his cardigan buttons as he sat in the corner.

"Not at all. There had been no arguments. Jackie did not talk to us as I would have liked. She was hard to pin down. Many a time, I would ask her to join me when I did the teas at church and give her the opportunity to meet some of the nice local teenagers but she was not at all social like that. She helped me with the fetes and things but she could be churlish. I really did my very best, Inspector.

"I have to wonder if she was flawed all along. Her birth mother was a teenage mother. Maybe, there was nothing we could do no matter how hard we tried. We have worried so much about the girl and I still think of her every day but really she had the best upbringing, everyone said so, we could not have done more for her," Meredith emphasised her message and she turned to her husband for his agreement, her little round body preened in the way of a pigeon fluffing out its feathers.

"Anything you can tell me would be helpful," Tom was prepared to sit patiently hoping for a nugget of information. He opened conversations rather than closed them down. He learnt more that way, although it could be time consuming.

Tom Wilkes listened attentively and took the occasional note but his observations extended to what he saw in their home and heard through the tone of the interchange. It became clear that Meredith was the controlling force and it was her husband's role to admire her, to placate her if necessary, to massage her ego and generally to respond to her performance. She was totally insular, showing her Christian charitable side for public view but she had an unmistakable hard core. She could not resist mentioning her good works and her abilities in home crafts.

In the corner of the room there were examples of her work cascading from a large sewing box. There were strategically placed photographs of her, one surveying the scene with the vicar at the church summer fete and another with a group of ladies having an afternoon tea as well as individual images of her on country walks or in their small garden. There was a photograph of her with the bell ringers from the church and catching Tom Wilkes eye she said that she had been asked to be Tower Captain. Her husband too was a ringer. They seemed eager to portray their involvement in church affairs both having served terms of office on the Parochial Church Council.

Mr and Mrs Pugh were obviously valued members of the community, that was according to their own estimation. Tom Wilkes as was his habit reserved judgement. He knew people so often were driven by the need for self-verification and sought influence in a variety of ways. This couple left no room for criticism and yet it was that very perfection that caused Tom to speculate on the limited life Jackie would have led here.

There were no photographs of Jackie and only one or two of Mr Pugh. Clearly he had been the photographer and she had been a willing subject. There were knick-knacks everywhere and examples of Meredith's craft skills. On the mantelpiece stood large letters interlinked to form the word 'Family.' The room was self-indulgent and claustrophobic. Tom began to form the opinion that any girl would have been stifled.

Meredith was gradually getting more animated and secure of her position with the Inspector so she expanded her comments. "I could not monitor her all the time. She became such a wilful child. She was spoilt, Inspector Wilkes, I admit it. I suppose adopting her I gave her all my attention. At times, she used to help me with my crafts which would have been good for her but as she got older she resisted. She had not the patience or the talent for creative ideas. I understood her mother had been young and came from a good background, clever; you know, so I expected Jackie to be the same but I did not expect her to be the same in having a baby like she did. We were shocked, weren't we, dear? But we would not turn her out. It was our duty to care for them both. That's what we signed up for when we took Jackie in the first place but I suppose it was her nature and our nurture counted for so little with her. If she came back and was suitably sorry, we would take her back even now but she has been gone so long that I fear the worst."

Tom said as little as possible and learnt little in a practical way. Jackie had few friends, all had to be approved by Meredith, and Jackie would see them at school or under the watchful eye of her mother. He could imagine Jackie bringing a friend home to have Meredith invading their play with supplies of biscuit or cake as she reorganised the activity of the girls. He imagined her dominance of the household, determining pastimes, determining routines, determining attitudes as long as she was central and her own desires met. Rarely had Tom Wilkes felt so initially repulsed by anyone.

It seemed that there was no boyfriend and little opportunity to have one. Tom had calculated a timeline and tried to push Meredith.

"Did you celebrate birthdays?" He asked in a general way.

"Oh yes, we always made a special effort." She beamed at him as he fed her the opportunity to be vindicated as parents and she turned to her husband for acknowledgement.

Taking his cue her husband recounted a couple of them when they had taken her to the zoo and the seaside. They both had the knack of portraying ideal parents without flaws.

"What about other occasions, say when she left school?" Tom had judged that this would have been about the time Jackie became pregnant. The question might open a door.

There was a definite pause before Meredith said. "We expected her to go to college and she had a job at a shop for the holidays. She'd been working there for some time. It was a nice little shop selling crafts and gifts. Sometimes, they would sell my creations. It was run by a nice lady called Mavis Smith. She attended our church and frankly I got Jackie the job. Of course, it's closed now. People don't seem to appreciate shops like that anymore."

Meredith looked wistful and Tom waited.

"That summer she went a bit wild. We clashed a lot and she would storm out and occasionally sneak out without us knowing. I remember, once in the sixth form she flounced out announcing she was seeing some friends at a new club that had opened in town. We were naturally very worried so was pleased when she got back. She had had the good sense to get a taxi. She quietened down a bit so we allowed her to meet friends but my husband always went out and brought her home at a reasonable time. We had done all we could to protect her and keep her out of harm's way so it was a complete shock to discover she was pregnant. The college course was out of the question so she did some secretarial training for a term."

"Have you any idea where she might have met the father of the child?" Tom felt he was unpicking the truth.

"Inspector Wilkes, she was obviously a vulnerable young girl, innocent of the ways of the world and some despicable male stole her virtue. He was probably much older and intimidated her. There was no lasting relationship and obviously he had no honour. We felt it was best to concentrate on Jackie and her welfare and not rake up the disreputable character. It was best not to know and Jackie seemed to have learnt her lesson and did not speak of him."

"Of course," Tom murmured. "So when she left it was all very sudden. There had been no difficult behaviour."

"That is the thing. There was nothing. We spent Christmas together. Jake was a poppet and he was baby Jesus in the church nativity. We were so proud weren't we George? We loved him as though he were our own. There was absolutely no reason for Jackie to go and she had left her job too. She still helped in the shop but we have no idea how she got her money when she left that. It was all totally out of the blue. She did not take much either so we thought she would be back with her tail between her legs but the days and weeks and then months went on. We had lost our precious little boy." Meredith took a handkerchief from her sleeve and dabbed her eyes.

"I know this must be very distressing for you revisiting it. Thank you for your time and please, if you think of anything else, any detail no matter how small, do get in touch with me," and he handed Meredith his card.

"I do hope you can find her," George spoke unexpectedly. "She was a bonny girl." Tom caught the slight frown Meredith sent his way. Tom ruminated about the relationships in the household.

Before leaving, Tom visited what had been Jackie's bedroom, although it had now been turned into a workroom for Meredith. Nothing of Jackie, their daughter remained. It was as though Jackie had never existed in their lives.

Chapter 12
Finding Your Feet

There is no point in work
Unless it absorbs you
Like an absorbing game
If it doesn't absorb you
If it's never any fun
Don't do it
When a man goes out into his work
He is alive like a tree in spring
He is living, not merely working

Work: D.H. Lawrence

2007: Jim

The burglary had affected Jim much more than he let on publicly. For a while he had felt frail and he had to admit he was vulnerable. It had been difficult to accept that his time was fast ebbing away. He was getting old not just physically, although that was a burden, but in his attitude. It was harder to have the resolution to survive. It was becoming easier to allow others to take control. He found he was gradually abdicating responsibilities.

After the burglary he had enjoyed the attention. He had found he liked the benefits of having help in the house. Barbara had been an asset. Life was taking on a different pattern, not unpleasant at all, but one that eased him from being an active independent man to someone who began to expect assistance and subdue his own efforts. He did not venture out so much on his own. Suddenly, he feared falling and, as if in tacit agreement to that fear, his balance began to shift and waver. Bending down caused a sensation of over indulgence in an alcoholic tipple and his steps became slow and hesitant. It took him much longer to do small jobs around the house and garden and he became reluctant to use the stairs so often. His time of recovery seemed to have rendered his muscles useless. He did not attempt to walk far or to lift even moderately heavy bags of shopping and his inactivity was making him tired in his heart as well as his body. He slept a lot dreaming of different times.

Neighbours would call and see if he was alright and people had got in touch from the football club. It was a new but welcome experience to be taken out on expeditions. Jake had been the most attentive. If only Ida was here, he thought, she would have doted on the lad and he would have become a sort of adopted grandson. Of course, if she had still been alive maybe a lot would have been different. Jim realised that in his head Jake had become the missing piece in his life.

Gradually, Jim shook himself out of his lethargy and as the summer progressed he managed to exert his mind to contemplate his position and regain something of his physical strength. He was pleased, although it had taken a lot of mental strength and grit.

At first, his thoughts were fixed on the past. There had been so many ambitions, so many hopes and dreams to fulfil. He had been young and eager in a post war Britain ready to take his place in the march to freedom and security. His football talents had earned him recognition. His father's breast had swelled with pride as his son was singled out as the new Stanley Matthews. He had seen the great man play and had been in awe of his deft feet as he guided the ball past the opposing full backs.

Jim had noted his fitness regime and the dedication to his sport and did his best to emulate him. Jim followed his example in walking everywhere, being careful with his diet even to the extent of drinking carrot juice as a way of detoxification and followed a strict regime of exercises that included half hour breathing exercises every day. By the time he was eighteen, there was every reason to hope for fame and fortune. The accident took that dream away. He was on the brink of stardom. His name had been spoken of as an international. He had been full of importance. Now in his seventies he knew how fickle fate could be.

There was a reserves' game and with his inflated ego he accepted the challenge to play. He could have opted out but he was young and invincible and wanted to show these also-rans what a real footballer could do. The ice on the pitch was brittle and covered scrapes of soft mud. Perhaps it had been the conditions. Certainly in his years of groundsman, he had been ever mindful of the way players relied on good strong turf to support the pounding of their boots.

The boy, his name now forgotten, had skidded into Jim as he was making his run. The tackle had been awkward and amateur. The boy had lacked the commitment and authority to make a genuine tackle. His lack of control in that moment of exhilaration as he sought to bring down the opposition's most renowned player was to have disastrous consequences. Jim was someone to be admired and if he could stop the run he would relish the glory forever after. He did stop the run but there was no glory.

The pain had shot through Jim bringing him at first airborne before lying prostrate on the ground. Jim reflected on the catastrophe over fifty years later. He still felt the anguish as he realised the break had been life changing. He had squashed the bitterness but could not quell the regret.

There was no-one left who could recall his playing days. He was a name, a footnote in the history of the club and as the years had gone by his name had been getting smaller and smaller. It would soon disappear altogether.

At times more reluctantly Jim would open the door in his memory to his days in Korea. The girl had lifted him from a depression after a sortie which had led to what he could only describe as a massacre of the occupants of the tight little village. There had been reports of insurgents and the unit had acted decisively. On inspection, the trail had been false. Jim grieved for the passing of his innocence.

It had been several weeks after the episode. Jim had not been able to shake the memory of the battered village and battered bodies. She had been drawing water from the well and seeing his thirst she offered him some. The innocence he had lost seemed to be epitomised in Ah-in, a name he later found to mean humanity and benevolence. She was graceful and kind and pure. She offered him a kind of salvation. They spent six weeks discovering another life in the other.

Each of them found beauty and forgiveness in love. They shared a language of look and touch. A few words of English were all that was required but they were enough to understand the essentials in their liaison. Then Ah-in had broken his heart by telling him she was to marry. He had been harbouring desires for a new different life with simple pleasures in a quiet village. He had known that was impossible but he had been seduced by the fantasy. He had left some of his heart and soul in that troubled corner of the world.

Jim could not remember her face. He vividly remembered his feelings of tenderness and hope. It had been nothing else but fool's gold.

He had recognised the hurt in Ida's face the instant he had seen her in her mother's kitchen. Ah-in had taught him that. He pledged to eradicate that pain and set about winning her trust. She had been closed much as Jim had been when Ah-in had entered his life. Jim knew a soul mate. He had patiently and determinably brought her to life and having done so he fell in love with the woman that had been revealed.

Underneath, he saw that Ida had had passions that had been untapped. He knew he would be a rich man indeed if he could unlock those passions but Ida had kept her passions hidden deep and rarely did she let go. Forbidden to enter Jim became obsessed with his garden and the football club. Jim had loved Ida with all his heart and she had loved him but at some point the chain of love they had tried to forge had a broken link and neither had found the tools to fix it.

It had not been an unhappy marriage. In fact, the marriage had qualities that few marriages had. There was trust and devotion and mutual respect. Each sought to satisfy the other even when they were aloof. There was humour too as they shared quick repartee but there had never been total honesty. Each of them had lost something in their youth that could not be regained.

Jim dearly wanted to fulfil a destiny. Men and women needed children. There had been none for Jim and Ida. He wanted to do something before it was too late.

Jim was not stupid. He had made a will. It had been sensible to do so. Now he would act out of character and seize the moment. If life was letting him go, then he would let go too.

Both Ida and Jim, starting their married life in the fifties, had known how to be frugal. Jim had inherited a small portion from his grandparents and parents which had not been squandered but had been put safely in the bank. They had added to the amount year by year and the inflation of recent years had brought rewards. Jim unbeknown to all but a few had another more valuable asset.

Bill had become keen on Jim's idea. It would enable him to reduce his hours at the nursery without lessoning his commitment. He had seen Jim, as with other customers, become older and while he and Anthea were together and with sound mind and body he should make plans not just for the benefit of the here and now but the future too. Jim's generosity could make that possible for a number of people.

They agreed to meet with Jake and Simon one summer afternoon as August was drawing to a close. It was thought appropriate that Simon and Bill came to Jim. It had crossed Jim's mind to ask Ken but then Bill reminded him that Jake was eighteen and already had the beginnings of a gardening business so perhaps it would be better to confine the conference to the main protagonists.

Actually, Bill who did not know Ken well feared he would influence proceedings and he would not see the greater good and ultimate aim of the arrangement that is as far as the nursery was concerned. Bill was very protective of the place and secretly wished all could go on as before. He hoped that this plan would preserve the nursery above all else as well as giving Simon a fair chance.

Jim invited them into his front room and got down to business. As it was his idea and he was the senior there and it was his house he felt it was his right.

"So young Jake, how's business then?" He began with a formal tone that seemed appropriate and Jake followed his lead.

"Good. I am getting really busy. I've been approached about a couple of small contracts for the council too which is exciting."

"That takes you away from the nursery does it?" Jim continued, probing Jake.

Jake anxious not to give Bill any excuse to stand him down replied, "No way. The nursery is the best thing. I love planting and growing. I do the gardening because it is good business sense I think and it honestly pays well so it's a win, win, really but you know all this already." Jake began to feel shades of embarrassment particularly under the glare of Simon.

"I understand from your dad that you would like some land to develop, make a name for yourself." It was Simon's turn to fall under the spotlight.

"I don't know about that," he replied with some caution. What was the old fellow getting at? What had he and his dad been cooking up? Simon feared an ambush.

"It's natural that a young fellow like you should want to get on. You should not leave it too late." Jim wanted to find out more about Simon whom he had not met often, although more recently after the burglary he had been impressed with how he had come and improved security at the house.

"That's exactly how I feel. Right now I have the energy. I'm not yet forty and I've made a few bob. There are opportunities out there and I intend to take them. It's not that I don't appreciate what you've done Dad. The nursery is great and it makes you happy." Bill felt patronised.

Simon continued trying to justify his attitude. "You know the guy I work with on renovations, I brought him here that time to help with the security, he is great but I look at him and wonder why he did not make a mint. He is so talented. His designs are inspiring and he has skill and knowledge too. He is in his late fifties now, so I suppose it is getting too late for him but not for me. You wait ten years from now I'll maybe have my million," Simon's natural exuberance carried him along before his father cut him down, butting in, "Thinking I will be dead by then do you?"

"Of course not, why do you never give credit? It always has to be your way. I can do it without you. I'm not after hand-outs." Simon ran his fingers through his hair exasperated with his father. He wanted his dad's pride and not his admonition.

The voices were rising and there was an edge that Jim had not envisaged. He did not like the way the conversation was going. Jake sat quietly feeling slightly embarrassed by the exchange.

Jim took the conversation back to Steve to allow tempers to cool.

"So this Steve knows his trade, does he? Maybe, he has not got a lot of business acumen. It seems that it is all figures these days and with things like Health and Safety a little guy cannot really compete with the bigger players."

"I think if he'd had a chance he could have made a fortune. He could have done with a leg-up. He deserved it but his ex-wife bled him dry." Simon had said too much in defence of his friend.

"Well, it's a leg-up we want to talk to you about."

Jim had his attention, although Simon had become defensive. He had always been arrogant, believing in his own ability and ready to take on the world. It was that that had made him a good soldier. Danger had been calculated and he was ready to take on risk. He had sought adventure as a kid and he had a taste for thrills.

His father's staid life had always narked him mainly because he saw the effort his mother had to make in support of it. He had never intended to stay at home for long after leaving the army but now six years later he was still there and he had accumulated a small fortune in the bank and somehow, had taken on the responsibility of the well-being of his parents. He could be tetchy about any suggestion he was a freeloader.

"What do you think about that patch of ground over there?" Jim pointed towards the front window and the view beyond.

Simon looked out of the window. Across the street he saw an ugly expanse of rough terrain. "Not much," was his answer.

Jake thought differently. That patch had been a lifeline when he was younger. He had spent many hours practising his ball skills or having a knock-a-bout. He felt he had known every blade of grass, every weed and every bush.

There had been a rush from the kids to get to the blackberries in the far corner before anyone else. On that piece of land his mate had caught his foot on a protruding root causing a broken leg. Some of the parents had been up in arms, saying it was unsafe and wanting it fenced off. The footballers vowed they would climb the fence anyway. Jake had had his first real kiss over there, at just fourteen. He had pecked at girls before as did the other boys but this was a sustained kiss with bodies close and tempting. The girl had pushed him away and shouted, "See ya," over her shoulder as she walked indifferently away. He knew there had been some petty deals done there. Carl had peddled a few sachets. Jake had kept away from the enterprise. By then Jim Woodhouse had told him about Stanley Matthews and the importance of respecting your body so when Carl sidled up to him with the spliff in his hand, Jake had told him where to stick it. That gesture had ensured he was an outsider as far as Carl was concerned.

Jake felt he should say something. "Learnt my football over there."

"Not many lads play there now, Jake. I suppose they're on their PlayStation. We are going a bit upmarket round here and people are saying it's a bit of an eyesore and the council ought to do something about it."

"You would hate that, Mr Woodhouse," said Jake.

"Yes, maybe I would, but things change over the years. When we moved here, Ida and me, the old house was still standing. Ida had been brought up there. I thought it would please her to be near the place but I'm not sure I was right. A word of advice for you two, don't always assume you know best for the women in your life. In the fifties the man made all the decisions and I thought she would like to be near her old home but I think a new start might have been a better idea. The house was empty, just the kind of place that your Steve would have loved.

"Gradually, the neglect and the vandals brought it down to the ground. There was a nasty fire one bonfire night which more or less destroyed the place. Then the children of the area started accumulating there. Before, Ida avoided looking out but suddenly she was engaged. She'd spend many a happy hour in this room, like I did when you were younger Jake, watching the antics.

"She used to take things out to them as well, biscuits she'd made, or cake and even toffee. She would collect the apples and distribute toffee apples. It was quite a thing. Those were happy years, me at the club and Ida watching over her flock. That was the past and now we have to think about the future."

Simon listening to Jim felt any tension subside. He had seen cities in ruins, the results of bombs spurred by human greed and power. The devastations had seared into his memory. However, the simple bomb dilapidation of one single home had haunted him. He could recall the child and her mother picking their way through the rubble looking for remnants of their life including the dead father and brothers. It was an image that was symbolic of all human pain. There had been great effort to build that house, great love to live in that house and then great heartache to lose the house. Jim had spoken of something universal.

"I want to make an investment," announced Jim.

So that was it thought Simon. He wants me to help him.

"I want to buy into the nursery."

This was completely unexpected and Simon felt his hackles rise once more.

"No way. Why would you want to do that?" Simon was still banking on the long-term goldmine.

"I want to buy as much as I can and I want to give it to Jake." There was silence in the room.

Jake was stunned. He had no words in his shock and then Simon spoke.

"I will stand in your way, Mr Woodhouse. Dad would not agree to it."

"I already have in principle," declared Bill. "Jim is making a good offer and I want you to hear him out. I have to accept your mother and I are getting older and you are not going to take on the nursery are you Simon? You will shut it down but I think Jake might do good things with it."

"But you would let it go out of the family?" Simon was astonished. He felt a sense of shock and betrayal not because of losing the financial entitlement but because he found he cared.

Jake had found his voice. "I couldn't let you do this Mr Woodhouse and anyway it would be a lot of money."

Jim could not seem to get his words out so Bill intervened, "It's an idea he's got, a plan to satisfy us all and a very generous one at that. It will need a lot of thinking about and discussion but it's a way forward that is exciting for us all. First of all, I will have the bungalow to live in and pass on to you and your sisters.

"I will sell a portion of the nursery, we would need to thrash out how much and Jake would have that share and so we would run it together. We thought maybe options to buy in over the next ten years might be something we could look at and then for you, Simon, a bit of inheritance now, up front, when you could do with it. Jim is offering you that land over the road. It's worth a pretty penny and you will have no trouble getting planning permission while I've checked and the planners would be unlikely to give you permission for the nursery land."

Jim added, "I bought the piece from the old estate. It was a lucky buy, I suppose, but I did not buy it as an investment, I bought it because it was Ida's old home and I could. I thought we might live there too but I had miscalculated and it seemed to upset Ida so I stayed quiet. I'm sure to have a compulsory purchase slapped on me soon. It would be much better for me to organise things for what I want to happen to it."

There was a quiet resolution in his voice that cast a sad veil over the four men.

Jake knew he should say something but at eighteen he was overwhelmed. He could only ask, "But what about you Mr Woodhouse? What would you get out of it?"

Jake felt desperate but Jim had regained his composure and said, "I would get the pleasure of seeing a young man I have become particularly fond of flourish and I know, my Ida would have been tickled pink. Besides this of course, I would want free plants for life and my garden tended as well for good measure." Jim smiled and his genuine glow transferred to the faces of the other three in the room.

"Maybe, we had better think on it all," said Simon, resolved to talk it over with Steve and the accountant.

"Don't think too long will you. I am not sure how many years I have left."

In the end, it had been a satisfying afternoon.

At first, Ken had been astounded at the proposal but quickly reasoned that it was an inspired plan. He felt he knew Jim well enough to have no doubt of his sincerity and frankly felt it was just reward for all the help Jake had given him. He had always thought that any inheritance would go to Ida's sisters and that had always irked him because they did not seem to care two hoots about Jim, and Ida when she was alive. The nephews and nieces seemed oblivious of their Uncle Jim and even when he was in hospital none of them to his knowledge had seen fit to visit. Jake had told him there had been a Get Well card but that seemed the extent of their interest. He guessed they were waiting for the hand-out after Jim had gone and did not want the trouble of getting involved with an old man before.

Jake was reticent, so would need to be talked round. It would be a topic of conversation for that weekend. The evening after the meeting Ken had other plans. It was Kathy's evening off from the pub and they had arranged to go to the pictures. Ken was nervous and was not going to tell Jake but he was forced to disclose why he could not chat that evening. Jake gave him a sideways look and grinned. "About time you got back in the saddle," he said. It seemed that things were looking up for the two males of that house.

Bill and Simon drove back in thoughtful silence. As they were drawing close to the nursery Bill ventured, "Always want the best for you. We want you to be happy son. I've been lucky. I've had the best years of my life here and selling a share will not take that away. If you don't like it, then that's the end of the matter. Do you hear me?" Simon nodded.

When they got back, Simon took off to the edge of the nursery and sat on a fallen log reflecting. He had grown up at the nursery and taken it for granted. He had always kicked against his father. He surveyed the scene. The nursery sloped towards the river. It was true, planning permission would never be granted for that section of the nursery. He recalled the floods from July that year.

The nursery had not flooded as many neighbouring properties had but the ground down there was sodden. It was a quagmire. Its charm was in the outlook. His father had tried to tier the land but as a one man band he had allowed nature to take its course at the bottom end. From this distance the grasses formed a fringe for the river beyond and there were occasional silver slivers of water separating the vegetation. The breeze skipped through the fronds as though a godly finger was lightly drawing a pattern in some sand. Jake had suggested planting trees along that section to help take up the moisture.

It was a revelation to Simon that he did not want to lose the nursery. When things had got raw for him in his army days, the thought of this scene healed trauma. It had been a constant in his life. It was a benchmark on what was good and worthwhile and noble. Without it in his life he would have been weaker. He knew in the pit of his stomach that it would be like a betrayal of his dad's work. He realised with something of a shock that he wanted to preserve it. He did not want that soft scene to be obliterated by diggers. There was nothing that he could create here that was better than what was here already. Sitting on that log he at last understood.

Chapter 13
All is Not Lost

O Rose thou art sick.
The invisible worm
That flies in the night
In the howling storm
Has found out thy bed
Of crimson joy;
And his dark secret love
Does thy life destroy.

O Rose Thou art Sick: William Blake

1994-1995: Diana

"Happy New Year," there was a chorus of voices and an abundance of hugs and kisses from those assembled. Diana reached over to her husband and planted an extra kiss on his cheek leaving a lipstick smear which she further smudged with her fingers. She was a little tipsy, she knew, but she was also deliriously happy. She took a moment to survey the scene here in their cosy flat.

The Christmas tree glittered invitingly in the corner, the table boasted the best food, champagne bottles that had begun the evening as soldiers on parade in tight formation had been disbanded and stood randomly and drunkenly on every surface and there was her family steeped in merriment, exchanging jokes and banter as they consumed the straw toned liquid. The music was blaring and Samantha had Phillip dancing looking hilarious but unconcerned. She saw Kirsten looking pensive. There was something wrong there, Diana thought. She would have to investigate. She had not been herself since coming home from university this Christmas. She was a serious girl who followed Antony in her mathematical aptitude.

"Here's to 1995," Antony whispered in her ear.

Diana whispered back, "Here's to us all. Gosh a couple of years ago I thought our world had come to an end but since then we've made a new life for ourselves and it could not be better. I never thought it could be like this. I had been so caught up in making an impression. How silly I was."

"We both had been sucked into a false world. I too enjoyed the rewards but I could never relax and I always felt I was part of something bad but I could not put my finger on why. It seduced me and I wanted you all to be proud of me and live in style."

"We did, though didn't we? We lived in some style," and Diana grinned.

Antony had been astounded by the transformation in Diana since they had left their former home. She had truly rediscovered herself. Instead of being the prima donna she had become a star player in a very different sense. During their first year in Midchester, she had been full of drive and her determination had carried him through. She had launched herself into the community.

In his business she had been his PA, his marketing manager, his receptionist and his confidante and his motivator. He was slightly ashamed that he had been so remote after she had told him about the baby. He would do all in his power to support her as she had supported him. His client list was growing steadily. Life was good.

"Mum, come and dance. You too Dad, let's see the inner you. We can put on some Beatles, if you'd rather."

Samantha pulled them both to the centre of the room. The balcony doors had been opened and they spilled outside, their laughter combining with the shouts and shrieks from the centre of town. The five of them were united and at ease. Samantha, the party animal of the group suggested they go into town and as she put it "Clock what was going on," and as usual, Phillip was up for the excursion.

Kirsten needed more persuasion but encouraged by the rest of them fell in with the proposition. Diana and Antony gracefully declined. They had other plans. The young guns peeled away and their parents watched them from the balcony waving and even blowing kisses in a ridiculous way.

"We have such nice children," said Diana. "Most kids would ignore their parents altogether on New Year's Eve. I know, all I wanted to do was go to a party of my own."

Antony when he was young had stayed at home. He had not been one for socialising until well after university. "I think your parents, especially your mum, would have driven even me to make the same choice."

He downed his glass of champagne.

"Bed?" He added and winked.

"Bed," she agreed.

Diana seized the first opportunity she could to tackle her daughter. The sales were in full swing and she had taken Kirsten off to a shopping outlet. Kirsten had a limited wardrobe, unlike Samantha and of course, Diana when she had been goddess of the winning wives. Samantha had pulled a face when she heard of the expedition but she had already arranged to meet some friends so was resigned. As she was still living at home Diana treated Samantha regularly, so it was only fair that the reserved and retiring daughter should have some attention.

Kirsten had always been quiet and studious. She was attractive but this was never forced and in contrast Diana was conscious of her own precociousness at her age. Sometimes, Diana had got impatient with Kirsten when she did not seem to join in, to seize life's pleasures, to be ambitious and switched on but she had now come to realise that Kirsten had a contentment that she, Diana, had only just managed to experience in her forties.

Kirsten was so like Antony in her abilities, her manner and her outlook, although Diana was gratified that she did have some physical resemblance to her mother with her blonde hair and striking blue eyes. Kirsten would be a beauty if she would only invest a little of her energy into the look. Maybe, Diana could bring a little glamour to her daughter.

Shopping with Samantha was always fun, Samantha darting from one clothes rail to the next, selecting a bundle of items to try on and encouraging her mother to do the same. There was never any hesitation with Samantha. She was a missile seeking out a target. Shopping for clothes was a passion which she indulged as frequently as possible and now she was learning the art of beauty therapies at the college she was emerging as a trendsetter.

Cost was not something high on her agenda either. She chose clothes on style, rarely looking at price until the decision to buy was being made. Diana often coughed up the funds probably because she felt conscious and even guilty about the change in fortunes for the family. She hoped Samantha managed to net a wealthy husband. She would need it.

Kirsten was entirely different. She was a casual, practical dresser and had always been cost conscious often to the exasperation of her mother who felt she was missing the point of using clothes for personal adornment. Diana wanted to promote both her daughters. She had spent most of her life so far in promotion of one type or another that it was hard to resist.

As usual, it was hard work shopping with Kirsten. The price tag was always examined first and with a shake of the head her daughter would move onto another rail. Diana tried to put temptation in her way.

"Just try it on to see what it looks like. You don't have to buy."

"This colour would really bring out the colour of your eyes."

She would then try another tack.

"You know this would be so useful for all kinds of occasions, simple and yet elegant. You could wear it during the day casually and with a few accessories it could look stunning for a night out."

"You will need to acquire outfits for the business world when you leave university so why not start now. It will stand you in good stead."

Eventually, with a little give and take the mother and daughter had made some progress with a few purchases and sought refuge in a favoured restaurant. A glass of wine was a welcome overture to both lunch and Diana's inquisition into what was troubling her daughter.

"Tell me all about university then," Diana began.

"There's nothing to tell. Same as last year really except more work, harder work and I am not in hall." Kirsten was concentrating on her food and answered automatically and innocuously.

"Work ok though? You could always ask Dad if it was too challenging. I know you, always independent and private, but you should take what advantages you can and your dad really is the best." Diana studied Kirsten carefully for any sign of anxiety. It had always been difficult to prize anything out of Kirsten. She could be a closed book.

"I know, and work is fine. I really enjoy it." She smiled reassuringly at her mother.

Not for the first time Diana wondered how anyone could actually enjoy row upon row of numbers, complex calculations and elaborate equations but she was glad there were family members that did to spare her the necessity.

"Well, of course, I did not go to university but I am told I missed out on a lot. What do you all get up to? Anything for a mother to be worried about? Any boyfriends on the scene?" Diana tried to give the questions a natural tone of voice even though she was prying.

Diana noticed a little start at the word boyfriend. She casually commented, "I expect there are lots of interesting people to meet." Diana knew that Kirsten would back off if she pressed to hard.

Kirsten had something on her mind but was not ready to divulge anything so ignored her mother's probing and tried to change the subject. "The lasagne is exceptionally good here isn't it? Thanks for bringing me. I really appreciate it," and on other matters she closed up like a clam.

Diana discussed her concerns with Antony who gave his opinion that Kirsten was a sensible girl who could be trusted to work out her own problems. As he put it an interfering mother was not in her best interest.

However, Diana's instincts proved true. At the beginning of the new term they both took Kirsten to her university lodgings.

"Alex has been looking for you. He keeps calling," her housemate told them.

Diana raised her eyebrows and Antony warned her. "Don't."

Alex turned up before they had unpacked the car. He looked a typical student wrapped in his duffle coat and university scarf but Diana with all her experience of men felt a warning shot. There was something too cocky and calculating about his approach. The look on her daughter's face seemed to confirm her intuition.

"Glad you're back at last," he was almost ignoring Antony and Diana.

"Hello," said Diana. "You must be a friend of Kirsten."

"Yes, we're good friends aren't we Kirsten? I don't know what I'd do without her. I'll wait inside the house, shall I, Kirsten?" There was a proprietorial air about the boy that Diana did not like. She had been taken aback by his affront and the way they were being effectively dismissed.

On impulse Diana said, "I am afraid you will have a long wait we are taking Kirsten out for a meal and no doubt will be some time."

Antony and Kirsten exchanged glances. That had not been the arrangement but each for different reasons was ready to comply.

Alex was clearly not pleased and stomped away.

When seated, Diana wasted no time, "Who was that?"

"His name's Alex and in fact he lives not far away from us in Midchester. He's on one of my courses."

"You haven't brought him home in the holiday. Are you keen?" Diana thought it best to begin with the obvious. There was no time to be lost and Antony's presence would make Kirsten less defensive.

"God, no! To be honest he's a pain." In response to her parents' inquisitive look she added, "He can't do the work and keeps using mine. He plagues me and now I can't shake him off. I felt sorry for him at first. It's awful not to understand so I helped him but he now seems to think I will help him all the time, do his work for him and honestly without me he'd have failed ages ago. I don't really know what to do. I can't tell a tutor, I really can't." Diana felt a moment's satisfaction that she had known something was wrong and had pursued it. She looked at Antony with a sort of 'I told you so' look so that he felt it necessary to respond.

"We can speak to him," Antony volunteered.

"No way, Dad. How do you think that would look? It will be alright. I can handle it. Don't worry. It's just a nuisance really. I will tell him I can't keep on sharing my work." Kirsten sounded decisive.

"Well, keep us informed and try not to let him upset you." Antony was relieved to settle the matter.

Unfortunately, Kirsten was not able to shake Alex off. She tried to repel him and avoided him as much as possible but Alex depended on her support and his approach became more and more threatening. He would follow her, he would interpose himself between Kirsten and her friends popularising himself by buying rounds of drinks in the Students' Union and suggesting if known by the tutors their collaboration would reflect badly on her. By Easter, she was ready to leave university altogether. She spoke to her parents.

Antony was horrified but at a loss. He was ready to speak to Alex if necessary but he was aware of his own limitations. It was up to Diana to tackle the problem. Apparently, Alex lived with his mother as his parents had recently separated. Alex resented his father and never mentioned him only suggesting he had another woman on the go. From the information he gleaned about Alex and his mother, Antony realised his father was actually a client of his but as the professional he was and concern that Diana would march in and upset the man he refused to give Diana any details, not even a name.

"No it's confidential Diana. Where would we be if it was found I divulged private information even to my own family? I can tell you that there is a divorce pending and his wife had wanted full disclosure of financial information for the courts so last year I was busy on his behalf. It has been difficult for him but my client hopes it will be concluded soon and he can move on. They separated years ago apparently even before he came to me. Now as usual I've told you too much," Antony as a last resort, would speak to Alex's father but he was mindful of his professional position and hoped to resolve it another way.

However, Kirsten was able to tell Diana where Alex and his mother lived and Diana decided to pay them a visit.

Diana dressed carefully. She wanted to give the right effect, a concerned mother, a person of significance, an empathetic and reasonable woman who understood that difficulties sometimes occur. It was a big ask, but Diana had not had all those years as a company wife for nothing. She chose a soft cream wool dress with an expensive tan leather jacket, nude shoes and a contrasting black and tan handbag. The effect with her blonde curls was stunning. There was a slight doubt that maybe she had overdone it but she dismissed it quickly, reasoning that her hesitation was because she was out of practice.

The house had been smart once upon a time, not even that long ago, but there was neglect in the way the door needed a fresh coat of paint, the side hedge needed trimming and a peak through the gate into the garden showed a mess of overgrown bushes and plants that had not had a winter prune. Diana rang the doorbell and waited.

The woman who answered the door was unimpressive. She was average in every respect. Her mouse coloured hair was of medium length without style, her face bland without animation and her general appearance showed a lack of care. She was colourless in every way and Diana stood there like some exotic lily.

"My name is Diana Carstairs. I wonder if I could have a word with you. My daughter, Kirsten is at university with Alex, your son and I want to iron out a little difficulty."

The woman stood obviously uncertain what to do.

"May I come in rather than discuss things on the doorstep?" Diana gave her most appealing smile.

Abigail turned and proceeded inside leaving Diana to follow and close the front door behind her. The woman had not uttered a word.

Diana glanced round the room, waiting for Alex's mother to invite her to sit down but nothing was forthcoming.

"This is a little awkward. It seems Alex is struggling with one of his courses. My daughter Kirsten has for some time been helping him with his difficulties and her father and I think that this reliance on Kirsten needs to stop. It is in both their interests I am sure you agree. We wondered if you would perhaps talk to him about it. After all, he will need to do exams soon and this situation will not help him there."

Diana felt she was delivering a monologue in an empty theatre.

"I am sorry, that probably did not come out well did it? University can be such a challenge. Of course, I did not go to university. Perhaps you did." She tried to be conciliatory and engage the woman.

Alex's mother gave no reaction.

"Is Alex here? Shall I speak with him?" Diana offered. "I am really sympathetic. My husband is an accountant so I suppose Kirsten has benefitted. Perhaps Alex could sign up for some extra tuition. The university are meant to be very supportive." Diana had not anticipated this.

The woman sat down flopping on to the armchair leaving Diana uncertain whether to join her and decided it would be a good idea and sank on to the settee tucking her legs elegantly to one side.

"Look, are you alright? Can I do anything? I am a good listener, really I am and I may be able to help. I do not even know your first name. I am Diana. We should swap notes on what it is like having a child all grown up at university." Diana tried her level best to be friendly and she was relieved to see a flicker of a response.

"Abigail, that's my name. I do not think I can do anything. Alex never listens to me." This answer did not surprise Diana and there was a sense of relief that at last the woman had spoken.

"Oh, I am sure he does. Boys always listen to their mothers. My son Phillip is full of bravado but I know, he goes away and thinks about what I have said." Diana was practiced at social matters and was gaining confidence.

"Well, he would wouldn't he? A woman like you." Abigail gave Diana a look of defeat.

"I am sure it is true for any mother," Diana bleated. She felt awkward suddenly and her mission seemed to be crumbling. Later in her assessment of the meeting she would realise that Abigail was like a limpet clinging to whatever rock she could find and sucking the algae. She seemed to drain even the room of energy.

"Your husband is an accountant you say," Diana was suddenly wary remembering that Antony was her husband's accountant so she only gave an affirmation.

"I bet he's a good one and successful." There was a scratch of jealousy in the statement that marked Diana's skin making her want to claw back at Abigail.

"Yes, he is a good one but not, especially successful. We are all proud of him."

Diana did not completely understand why she suddenly felt wary. There had been an insinuation in the woman's comment and she seemed to be picking up the vibe with her own comments.

"Lucky you," Abigail had a soft, flat voice. She spoke on monotone and to Diana seemed to live in monochrome.

"My husband has always been a disappointment."

The coldness of the statement made Diana shudder. Diana felt for Abigail in her divorced state so naturally Abigail was hurt and therefore critical. Diana was patient enough to listen and could tolerate a little self-pity but she knew she had not the character to be a counsellor. Her manner had always been to have a paddy about whatever it was and then pick yourself up and forge a way through. This woman was clearly wallowing.

"I understand it is difficult for you but things can get better." It was a trite thing to say but Diana felt she was in no position to say anything else.

"What do you know with your perfect life? You have it all." It was the first bit of anger that the woman had shown.

"You have your son. I am sure he needs you and he has done so well to go to university. We were delighted with Kirsten, you know, the competition for places is fierce. I did not want to make things more difficult coming here but we thought you should know he is struggling. He needs support but not through my daughter. If he continues to rely on her, he will ultimately fail his exams and before that happens we will inform the university. Of course, we would much rather he made his own decisions in this matter," Diana was adamant that Abigail had understood. She made a move to depart picking up her chic black and tan handbag.

"His father will have to deal with it. You can speak to him if you like," Diana really wanted to shake the woman.

"Perhaps, it would be better for you to explain to him."

Diana was getting tired and impatient. "He never listens to me either."

Diana wondered if Abigail ever gave him anything worth listening to.

"I know, I should never have married him but at the time he seemed a good catch. He was working and had a good wage so he could afford a wife. I picked the wrong horse there, didn't I? I should have found myself a nice accountant to look after me."

Diana found her hackles rising, maybe because it was true that she had gone for Antony because he was a safe bet but also because they had worked at their marriage and now she truly loved him.

Diana was now on her feet eager to be gone.

"I could have had anyone I wanted you know. All the boys fancied me but I could not wait. Steve was older and I thought he would go far. How wrong I was." It was almost as if she was reasoning with herself.

"That's him." She picked up a photograph that had been pushed to the back on the sideboard. Diana was not in the least interested but took hold of the small frame showing a small group, a father, mother and young son.

"That was taken ages ago. He was miserable then too. I liked to go out, go to parties. Still, he didn't mind looking after Alex if I wanted to go anywhere so it wasn't too bad at first. He's very dull, always has been. A woman needs attention and pampering. He was always out working and would come home in dirty smelly work clothes expecting me to wash them.

"That was not what I had signed up for at all. I was not going to be any man's skivvy. I think he has another woman now. I don't know how he's managed that. She's a spinster. She would be. Who else would be so desperate?"

From saying nothing when she had first arrived Diana was taken aback by the torrent. Diana looked more carefully at the photograph interested to see the man in question who had had the misfortune to be married to Alex's mother. For a nanosecond her self-control faltered for there, quite unmistakably was a man she had known in the past, in fact a man she had known rather too well at the time and her stomach lurched. She handed the frame back and made her excuses.

"It has been interesting meeting you and all the best. Please speak to Alex. It would be in his best interests. I am afraid I must go. I am meeting someone. Thank you."

Diana left as quickly and smartly as she was able with Abigail's parting words ringing in her ears, "Do come again soon. Maybe, we could go out sometime."

Diana never wanted to see the woman again. She drove home as quickly as she could, doing her best to banish the encounter from her mind. Alex was his son. Alex that arrogant, lazy toad was Steve's son. There was in her view not an ounce of Steve about him. Steve had been considerate and thoughtful when she had met him. He was good looking too. How on earth did he land up with Abigail; she thought?

Diana reported back to Kirsten embellishing her account to give Kirsten more confidence to detach herself from Alex. He must she emphasised face his own consequences. Through her visit to Abigail he had been warned.

Later after work she recounted the meeting to Antony. She tried hard to probe him about Steve but Antony would not divulge anything. If she wanted to know any more, she would have to use subterfuge and look through his files or gain access to his computer. She was intrigued but not sufficiently to jeopardise her relationship with her husband. That had been tested sufficiently when she had told him about the baby. She hoped she would not run into Steve.

In her own mind, she looked back to the time she had known Steve.

To Diana, at eighteen, Steve had seemed so worldly. She almost worshipped the ground he walked upon. He had a sort of sardonic grin she remembered, completely opposite to his character. The girls spoke about him endlessly. He had become a prize. Her group of friends had been very competitive, flirting shamelessly and hitching skirts to show as much leg as possible. While the boys responded in kind, Steve kept a distance and thwarted their rather obvious attempts at seduction. He did not attend many parties either, which made his presence even more compelling.

The party organised by Nicola's brother was not the usual gathering. Their parents were away and the house sat at the end of a country lane so they could make as much noise as they wanted. There was a lot of alcohol and a few drugs. Diana restricted herself to the alcohol. Steve was there and Diana was overcome with jealousy as she watched Pat pawing him, demanding his attentions.

Diana seized her opportunity when Pat departed for the bathroom. She gave him her best smile and shook her hair seductively. He sauntered over, "please rescue me," he said.

Diana remembered the thrill of those words and the dismay on the face of Pat when she returned to see Steve and Diana in an embrace. They had both drunk too much, too much to prevent the coupling but not enough to render them incapable. Diana had known this was her moment and she had seized it leading him upstairs. She had always been glad to have lost her innocence with Steve. She secretly hoped for a relationship but then sense had kicked in and she saw him as a nice fling but not a prospect so she began to avoid him. She had won the competition as far as the girls were concerned. She could move on and keep upgrading.

Of course, a couple of months later she knew that consequences could be very different. There was never any question about informing Steve of her predicament. He was the sort of man who would stand up and be counted. She did not want that kind of attachment. Indeed she did not want any kind of attachment in those days. She wanted a good time.

In fact, Diana was not to meet Steve for many more years. This was a shame. If she had not so studiously avoided him, she would have rediscovered her old school friend Gillian.

Time and circumstance can play games with lives but, although decisions are driven by outside forces, ultimately every individual must take ownership for their destinies.

Chapter 14
Finders Keepers, Losers Weepers

*Better by far you should forget and smile
Than that you should remember and be sad*

Remember: Christina Rossetti

2000: Jim: Simon: Diana: Gillian

The Millennium had burst into everyone's consciousness. The old century was now a history of wars and servitude. The old ways of duty and family ties had been broken. Familiar faces in a broken society had faded and became like sepia photographs to be examined as if in a lesson. Some of the old brigade clung to their ways but most cast aside these doubters and pushed into new beginnings and a new century not yet tainted by human greed and misery. All was another time, another place and for most the beam of opportunity shone. Decisions were made, regrets buried and inevitably the same mistakes would be resurrected all over again.

Jim Woodhouse, at sixty-eight years old, opened a bottle of single malt, pulled his curtains open in order to study the night sky. Gradually, the early evening random flickering of fireworks mounted into wild explosions whose brilliance shattered his normally quiet sitting room. The vibrant colours intermittently painted the walls in vivid shades streaking their way in one sudden flash after another exposing Jim as he sat absorbed in the extravagant display. In the corner of his room, he tried to hide from the full impact. It was a time for exhilaration. Celebrations continued throughout the night but about one o'clock in the morning Jim had had enough and closed his curtains against the invasion.

He thought he had got used to living alone but that night he missed his Ida. The whole world outside his home seemed to have joined together and left him in isolation, a non-participant, a mere onlooker, someone who marked time and time was relentlessly escaping through his open fingers. Ida would have been excited and entranced. She would have baked special cakes to nibble as she sipped her Amontillado and insisted on watching the television to laugh at the comedians and follow the progress of the New Millennium as it travelled around the world.

Jim needed her inspiration and without her he was mundane. From news reports he would be aware of the Millennium Dome, somewhere he had no inclination to visit, but full that night of important guests including the Queen and Prince Philip and there would be splendid performances. The cost to do all this had not escaped his notice and to him it had seemed senseless. He knew Ida would have revelled in the occasion and told him not to be grumpy and difficult. Human happiness was money well spent. She had made every day precious and without her it was him that was squandering the life he had left.

On his second glass of single malt, just as the fireworks became more intense, he felt the conviction that he needed to change. He paused in his thoughts swirling the mellow amber liquid around the sides of the heavy glass. He allowed himself the luxury of imagining a different lifestyle. He was nigh on sixty-nine and would be seventy in another year as old as Ida had been when she had died. The century was quickly drawing to a close and a new century was beckoning. Ida would have been making plans.

When she was alive, she had urged him to take holidays, although to have prised him away from his garden and his routines, particularly at the club, had been almost impossible. He had been groundsman since 1957, over forty years and he had seen no reason to call it a day. It was such a long time but so absorbed he had been in his occupation he had not noticed how the years had slipped by and more importantly the effect on his wife. He resisted holidays as much as he could, continually mindful of the need to care for the football pitches and his garden whatever the season. He was the one to organise the correct amount of watering, to ensure the correct use of rollers on the pitch, to cut the grass to the correct length and to ensure that all pitch lines were correct. He had been a proud man but in his pride had forgotten that he was a husband first and foremost. His wife had sacrificed much to enable him to carry his load.

They had gone away occasionally but never for more than a week and he found it difficult to settle wondering about the consequences of his absence for his grass and plants. He was not a natural delegator except as most men of his generation he entrusted the management of his home to his wife. He had received praise and acclaim for his efforts in maintaining the sports field of play.

Whatever the weather, the pitch at the club was firm with lush grass groomed to produce a perfect finish and players, managers and fans had shown their admiration and appreciation with a number of awards kept on display at the club. Most did not acknowledge Jim personally, that was not to be expected, but those who mattered knew he had been responsible. Over the years, he had produced vegetables and flowers for exhibition at local shows. There was a drawer full of winning certificates to prove his prowess. Ida was always first in her congratulations demonstrating her delight with her hugs. As he sipped his drink he thought he had been selfish.

Midnight had come and gone and throwing caution to the wind he poured a third glass of whisky. He remembered Ida coming home after her first trip to the hairdresser that Jackie had taken her to and he felt a pang of regret that he had not complimented her on her new look. He should have kissed her and taken her out for a meal in a smart restaurant but all he did was say she looked nice but he had liked her the way she had been and he even joked about the cost. She had set to and donned her apron to make their supper.

It was not as if they did not have the money to pay for anything. At the club some of the directors and even other staff members took their wives on cruises. Ida would have been satisfied with a trip to Spain, although he knew she had longed to go to Venice. He did collect brochures one year but he found the prices eye watering. However, now when it was too late, he admitted that he had not wanted to abandon the football ground and his garden even for a few days. He had caught her looking longingly at the pages in the brochure but he determinably ignored the desire he had witnessed. It was certainly not the thought of the cost that now made Jim's eyes water. He closed the curtains trying also to close his feelings of shame and regret.

Ida had clearly loved having Jackie and Jake in her life. Jim knew she would have made a wonderful mother but they had been unlucky. Ida seemed to have a premonition that there would be no children and warned him prior to their wedding. He suddenly had the notion that it was more than a premonition.

He recalled her mother, Molly, commenting one Christmas as they all fussed over Daisy's children, "Pity you won't have children our Ida."

Jim had responded, "There's still time and it's fun trying," so they all laughed but Jim had remembered the look Molly had given Ida.

Ida knew more about Jackie than she had ever let on. Again, he felt the guilt. Before she died, Ida had made him promise to look out for Jake and actually take care he was alright but he had not done even this for her. He noticed Jake of course, when he played with the other local lads on the waste ground opposite.

Who wouldn't, he thought? Jake was a smart little footballer. He was a natural and only needed the guidance of a good coach. Jim knew he should have taken an active interest. Ken was a decent man but it was hard for him and Jake was not his son. He liked Ken, an open, honest man who had been a bit of a lad in his time and given his widowed mother the run around.

From time to time, they had even sat over a pint together. After Ida had gone and after the interlude of sympathetic interventions by neighbours Jim had raised the drawbridge and divided his time between work at the ground and his garden. He made that his world.

Shaken by the clamour of the Millennium fireworks and dazzled by the spectacle at odds with the dark world he had created after his wife had died Jim made a belated promise to Ida. It was as though she had visited him that night and had illuminated his being. His job had been getting harder and he resented the new management strategies under Clive Corneille so he would take his retirement, he would seek out Jake and support him and become more social and outgoing as Ida would have wanted. The decisions had been a long time coming but when they did they began to excite him and soothe his troubled mind. Ida would be his guide and he would not let her down again.

****

Jim's friend Bill, who owned Jim's favoured nursery for plants had also reason for optimism. His son, Simon had finally decided to leave the army and make his way in 'Civvy' Street. Bill's wife was over the moon. They had two daughters but Simon was their son and more than that his army career had taken him into some dangerous situations. He would not talk about his missions but they knew he was based at Hereford and drew their own conclusions.

The SAS had a formidable reputation but there were always casualties. Simon had been lucky with only a few minor injuries but others had not been. He had joined up when he was eighteen and had completed fifteen years which his parents considered was quite enough. He had discussed things with them on his last leave. He felt that he would have to make a decision about his future. He could stay in the army and in some ways that was appealing, although if he signed on again it would mean that the army would be his career for life. To leave when he was thirty three, meant there was every chance he could make a career outside the military. Simon calculated that to leave was the better option. He did not want to leave when he was over forty and there would be fewer opportunities. He would return to his home town of Marketborough briefly and then see where life took him. He was someone who was not without ambition. Simon had asked them to look out for work possibilities. They hoped he would never leave again.

****

In the next county in Midchester, the two school friends Diana and Gillian were experiencing contrasting and separate Millennium experiences. Now thirty years since they had shared Diana's shame they each had trodden very different paths. Diana as in the song had trodden the high road. It had been rocky in places and there had been sheer drops where anyone with less determination for survival might have fallen into an abyss. Diana had been self-seeking, craving the light and the pinnacle beyond her. Her steps towards her goals had generally been calculated. She had used society as clamp-ons to support her climb and as she had drawn nearer the summit had discarded any unnecessary baggage that could be an impediment to her assent. It was only as she stood at the peak she began to realise that however fine and spectacular the view was it had been remote and lonely and when she surveyed the scene she saw other peaks higher, steeper and more treacherous waiting to be conquered. She could never climb them all. Her life with Antony had given her a perspective and eventually shown her new horizons. She did not need to stand above everyone else as some intrepid mountaineer to feel worthy.

Gillian had taken the low road on the outskirts of life. It had been long and monotonous. She had been sure footed and like Diana had determination but while Diana had vision and was able to lift her head as she journeyed fixing her eyes on distant vistas Gillian had both literally and metaphorically kept her head down. Her road had been edged with high hedges and walls and while they seemed to keep her safe and warm their protection also obscured any view and did not allow hot sun to penetrate the shadows cast over the narrow track. Of course, she was sheltered from the extreme storms of life, although her endurance had been tested as she battled against winds of change. She walked stalwartly until eventually tired she had paused by a gate and temptation had consumed her so she had forced the gate open to breathe in the scents of the spring meadow, a heady concoction of life. Steve had been invited to follow her path. He had tried to show her other ways but Gillian had stuck rigidly to her route convinced of her destination.

Diana and Antony hosted a dinner of select friends at their town house. They had left the flat at the end of 1996 and decided that a town house close to all the amenities they so enjoyed and near the office Antony had by then opened would suit them better than a sprawling country residence as they had before. It had cheered Diana and occupied her when they had failed miserably to locate Jackie. It had been a temporary consolation. The house over three storeys boasted a spacious kitchen with huge glass doors leading to the private walled garden. They spent most of their time in the kitchen with its sleek units and up to the minute appliances. It had a large work island strategically placed to divide the work centre with the more relaxed dining and lounge areas where they could eat, watch television in comfort, work if really necessary and informally socialise. On this the Millennium Eve they opened up the rather splendid Victorian dining room.

Their guests were a random collection of friends, none of them chosen for their status or position, those days of trying to please the city elite were well behind them. Here, they gathered together people they valued in very different ways. There was Michael and his wife Margaret. Antony had been grateful to Michael for his input when he had wrestled with Diana's revelation about her baby. In turn, Antony had helped Michael to extricate himself from the Veterinary Practice so that he and Margaret could enjoy retirement. Antony liked being a part of his client's lifestyle choices, helping them to see financial pictures more clearly. In his city life he had been a well-paid but very dispensable cog in a mighty wheel of fortune but his new life had shown him that money served people rather than the reverse. He did not put a clock on the time he spent with clients to calculate charges as most of his competitors did.

Diana had enjoyed using her abilities to good effect for the dinner party. She had combined the use of a local caterer with her own culinary skills and brought a magical quality to the room, strategically placing candles and table lamps to cast a glow that reached from the oak panelled walls to the splendour of the large walnut table boasting a floral centrepiece of poinsettias and Christmas roses expertly entwined with ivy and other greenery.

Each guest gasped as they were shown into the room. They had all been to Diana's many times but usually these social calls were confined to the kitchen or sitting room. Here was the epitome of a sumptuous and regal Victorian banquet. Diana glowed too but not with the pride of her former life. It was the pride of bringing warmth and hospitality to good friends. She was glad that she had kept the Royal Worcester dinner service that had twelve place settings and the beautiful Waterford crystal glasses, rather old fashioned in style but their shimmer could not be outdone.

The ladies had dressed for the occasion as much as possible, although all of them had warm coats and boots ready for the departure after the meal to a firework display at a country park. Antony and Diana had been meticulous in their preparation. Three taxies were to transport them at ten thirty to take the whole party to the venue. They would return at twelve thirty to whisk everyone back to their respective homes. Diana and Antony had spared no expense as host and hostess. It was not an investment for personal advancements but an investment in relationships. Diana had kept the food simple in concept to make it easy to deliver. There was no competition to provide a lavish and wasteful meal. These guests were appreciative of the occasion and spending the evening with friends.

At first, when she moved from her previous life Diana had still tried to impress before gradually realising that people could like her for who she was whether she served Chateaubriand or cheese on toast. Relaxing in their company made the world more enjoyable.

As well as Margaret and Michael, there was Marjorie and Malcolm. Diana wanted to find out the maiden names of the two women, reminded of the old saying, 'change the name but not the letter, change for the worse and not the better.' However, as both couples seemed unashamedly happy in their marriages she discounted any coincidences of surnames. She had met Marjorie at the charity shop where Diana helped.

At the time of arrival in Midchester, she had thought it would be seen as a worthy thing to do and promote their entrance into local society with the plan to relinquish the role after a short period but she was still there almost seven years later and Marjorie had been a good reason for this. She was the kind of fussy plump woman Diana's old self would have dismissed but she had found her to be a wonderful soul.

Marjorie and Malcolm lived in a little terraced house not far from the town centre. His work on the shop floor of a factory was boring to say the least. They had lost their only daughter from a complication following an operation when she had been a child. The loss was never hidden and tidied away. Instead it had inspired the couple to foster children on short term stays. Malcolm read a great deal so he was an asset in any quiz team and Marjorie loved the soaps so was always worth her place in a team. Marjorie and Diana would keep Malcolm well supplied with books from the charity shop. There had been several occasions when Diana had been tempted to talk to Marjorie about her own lost daughter but she felt ashamed. Marjorie in her simple way had provided Diana with a sympathetic view of humanity.

Other guests included Elaine and James from the bridge club and Pauline and Frank another couple from the walking group making ten in all. They knew each other well so there was no ceremony. Both Diana and Antony recalled the stuffy dinners of a previous era.

Kirsten and Samantha had both left home. Samantha had gravitated to London and had landed a job in a fashionable beauty salon. She shared a flat with one of the other girls and had a steady boyfriend. Somehow, Samantha's future had always been predictable. Kirsten on the other hand was feeling her feet. She had left university with a first class degree and angled for a job with Antony but both parents had resisted gently urging her to gain outside experience. She did not want a job on Antony's patch as she put it so reluctantly sought work in Manchester where a friend from university was living. She found she enjoyed the challenge and made progress. She had warned Antony that soon she would be ready to take over his accountancy practice. That year, Phillip had gone to university to study medicine and had travelled to Australia for Christmas and New Year with a couple of other students. Diana hardly dared to think what he might have been up to that evening.

The men gathered in the lounge where Frank was getting the evening started with some rather crude jokes. Antony stood on the edge conscientiously filling glasses. He was never quite at ease in these situations feeling stiff and self-conscious even though he was the host and he had a superior intellect.

James suggested a game of golf in the New Year. There was a good deal on offer at his club for reduced green fees. Antony who was no sportsman said he would decline leaving the other men to arrange a foursome. Antony had often felt his time in the boardroom had been hampered by his inability to join in these excursions.

The five women were consuming champagne in the kitchen. Diana made the last adjustments to the casserole. Marjorie was taking cling film off the plates of smoked salmon salad as starters before delivering the plates to the dining room. She was not so used to champagne and intermittently sipped delicately from her glass.

Diana in times past would not have allowed the intrusion into a private space or the interference with her arrangements and even now she had momentary panic as Marjorie fumbled with a plate and then taking a fork rearranged the presentation of food. Diana bit her tongue and pursed her lips much in the fashion of her mother. She glanced towards the plate glass doors now reflecting the bright room against the darkness outside and caught the scene inside, and, for a brief moment, was horrified to see a woman who resembled her mother asking if she had really gate crashed the party before relaxing her stance to become Diana again. Margaret, Elaine and Pauline were discussing the failures of their menfolk over the festive period.

"I don't know what we would have been doing tonight if you had not sorted this out," Elaine declared. "James might have dragged me to the golf club I suppose."

Pauline said, "Don't knock it Elaine. Frank never wants to go anywhere. He's a real stick in the mud these days and we would have been at home. He probably would be snoring in the chair after too much to drink earlier. I don't know what happens to them, men I mean, you give them your best years and then you might as well be invisible."

"What did he get you for Christmas?" Elaine sparked.

"I'd seen a coat in Percival's but you know it was a bit pricey. It has a lovely sheen and I so wanted to wear it tonight but Frank thought we should wait for the sale which starts next week. I bet someone will nab it before me. He used to be extravagant but now he seems to think money should be kept in the bank. I blame your husband, Diana."

"I don't think you can blame Antony," Margaret retorted, "Diana always has fabulous clothes and look at those diamonds. Are they real?" She pointed to Diana's necklace.

"Of course, I would expect nothing else," interposed Elaine.

Diana fingered the necklace. It had been a gift from Antony. It had been eight years since the fateful garden party when Jackie had turned up and seemed to signal the start of her life spiralling out of control. That previous life existed in her memory box but it had become insubstantial. It had all seemed so important and vital. She had stopped running.

"Yes, it is a Christmas gift from Antony," she almost felt embarrassed before the admiration.

After her confession to Antony about her daughter they had made efforts to locate Jackie but as months turned to years she had felt demoralised and underneath her perfect exterior her confidence had gradually disintegrated. Antony had watched the suffering and his heart was moved. He knew they might never find her and he wanted to capture something of his old wife to give her strength.

It had not worked and Diana had melted on Christmas Day. She had been vicious in her attack accusing him of having no feeling and how could flashy expensive jewellery ever make up for a broken heart. He had told her she was selfish and pitiful and needed to wake up. She should not pretend. She had given the baby away. She had not thought about her for years and now she was being unreasonable. He said he would return the necklace and took off for a long walk in the winter sun.

Diana was left alone until the girls descended for their Christmas dinner. She had squirmed and she had despaired and she had raged. She wanted to lash out. She wanted others to suffer as she did. Resentment had bubbled up. She made no effort to disguise it. When the girls arrived, she was still deep in this miasma leaving them to cope with the meal saying she had eaten something that had made her sick.

As the day unfolded, each of them played a part, but Diana watching her daughters with Antony, felt an outsider. Even later when they rang Phillip who was travelling in Australia until he was due back at university and he had teased his mother in his usual cheeky manner did not lift her spirits. The girls were reminded of the disgrace when Antony had been sacked. It had been uncomfortable at home and school.

Kirsten had been more immune to any taunts as a valued sixth former but Samantha and Phillip had fielded the remarks. Samantha was glad to quit school but Phillip underneath his jocular manner had a steely character. Either his quick wit or his spunk could deal with any onslaught and soon it all subsided.

On the last Christmas Day of the twentieth century the four had taken an early night. All had been exhausted by the efforts of the day. It allowed Diana and Antony the opportunity to come together and by the next morning the squall had subsided. The New Year's Eve party was the perfect opportunity to show Antony he was valued and she wore the necklace.

"Let's eat, shall we?" Diana called. "We can collect the men on the way."

The meal proceeded with much banter and the attention of the other men had been drawn by their wives to the diamond necklace. Their admiration had been tarnished only by their fear of future expense. Antony and Diana were once more in harmony.

****

While there was pleasure and spontaneity in Diana and Antony's household her former school friend Gillian was experiencing anything but. While Diana lived in the centre of town in the same way as she lived in the centre of a vibrant social life Gillian lived on the outskirts in a quiet hidden road that branched into a cul-de-sac as was her life.

Steve's latest project had not been going well. It had been taking him far too long to complete the renovation and time cost money. He had taken out a larger than usual mortgage and the delay in completion was going to eat into any profit. One of his suppliers had gone bankrupt and not supplied the materials so he had to buy from elsewhere at increased cost and he had lost his deposit for goods with his usual supplier. He felt sorry for Bruce with whom he had dealt over ten years. He knew the strains of cash flow, the ramifications of which he had to face several times in the past so he understood the fine line between success and failure.

It had become a lot easier for Steve with Gillian as his wife. With her job as a teacher, she shouldered the financial burden equally so if things got tight he could adjust payments into the home pot making up for any deficit at a later date. With Abigail, he had had no such luxury.

It was decided that Steve would work as late as he could and then take the next day off. They would eat late and open the bottle of Chablis that they had been saving. Gillian would prepare a supper. She would poach a whole salmon, serving it with a lemon butter sauce and then cold with salads the following day. She would serve home-made mushroom soup and complete the meal with a roulade. Gillian would have a happy afternoon preparing and then they would celebrate in style on Steve's return. The next day was to be pure relaxation together. She was full of anticipation.

The phone call came about five minutes after Steve had returned home. Gillian took the call, urging Steve to shower and change.

The strangled voice at the end of the line said, "I need to speak to Steve urgently."

Gillian knew the caller. She had heard the voice many times.

"Can I help? He's having a shower," Gillian tried to keep a cool head.

"No you can't bloody help. Get me Steve. NOW!" The voice was aggressive and frightening.

"Wait a minute."

Gillian thought much later whether she should have fended her off and been adamant that he was unavailable but she did not. She always felt weak in the face of conflict.

Steve took the call while Gillian hovered. "It's Alex. He's in hospital. It seems serious. He's taken something. I'm going to have to go," and as an afterthought, "Sorry."

Gillian felt a net fall on her shoulders and over her body, tightening and keeping her prisoner.

Gillian had to agree. There was no choice. Her practicality kicked in so while he dressed she made a sandwich, thrusting this into his hand with a carton of juice as he left. She was alone. The supper would have to wait. She switched the oven off and sank to the floor.

Steve picked Abigail up and drove to the hospital. She had waited for him not daring to go by herself, so typical of his ex-wife he thought with exasperation always needing a man to lean on. By the time they arrived Alex was out of danger, having had a stomach pump and antidote but he was weak and feverish. His parents meeting the doctors and nurses felt the weight of responsibility, at least Steve did.

Alex at twenty-four had become no less a worry than he had been at fifteen. He had quit university at the end of his second year, having failed his exams and not wanting the trouble of a retake. He had since drifted in and out of jobs, using his mother's home as a base and using his father for funds when required. There had however been a change in the last few months and Steve had dared to hope that things would be better.

Clive Corneille, it seemed had taken him in hand. Steve was not sure what the job entailed and sometimes it seemed that Alex was a glorified errand boy but it was regular work. Steve had not asked many details partly because Alex would not tell him anyway and partly from the release of having to fund his son. Steve had grown tired and frustrated from the demands. It had become a drain not only affecting his income but at times his relationship with Gillian. He had been pleased that his son seemed more settled.

Things were better at home with Gillian when he was not chasing around after Alex. Abigail too had drawn away from him which was a bonus. In fact, she was looking smarter and seeming more positive. Her current relationship must be working for her. Even now he found it hard to admit the frailty of their marriage. Being with Gillian had proved a revelation.

Gillian was not easy to live with, she had too many insecurities but she was wholeheartedly in his corner. Her actions were in support of him and he was in no doubt that her thoughts were always directed towards his well-being. She worked hard too, sometimes to the detriment of her health and welfare as well as intruding into their time together. Abigail would whine if he had left her alone too long. Abigail had no compunction about using any income for her own needs. She had no desire to work for a living, especially after having Alex. There had always been an air of entitlement about Abigail. She could be enticing, especially in the beginning of their relationship, but more often she would denigrate his efforts and repel any approaches.

Yet Abigail relished social attention. She fed off attention at any gatherings particularly from men. She had flirted shamelessly with Steve when they had first met. He had been no match for her whiles. With the suggestion of a pregnancy they had married within months, him full of enthusiasm, her full of satisfaction. She insisted on a vibrant social life which befitted her personality. Like a great actress she craved the limelight and disappeared inside herself when the footlights dimmed. Steve in his solid dependable way had never been the jealous type which allowed Abigail scope to manoeuvre her lifestyle to include a posse of admirers. Of course, the birth of Alex temporarily prevented socialising but soon Abigail emerged to reconnect with her fans and Steve invariably chose to stay at home with Alex.

Hindsight told him that he had contributed to the disintegration of their marriage by his inactivity. It had suited him. He was honest enough to realise that they would have separated many years before had it not been for Alex.

Alex had not been an easy child. He had resisted Steve's attempts to teach him woodcraft or in fact any other skills. He was not interested in any sports and threw tantrums if he lost at any games. His black hair had been a mystery. Although Steve was the parent who spent time and effort with Alex, it was his mother who the boy seemed to admire.

They remained at the hospital until early on New Year's Day. There had been a strange mixed atmosphere as the new century broke. There had been a rather feeble cheer in the waiting room and random greetings but interspersed by a woman crying and the shouts of a drunk in pain after a fall down an escalator.

Steve and Abigail sipped their machine coffee, each resigned to their wasted evening, underneath Steve was calm but concerned about Gillian and Abigail bitter and resentful. Alex drifted in and out of consciousness until he became alert as the reluctant dawn began to break.

Steve took them all back to Abigail's where she disappeared to have a soak in a hot bath. Steve found some eggs which he scrambled for breakfast. They had been given firm instructions to monitor Alex. He did not ring Gillian who he hoped was sleeping peacefully. He had of course, spoken to her at the turn of the year but their less than private conversation had been strained and stilted. He could not wait to get back to his wife.

Abigail had other ideas.

She had taken the opportunity to go to bed for a couple of hours while Steve watched over Alex. She was warm from her bath, replete from the breakfast he had cooked and ready to drift into sleep. She had almost been tempted in her haze to invite Steve along too for old time's sake. Steve, willing as ever to accede to his ex-wife's demands to mind Alex, contented himself that he would be with Gillian for lunch. Alex had been surly but quiet.

Gillian had eventually fallen asleep about four in the morning. It was a fitful sleep with twists of dreams, incomplete but disturbing as she alternately dodged some stalker or plummeted down some precipice waking briefly to note the reassuring familiar surroundings but with the absence of her husband making her feel empty and abandoned. Eventually, as light began to drift through the curtain cracks she slumbered. It was mid-morning when she finally emerged.

Gillian scolded herself for her weakness. To be jealous of Alex and Abigail was corrosive. If Steve was a different man, harder in rejecting his past responsibilities she would have found him less appealing. She basked in his sincerity and genuine human warmth. Neither of them could alter the past. They had to come to terms with it, although sometimes it was nigh on impossible not to feel outrage. Gillian would wait patiently and welcome him home despite her inner resentments. He would be home for lunch.

Steve had been shocked when Abigail came down from her nap.

"Can you fix my necklace?" She came close and turned away one hand clutching a gaudy necklace to her throat and the other lifting her hair at the back of her head.

Steve automatically fastened the clasp at the back of her neck.

"I'll be off now," he reached for his jacket nodding at Alex who glared back.

"The hospital said Alex should not be left. You will have to stay with him," Abigail was checking herself in the mirror. It was an action he had witnessed many times before.

"Come on Abigail. I need to get back. I've been gone all night. It's New Year's Day. In fact, it's a new Millennium. Gillian will be waiting for me."

Steve could almost feel the heat of the flame in Abigail when he said Gillian.

"Why? You are not going anywhere or doing anything. You told me you had no plans."

"I told you we had no plans for today except to spend it quietly together. That is a plan." Steve tried to emphasise his point and was aware of Alex watching the charade.

"Steve I have a luncheon to go to. It was expensive and I am not about to forego it. Alex is fine really so won't be any trouble, will you Alex?" Alex smiled as if part of a conspiracy.

Alex had been watching his parents with interest. He knew who would win.

"I am being picked up in five minutes Steve. You can ring her and explain. She'll understand and I should be back by say six. Honestly, Steve you should not leave everything to me. You should do your bit. Alex needs someone here. It's obviously got to be you."

On glancing out of the window she noticed a black sleek car draw up before the gate. "They're here. Be good you two." She grabbed her coat and was gone; leaving Steve seething with fury and frightened of conveying the news to Gillian. It was not the immediate anger she would undoubtedly feel and any cross words that would be exchanged that upset him but the way he felt he was betraying her. Gillian depended on him and he was incapable of not letting her down.

Gillian took the phone call from Steve resisting any urge to stomp and shout. In fact, she had felt flattened even before discussion. At first, her thoughts were mundane masking despair. She wondered if Steve would be able to watch the racing from Cheltenham as he was accustomed to do on New Year's Day. She had the impulse to finish her sixth form marking while the house was quiet but dismissed that idea.

That would, in her view, add insult to injury. Since childhood and her parent's careful arrangement of life she had thought that what happened at New Year would prove to be a motif for the rest of the year. She would therefore avoid work and much more significantly she would avoid argument. She did not want to carry the psychological significance for the rest of the year and horror of horrors the century.

The problem was that, she could not avoid the ache that permeated her centre. She did not seem to have any remedy for her inner misery.

Gillian wandered round her home fingering her treasured possessions trying to find comfort in the familiar touch of a porcelain figurine, a cut glass vase filled with chrysanthemums from Christmas. Their petals were wilting and as they did so had lost some of their colour. Gillian was also wilting. The Christmas decorations that she had thought so tasteful and effective now seemed gaudy and tasteless.

The Christmas tree in the corner had become oppressive. The dropped needles around the base created a dusky pattern on the cream carpet, the angel on the top had fallen drunkenly to her side, desperate to be rescued and reinstated on the pinnacle. Gillian switched on the fairy lights but their sparkle was lost on her. Pale berries remained on the mistletoe wreath. Kisses had not been plentiful. As usual, having been brought up in the Christian tradition the red holly berries reminded her of blood drops from the crown of thorns. She knew that the Druids believed that holly represented fertility. The humour was not lost on her as she fingered the stiff leaves. There were no children in this house but the child of her husband had claimed him from her.

Gillian felt wretched. She wanted to scream but seemed to have no voice. She felt she was being strangled and her breath was shallow like her life. She was lonely and feared being alone. The busy school life was a mere façade. She covered up her true feelings. Steve had entered her life at a low point. She had been vulnerable and needy or she might have fought the need that had led her to desire him and try to own him, but now she felt it was all a sham and really he inevitably belonged to Abigail and Alex.

She had pretended and here was the manifestation of that pretence. She felt hollow inside. He had made lifelong vows to Abigail. She could not escape that. They had made commitments. They belonged to each other and Alex was a product of their relationship. Gillian thought they would have stayed together if she had not presented him with the allure of a different life. She felt the guilt.

She could only despise herself for all her weakness or for not rising above the situation.

Her mother had made clear the importance of the matrimonial promise in a conversation she had accidentally overheard when she was a young teenager. Her mother had been sympathising with a cousin who had been unhappy with her lot.

"It is hard," Gillian's mother had sympathised, "but you are not alone you know. Women have to bear the brunt of a marriage and if they are clever and wise they can handle any situation. You need to take a step back. He is not a bad man but all men can be stupid and selfish so you have to flatter him, allow him some freedoms and then choose what you can control and how you can influence. A broken marriage is the worst of all outcomes for you. You must hang in there and you have family and friends to help you. You will not survive alone. Do not abandon your responsibilities. Do not shame your family with divorce."

The young Gillian had witnessed the friction between the couple and had seen how her cousin had strived to survive the situation. Gillian wondered why Mary had married him in the first place but she also remembered the excitement of being a seven year old bridesmaid and the way everyone showered the couple with congratulations and good will. It was scenes like this that had encouraged her belief in true everlasting love and then the scene with her mother and cousin that had shattered that illusion.

Gillian wanted true love. She did not realise that real love had its flaws.

Diana slipped into Gillian's consciousness. She wondered what had happened to her and the baby Louise who would now be grown up and possibly with a family of her own. The image caused a storm of tears, hot in her passion, cold in their touch.

What would have been Gillian's reaction if she had known that Diana had returned to Midchester with her family and had been hoping to reconnect with her? What would Gillian have thought to discover the baby, as a young woman had come looking for Diana? Even worse with all the love Gillian had to give, what would have been her despair to learn of Diana's rejection of the girl?

The two women had lived so close in many ways, born in the same town, although from different backgrounds, colliding briefly at school to share a fundamental human need that had encouraged a deep bond, separating in their situations of adulthood and currently living a mere stone's throw from the other. Furthermore, Steve was a client of Diana's husband and moreover had previously had an even closer association with his wife. Diana too had confronted Abigail, Steve's ex-wife and formed opinions regarding her and her son. Yet the two women had remained apart, in their own worlds oblivious to the other and for the time being out of reach.

If Steve had returned at that moment, then Gillian would not have been responsible for her actions. She would have railed at him and hit him and probably forfeited her marriage. Much, much later, she had wondered if that would have exploded the myth forever and left her with more dignity.

Somehow, she was glad that Steve had gone and she was alone with her thoughts and feelings. Inside her, the little black spiders crawled, confining the very essence of her, creating thin layers of silvery webs around her very being, enclosing her in their soft, silky strands. Her mind rebelled and tried to assert dominance, but the little spiders would not be suppressed and would constantly weave. She knew she must assert herself. She knew she had much for which to be grateful. She knew that people thought she was fortunate but somehow lately her feelings had betrayed her more and more.

There was irreverence in the emotion she felt. She did not recognise it. She did not acknowledge it. She did not want it. It cast a shadow, sometimes deep and purple but often the merest fleck passing over to mar the moment. Today she felt her shortcomings. Desperately on this new day as it melted into the afternoon and a new century she wanted some little sign, some little gesture that would begin to cast a light into the grey shade and impact those little black spiders that crawled around inside her.

By the time Steve returned they had both quelled any emotional response. Steve by then was physically exhausted as well as emotionally drained and Gillian had compressed her feelings into a little tight ball. They agreed to leave any discussion to the next day and settled before the television. Gillian put the cold salmon and salads on the coffee table to pick at as they viewed.

Although they shared the settee there was an intangible distance between them that was soon further confirmed when Steve fell asleep even before finishing the glass of Chablis she had poured for him. She shook him encouraging him to go to bed and rest leaving her to clear away and sit in the darkened room alone.

Chapter 15
Win Some, Lose Some

The Moving Finger writes; and, having, writ,
Moves on: nor all thy Piety nor Wit
Shall lure it back to cancel half a Line,
Nor all thy Tears wash out a Word of it

Omar Khayyam

2001: Steve and Simon

The function room at the hotel was beginning to fill with a steady flow of interested parties. Tables had been pushed to the edges of the room. The one nearest the entrance had piles of pamphlets neatly arranged, flanked by advertising easels with bright displays. Suited receptionists compiled names of attendees who registered interest and then were given the appropriate literature.

Chairs elegant with their arched cream backs and soft blue upholstered seats, normally used for diners at smart celebrations, had been arranged in spacious rows and small knots of people were availing themselves of them as they alternately chatted and perused the documentation in their hands. There was always an air of anticipation before a property auction.

Steve had arrived in good time, picking up the folder for his focus properties before purchasing a coffee and choosing a spot from which to observe the auction and make his bid. He had ventured further afield to Marketborough for this auction because his interest had been piqued by the derelict properties he had seen.

Usually, his property purchases were restricted to his immediate neighbourhood. It was advantageous not to have to travel far for renovations. This could be time consuming and costly, plus he had his small army of tradesmen and suppliers to call on when required. Steve could fill all his days with carpentry work and indeed, earn a good living by doing so but his real thrill was in taking a property and transforming it from a run-down neglected shell to an eye catching modern dwelling. He loved design.

As a property developer, he would have been far more successful financially if he had efficiently restored the place for minimum cost giving a smart look and moved on to his next project but Steve sought perfection and his own satisfaction was at stake so inevitably he spent time and effort to bring originality and panache to any project. Therefore, Steve could not afford to be a property magnate. He would have to be content with more minor and intermittently spaced developments.

The small cottages were exactly what excited Steve. They were a pair of farm workers cottages, detached from each other by a narrow strip of land. They had gradually been swallowed up by the growth of suburbia. They had been completely neglected as apparently there had been protracted legal wrangling regarding ownership but now it had become important to dispose of them quickly.

Steve had taken Gillian to see them the previous week.

Gillian trod with care over the broken wicket gate crunching rotting wood and stepped gingerly through the portico entrance. She saw nothing but debris and dust. The front room was tiny, made even more so by a large featureless brick grate probably introduced in the seventies stretching across one wall which had at some point supported a television judging by the mess of cables.

There were great gouges in the plasterwork and a dated brown light cord hung from the ceiling. There was no inner door to speak off, it had been battered down and lay defeated on the floor. Steve pushed forward eagerly into a larger second room clearly a more established living area judging from the grimy flocked wallpaper in places hanging in tendrils. Some wallpaper curls lay on the floor like the cut ends of locks of hair on a hairdresser's floor. There were some wooden cupboards, again decrepit and unsightly.

Gillian's eye caught the dark stains of mould that also feathered the walls and ceiling. Gillian was repulsed by the dank smell which crept nauseatingly into her nostrils and that, coupled with the dust, made her sneeze. She had really seen enough and conscious of the odours permeating her clothes said she would wait outside. Steve had already advanced and looking back from the rear room his face crumbled.

"I know, it's not your thing Gill but look it has such possibilities. Let me show you."

Men have such a way of carrying you along with their fervour she thought and we women can't help but respond to their appeals as if they are little boys at Christmas. She smiled and plodded forward. There had been a space between them since the Millennium over a year before. The consequence had been a no-man's land and neither could venture into the area. Each was on the defensive fearing the ramifications of an attack by the other and clinging to their positions. Neither had wanted to relinquish ground. They had become stuck in the gooey mud of hurt. Gillian had felt aggrieved that even his explanation did not seem to choose her and Steve could not rouse his wife to move on and leave it behind. They were not the kind of people to have an explosive row. Life became a waiting game with small detonations as warning shots. Gillian became more absorbed in her school work allowing that to take the brunt of her feelings while Steve lost himself in plotting the next assault on the property front. Both hoped somehow things would get better. Meanwhile, it was a small war of attrition.

To her there was very little to see but Steve was in his element. He explained his thoughts for joining the rooms and adding a conservatory. The bathroom tucked away at the rear could, he said, be relocated upstairs and the existing cupboard of a bathroom incorporated into the rear scullery room to make a dining kitchen and if they could add a garden room or conservatory then it would be a stunning transformation.

'Better still,' he had said, and she could see him trying to curb his enthusiasm so she would not reject the idea altogether, 'a small extension could support extra space upstairs, invaluable he said for selling a property like this.'

She could, through his eyes, begin to see the recreation by taking out the oppressive brick surround of the front room and joining the two rooms into a more spacious and versatile living area and then the grand designs for the rear room. He assured her that he would keep the essence of the place. Gillian knew that Steve always treated any renovation sympathetically and indeed, sometimes projects became restorations at increased costs. She would never fault him for that.

There were two cottages and Steve knew he could not afford both which he would have dearly loved. He would take whichever but he needed to convince Gillian. His mortgage adviser had said that there would be limited loans available and it would take time to put any in place. He would need twenty percent deposit on auction day if he was successful, the terms of the auction required full payment within twenty-eight days. His last house had only netted him thirty thousand.

This house could go for a song but it was worth he thought seventy and even a bit more at a stretch. To buy one he would need to borrow from their joint savings and if possible the last of the inheritance that Gillian kept tucked away for a rainy day. He had one week before the auction to convince his wife.

Gillian had said nothing after the visit. They had gone into the town and found a smart café for lunch not far from the football ground. Steve had followed the team when he was young but he was more a cricket and rugby fan, although not actively these days, only viewing important games on the television when he was able. The town showed prosperity. There was enough retail therapy for Gillian in the afternoon with little independent shops and bigger stores. Steve was happy to tag along absorbed as he was with the project. Gillian enjoyed fashion and spent a happy hour or so ferreting through the rails and trying on choices. At almost fifty, she still had a trim figure and her dark features meant she had a wide range of suitable clothes from which to pick. Steve encouraged her to be daring but she was as ever mindful of cost and tended to buy with her job in mind. That day she was happy to make one or two successful purchases. That self-indulgence tended to make her feel guilty.

Steve brought up the topic the next evening. "The auction is next week. I will go and see what they fetch."

"Mmmm," she said. She was not going to be drawn.

"I reckon if the purchase price was about seventy and then a spend on renovation of about fifty each cottage would sell for say for at least one sixty, probably a lot more in that area. It would be a good investment in anybody's money." He leaned towards her.

You have to put money up front at auction, don't you?" Gillian reached for a tendril of hair and twisted it in her finger.

"Yes, and that's why you can get a bargain. Most people can't do that. Of course, there might be builders who might be interested and put the price up. They would probably want to knock them down and do a new build. I think that would be a shame, don't you?" He could not hide his interest.

"I suppose it would." Gillian as ever was non-committal while inside she felt her nerves flutter.

She looked at him and could feel the adrenalin pumping through his veins.

"I've got the twenty percent for the day Gill but if I bought one I would need some cash to complete. Of course, anything would go right back into the pot when I sold." He did not see any risk, confident of the outcome while she felt like a rabbit caught in headlights.

Gillian did not know how to respond. Their relationship seemed at stake and one false move could jeopardise it but she was not brave. She had known he would want to do this and almost her purchases the previous day had been in defiance of the prospective outlay. It frightened her not to have hard cash in the bank.

"I am keen, Gill." He said gently, "I would not go ahead without you."

Gillian felt the weight of his dreams.

"Steve, it's a long way away. How will you manage, back and forth and you really ought to be beginning to take it easier and consolidate, not take on daunting challenges that will take time away from your day job. I thought your accountant said something about investing more in a pension," Gillian felt the guilt for throwing cold water on the scheme.

Steve began to look crestfallen before rallying, "Are you implying I am past it? You didn't say that last night." He smiled engagingly before adding boastfully. "I'm a man in my prime. I can prove it anytime."

Gillian relieved from his teasing laughed.

There were little skirmishes during the week but no resolution. Gillian would never say no absolutely. It was not in her nature. Steve tried different tactics and did his homework. He visited the planning office and discovered that despite the state of the cottages there was no appetite to see them demolished. Steve was happy that the smash and grab builders would leave the project alone. He was convinced that they would go cheaply. The cottages had reserve figures of forty and thirty five thousand, respectively but he knew they would exceed this figure.

"I'd never let you down," he had cajoled and she demurred remembering how let down she had felt at that New Year. She knew he did not mean like this but the feelings that she had suppressed were even sharper over a year later. Fleetingly, she thought of Abigail, still living in the house she had shared with Steve, rent free, still claiming his patronage while she was called upon to serve his requirements. Gillian had long ago accepted the situation putting the justice of it to the back of her mind. She wanted to feel important and that she mattered but it was inherent within her to comply. To shake the structure of their marriage was a risk she was not prepared to take. She feared that the foundations would give way. Deep down, she trusted him.

Gillian had been busy as usual. March was always a difficult month with coursework to be finalised and moderated, predicted grades discussed and entered plus the extra lessons offered to struggling students at one end of the scale and high fliers at the other to ensure their optimum grades.

Each year, the pressure was mounting, although Gillian had not succumbed as other staff had. Her determination and meticulous planning had always seen her through. However, her single-mindedness did make conversation about the cottage difficult so somehow the day of the auction dawned and she realised her silence was giving tacit agreement. She hoped someone would bid well over the odds so she could sympathise with Steve on his return while assuaging her fears of over commitment.

During the afternoon her mind wandered from Cordelia's relationship with Lear in her sixth form lesson and Scout's relationship with Atticus with her year eleven. Her worksheets were exemplary. She needed them to be while her mind was so diverted.

Steve watched the crowd grow in the function room. He recognised one or two big players but he knew they were after some larger properties that could be turned into flats and there were a couple of nice building plots for detached houses. As auctions go there were not many attendees so again Steve felt elated. He tried to assess the opposition.

The cottages were lots six and seven and having seen the earlier properties go he assessed that there would be very little in the way of counter bids. He tried to relax but tension grabbed him. He had been to many auctions so he knew the form. He could be cold and calculating in mind but his emotion betrayed that level headedness particularly if he had a particular penchant for a property.

Steve never made an early bid, biding his time and judging the capability of other bidders. The first cottage had a slow start. The prime mover was a guy sitting with an older man three rows in front of him so he could only make a judgement from his back. He looked about thirty and sat alert. He was dressed in a tee shirt that pulled against strong muscles. Steve had never seen him before so presumed he was bidding for personal motivation maybe on behalf of the older guy who was displaying signs of anxiety by his fidgeting hands.

There was a lull and the auctioneer surveyed the scene ready to bring down the gavel when Steve seized his opportunity hoping to get the place at a rock bottom price. "Sixty," his bid was registered. The guy nearer the front took up the challenge and Steve found himself in a bidding war. The sums steadily increased and Steve realised his limit was fast approaching. He felt the quiet stillness of the room, the little glances as other attendees watched for the outcome.

The bids were made leisurely and quietly, belying the intensity and pressure. Steve pushed his limit. He had now bid seventy five and a few minutes later eighty. He knew he was being foolhardy but he kept pushing curious to see how far the younger man would go and fired up by the passion of his desire.

At ninety, he suddenly saw Gillian in his mind's eye. He knew he was in unfamiliar territory. He had never been carried away before and he felt the beginning of nausea. He began to panic. His bid rested in the hands of the auctioneer. He could see the gavel poised. Little beads of sweat gathered on his forehead. He kept his face as impassive as he could. The seconds stretched before him.

"Ninety-two."

Steve stared straight ahead. Had he heard correctly? The auctioneer looked across at him for a response. Steve managed to shake his head. The cottage was not to be his.

The auctioneer concluded the sale and opened the bidding on the second cottage. Steve entered the fray at an earlier point. He had already shown his hand with the previous cottage. He thought his voice shook slightly as he became involved but there was little opposition and he concluded the purchase at sixty-five thousand. He was ecstatic.

The second cottage did not have quite the same scope as the first and he would have to rethink his design ideas but he was more than confident he could turn it round. He had been lucky. Ninety-two thousand, Steve thought, was excessive and relieved that he had not been so foolhardy to continue with the bids and wondered about the purchaser. He knew he had had a lucky escape which subdued his elation.

He did not meet the purchaser of the other cottage until several weeks later when he visited his cottage to take internal measurements. There had been some cosmetic improvements to the other cottage. The fence and gate had been fixed and an attempt had been made to calm the outdoor space. The older man was cutting back the mini wilderness at the side, carefully leaving any nesting habitation. He clearly knew what he was doing.

As he left Steve nodded to the man who was taking a break. He had been joined by the younger man who was pouring a hot drink from a Thermos.

"You're the blighter who got me to pay too much at the auction," the younger man shouted across.

"Name of the game," Simon retorted and then more placatory, "You got the best cottage though. You can do a lot with that one."

The man looked across with interest. "I'll swap you for the price."

Steve would not be drawn.

"You a builder?" He asked Steve.

"I enjoy renovating property. I'm a carpenter by trade. What about you?" Steve was well aware he was a novice regarding building.

"I'm in security I suppose."

Steve sauntered across and introduced himself discovering Bill was Simon's father. It was always preferable to get on with neighbours. It led to less hassle in the end and Steve was a conciliatory guy.

He learnt that Simon had left the army the year before and had taken a job in a security firm fitting alarms and other devices. Steve recognised the enthusiasm the younger man had to make his mark and the appeal for property renovation. He was reminded of a younger self. Steve asked him about his plans.

Simon was vague in his proposals and hesitant in his delivery. There were lots of "I might," and "Maybe," and of course, "If." Simon was clearly wary of knocking through so he was banking on clearing up, re-plastering, hopefully dealing with damp issues in the process and giving the whole a makeover. Steve was disappointed and began telling him of his vision. By the end of the discussion, the two men had agreed to meet further and discuss the possibility of working together.

Simon recognised the value of a skilled man like Steve. He was happy to do the physical work but he was realising he had bitten off more than he could chew. This guy could be an asset. Each man through their different life experiences were good judges of character and this early meeting prompted a co-operation that was to last many years.

Simon was a quick learner and Steve a knowledgeable teacher. Steve knew about such things as building regulations and planning laws. Simon lived relatively close to the cottages so would supervise arrivals and departures of trades people and the numerous skips they needed to clear the properties.

Simon's security work hours seemed to be flexible. Steve had the connections and the vision.

Steve had never been so happy in his work. It was good to have a younger man at his back. Simon felt in those early days it was an unequal partnership as it was Steve who gradually asserted his expertise with Simon following his guidance. They worked in tandem timing the employment of trades for both sites which helped costing. It would not have worked if each man had not been fundamentally honest.

The cottages occupied Steve most of that summer. He would leave home early and arrive home late, travelling when the traffic on the roads was light, making sure he visited and, more often than not, worked on the project every day but still trying to fit this in with his bread and butter work. He reasoned that Gillian would be absorbed in her examination marking and was quite self-sufficient, a quality he had found attractive when they had first met after the cloying Abigail.

He did not really understand that Gillian had had years in this vein living with her parents and as her parents aged having to be more and more independent. There were times she would have liked someone to lean on and take care of her in the fashion of fairy tales even though she valued the equality of their marriage. She felt such thoughts were rather perverse.

It seemed Bill had a nursery not far from the cottages. Simon and Steve would migrate there if they wanted a place to sit, drink tea and spread plans out on the pine table to cogitate in the sunshine. Bill enjoyed their company too and in between customers would sit and chat. The nursery extended five acres on the slopes of the river valley. It was an attractive spot. It was clear that Bill did the lion's share of the work with his wife helping with planting and occasionally sales. He would call on extra support when necessary, with his daughters providing some back-up in between child care and part time jobs but it was clear to Steve that the business was more of a hobby than a profit making concern. Not all the site was used effectively, especially towards the river. Bill did what he could or rather what he wanted to do. His needs were modest. Simon released from the high octave army life found it difficult to contain his impatience, although Steve saw the deep regard father and son had for the other.

The peace of the nursery prompted Steve to reflect on his own life. He knew he was content. There had never been ambition in a worldly sense but he did have determination and a desire for accomplishment. He saw achievement in a job well done, a satisfied customer and a sense of making things better. He wanted to leave his mark on the world around him. He did not want that world to be poorer from his presence. He had seen how greed could corrupt and spoil. He was proud too of Gillian. She was making a difference. She cared about her students. She cared about the standard of her work. He decided to take something home for her. Bill took him over to the pots of roses.

"You can't go wrong with a good rose," he said. Steve was ready to be guided. "If you want a good strong grower with lovely coral blooms and a strong scent, I'd take this one, Fragrant Cloud. It's been a favourite for years. Put it in a sunny spot and it should do well. It's getting a bit late for planting but this one is pot grown so should be fine. If not, I'll replace it and you can plant in the autumn or better still early next spring."

Steve agreed and reached in his pocket for the cash noting the price ticket.

"No. I don't need that."

"You'll never make a fortune if you don't charge."

"You've given my lad much more than the cost of this rose. Give it to your lady wife and bring her over to see me sometime." Bill thrust the pot into Steve's arms.

"Thanks Bill. I don't know what to say."

"Nothing. You've earned it. I don't know what mess Simon would have got into without you."

Steve took the rose for him symbolic of a good life, a life where people cared and co-operated and shared common principles. Steve was genuinely touched not only with the rose but from Bill's comment. There had not been many compliments in his life.

Gillian was delighted and chose a spot in the front garden outside the study window where she would be able to have this emblem of summer in her sight as she wrestled with papers. Steve planted the rose. They shared a glass of Chablis in honour of the occasion as though the lost Millennium had been found.

The cottages proved to be a successful venture in every respect. They sold for a tidy profit so at the end of the summer Steve was able to replenish the savings pot much to Gillian's relief. While Steve's cottage seemed to make more profit calculated on the initial auction purchase he had spent more time on both cottages neglecting his own income so in the end things were more even. Both men were pleased and decided to look for joint ventures in the future. Neither wanted to form a partnership but each could see advantages in co-operation leaving the freedom for independent work when it suited. The association proved profitable in other ways. They enjoyed working together. For Steve, having worked on his own for many years, it proved to be a welcome change to have company as well as someone to provide muscle and give back up in organisation. Simon soon admired Steve for his skills and his approach. Neither man suffered fools gladly. What had started out as practical co-operation, built to become a strong friendship over the next few years.

Gillian did visit Bill at his nursery. She was treated as an honoured guest. Like Steve she found the place relaxing. There seemed to be a harmony there, particularly between man and nature. It was such a pity it took almost an hour to get there. She found Bill's wife a departure from her usual crowd. Anthea was a practical, no-nonsense woman who took life as it came. She and Bill would dovetail perfectly but they would bicker and jostle in their day to day confrontations.

Gillian's natural humility and reserve was not affronted by the woman's mettle rather she enjoyed her warmth. Anthea was used to directing her family and she recognised in Gillian a repressed spirit who needed her ebullience to bring out her personality. Anthea thought that Gillian had too often taken a back seat and too often allowed others to bully her albeit in a mild way. She noticed Gillian's deference to Steve, the way she avoided confrontation of any sort, the sensitive response to any personal slight whether intended or not and yet also she saw strength in the way she supported her husband and the way she spoke of her teaching. The older woman became a friend just as her son had become a friend of Steve.

Anthea had a knack of getting to the truth. Her children had learnt this sometimes to their cost over the years. It was no good faking illness to get a day off from school or trying to cover up a misdemeanour. She had a sharp brain and a sharp tongue to go with it. She had had a hard start in life, one of nine children from a back street in Liverpool. Her dad was as often out of work as in work and the family had lurched from one crisis to the next. She had learnt to be tough and she had learnt how to assert herself.

She had left home at fifteen, at first living with an older married sibling and then getting a room in a boarding house to give her sister space for her growing family. Her people were proud and resilient. They seemed to have an unwritten code on survival. They adjusted to circumstance. Some of her neighbours fell by the wayside as was inevitable but she had felt the heart of Liverpool that was strong at the time when Anthea was growing up.

Liverpool was emerging from its war wearied streets and its heart was beginning to beat insistently to other tunes. There had been a clamour for noise, for deeds, for life and Anthea made sure she danced to that rhythm.

She had been young when she married Bill and he had whisked her south where she danced to a much mellower tune but she never completely left the throbbing city behind returning periodically to be reunited with her siblings and be swept along to dance at their wild parties or sing a sentimental tune. She could be brash and excitable but also tender and compassionate.

Many would say, she had experienced a cruel beginning to life living in poverty. They would say she had been deprived. Anthea thought differently. Her early life had been full of laughter and hope. At times they were hungry but a good dish of scouse or corned beef hash could fill their bellies and then all was right with their world. Their needs were small but their ambitions were big and the children took jobs as soon as they were able. They were adaptable and not work shy, not like some of the slovenly families in the area.

Anthea and her siblings built a better future, although they never left their origins. Each of them, even living as far as Australia and America, were 'scousers' at their core. They might have trodden different paths, but forever they would be drawn back to where they had started. This gave Anthea her inner steel. She could trust life. It did not scare her as it seemed to scare Gillian.

They did not see each other often. Gillian was always too busy but they bonded. When they met, there was no polite preamble. Conversations got to the heart of the matter.

Gillian was drawn to the family. There was no embarrassment in witnessing Bill and Anthea squabbling and scoring points in silly arguments. There was never any heat in the exchanges. It was understood that each was playing a part in a long running drama. There was nothing to prove. No-one held back in opinions and no-one took personal offence.

Simon would badger his parents about the goldmine he saw in the nursery land and his parents would tell him he could wait until they were pushing up daisies before he'd get his hands on it. Then Simon would set to and help his dad with some heavy digging as though nothing had been said.

Simon and Steve settled into a routine. They each pursued their own employment and took on one or even two projects most years. Occasionally if it suited, Steve would do an independent renovation. Gillian liked Simon and wondered why he was still single in his mid-thirties and living with his parents. From time to time, she had nudged him in the direction of someone she thought suitable but he never took the bait. She spoke with Anthea one spring day, a couple of years after first meeting her.

"I hated going on my own to things," Gillian confided, "of course, I would put on a front but the worst places were people's homes where I made it an odd number. I felt conspicuous, made even worse by the attention of all the married men. The wives never really showed they minded but I always knew they did."

"It's different for a bloke," said Anthea. "I don't think Simon is at all bothered right now. He has never mentioned any women in his life. Bill tells me he's the type to fall suddenly head over heels. I don't know. I have the feeling he might have met someone a while ago but it did not work out. He wouldn't say of course, and we wouldn't ask. It's just my intuition. He can be a bit shifty when I say something. Perhaps you and Steve can find out. It would be nice to see him settled like his sisters."

Gillian doubted she would learn anything and she knew Steve would never have this conversation unless prodded. She agreed that having someone special in your life was an ideal and she wished she had met Steve earlier and maybe they might have had a family of their own. She spoke about this to Anthea who had more sense than to commiserate. Gillian had missed her opportunity and it would not do any good to ignore the fact or to try to smooth things over with platitudes.

"It's a crying shame. You would have made a brilliant mum. Did you try when you first got together? I know, you were a bit old but not impossible."

"I was forty four when we married. Of course, we got together when I was forty one but we had to wait for the divorce to come through."

"If only you'd been a bit more reckless." Anthea gave her a sideways look. With a shock Gillian realised she was serious.

Gillian thought about this but it would have been absurd. "Well, of course, Steve had Alex and I had my dad and then there was my job. I could not turn up at my age as a single mother to be. What would everyone have said?" Gillian felt she had summarised the position which dismissed the notion but Anthea had more to say.

"I'm sure you could have coped and you might have been surprised about other people. Not sure you can count Alex from what I hear," retorted Anthea.

"Only met him once or twice but I'm not impressed. Don't want to offend you but I've not heard much to make me think differently. Not very much like Steve, is he?"

Gillian felt torn. She completely agreed but felt disloyal to admit it.

"I'm not getting at you love but you need to face facts and decide what makes you happy. Best thing is to move on and enjoy what you have now. Have some fun. You seemed to miss a lot of that when you were younger."

"Trouble is, Anthea, I don't think I know how." Gillian had found a truth.

"Well, you learn and learn quickly or life will be gone. Don't let there be any more wasted opportunities and for goodness sake stop trying to please everyone else and forgetting yourself in the process. You are not the queen having to do your duty at the expense of your true feelings. Steve is a nice guy but he is lucky to have you. Don't forget it."

The years slipped away. Work at the nursery became easier when Bill took on a young school leaver at the recommendation of a friend Jim Woodhouse. Jim had been groundsman at the football and if he endorsed the lad he was prepared to give it a go. Jake fitted in perfectly. He was a hard worker and eager to learn, although did not come without skills and knowledge gained from helping Jim. He attended college two days a week so wages could be found, especially as it meant Anthea could take a step back and once Jake found his feet, Bill could take an afternoon off to go out with his wife.

Simon liked to see his parents having more time and he found Jake an asset sometimes offering him extra work labouring on property renovation. Gillian could not but think she had gained a surrogate family.

Chapter 16
Find the Lady

All the world's a stage,
And all the men and women merely players:
They have their exits and their entrances

Jaque's Seven Ages of Man: William Shakespeare

2006: Diana and Kirsten

Both Steve and Simon were practical people and while each of them made a valiant attempt to keep track of paperwork it became almost impossible to manage after a day of labour and juggling their day to day work. Trades people they employed were not always efficient regarding invoices and sometimes it was difficult to separate out costs and profits. Incidental expenses could easily be overlooked as well as the way cash payments were occasionally made. The fact that they might collaborate on a time to time basis was also a hindrance to organisational matters.

The pressures, at times could make them neglectful of accounting and this was particularly true for Simon who was new to it all. Steve up until the liaison had managed to keep a reasonable record enough for Antony his accountant to make sense of it all but they both realised they were wasting a lot of valuable time trying to work out the divisions of financial input and of course, output.

It was to their credit, that their association survived what would have been a bone of contention to many others. After some four years or so of joint enterprises it was time to regularise things and to do that they took the advice of Antony Carstairs Steve's accountant. Steve had first used him ten years before when his previous accountant had retired and had been impressed with Antony, who had helped him through the treacherous waters of divorce.

Neither of them wanted a legal partnership to make them interdependent as both men wanted scope for personal projects. Antony discussed the implications of taxation, and V.A.T. Steve had always made V.A.T. returns but Simon had not registered. He was an employee at the security firm and any property projects were additional to that. He was unsure about having an independent business. He said he had seen the worry all this brought to his parents at the nursery. After several meetings they decided that any project would be officially in Steve's name and thus all accounts would be kept by him, overseen by Antony who would arrange for the profit share. Antony would act for both of them for a modest fee in the capacity of a financial manager. They would meet regularly to review matters.

"Fancy a beer," Simon asked Steve after one of these meeting. "I need it after that."

"Why not? I think Gillian has a meeting tonight anyway so it's an empty house."

"That accountant is pretty impressive isn't he? I could not understand half of what he was saying."

"I think he will look after us alright. He's what we need if we are to move on to bigger things. I think he is right that we need a separate bank account for projects. It has all been difficult to track and I don't feel some of it has been fair on Gillian when she tries to help me unravel things. A completely separate pot will help stop the muddle." It had been a satisfying meeting.

Simon agreed relieved that their future was much more assured. "Having a man like Antony supervising things will keep it business-like. I know I don't keep my personal money and property money separate now. In fact, I sometimes wonder if I support the project or the project supports me. I really hate the paperwork. It would all be so much easier if I could just go and do the job and that's all," admitted Simon.

Steve had to acknowledge that there were times in the past when he had allowed things to blur. He knew Antony would keep them on the straight and narrow.

Antony had enjoyed meeting Simon. He always looked forward to seeing Steve and at first had been worried that taking on someone who was essentially a partner might not be in Steve's best interest. He could see the camaraderie between the two of them and the deference Simon showed Steve in business matters. Antony would keep a close eye on their accounts and make sure he spotted any danger points. The loose arrangement was not usually to be recommended but in this case as there were such few projects and it was not the main source of income for either of them he thought it would work. He was even tempted to invest a little into a project. He liked his job because he liked order but it might be quite exciting to become part of a different type of enterprise occasionally. He thought Diana would agree, especially if she could make one or two suggestions for interior design. As he left his office he smiled to himself at the prospect. It could be fun. He should introduce Steve and Simon to Diana.

Diana was quite aware of Steve after her uncomfortable meeting with Abigail when Kirsten was at university. Later she had used the opportunity when in the office to dip into the files and learn what she could about him. She found his address, determined to avoid the area in her day to day life. In her view he had done well and there was evidence of hard work and enterprise.

The marriage to Abigail seemed to have been a constant drain but his present marriage to a teacher seemed the opposite and she had noted the presence of Simon periodically in his file. His son, Alex, did not figure in his financial life. Steve apparently did not live a complicated life. There were a few shares and he had a couple of ISA's plus a modest pension pot.

It all told the story of a dependable and sensible man who from time to time had a fling with a renovation, nothing big but definitely bigger and more profitable more recently. She wondered how far Abigail might have been a millstone for the majority of his working life. She would have liked to know much more but reluctantly closed the file.

Kirsten was due to visit at the weekend. Diana relished these visits and spent the preceding days considering and buying food to indulge her daughter and making sure her room was spotless. Kirsten was an easy going daughter and it was almost because of this that Diana gave her these attentions to spoil her eldest child. Samantha's visits on the other hand produced comments such as, "That shade does not really go in here does it?" About the new cushions.

"I thought you were going to have your kitchen units painted. They're getting a bit dingy and it's not a fashionable look is it?"

"Oh Mum you are not cooking a roast. I thought I had told you I need to lose a few pounds and not put them on. You're not being helpful are you?" She would gently scold.

Diana knew exactly where these traits came from and would cringe as she remembered, as well as feeling tense from the visit. She knew Samantha adored coming home and feeding off her parents with their attentions which made her visits frequent and, although delightful as they were to Antony and Diana, the experience could at times be exhausting.

Kirsten, with her quiet appreciative manner offered balm on her visits. Phillip their youngest came home when he could to sleep after busy shifts in the A and E department as a junior doctor.

The weekend in question was intriguing on two counts. Kirsten had said she wanted to discuss something important and she wanted to go out for dinner to introduce them to someone. Diana was a flutter with excitement and even cool headed Antony was on edge. He postponed talking to Diana about investing in Steve, guessing they might have another investment to make before too long.

Kirsten drove down from Manchester on a cool summer day. She had taken a couple of days off so she would not have to rush to her parents and she could avoid the rush hour which would have meant hours of queues even to leave the city. She had enjoyed city life more than she had expected. There was a buzz everywhere and an energy that injected pace and urgency to life. It could be exhilarating.

However, as she travelled south and the countryside opened up beside the motorway she felt she could breathe more deeply and fully. The landscape of neat farms and summer grass fields edged with verdant hedgerows sped past her. She anticipated arriving at the small market town of home and the sanctuary it afforded her. She was perennially grateful to have this luxury.

Her parent's house stood just below the town square in a discreet side street that made its downward curve to the river. The house was elegant. It had been built for a prosperous merchant at the beginning of Victoria's reign but had a regency feel about its structure. It was a balanced house similar to a child's square drawing of a house with a central entrance and five large square windows, a generous window either side of the door and three further windows positioned above those on the lower floor and a middle one over the door. There were two smaller windows above neatly placed under the eaves.

There was a satisfying symmetry to the house which appealed to Kirsten's mathematical brain. The crescent driveway reached between a hedge of copper beech, which formed the straight line to its arc, each end marked by classical Doric style pillars. The central point of the semi-circle brushed against the wide commanding steps to the house. Tucked to the sides was room for three or four cars. Rhododendron bushes in full bloom further flanked the drive. Coming home for Kirsten brought peace and order.

"Well, what is so important?" Diana could not contain her curiosity. She had waited until they had eaten and sat with coffee looking through the enormous panes of glass that made up the patio doors out onto the patio and beyond it the cultured small garden.

"I've been offered a promotion." Kirsten was nonplussed in her declaration.

"That's brilliant, darling," although Diana could not help feel disappointed. She had expected a different announcement.

"Yes, it is a brilliant opportunity and there would be a good pay increase. I would be managing a small team and it would be my head on the block if things went wrong." Kirsten still seemed restrained.

"You don't sound wildly enthused." Antony commented.

"I'm not Dad and that's the point. I should be, I know."

"Does it worry you?" Antony continued. "I am sure you are more than capable. These things can seem daunting but it is surprising how quickly you can settle into the new responsibilities."

"It's not that. Actually, I would be thrilled and excited by it. No it's more fundamental than that. It's a great company to work for with lots going on and I have learnt a lot. Thing is I've realised I am not at heart a city girl. If I took this, I feel I will never escape and I really want to come back here. If you could contemplate it, I would like to work with you, Dad." Kirsten seemed to hold her breath.

"I thought you were well settled and happy," Diana asked. She hated any of her children to feel unhappy feeling it was a personal insult.

"Yes, I am, Mum. It's been great and I am so pleased you both persuaded me to go and I could be content to stay if that's for the best but in my heart I dream of coming here and being your partner, Dad."

Antony felt he could burst but knew he should remain nonplussed. There were issues to discuss.

"I won't deny the practice has been growing steadily and I do need to take someone on soon but there aren't the wages you are used to Kirsten and actually you would be over-qualified."

"Dad you always told me I could never be over-qualified," and she laughed before adding, "So it's a no, then."

"Not at all. It's me looking at all angles, something I would expect any partner of mine to do." He winked at her. "Tell you what let's go to the office in the morning and I can show you what's what. You don't want to make any rash decisions."

Kirsten hugged him and kissed her mother.

Another coffee poured and Diana ventured, "I've booked Benedicto's for tomorrow night. I hope that will suit. Are you going to tell us about the fourth diner?" Diana tried to be nonchalant but the quickness to her question betrayed her.

"It's someone I knew at university. He's a couple of years older than me so he left when I started my second year. I did not know him very well but then we came across each other at a couple of conferences and then he got in touch and we've been seeing each other. His name is Mark. I hope you will like him." Kirsten unusually was blushing.

"If he's a friend of yours, I am sure we will," interposed Antony.

"Boyfriend you mean," Diana added meaningfully.

They discovered that Mark was in the police and used his skills as a forensic accountant to examine possible frauds. It was a demanding job and he had been involved in some high profile cases. Generally he had worked in London but like Kirsten wanted a more fulfilling life in the country. He had been brought up on a farm and missed the open space and the opportunity for country pursuits. He had said there were too many criminals and with the increasing complexities of their operations he could never seem to break away.

It was clear from the way Kirsten spoke of him that she was fond of him and admired him too. Each parent hoped they would feel the same.

Brown haired and brown eyed Mark proved to be a welcome addition. Kirsten shone which pleased Diana who always knew she was a natural beauty who hid behind a serious face and plain practical dress. Diana liked the chivalry with which he treated Kirsten. Nothing was forced. She found he had natural good manners that he applied to them all. They talked of a range of topics.

Mark was quite open and honest about his job but did not divulge any content. He clearly preferred talking about environmental issues and his sporting interests. Antony was pleased to note he enjoyed cricket rather than football. Ideally he said he would like to settle in a place with land so he could have horses but he would need to change career to do that so he had to be content with the occasional ride when he visited his parents. On this visit Mark was staying with a friend who lived nearby but it became clear that on future visits if Kirsten returned home it was expected that he would stay at her home.

Diana watched her daughter flirt, sometimes outrageously which was completely out of character. She even giggled from time to time. Both Antony and Diana wondered what had happened to their retiring daughter and as they rolled into their own bed agreed it must be love.

Kirsten took up her position at the practice six weeks later. She felt it was a new beginning but one she had strived for in her apprenticeship. She was an asset, although she had a lot to learn, not least about the foibles of her clients. She had been used to a fast paced competitive office mainly dealing with commercial accounts and the wealthier clients but now she had to scrutinise scribbled accounts and make sense of flimsy invoices. She had to curb her impatience at times and realise that many of their customers ran small businesses on a shoestring with little or no education. Some of them she came to admire for their dogged determination in the face of adversity. As her father before her she too became connected to her clients as she became familiar with their circumstances. It meant the accounts were more meaningful and personal. She was no longer dealing with abstract numbers on spreadsheets where she was unaware of consequence. She knew her input mattered and she cared fiercely about the financial well-being of the people who engaged her services.

Coming home on a more permanent basis brought a shift to all participants. Kirsten was quickly swallowed up into her old home and more particularly the office. She and her father would talk endlessly about new financial regulations and their application to clients. Antony should have been able to take more time away from the office leaving Kirsten to take the strain but his enjoyment level was raised considerably by her presence so he became even more involved.

Diana felt left in the cold. She could not join in their discussions because she had not got the knowledge. She still helped in the charity shop with Marjorie and still helped at the office when required as well as play bridge when Antony joined her but she found now that things were settled she needed something more. She had been disappointed that she had not found any leads regarding her daughter but Jackie seemed to have completely disappeared.

As she got to know Mark better she thought she might enlist his help as a police officer but then she remembered her position as potential mother-in-law and decided to keep her dignity. She found herself resorting to shopping but it did not have the appeal of her youth. She felt discontent when she knew she should feel satisfaction. She realised that she operated best when there was a challenge.

Then a year later in 2006, Steve had some news which he shared with Antony and Simon at their regular meeting. He hoped it would make a difference to his financial responsibility and more particularly his peace of mind, especially as Gillian was certain to be made redundant at the end of the summer term. Abigail was to marry. It seemed she had been seeing Alex's employer Clive Corneille. She would be a lady of some repute and wealth.

"It will suit her," said Steve. "I could never give her the life she craved."

Antony assessed the implications. "Will you sell the house? You still have a majority share."

"I am hoping so. It would make a big difference to us but she's said Alex should live there while they are getting settled and sorting things out."

"You know you are really too soft there. You should have some rent at least," Antony pointed out.

"Yes, well, I know, but we are happy and money isn't everything." It seemed a feeble excuse and one that he had so often used to cover up his guilt, especially concerning Gillian.

"You're saying that to an accountant," Antony retorted. They laughed and resumed their exploration of accounts. Simon tended to hold back, confident in the other two. He hoped he could find the happiness that the other men seemed to exude.

Simon had had a number of girlfriends since leaving the army but none had fired his passion. Maybe, he was getting too old to feel as he did as a young man. He should be married with kids, not living with his mum and dad by the nursery. He did have a healthy bank account and could easily move out but he could not see the point when he knew he would be at the nursery helping out whenever he could. He remembered that magical weekend when he had turned twenty-one and on leave from the army and had met her.

She was lovely, fragile, so he immediately wanted to protect her, appealing in her short skirt and 'come hither' look and an old fashioned manner of speaking that separated her from the other girls who were out that weekend. She had been trying too hard showing her lack of experience and a sheltered upbringing. She was even then at almost eighteen in trouble if she was late home so they had made the most of the daylight.

He had singled her out as the other soldiers pursued the other females. She had seemed uncomfortable with the seduction routines and he had been her champion. In the few days of his leave he had extricated himself from the raucous crowd and sought her company, finding her gentle thoughtfulness alluring. There was no glamour in her person but to him she was beautiful with her fair curls and blue eyes. He could drown in their look and by the end of his leave he had.

He had treated her with the utmost respect. It had been conversely both easy and hard, easy because she was perfection, a porcelain doll that must not be broken, and hard because of his carnal desire that leapt unbidden into his loins. He had never felt so confused and so feeble. They walked for miles talking about their lives and their hopes and dreams. They sat beside the gentle flow of the river in silence resting in each other's arms.

Their kisses were sweet and not provoking, that is until the last afternoon. It had been a beautiful day, the sun bright and benign, beaming down on the radiant couple who had sought shelter in the apple grove. He had brought a picnic blanket and she had brought ham sandwiches and a flask of tea. They lay comfortable and relaxed, soaking up the benevolence of the day and each other. It was she that had shifted first disturbing his quiet pleasure and awakening something in his inner soul. She nestled against him and touched his chest through his open shirt her legs resting against his thighs. Automatically, he had reached across and sought her small pert breasts under her blouse. The door had been opened and they had both been glad.

It was the first time he had not wanted to return to Hereford. He had always been excited about new missions and being committed to a new test of his strength and resilience. He loved being an action man but this was a yearning he had never experienced and he had been torn. On his return to camp, he had written to her several times but Jackie had never replied.

Now all these years later, he wondered if she was happy and knew he would never find anyone to equal her.

"Is that alright with you?" Steve questioned Simon.

Simon scrambled, "If you both think so, it's fine," as he wondered to what on earth he had agreed.

As predicted by her parents she and Mark did become engaged. Mark was engaged on a big case which he warned could have wide reaching consequences and he knew the next twelve months or so would be incredibly busy and stressful. Never one to rush into things Kirsten decided to marry in the summer of 2008. Kirsten was content to allow her mother to do the lion's share of the organisation but warning her she did not want anything flashy.

"As if I would," Diana replied and launched into the arrangements. Diana knew the best venues could be booked for years in advance so welcomed the time and decided to get on it to it immediately. At last she felt motivated.

Diana had not used Marcus for years but something like her eldest daughter's wedding deserved the best and his company she knew had certainly flourished. She would contact him and perhaps be that exacting woman again. She relished the thought. It would add fun to the occasion.

Kirsten allowed her mother scope. She had never been exuberant and ostentatious and thought she would be able to rein in her mother gradually without causing friction. She also trusted in her mother's good taste.

Further to this, Mark, whose parents had a farm in the west country, had a large extended family and there would be plenty of logistical problems in accommodating them and entertaining them prior to and post wedding. Diana would be in her element, while Kirsten's natural reserve would inhibit proceedings.

Marcus remembered Diana Carstairs only too well. At times she had been a difficult woman but she had been predictable so Marcus could placate her and satisfy her whims. She never quibbled about the bill either as some of his clients did. He had learnt to be careful with contracts as in running events it was all too easy for a client to add on the little extras and then refuse to pay for them at a later date.

Diana was not in that mould. She had a clear head and her accountant husband kept a firm control of expenditure. Everyone had always known where they stood. An appointment was booked for the following month. It was a pity that Marcus could not take his assistant Louise after the debacle some years ago.

Louise gave very little comment except that it would be interesting to discover the family set up. By then Louise had become resigned to leaving her past buried. Certainly that was true about any connection with Diana and Meredith. She had not expected to make a new life and a successful one at that when she left in January 1993 but she had and must accept her fate.

The only loss she never accepted was the loss of Jake. Inside when she thought of him, which was daily, she felt completely hollow. She had fond memories of Ken but in her new successful career believed she had no yearning to return to that way of life. She had managed to plot Jake's progress from afar and at times as she had watched him from a vantage point had been tempted to accost him but the spectre of Clive Corneille stopped her. Ida had thought she could return and pick up life again but there was in reality no way back. She had walked away and as she did so the path that she had taken had become overgrown behind her. One day, she hoped to make amends. Marcus would come to the house to meet Diana, Antony and their daughter. Marcus was ready to handle this himself rather than delegate to one of his team.

Antony answered the door to Marcus ushering him into the sitting room. Diana with a bright smile greeted him pressing his hand before pushing her blushing daughter forward. Marcus assessed Diana. Here was not the frantic woman of the past. Her movements were slower and more relaxed. He had expected the usual agitation and a demanding list of requirements for him to fulfil. She was not subdued but there was a calm that exuded from her posture and conversation. Instead of attacking him with a series of "I want," she asked him how he fared and enquired about the business congratulating him on the renown he enjoyed and joking that she hoped it would not be reflected in the cost. He assured her he was always competitive in price and he added that she had been a valued customer so it would be good to work with her.

"You have lost none of your charm," Diana observed.

Marcus listened to the mature woman guiding her daughter through ideas. 'Where was the self-obsessed and domineering duchess he had worked with years ago?' He wondered. He warned himself to be careful as she must be hidden inside. Diana recognised his look of curiosity and admiration. She thought she could give him a run for his money.

Marcus recalled that September afternoon garden party at the Cotswold residence. Diana had been one of his early customers and initially through her he had made profitable connections. The afternoon had proved ugly and enlightening. Diana had a past and it was clear she had been anxious to hide it from her straight laced husband.

Marcus had schooled himself not to make judgements on his customers but at times it was hard. That day he had despised Diana for her arrogance and her calculated control. She had in front of his eyes abandoned her daughter, meaning she had abandoned her twice, something he found unforgiveable. Jackie had been a lost soul who needed his help, especially after Corneille had turned up. Marcus was assessing whether he would work with Diana again. He could afford to be choosy but at that moment he felt he was being reeled in by an expert angler.

Diana was enjoying herself more than she had for a long time. She was smooth and articulate as she indicated the requirements, emphasising that Kirsten must make any final decisions. Diana had not lost the knack of working an audience and fleetingly in her head she recalled her exploits in the South of France when she worked as an au pair. What a minx she had been!

Marcus agreed to make a few suggestions and see them again with some brochures when they could come to a firmer understanding. He found he was looking forward to the job, although he would need to run it past Louise his assistant. She might have strong objections.

Kirsten had been happy with the meeting and felt reassured. Mark had this big case on the go and she could see his fatigue from long hours when he visited. He let slip there were connections with the area and he might be down more often. She was glad but hoped it would not disturb the equilibrium of the local community. She wondered who was in their sights. She shrugged knowing it would not affect anyone they knew.

Chapter 17
Losing Your Nerve

If you can keep your head when all about you
Are losing theirs and blaming it on you,
If you can trust yourself when all men doubt you,
But make allowance for their doubting too;

If: Rudyard Kipling

2007: Kirsten and Alex

Steve could not help comparing Jake with Alex his son. There were thirteen years' difference in age but it was Jake that had the work ethic and it was Jake who had the common sense. Alex seemed to want anything with too little effort and his conduct left much to be desired. Jake seemed mature while Alex still seemed juvenile. Steve worried about his son. He had continued to help out financially from time to time even though Alex now had a well-paid job with the Corneille group of companies mainly because Alex could not curb his spending and had transgressed driving rules with his speed and parking which meant fines he never had the money to pay. It was exasperating and Steve would think about his upbringing comparing it with Jake. Alex had had all life's advantages, a warm and comfortable home, toys when he was young and technology when he was older, good food, regular holidays and two parents who were interested in him and loved him.

Steve realised that he had been very busy at times with his work but he had never let him down regarding parent and teacher meetings at school and all his spare time was spent with Alex. It was not so with Abigail but then she did not work and after days at home needed the release of a social life. Steve did not begrudge her that.

Jake, Steve knew, lived with his dad, a single parent. His mum had abandoned him. He had never been neglected as such but he had had to fend for himself and home was safe but could not be described as very comfortable. Jake had left school at sixteen and got on with things while Alex had support throughout his school life, even private lessons to get him through GCSE and later 'A' levels. Steve had managed to fund him through his two years at university before he had quit under a cloud. Even then Alex had not put himself out to find work. He said he deserved better than that on offer. Had they spoilt him?

Jake, on the other hand, was making his own way. He took home scant wages, did his chores at home and helped the neighbour Jim. He was prepared to work long hours and travel by public transport or take his bike to get to work and college always punctual for labour or learning. He was polite and respectful too. It seemed he had been a useful footballer with aspirations to be a professional but instead of chasing an unreliable dream he changed direction and it looked to Steve as if he would make a success of whatever he chose to do. Steve had met Ken once or twice and thought how lucky Ken was with his son and wondered what Ken had done right and what he had done wrong.

Recently there had been a horrible incident when Jake's neighbour had been burgled. Jake had been beside himself. It had been one of the few times he had heard Jake swear and Simon had to hold him back from going over to attack Carl the perpetrator.

Jake had apparently known Carl since school and they had played in the same football team and Jake complained that Carl had been a dirty player then but he never thought he was so callous. There had been much discussion at the nursery about the rights and wrongs of the actions and what was going on in society in general as well as heated exchanges about justice and punishment.

Simon had gone with Jake to advice Jim about security and Steve had later helped Simon put extra measures in place. Jim had been grateful and wanted an invoice but of course, they had ignored the request and settled for a cup of tea instead. Ken had popped round as well to inspect what was happening. The five males tumbled into the front room clutching their mugs of tea cajoling each other and then deciding it would be a good idea to visit the local hostelry to do some further bonding. Steve could not imagine Alex fitting in a scenario like this which pulled at his heartstrings.

Gradually, Steve had begun to fret less about Alex. Since marrying Gillian and even more since they had got over the Millennium episode his own life was good. He had a wife who cared for him and allowed him scope to follow his own passions and not grumble about the time he spent on them. He was making more money than he had ever done through his association with Simon and it was good to share responsibility with someone.

Gillian had become a lot more relaxed since she had left school the previous summer and was contributing to his business which made things easier for him and provided him with more opportunity to do what he was good at. To him she was a very special lady. She accepted his commitments regarding Alex and indeed, Abigail. He was lucky.

However, since the turn of the century Abigail had begun not to be so dependent on him and Steve had rightly guessed that she had her sights on another man, not before time in Steve's view. Then there was the shock that she was to marry Clive Corneille. Steve had never met him but he featured often in local newspapers and sometimes in national papers. He had listened to Jim and Ken talk about the management of the football club and the influence of Corneille. To them he was a leech sucking the life blood of the club. Jim had a handle on things and commented that the club's assets had been shrinking for some time. Corneille blamed the financial markets but Jim felt the problems were much nearer home. Clive Corneille had invested into the club which convinced some supporters of his commitment to the club but Jim said it was not genuine investment. It was all smoke and mirrors. It was not his money that had been invested it was all loans that the club had to repay. Corneille took his profits and the loan companies took theirs. Jim was convinced that if one dug deep enough Clive Corneille would have his fingers in the loan companies' pie as well.

Corneille was a slippery customer. Jim could feel his heart racing when he got on to this hobby horse. "If only the club could get shut of him," was Jim's perennial and closing cry to the argument. Ken agreed but some people thought Jim was getting old and did not move with the times and understand modern finance and football. They said that the club had to be competitive or it would completely go under.

Jim, for different reasons, could see his beloved club going bankrupt. Steve listened and said little, not being an ardent supporter or living in the town. He liked Jim and felt there was wisdom in Jim's words.

In his mid-fifties Steve was still fit and healthy. Alex having reached his thirties should really be able make his own way with the interest of his father and not so much with his practical support. He could take a step back and enjoy some of the fruits of his labours with his wife.

Abigail had left his sphere of influence and he had been feeling the effects of the release. Looking back he saw things more clearly and what he had thought was loyalty had often been stubbornness. He did not like failure in any respect and the way his marriage had faltered and crumbled was to him abject failure. He had not provided his wife with the happiness and fulfilment she had looked for in a husband. He had been found wanting and deep down it hurt.

He remembered the days when he had first encountered girls of that set, most of them students while he had been a little older and had emerged from his apprenticeship. They had been enticing to a solid workman. He had enjoyed flirtations, bedding one or two and even bragging to the lads at the building site. Abigail had been a fascinating creature then and he had enjoyed his status as stud. What a conceited bloke he had been! He had let the girls come to him in those days. He supposed they liked him as a bit of rough.

Certainly, he was never short of supply. Abigail had clung a little more effectively and when she had said she was pregnant he knew he had to throw in his cards and accept defeat. Abigail was very attractive and came from a professional background. He remembered introducing her to his mum and dad and the rest of them. Abigail glided into the house and everyone fussed around the swan who had suddenly arrived in their midst. Of course, Abigail did not want to associate with his family after they married. She was from a different background altogether and Steve resented the slights she afforded to his family particularly to his mother. Mike, his brother to whom he had always been close began to avoid coming to the house and Steve only saw his parents if he went to them without Abigail. She would resent these visits too saying he should be helping her and not skedaddling back to his mum and dad at every opportunity. There was no baby. It had been a false alarm but Steve had already proposed and was overwhelmed by the amount that Abigail's parents were spending on the wedding. He could not be such a cad as to withdraw and she did have physical allure. He did not face the question of whether he loved Abigail or not. The commitment hardened when Abigail gave birth to Alex a couple of years or so into the marriage. She had sworn never to go through that agony again. It had become easy to take charge of Alex while Abigail had her social life. It had been a bitter pill to swallow that Alex had resisted his parenting.

Alex had at last found his niche with the Corneille organisation and now he had an even closer link with Clive Corneille Steve thought he should shed his personal feelings about him and move forward. He knew Gillian lamented her childless state and he had felt the bitter twist of the knife from the rejection of an only child. It was up to them both to turn to the future.

Kirsten had found it was nice to be at home and catch up with old friends. The girls discussed their various careers, their boyfriends or husbands and even children and holidays as well as weddings. That was a favourite topic of conversation. On one such occasion, Kirsten making her way out of the bar noticed a familiar face in the corner. She hesitated which was silly as she would normally make a quick exit but there had been something forlorn about the figure in the corner. Against her better judgement, she approached him.

"Hello Alex. How are you?"

Alex had been so absorbed in his thoughts he started. "Kirsten, the calculator," he said.

Kirsten had known this was her nickname at college. She did not answer with his nickname 'parasite.'

"Join me for a drink," he invited.

"I haven't long," she replied through courtesy trying to hide her reluctance.

"Please I could do with the company," he added.

He stood politely and offered her a seat. She could not refuse. A glass of wine in hand they exchanged pleasantries. She told him she had worked in Manchester before joining her father and that she was to be married. She felt she should mark his card somehow. He could not remember Mark, of course, who had been two years their senior and a high flying student. When he learnt Mark worked in London, Alex assumed he was some company accountant. It would never cross his mind that he was a police officer.

Alex was subdued. He was working for his new father-in-law which did not seem to inspire him. Eventually, he paused and then deliberately caught her attention and said, "I was not very nice to you at uni, was I?"

She felt she could not reply. "I know, I was a heel and used you. You were incredibly patient and you did not deserve it all." Kirsten thought he was probably buttering her up for something.

He took a long swig of his lager. "I could do with some help, Kirsten." Her stomach churned and she prepared to go. "No don't leave. I meant I could really do with some advice. I know, I wasn't nice to you before and I can appreciate why not, but meeting you here like this, well, please give me a chance. It is just advice I need. I have no-one to turn to and I don't want to get into trouble."

Kirsten still hesitated and looked across the room for reassurance.

"Only advice?" She asked. "You know if you came to the office I would charge you."

"I would pay you too. It is not that kind of advice. It is more personal. I need someone I can trust." Alex seemed different, abashed and uncertain.

Kirsten was intrigued and sat back in her seat.

"Did you know I work for my stepdad?"

Kirsten nodded. "I had heard something on the grapevine. You've done well Alex. What you wanted isn't it?" He looked intently at her before gathering himself and launching into an explanation that would change her world.

"I thought so. I really did. I watched my dad give all he had to me and Mum and doing without and working hard, scratching a living and I did not want the same. When I was a kid, he tried to take me to football and cricket but I was no good and I hated it. I got embarrassed. If they put me in a team and, like, I would drop an easy catch, someone would shout butterfingers and football was worse. The parents on the side lines would yell at me, 'get the ball,' 'pass you idiot,' 'shoot you clown' and always 'get him off the pitch he's a liability,' and those were the more polite things. Dad tried to encourage me, I know, and thought I could work with him but by then I was so angry with everything. It was a lot easier to make him think I did not care. It got to be a habit I suppose in my teens. I hated it all. It got worse and worse."

Kirsten sat mesmerised by his admissions. She did not know how to respond.

"You think I'm an idiot too, don't you?" He looked her straight in the eye.

"No never an idiot. Misguided perhaps," was her feeble reply.

"God, Kirsten, you are just too nice for your own good. You know I used you and bullied you. I sort of couldn't help myself and I hated it. I wanted you to like me. I always did."

Kirsten began to feel little panicky flutters in her stomach. What was he telling her? Would he make trouble between her and Mark? Alex had always been a loose cannon.

"I'm not sure, I am the right person to help you, Alex? We've moved on. That was more than ten years ago."

"I'm not coming on to you. I wish I had all those years ago but too late I know. You're the nearest anybody has been to me as a friend and right now I really need a friend."

Kirsten's intuition told her to leave, to run away, Alex had always been trouble but she was basically kind and she could see his distress. It would not have surprised her if he had even cried so absolute seemed his misery.

"What has happened Alex? Where's the 'I'm the king of the castle' Alex that I knew?" Her voice was sympathetic and gave Alex heart.

"I'm scared Kirsten, really scared." Kirsten could see it was the truth.

"I'm not sure I can help but you can try me," she encouraged.

A few minutes later she wished she had not been so encouraging. "You can't keep this to yourself, Alex. You should alert the authorities."

"I can't Kirsten. I really can't. Mum's happy now and you don't know how she can be when she's not. Believe me she's impossible and I could not do it to her. She would hate me forever."

"What about your dad? He seems a decent guy. Dad always speaks very highly of him."

"He does not have much to do with me now. He used to ring a lot but he hardly ever does now so I suppose he's washed his hands of me." He looked down at his hands splaying his fingers to release the tension.

"Ring him, Alex, or better still, go and see him."

"I've not rung him for years. He'd probably have a heart attack or think I needed a large amount of cash. I always rely on him to get in touch with me. Mum rings him from time to time, especially before she married Clive." Kirsten who had never been at odds with her parents even in troubled times, was sad.

"You can't be dragged down by this, Alex. You will certainly have to quit your job, at least."

"Oh yes, and what would I do for money and how could I explain it. He'd be down on me like a ton of bricks. I've seen something of the way he operates and it's not very nice. He has the power. It would be like committing suicide."

This was so completely out of her sphere and Kirsten was weighed down with the knowledge. She could just walk away and forget about it. For her that would be the best option but she had knowledge now and like Eve after a bite of the apple from the tree of knowledge she could not ignore it. In fact, if Alex did not come clean, she knew she would have to and at that moment she wished Mark was around, but she would not see him until the weekend, almost another week, and to her time was of the essence. Alex picked up on her dilemma.

"You can't say anything, Kirsten. They would know I have been talking to you and the police would arrest me for involvement. I could face years." He pleaded scared to have confided in her, and even more scared to be alone.

"Well, you and now me can't sit here and ignore it can we? Maybe, Alex, it is time for you to take responsibility. It's scary, but you are a decent person and you have to grow up."

Alex almost crumbled before her eyes.

"What did you expect, Alex, when you told me? You know most people confide in people they know will give them the answer they want deep down. You wanted me to tell you to do the right thing. You wanted me to make you behave honourably. You wanted me to tell you to be brave. You can do this Alex. You can sort it and you will be protecting your mother in the long run. Think long and hard but do not leave it too long. Look get in touch with me tomorrow or the next day at the latest or I will have to act. It would be better if you did. You know that." Her voice had softened from its earlier force.

Kirsten made sure he had her current number and insisted he leave with her because she was worried he would try to drink his way out of his misery. They parted at the taxi rank where Alex took a cab for home and Kirsten walked thoughtfully back to her parents.

Kirsten could not sleep that night. All kinds of scenarios tumbled through her brain. The large cash payments were undoubtedly bribes, the evidence of false companies hid the illegitimate trading and almost certainly money laundering. There was the property portfolio that indicated an income that far exceeded the declared earnings.

It all added up to major and consistent fraud which had been going on for years. Alex had mentioned one or two names and she planned to research the companies and individuals mentioned. They were powerful people she already knew. She was afraid and if she felt this way by only knowing the tip of the iceberg then how must Alex feel. He would not hold it together and suddenly she was scared for another reason. Supposing it was too much for a flaky character like Alex, who was so desperate he had turned to her, someone who had been out of his life for years, so that he did something stupid in his anguish. She would have to check up on him and not wait for him to get in touch.

She could not sleep that night. Her bed seemed cold and yet beads of sweat prickled her body. Little darting thoughts shot through her brain each one jabbing and prodding her into submission.

Kirsten thought of confiding in her dad. She knew he had worked for Corneille many years before so would have an idea what Alex was up against and she relied on her father for cool common sense. He could be dispassionate and any assessments seemed to have an almost surgical application. Logic was his key and Kirsten was not sure whether it would be fair to her father to bring him into the confidence or indeed at this point wise. She could live with it for a couple of days.

"What's wrong?" Mark asked when he phoned.

"Nothing, just tired and some knotty problems workwise," she half lied.

"I hope you clear your desk for me when I come, and get some beauty sleep. I want a lot of attention you know. We accountants can get very demanding and police officers are even worse." His voice sounded sexy and she longed for his touch.

"I can't wait to see you," Kirsten said with feeling.

"See you soon darling. Be good and relax. Don't take everything so seriously. Got to go now. See you Friday. Love you," and he was gone. Kirsten burst into tears.

Alex could not be persuaded to go to the police. He thought they could not be trusted and there were some officers who in all probability were in the pay of Corneille and his group. Kirsten could not deny that possibility. She had done her research and found to her horror something of the extent of the network.

There were some very high profile figures linked to Corneille and it was impossible to tell if they were participants or innocent bystanders. These were murky waters indeed.

She met Alex again and they began to piece together evidence and what it meant. Although Alex had worked for Corneille for a few years, in that time he had not been privy to any really incriminating evidence. Looking back and adding things up a picture began to emerge but some of it was conjecture. It was only after the marriage with his mum that Corneille seemed to up Alex's involvement and divulge details. Clive Corneille seemed to treat him like a son rather than a new step-son.

Alex had felt uncomfortable and resisted playing happy families. He was glad he was able to convince them to let him live at his mum's old house. He had told them he wanted to strike out on his own. Clive seemed to be proud of Alex and introduced him to the great and the good at every opportunity. Alex had felt he was being wheeled out as an expensive accessory and he missed his real dad.

Mark arrived Friday evening after a late departure from London. He was sufficiently at home there to flop into an armchair relieved to be there and grinning from expectation of later lovemaking. Diana and Antony tactfully lurked in the kitchen until the young couple were prepared to join them. Some cheese, pork pie, pickles and salads satisfied any hunger while tea sufficed as a drink. Samantha was planning to join them the next day. As chief bridesmaid she was anxious to get in on the act. She was also between boyfriends so was a little at a loss for activity in London and thought she deserved a weekend of spoiling.

Kirsten and Mark retired for the night. He quickly caught her in his arms impatient to fulfil his needs. She was unusually reticent but he had excellent persuasive techniques and Kirsten left her anxieties behind until afterwards when they pressed again into her mind. They lay absorbed in their personal satisfactions drifting into a night's rest. Kirsten thought this was a good moment.

"I want to ask you something, Mark," she whispered.

"Anything," he said "especially after that. You know exactly when to use your feminine wiles." He planted a kiss on her head before shuffling to a more comfortable position.

"No it's advice and maybe help," she suddenly felt as though she were Alex the week before.

"Can it not wait until the morning? I'm tired and it's late."

"We have to go to see the venue first thing. We'll be in a rush." Kirsten did not want to delay but he did look tired and so was she. It was good to have his presence.

"Later, then. Sleep now. Come here. I'll hold you. You will feel better."

Of course, Kirsten despite feeling tired could not sleep. She had been waiting for Mark with whom to share the confidence as though he were going to be her knight, relieving her of the weight of the problem, reassuring her that nothing was fundamentally amiss, but no, he wanted sleep, he could not recognise the plea in her voice. The next day proved as Kirsten predicted: a merry-go-round of appointments her mother had scheduled for them. Samantha commandeered Mark, quizzing him about who was to be the best man and would he be boyfriend material.

It was late again, when they were alone and she did not feel as brave about seeking his support. The day of wedding fever had somehow diminished the need to talk and the topic seemed too fantastical amidst the normality of planning a wedding. It would be easy to let things slide. After all, if there was a problem it was a problem for Alex and not for her, and she began to understand how Alex and anyone else in the position could evade the problem and choose not to rock the boat.

It was Mark who broached the subject or Kirsten might have resisted altogether.

"What was so important last night? Wedding nerves? You're not having second thoughts, can't blame you if you were, after all that today. Sometimes, think it would be nice to forget the whole thing and run away together." He tickled her before pulling her close. "But I have to tell you my mother would never forgive you as she has already bought the most outrageous hat which she would never wear to anything else so that's it really, do we go through all this palaver and win my mother's lifetime approval or ditch it and face the consequences. No contest really, is it?"

He was convinced his shy bride only needed reassurance. She pulled herself away and prepared for his reaction.

"Do you remember Alex Mason from university? He was in my year, so maybe not."

"The infamous Alex, you mean. Didn't know him personally but his antics got broadcast and he was always in the union bar so yes I do. You are not leaving me for him, are you?" Mark could say this in jest as he was quite certain this was not happening and once Kirsten had told him she had a few difficulties in that quarter.

Mark collapsed on the bed giving her a come hither look but she took the chair by her dressing table.

"He's in trouble and asked for my advice."

"The damn cheek! Kirsten, ignore him. Let him sort out his own stupid issues."

"I can't Mark, not after what he told me," and she launched into an explanation.

"Christ Kirsten. What have you got yourself into? You should have walked away and now you are dragging me into it. This might cost me my job and you yours and might ruin the accountancy business. You are now complicit. How long have you known? Who else knows? What on earth were you thinking about?" The questions in the accusative tone came thick and fast.

"I didn't know he would tell me this. He looked miserable." It sounded pathetic even to her.

After the exhausting day when she wanted his reassurance all she got was his venom and tears bubbled inside. Her voice wavered and the volume increased by an octave. "I was talking to someone I knew. I haven't done anything wrong. I thought I could ask you what to do. Obviously I should have dealt with it myself and left you out of it."

"What do you expect?" He retorted. "I thought you had more sense. How long have you known, Kirsten? Has he told anyone else?"

"Only for a week. I saw him last Monday and then again on Wednesday I don't know if anyone else knows."

"You can't see him again or speak to him or text or anything. Understand." His voice was forceful and sharp.

In the other bedroom Diana and Antony were aware of raised voices.

"Why not? He's desperate Mark. I said I would meet him on Tuesday. He's coming to the office at lunchtime."

"It gets worse and worse," By this time Mark was on his feet pacing and prowling round the room looking at her with something that alternated between contempt and panic. He was losing his temper.

"Have you been in touch with him? Tell me you haven't Kirsten," and seeing her face, "It can all be tracked you careless, stupid girl. He must not, absolutely not, meet you at the office. In fact, he must not meet you anywhere," There was a strength and power in his tone that Kirsten did not know he possessed. The force overwhelmed her.

"I was worried he would do something stupid so I've been calling him and texting." Kirsten's voice shook, but Mark did not seem to register her discomfort.

"How often?" He demanded.

"Every day I suppose." It was like admitting to an infidelity and she felt ashamed.

"Even today, when we were at lunch, you were messaging."

"I'm sorry Mark. I thought he was suicidal. I could not have that on my conscience." She was partly crying as she spoke and Mark altered his tone slightly.

"Well, sometimes, Kirsten, you have to cover your own back and think of your family and not get dragged into a whole load of shit." She hated his superiority and by implication her failure which rallied her senses.

"Anyone would think I was to blame. Forget it Mark. Can't have you tainted by it can we?" Her sarcastic tone cut into him and he glared.

In the bedroom across the landing Diana and Antony strained their ears but could not make out the content. They did know that there was blame and accusations from the odd word and tone. "Maybe, pre-wedding stress" murmured Diana but, neither of them was convinced.

The passion of the argument gradually dwindled. Kirsten sat slumped beside her dressing table. She had picked up her old teddy bear that had lain unloved for many years on the shelf nearby, now clutching it to her and burying her head in the soft fur. Mark, with his anger dissipated, stared unblinking at the family photographs she kept on the chest of drawers. He became more resolute. The silence pervaded the room.

Eventually, Kirsten muttered, "Sorry, Mark." Wrenched from his thoughts he studied her and felt an upsurge of affection.

"Let's get to bed and talk tomorrow. I can't deal with it now," and he moved resignedly to the en-suite to prepare for bed.

They climbed into bed like two strangers stranded in a remote location forced to spend the night together and guarding their modesty. They lay in parallel lines. They did not provoke the steel barrier between them.

Sunday dawned and Mark dressed early. Kirsten had eventually fallen asleep and peered through the half-light to see her fiancée putting his things together. "Where are you going?"

"I have to go Kirsten. I'll call you before Tuesday. Don't contact Alex and don't answer his calls."

"Mark you can't go. I don't understand. We were going to talk."

"There's nothing to say Kirsten. Go back to bed. I'll be in touch."

"Don't leave Mark. Please don't go. I love you." Desperation was in her voice.

"I can't stay here, Kirsten. You must see that. Take care." He was gone. She looked out of her window and saw the rear of his sports car as it turned through the gate. She had comforted many friends after a break up and could not believe it was happening to her. They were strong. What had just happened? She hated Alex.

As far as Kirsten was concerned time had slowed to an excruciatingly slow pace and Sunday crawled interminably to a close. She shut the bedroom door telling her parents that something had come up. She waited for him to ring and periodically tried to call him. She felt weak as she texted "Love you. Please call," but there was no response.

Chapter 18
He Who Hesitates Is Lost

"Truth," said a traveller,
"Is a rock, a mighty fortress;
Often have I been to it,
Even to its highest tower,
From whence the world looks black."

"Truth," said a traveller: Stephen Crane

2007: Alex

Tom Wilkes received the call Sunday afternoon. Things were coming to a head and he was being given a crucial role. He spent the rest of the day doing his homework, preparing for his part. He was excited and pleased to be a part of momentous events. To have a family member of Clive Corneille to co-operate would complete the picture. He would need his A game.

He had already tracked down Jackie now known as Louise. He had been genuinely surprised to find a capable, smartly dressed woman, having expected someone more desperate and care worn. She had calmly recounted her association with Clive Corneille which had been disappointingly brief.

The contents of the box had been given to her by her friend for safe keeping just before she had died so she had not been directly involved like her friend. On one occasion, she had attended a party but had quickly exited when it became apparent that the young girls were assembled as eye candy for the uncles who would take their pick to satisfy their further appetites.

Louise had kept to a script. She had been low key and Tom knew he would have a dig a little harder if he wanted her full co-operation. None of what she had said really answered the question of why a doting mother had abandoned her son. Meanwhile, he would gather what he could from the stepson.

Alex was not happy to have his meeting with Kirsten cancelled. A secretary had conveyed the message and none of his calls and texts had been answered. What was she playing at? Had she got cold feet? Was she running away? Was he to be left alone? The whole sorry mess horrified him. He felt cowardly. He wanted escape. He wanted his dad more than ever. He wanted that solid presence, the calm rational approach, but more than anything, his kindness and his love.

Clive had called him that morning and given him another job and he could not find a way out. He was to collect a package later that afternoon and bring it to Clive at the house. He had done this before, in fact quite often, but then he had not understood the implications. Now there was no doubt he was part of a criminal enterprise. He had become a willing participator. There seemed no way out.

He spent the morning at the football club. His mind elsewhere he pretended his interest in the schedules and wandered down to pitch side to watch the ground staff. He recognised an elderly man talking to the new groundsman and sauntered over.

"Hello Jim. What are you doing here?"

"I asked him to come, Mr Mason. We've got a problem with the grass. Look there are these small brown patches here and there. Thought Jim's experience would be useful," Lewis volunteered.

Alex inspected the small patch of brown. There was obviously a disease.

Jim gave them his opinion. "You've a problem with the fertiliser and then the excessively wet July has not helped. If it's not sorted, they'll be major problems and with the start of the season days away you don't need it."

Lewis had good qualifications but he was new to the demands of a football club. His job was on the line. One of the ex-players had told him to get old Jim in to have a look.

"Can it be sorted?" Alex asked.

"Oh yes, easily. It's not serious but needs doing now. What fertiliser are you using?" Jim was enjoying being needed and felt his self-esteem rise.

"I'll show you," and Lewis prepared to leave with Jim. Alex, in a rare moment of appreciation, invited Jim to the directors' suite when he had finished. Jim usually nonplussed had a flutter of excitement and agreed, with the thought that it would be something to report to Jake and Ken when he saw them later.

Alex met Jim at the top of the steps and took him into the inner sanctum.

"Would you like tea, coffee or something stronger?" Alex asked.

"Tea is fine for me, Mr Mason," Alex indicated one of the easy chairs in the club colours.

"Call me Alex. You are an honoured guest and a valued past employee. No ceremony. I'll order some sandwiches too, it's nearly lunch time." Alex needed the distraction.

Jim was staggered. He had not had much to do with young Alex Mason when he had first arrived at the club in 1999. Despite his decision at Millennium to retire Jim had been reluctant to retire fully and had spent a couple of years still working in a part time support capacity before admitting his age had become a hindrance.

Alex had been a cocky individual who was abrupt in his dealings with general staff. Jim had since been told about his new position as Clive Corneille's stepson and could only imagine the inflation to his ego in consequence, but studying Alex closely as he ordered the refreshments through the intercom, he thought he detected an uncertain boy so he wondered how much of his previous behaviour had been bluster. Jim sat on the easy chair appraising the situation.

"Did you get it sorted?" Alex could talk easily when he wanted.

"Yes. Think you need to change your fertiliser though. I know, you have to be cost effective these days but cutting corners on some products can be a mistake."

Alex remembered how Clive had cancelled the contract for fertiliser for another brand. Alex had not understood the reason at the time but after his analysis with Kirsten it had become obvious that this was one of the scams of his step-father. His hand shook slightly and he rested it firmly on his knee. He thought it might have been a mistake inviting Jim but he needed the company of an outsider. Kirsten had become unavailable. Jim's quiet manner was some comfort.

Jim had always been a good judge of character. His estimation of Alex was out of kilter. If he did not know better, he would say that Alex had the demeanour of a frightened schoolboy.

"I was sorry to hear of your trouble," Alex commented. "Are you fully recovered?"

"Oh yes. I'm tough. Everyone has been so kind and I have been enjoying the fuss. I met your dad. He was very nice."

For a moment Alex so consumed by his thoughts of his step-father and being at the football club thought he meant Clive but quickly adjusted his thoughts, realising he meant Steve.

"Did you? How was that?" He automatically took the conversation forward giving half his attention to Jim.

"He came over with a friend's son to sort out my security. Nice bloke. He was very helpful." The comment prompted a spontaneous vision of his dad in his mind's eye. He felt the loss.

"I don't see him now as much as I should." Alex sounded wistful.

"Well, I think he misses you. We went to the pub and he said how well you were doing and how busy you were. Jake my neighbour asked him about you and he told him how you would do things together when you were young. I bet you had a great time." Jim watched the young man and was acutely aware of the chinks in his armour.

Alex was taken aback. He had always taken Steve for granted, encouraged by his mother. He felt shame kick him. He was a loser. He had lost his dad, he had lost any friends, he was about to lose his freedom.

There was a knock and the refreshments were brought forward.

"There's a police officer asking to see you. He apologised for not making an appointment but there are some queries regarding the police charity function next month."

Alex looked across at Jim. "Do you mind if I see him. It's probably something straightforward and should not take long. Tuck in," he said invitingly. Alex wanted an excuse not to engage with the police at this point in time and Jim would provide the diversion.

Tom Wilkes was shown up to the suite of rooms.

"Well, this is a surprise," he greeted Jim with a smile.

"A surprise for me too Inspector, Mr Mason here is giving me a nice lunch after a little bit of pitch advice."

Jim turned to Alex, "one of the best officers on the force. Inspector Wilkes sorted everything when I had the break-in. He brought back Ida's bracelet personally as well. I am so very grateful."

"Perhaps you would like some tea, Inspector?" Alex resorted to polite conversation and wanted to take the lead.

Tom agreed. He had hoped to confront Alex alone but maybe Jim's presence was fortuitous giving him an inside track.

"Catching many criminals?" Jim chuckled.

"One or two," was Tom's retort.

Jim sensed an undercurrent. A man like Inspector Wilkes would not be wasting his time sorting out police charity events. He thought he would play along. Alex sat still as if willing his body to blend into the background. Jim tucked into the sandwiches passing comment about the fillings before offering some parting advice.

"You know, Mr Mason," he felt emboldened, "Alex. If you have got something on your mind, then you could not do any worse than get an opinion from Inspector Wilkes here. He has the knack of putting your mind at rest. He not only looked after me but he is helping my young friend Jake and his dad and going out of his way to do so. He will put you straight if there's anything bothering you." By which time he had stood ready to go. "I'll see myself out."

He turned and shook their hands, leaving Tom bemused and Alex astounded.

Tom appraised the situation. He sat quietly without malice willing Alex to seize the moment.

Eventually, Alex said, "You haven't come here about the charity event have you?"

"No but I wanted to see you alone and not arouse suspicion. I think you have things to get off your chest." Tom spoke quietly and intently and sat drinking his tea, watching and waiting.

Again, there was silence. Alex was desperately trying to process his options. He knew one response would be to tell this Inspector that he had nothing to say and he was a busy man and usher him out, firmly closing the door, both literally and metaphorically. Then he would tell Clive of the encounter and maybe all his anxiety would go away. He would have been strong in a crisis. He would have earned his step father's approval too. He would have proved his loyalty. It was an obvious choice.

Little beads of sweat warmed his neck.

This was a crossroads and Alex had to make a lifetime choice. He sat in the sumptuous boardroom, occupied so often by the bulk of his step-father, controlling affairs with a ruthless iron fist. Alex gazed out over an expanse of lush green pitch, no defect apparent from on high, where men became boys both on and off the pitch, putting all their energy, skill and guile into controlling the ball and demolishing the opposition with one cool strike of it into the net. Spectators were ardent in their support, unflinching in their partisanship, often mindless in their commitment and forever unwavering in passionate support. A game could turn in an instant. One player could seize an opportunity and tear through a defence or another player could fumble his chance and humiliatingly score an own goal. In his mind, Alex was on that field of play. His heart was beating, pounding in his chest and he could visualise his dad, Steve, anxious and alert on the touchline willing him to concentrate, willing him to do the right thing, while Alex would invariably kick the ball away in a fit of pique or stand idly by without any attempt to get involved, leaving a defence wide open. The jeers still echoed in his ears which at the time he had rebuffed with his anger and spite, but he could never erase the look on his dad's face of disappointment and resignation. Even then, his dad would scoop him up and buy him a burger or ice cream to commiserate, telling him better luck next time, encouraging him and sticking by him, although he must have felt the embarrassment of having an ineffectual son. Alex would give anything not to disappoint his dad ever again.

"How can I trust you?"

The question told both parties all they needed to know. Alex had capitulated. He was not strong enough to bear the brunt of deceit and treachery. It was fundamentally that he had been brought up with the examples of integrity and dignity and kindness. He had tested the world of selfish greed and he had been perennially uncomfortable. He had watched his step-father shirk away from the kind of responsibility that his father embraced. Clive Corneille relished power. People had been crushed by such men. Alex terrified had shrunk away from reality.

Tom quietly in that moderated and gentle tone replied, "You can never really know who to trust but I suppose my greatest recommendation is a person like Jim Woodhouse, a decent, honest, genuine man who has lived a life that has taught him values. The respect of a man like Jim counts for everything. I think in the end you have to trust yourself."

The die had been cast. For the next hour Alex leg go. He poured out his heart and he emptied his mind. Tom Wilkes was exactly the right man to extricate Alex from his demons. His patience, perseverance and reassuring presence allowed Alex the scope to come to terms with his situation. Tom was honest enough to say that Alex may well face prosecution. It was not in his remit to grant otherwise but his co-operation would be noted and probably carry sway. Alex would have to divulge even more to specialist brains but for the moment Tom Wilkes would be his contact and his confidante.

Alex told Tom about the errand he was to perform later that day. Tom reassured him that he should go ahead. He was to carry on as normal, although both knew that would be difficult. Tom provided Alex with a mobile phone with pertinent numbers already logged. They would probably not meet at the club again but either party could communicate to arrange a liaison. Alex promised to provide what hard evidence he could and Tom's faith in him, reminding him of his dad, strengthened his resolve. Tom told him to try not to worry and good things were happening in the background.

When Tom Wilkes had left, Alex made a decision. He called his dad. Steve, working on some spare room wardrobes for one of his regular customers, was taken aback to receive the call.

"Hello son, how are you?"

"I'm fine, Dad. I'm good."

Somehow, he did not know what else to say. There was a short silence while each of them assessed the situation.

"Do you need anything, Alex?" Steve was the only person who had ever asked this question of Alex and for the first time Alex was completely humbled. He was full of regret.

"No, Dad, I wondered what you were up to. I had a few minutes and thought I would give you a call."

"That's great, Alex. I'm at Mrs Roberts, you know the lady who used to run the Black Bear. She wants some fitted wardrobes in her spare room." Steve had always been willing to take on any job big or small, something that Alex had learnt through Abigail to berate him for but listening to him now Alex loved the normality.

"No renovations on the go, then?" He asked.

"No not right now. I'm on the look-out of course, but I've got plenty to do otherwise."

"I saw Jim Woodhouse today. He said you'd done some work at his house."

"Not much really. We sorted out the doors and Simon put up some security lights. He's an interesting man. We had a good chat. He's a mate of Bill Cartwright, Simon's dad, you know, he's got the nursery at Rainwick." Alex realised that his dad had been perennially self-effacing and yet as a skilled workman there was much for which he should be proud and more than that he was a genuinely good, kind man. Alex dreaded the outcome of the police investigation and acutely felt the shame of his own behaviour.

Alex had never shown any interest in Steve's work and Steve was puzzled. He was even more astonished when Alex asked, "How's Gillian?"

"Gillian. Yes, she's ok. Getting used to retirement so not so stressed," suddenly Steve felt disloyal as though he had criticised Gillian.

"And how's your mum?" Steve felt he had to reciprocate.

"Oh you know Mum, she's happy in the big house. Thanks for letting me stay at the old house. Really appreciate it."

To Steve the whole conversation seemed bizarre. Something was afoot. He had the conviction that Alex needed him. The call had been an aspect of a Crie de Coeur.

"We'll meet up sometime shall we? You can always come to us here at Primrose Crescent, or maybe meet for a drink or something to eat." Alex had avoided visiting his dad and Gillian at their home. It had been seen as an act of betrayal to his mum and Alex had been jealous of their obvious pleasure in each other. "It's always good to see you Alex. Always welcome," his voice was tailing off.

"Yes, Dad that would be good. I will. Look I'll call you and fix something up."

"Don't wait too long Alex. It really is great to hear from you. You've made my day. I'm always here for you." Steve was scared of pushing him away with too much sentiment.

"Yes, Dad, must go, will be in touch." Alex cut the call as his voice finally gave way and he collapsed, a heaving head in his hands. When he emerged, he felt lighter and more at peace. He began to feel he had a future.

Alex collected the package as instructed, safer in the knowledge that Inspector Wilkes had his back. It had been a substantial envelope and would not fit in the glove compartment so he placed it visibly on the seat. He confidently drove the BMW to the fortress, the nickname he gave the mansion where his mother now lived with Clive. Simon had been involved in securing the property against intruders and had reported to Steve it was like Fort Knox.

Alex sailed along the link road joining the mass exodus of end of day traffic. He was feeling pleased with himself. His dad had given him a perspective and Inspector Wilkes a reassurance and calmness. He had not experienced this for weeks, or rather months. It was pleasant. He turned off towards the genteel neighbourhood. It always tickled him how career criminals would seek to hide in respectable neighbourhoods, or maybe he mused they were all lawbreakers.

Clive Corneille lived cheek by jowl with high court judges, medical consultants and famous faces seeking retreat.

Suddenly, his reverie was interrupted by a police siren and a signal to pull over. His whole demeanour changed. Had he misjudged? Was this an arrest? Had he made a mess of things? He pulled to the side and sat with violent palpitations in his chest waiting for the axe to fall.

"Do you know what the speed restriction is here and the speed you were doing sir?" The policeman began.

"It's thirty and I thought I was within that?" Alex desperately tried to hold himself together.

"You were doing thirty-five." Alex realised he may have been a little too carefree.

"I am sorry, officer. It was quite unintentional and must have been only for a brief period."

"You have a break light missing too."

Alex waited, trying to convince himself it was just a routine stop.

"Well, we will give you a warning this time but please take more care. While we are here I had better check your details." Alex provided his driving licence and explained the car belonged to Clive Corneille's organisation for which he was insured. One of the officers checked while the other asked him where he had been and the purpose of his journey. He was caught out. His brain could not think of any alternatives so he blurted out the addresses, hoping the policeman would not dig any further. Guilt swept over him.

"Present for Mr Corneille?" The policeman asked, seeing the bulging envelope with Clive's name scrawled across in large loopy letters. Alex felt his heart stop and could only nod.

"Well, take more care and get that light fixed." With that the policeman returned to his vehicle. Alex more than ever knew he had not the stomach for crime.

Clive took the package and disappeared into his study while Alex sought his mother in the drawing room. She kissed him but looked slightly distracted. Alex was not intending to stay long so moseyed over to the window rather than settling into a chair. Clive's chauffeur was changing the break light.

"We need to talk to you, Alex. There are plans."

Alex was immediately alert. Every nuance affected him detrimentally. He hoped any plans did not include him. He turned to look at his mother. Abigail had found her level. She fitted in perfectly. Alex had not noticed before how his parents had been an ill-fit. They had no shared interests, although it was more than this. They were irritated with each other. It had been always there, hidden and not apparent but conversations would scratch and chafe. There had as long as he could remember been a distance. When he was little, he would play with his toys aware of the vibes and as he grew older he had begun to invade their space, thrusting between them and testing their unity. It was not something that was conscious. It could only be discerned through hindsight. Alex felt sorry for his parents.

Clive bustled in, seeming pleased. "Do you want a drink, Alex?"

"No I shouldn't. I need to be careful. I was stopped by the police on my way here."

Clive's happy face slipped into a scowl. "What for?" He probed.

"Nothing. A brake light out and it seemed I had crept over thirty on that stretch by the golf club. They did not say anything except fix the light and watch my speed."

"That road is a real speed trap. It catches a lot of drivers out." Clearly Clive was relieved, although again Alex detected tension in the air.

"We are moving away," Clive got straight to the point. Alex was surprised. They had not lived in the house very long and had spent a lot on interior decoration.

"Of course, you will come with us," his mother added.

"Where are you going?" Alex felt duplicitous in asking.

"Spain. To the villa, initially and then we will take stock. We fly out in the morning."

"Not for a holiday then?" Alex queried.

"Things are getting a bit uncomfortable over here. The markets are getting unstable. We need to consolidate. It's going to be survival of the fittest. Believe me a lot will go under. Cash is going to be king, you mark my words, and I'm selling what I can before it goes belly-up." Clive had poured another large brandy.

This capped Alex's extraordinary day but there was one more shocking detail to learn.

Clive downed most of his drink and for once looked uncertain.

"Your mother and I have something to tell you which we hope will influence your decision."

Alex could not imagine what new declaration could affect his day but he was about to be shattered by the revelation.

"Alex, dear," his mother began, reaching out to him, although Alex remained statue like. "I have known Clive a long time. In fact, I knew him about the time I met your father. I used to go to some wonderful parties and Clive was there, in fact he often organised them. Clive was busy empire building and I got to know Steve and married him but I still saw Clive from time to time."

Abigail watched her son and Clive stood behind her. Alex was not stupid. He looked at them both, together, black hair and eyes of flint and he knew, he knew without a doubt he was a blend of these two people.

"No," he stuttered.

"Why do you think I took you on Alex and why have I trusted you like no other. You are my son. You are my heir. I have no other children. We are a family. We can leave here and live a wonderful life. I have funds ready and waiting. Tomorrow we can be gone." The smile seemed more like a leer.

Alex was lost for words and then unbidden, curdling through his stomach and rising through his throat, a giggle and then a chuckle and finally Alex convulsed into loud unmitigated laughter. Abigail and Clive hesitantly joined in and very soon the three were howling uncontrollably. Alex recovered first and looked at the remnants of his family.

"I'm going home," he announced.

"You'll be back. You will come with us." His mother merely checked having no doubt that he would be there.

"I'll let you know." His mother smiled with self-satisfaction.

Alex took the car with the faulty break light fixed. He drove sharply but in snatches as his attention was lost. In one horrifying moment he had lost his dad, the man who had brought him up, the man he wanted more than anything to be his dad, the man he loved. He hated his mum for her deceptions and he hated Clive for claiming him, in fact for stealing him from whom he had been and who he wanted to be. Tears coursed down his cheeks. He did not see the cyclist until the last moment and swerved automatically into the path of the lorry.

Steve took the call and as at the Millennium rushed to the hospital but this time accompanied by Gillian. Phillip Carstairs the A & E doctor took them to one side.

"He's been lucky. It was a nasty crash. He has a head injury which we must monitor and some broken bones, a couple of ribs and we had to re-inflate the lung, and a broken leg that will need surgery."

"Can we see him?" Steve asked.

"Yes, but he's had an ordeal and needs to rest so maybe for a few minutes."

"What about his mother? Is she here?" Gillian asked before there was any embarrassment in the meeting.

"No we have left a message on her phone and I have explained to his stepfather as I have done for you. That was a while ago now but they have not arrived yet."

Alex lay immobile heavily drugged and surrounded by monitors. He was lucid which had been a relief and Steve took his hand in comfort.

"There's a phone in my inside pocket." Alex could hardly get the words out. "I need to ring someone."

"Surely in the morning." Steve soothed.

Alex gripped Steve's hand as hard as he could. "No now, the morning will be too late."

Gillian retrieved the phone and asked about the name and what she should say. "Tom," he muttered. "Tell him to come," Alex fell into temporary oblivion.

Gillian made the call curious to know who Tom was and how he figured so hugely in Alex's life. Alex had dated many girls to their knowledge so it was difficult to believe he had a boyfriend. At the very least this Tom was special to him.

The call was answered immediately almost as if he had been waiting. He said little except that he was on his way.

Tom Wilkes got to the hospital as quickly as he could and was admitted by a side door. The last thing he needed was to run into Clive Corneille.

Steve and Gillian were asked to wait in the relatives' room while they ran some tests. They were provided with a welcome cup of coffee and a biscuit. Meanwhile, Tom stole into the side room where he found Alex.

"Well, then? What's happened to you young man?" Tom looked sympathetically at the inert figure wondering about the circumstances of the crash. He had made his report to his seniors who had been full of enthusiasm, congratulating him on the pressure he had managed to exert on Alex. Tom had not liked the word 'pressure.' He had seen decency in Alex and had encouraged his confidence rather than demanded it.

Any pressure had come from the society around Alex as was so often the case for young people. There was the need to make their mark and there was continual fear of failure which bounced them into the path of the unscrupulous in society like Clive Corneille. Tom saw Alex as a victim and vowed to support him as much as possible.

Tom had to put his ear close to Alex to hear him. "They're leaving tomorrow morning—for good," he added. Alex gave him the details he knew.

Tom grasped the situation. "I'll be back," he said. "You've done well, Alex. Relax now and leave everything to me." Alex sank gratefully back on to the pillow.

Steve remarked to Gillian in the waiting room. "Funny when I went to the toilet a minute ago I could have sworn I saw that Inspector I met at Jim Woodhouse's coming out of Alex's room. He seems a bit senior to bother about a road traffic accident."

Steve and Gillian remained at the hospital throughout the night. Alex slept sporadically and occasionally moaned from the hurt. Steve kept a silent vigil and Gillian kept spirits up with encouraging words and coffee. She was able to observe father and son and was moved by the bond that she saw existed. She sat close to Steve who held her hand as he sought reassurance from his wife and for the first time she felt she belonged in the group.

Abigail remained absent and as a new day dawned Gillian felt more confident of her role as she pitied the prostrate Alex. She felt proud of Steve in his constancy while condemning Abigail for her absence. At one point when Steve felt he should telephone Abigail Alex had shown agitation and implored his dad to leave it. Gillian wondered if she had withdrawn from Steve's previous life too easily allowing a separation both between past and present as well as in her own marriage. Since the divorce, Steve had seen Alex independently and that had only emphasised any rift. Gillian acknowledged she should have made her presence felt. It had been a long night but as they waited for a bed to become available in a ward they drew together ready to redefine the future.

Chapter 19
Finding Hidden Depths

Does the road wind uphill all the way?
Yes, to the very end.
Will the day's journey take the whole long day?
From morn to night, my friend.

Uphill: Christina Rosetti

2007: Diana and Antony—Kirsten and Mark

Kirsten found out about Alex through her brother.

"You don't think it was deliberate do you?" Kirsten was terrified that her actions or rather lack of them had caused the accident. She had never in her life felt this guilty and this responsible. It was a burden that she shouldered while it also deepened her resentment towards Mark.

Phillip thought not but asked if she thought he had mental problems. Kirsten kept her counsel when she had heard that there had been a clandestine visit from a senior police officer but she feared the worst. There had been no word from Mark so another sleepless anxious night loomed. After two days of silence she was in a deep depression. Her mother hovered in her vicinity poised to listen to the difficulties and prepared to offer commiseration.

Kirsten's life had always been predictable, that was until her father's change in career and that had hardly affected her. She had already had her university place and completed her boarding school life before going trekking round Europe with a friend, so had not witnessed the stress and uncertainty as did her younger siblings.

Kirsten was also pragmatic and sensible with modest needs and little love for the high life so did not really miss the country residence. She knew though that Phillip had felt guilty for the cost of his final years of school which was an additional incentive to drive him to achieve highly. Although he was a 'jack the lad,' an attitude which had made him popular, he was underneath it all a sensitive human being with a strong work ethic. Medicine had been the right choice.

Kirsten could imagine his cheery face reassuring his patients but, also coupled with this caring nature, he had a toughness and resilience to fight off the inevitable results of dire days in casualty which could mentally cripple someone of less calibre. Phillip had his father's analytical brain and his mother's passion for life. He never held back and would dive into any opportunity and then decide if it was worth pursuing or dumping. There was always ruthlessness about Phillip in the way he dealt with life.

Samantha was a joy. She had a devil may care attitude, probably Kirsten thought, a bit like her mother would have had in her youth. Consequence did not seem to engulf her as it did Kirsten. She could pass blithely from one disaster to another and glide through to emerge brighter after leaving carnage in her wake. She could be at the depths of despair one minute and then ecstatic the next. People warmed to her and wanted to bask in her sunshine. Samantha did not see the need to hold back. Life was for living, she said often, especially when she was trying to inveigle herself out of a predicament. She was good at her job too. She was never floored by the attitude of wealthy clients treating all and sundry in exactly the same manner. They loved it and time and time again came up for more. If someone asked for her opinion, she gave it. She was never rude exactly but she could be blunt. She was the only one in the family who could intimidate Diana, although at times there could be a real tussle of wills between them that could either provide amusement for everyone else or create an unwelcome tension. Both Antony and Diana had worried that Samantha would fall by the wayside leaving school at sixteen and then taking the beauty course at the local college because it seemed an insignificant choice but Samantha had forged ahead, her personality being her advantage. She had a posse of admirers.

It was Samantha for whom Kirsten craved in her present distress. Samantha would bolster her up whatever answer she gave. She craved her company to dispel her utter gloom.

Kirsten was a product of her upbringing and had profited from it. Her early life spent in the gracious Cotswold village had a wealth of activities. There had been her riding, her dancing which she enjoyed, although at a level that would earn her praise for her sweet portrayals rather than for talented performances, her Brownie pack, her piano lessons and her French lessons. She had a busy schedule and luckily she had an excellent brain so excelled at the village school and a placid personality that enabled her to cope with the demands of life outside school.

There had always been someone to ferry her back and forth if her mother had not been available which was a regular occurrence because she was at a function with Antony, or had one of her headaches or needed to deal with her less amenable second child, Samantha. Kirsten hated attention so had not an ounce of jealousy for Samantha. In fact, she would do her best to divert her sister and therefore placate her mother. Kirsten strove to be the model daughter.

Kirsten had loved boarding school too. She was self-sufficient in a practical as well as an emotional sense and her ability particularly mathematically and scientifically separated her out from the common herd as someone with special aptitude to be nurtured. The teachers became her friends. They were charmed by the quiet, serious girl. She was obedient to their wishes in the nicest possible way, reasoning the sense of the instruction rather than feeling belittled by it. It all encouraged harmony and purpose.

The school welcomed the second daughter but Samantha soon showed she was not a shrinking violet in the same way as her elder sister. At times Kirsten would intervene to keep Samantha on the straight and narrow. The two sisters seemingly so different in personality became a forceful coalition to their mutual benefit. Samantha managed to negotiate school without incurring too many penalties thanks to Kirsten's help and Kirsten had an ardent supporter to raise her confidence and her profile.

By Tuesday afternoon, almost three days since Mark's hurried departure, Kirsten had gone through a kaleidoscope of emotions. Mark seemed to be blocking her calls and for really the first time in her life she had felt deep humiliation. She had trusted him. She had relied on him. Now she hated him or rather what he was doing to her. She was crushed by the intensity of feeling. She felt that whatever the outcome their relationship was blighted. It would not, it could not recover. She argued he had left her at the first real test. She had not done anything wrong but he had condemned her. She put the relationship under a microscope and forensically examined it, interpreting every action and every word she could remember. She agonised over text messages and looked at the photographs taken together remembering the occasions and her feelings. He had made her feel special. He had given her certainty. They were to shape their lives together, but, now they were not together, she felt alone and abandoned. That afternoon she took off her engagement ring and put it back in the box. Avoiding her mother she went for a long soak in a bath.

The warm water cleansed her body and her soul and temporarily brought respite. The gentle lap of the water against her skin as she moved made her feel desirable and the privacy brought some solace. She could think on a wider scale. She could allow her thoughts to drift and project them into the unknown and untested. She began to think more purposefully and deeply. She thought of Alex and what she had learnt about him.

No longer did he frighten her as he did at university but she was frightened for him. To her he had become a victim and not a perpetrator. She wondered what she would do in his position but it was impossible to imagine. Her father was not like his step-father Clive Corneille. She believed Antony would never do anything dishonest or even self-seeking.

She recalled seeing Clive at her parents' house one Christmas Eve when they used to host a party. Home from school she and Samantha would linger at the top of the staircase peering through the balustrade. Samantha's interest was in the fashion and she would inspect every lady as they arrived handing down her judgement of their attire to Kirsten who was much more interested in the personalities.

Kirsten knew the guest list. Her mother had always entrusted Kirsten with duties such as place names for dinner parties or distributing the little dishes of nuts and nibbles on the various occasional tables. Her mother liked to check too who had arrived and at what time as a sort of judgement for future consideration so Kirsten dutifully marked the attendance sheet with time of arrival.

Diana left nothing to chance. That had always been her way. Kirsten had not been impressed with Clive Corneille. The most striking thing about him was his raven hair. He peered through his dark framed glasses over his beaked nose scrutinising the guests as well as the setting.

From her vantage point, Kirsten would see him inspect a fine piece of porcelain, picking it up from the open cabinet and checking its authenticity by peering at the base. He would command attention of a group and dismiss inconsequential people easily, removing to another person who better warranted his time. That evening Kirsten had been absorbed in considering his artifice. To her as onlooker even at her young age she saw how he plundered the party. He was there for self-gratification and self-advancement. There had been students who were like that at school.

Of course, she knew Alex's real father was a decent man. She had met him through work and was struck by his open natural manner. She hoped he would not spurn Alex. He would need good people around him, although she feared Alex had pushed away too many of those good people. Phillip had told her that Steve and his wife had been to the hospital, sitting with Alex through the difficult early hours of admission but his mother to Phillip's knowledge had been noticeably absent.

Of course, she probably knew Steve had been there, Kirsten reasoned, and would have visited by now, especially as Alex was on a ward. Kirsten would have liked to go and see Alex too but Mark's words still resonated in her brain. She decided she would go when she felt more controlled. She would be no good to him in her current emotional state.

The water was getting colder. Kirsten unwilling to emerge raised the plug to allow the water to escape and then replenished the bath with fresh hot water. Considering the predicament of Alex had distracted her from her own situation and she began to feel tension rise again and tears prick her eyes. She had to fight to keep them at bay. She tried to convince herself that it was for the best and a marriage partner needed commitment.

As she lay immersed in the water, it seemed to her that Mark had acted selfishly, protecting his own career and reputation and not caring for or trusting in his wife to be. Kirsten used her mind to push away emotion. It was best to be cold in her heart. She could not contemplate any alternative.

When she had dressed, she felt capable of facing her mother. She would keep her at arm's length, anything less would be her undoing.

Diana looked up and smiled, "Mark rang while you were in the bath. He's coming here tomorrow."

Kirsten was suddenly aghast. She was angry she had missed the call. There had been nothing on her mobile. Why had he rung the house phone and spoken to her mother? She knew he was coming to sever the relationship. It was confirmation and she hardened her heart.

Wednesday was a busy day at the office. Kirsten had a full diary which kept her occupied but it meant she would be late arriving home. She saw Mark's car parked in the driveway and her heart quickened.

Diana met her at the door.

"They're in there," and she pointed to the study. Kirsten glanced at the mirror to check her appearance before going in but her mother reached out and took her arm. "We are not to go in apparently. They were both adamant."

Kirsten was puzzled. "They've been rummaging in the loft too."

"Let's have some tea and a talk." Diana pushed her daughter to the kitchen.

"What's going on Kirsten? Your dad looked dreadful. He said to stay out of it, whatever 'it' is."

Kirsten felt the weight of responsibility descend on her. She had brought trouble on this house. Just over a week ago they had all been sailing along in a benign wind but now there was a squall which seemed to be developing into a full blown storm and threatened to engulf them as in a seasonal hurricane.

"You know don't you, Kirsten? Is something wrong at work? Why is Mark here with your father?" Diana had had most of the afternoon to feed her anger.

Diana waiting for answers was getting impatient. She was seething and ready to attack anyone who stood in her way and at Kirsten's reticence she let rip.

"I'm sick of being ignored and pushed out by everyone in this house. You all think I'm stupid but I'm not, and I won't have the lot of you treating me as though I am. I've worked for this family as much as anyone else, in fact more. I'm here looking after everything, being ignored, while you go to your offices and expect me to be here backing you all up, never including me, never bothered if I am happy. You all take me for granted and I'm sick of it. I won't stand for it, I won't, so whatever it is, you had better start telling me or I won't be responsible for my actions."

This was the Diana of the past, her temper rising quickly. She was angry and resentful. She was a woman who had learnt to love her life since moving to Midchester but felt under threat. It had started when Kirsten had returned home and feeling excluded. Antony had become wrapped up in his affairs. Diana had been belittled. She had soldiered on but increasingly had been outpaced and out-gunned by her own army, daily irked by the treatment and now she felt she was fighting for survival. She was prepared to lash out at anyone and everyone.

"I don't know what's going on between Dad and Mark. I really don't. As for me and Mark, I can't say. I'm sorry, Mum, I can't help. It's not easy for any of us," and she took off to her bedroom waiting for the next development.

Diana had been incandescent but now she deflated like a burst balloon. She was almost fifty-six years old and she felt it. Outside the year was turning. In the little outside space beyond the patio area she could see the changing colours. The air too was heavier making the light opaque. The nights were drawing in and they required more heat in the house. Time she felt had a way of creeping up. It was relentless and she had for a while felt in its grip. When she was young, time had been her friend but lately it had seemed her enemy. To her life had been divided into four. The first part nonchalant and curious, acceding to temptations, relishing the sensual world at her disposal, often defiant and generally selfish and then there was a second quarter when life had taken on, she had thought, more meaning. They had been climbing the ladder. It had been dizzying sometimes but at the time always satisfying.

Looking back, Diana could only recall the momentum. Speed and purpose were of the essence, moving on to the next rung as though there was some master plan. She had had her children in that quarter too. Childbirth had not been difficult for Diana. It had been merely an inconvenience and so when the son arrived, she could leave childbearing behind. Four pregnancies and births were quite enough for any woman. It was only in the third quarter that she had begun to appreciate her children as a mother and she was honest enough to realise that her input into their upbringing had been woeful. That third quarter of life had been surprising in so many ways. It was as if, she had previously covered herself in a fur coat but rather than keep her warm it had smothered her and choked the life out of her and then the coat she had worn had become unfashionable and even deplorable for the killing it had involved. She was out of kilter.

The remnants of her parents' world had been cast aside as she was forced to cast aside the trappings of wealth to rediscover something from her early life. The abyss she had feared became a change of landscape. She found friendships and she found her family, marvelling that she had been given this chance through being forced to leave the pretence of an idyllic life. The experience of a different better life from seeing people close-up and personal had been a rebirth.

Now she was conscious that she was on the brink of her final quarter. The winter winds were gathering strength. She felt cold. Physically there were signs of middle age which no creams or potions could remove. Her skin hung more loosely about her face and her eyes lacked lustre. She would stare at her reflection willing her expression to take on a missing vitality. Her mouth had a downturn emphasised by the little creases at the edges. Her figure had begun to take on the stoutness of her mother, much to her dismay.

She knew she could still be attractive with careful applications of make-up and clever clothing but it all took so much more effort and by the time she had imposed the restrictions of strategic undergarments she had lost any spontaneity.

Diana had always relished a goal. There had been some undertaking for her energy which would result in the satisfaction of achievement. She had chosen a suitable husband, she had advanced his career, she had become a lady of the manor and on moving she had reinvented herself and Antony as a couple of repute.

Their life in Midchester had earned them a different kind of prestige, but prestige none the less. They were people of consequence and status, although in a more mature and secure fashion. People gravitated to them because they had personal worth, while previously people had gravitated to them because of a different kind of worth.

Things had been changing for a while. Margaret and Michael had left the town to settle on a smallholding in Shropshire. It was big enough to satisfy the ex-vet's need for livestock without being overwhelming. The walking group had had an influx of new members who were younger and more energetic seeing the group as a means to exercise rather than a stroll to enjoy companionship. They would design hikes requiring sturdy walking boots.

Diana was not really up for the challenge. She still helped at the charity shop but the routine was undemanding. The quality of the donations had deteriorated too. At one time she could find gems of designer clothing and fine china and glassware but now the items more resembled those that could be found in a skip only thrown their way to appease a conscience. Even Marjorie seemed to be running out of steam but she had the acclaim of the many foster children that had gone through her hands. Diana admired this popularity. She was also a little jealous of the attention they bestowed on the little woman.

Diana could not take credit for her own children. As a parent she knew she had been self-centred, palming them off at any opportunity. It was the way she had known from her own childhood. Her own parents had been remote which had the advantage of allowing her to exploit her freedom from undue attention.

However, they exercised control with an omnipotence that brought consequence as epitomised with the birth of Louise. Her mother was the determining factor. If it had not been for Antony's downfall as her mother termed it, she would not have had the relationship with her own offspring that she relished so much. The children had exceeded expectations and at times she could even be in awe of them.

Perhaps because of her own upbringing or her avoidance of hands on parenting when they were younger, she never felt the power of belonging to them. She had been left behind. She was now adrift. That Wednesday she did not know what was going on but she did know that in the rough seas of the household in this hurricane season she felt completely at the mercy of the waves. She was rudderless and alone. The others were clinging together in their lifeboat.

An hour later, Antony showed his face requiring sustenance but refused to be drawn by Diana. Meanwhile, Kirsten heard a light tap on her bedroom door. She had lain on her bed clutching the teddy bear as she had when Mark had first grappled with what she had told him of Alex. She had made up her mind that the axe would fall on their relationship and the little knock was the death knell. She gave no answer. It was impossible to answer. She would not voluntarily mount the scaffold.

The door gently opened and she saw Mark in the frame. He looked drawn and tired, his shoulders were sagging into his body, his hair was dishevelled and there was dark stubble round his chin giving him a swarthy and haggard look. She hardly recognised the clean cut man of her fiancée. There were no words from either of them. She gathered him to her as he caressed her hair and sought her mouth his bristles burning her skin with the intensity of the kiss.

Mark lay in her arms and recounted events as far as he knew. Neither questioned the power of their love for each other or the decisions that had been made. Mark, privy to highly confidential information, had realised the catastrophic potential of Alex's confidences to Kirsten and so he had acted quickly. His superiors had been informed and things had escalated at an alarming rate. A trusted police officer had made contact with Alex who had been co-operative to the extent that his step-father had been arrested early Tuesday morning along with other prominent people. It had been up to Mark and other members of the team to generate the evidence for these arrests.

It had been complex and Alex had been able to join some of the dots. There was still a lot of work to be done but Mark had worked round the clock to enable charges to be brought. These were clever men, used to hiding their affairs, and they had top lawyers at their disposal to defend them.

Time had been of the essence as they had been given reliable information that Clive Corneille was leaving the country so it was even more imperative not to delay. Mark had no opportunity to return her calls. He had hoped she would understand.

"And what about Dad?" Kirsten asked. "Why have you two been holed up in the study?"

"That may be something that he should tell you." He was being evasive.

"It's something to do with the case then?" His silence was her answer.

"Is there anything I can do?" Kirsten was frightened but now that Mark was there she had courage.

Mark looked at her softly. "Feed me, I'm famished," he implored, "And hold me in bed tonight so I can sleep. I need to get back to your dad. There is something else too. Cover for your dad at the office in the next couple of days. We need time."

Kirsten hugged him before she left to source something to eat. He followed her to the kitchen where Antony was scoffing an omelette. Kirsten was already beating the eggs.

Antony coughed before speaking to Diana and Kirsten. "We might be in for a difficult time. I will explain when I can but right now lie low and say nothing."

"I should also warn you," added Mark, "that prominent people have been arrested for serious fraud and there will be repercussions. The news will break in the next couple of days. It's a big case with ramifications." Diana dreaded those ramifications wondering about Mark and never guessing Antony would be touched.

When Antony had arrived home from the office earlier that day, he had found Mark waiting for him.

"Can we have a word in private?" Mark had begun. Antony knew there had been some sort of argument, the atmosphere in the house and at work with Kirsten had been an indication of a serious issue. Kirsten took most things in her stride unlike her mother. He expected a genial chat, a smoothing of ruffled feathers and maybe even some practical help but he did not expect the bombshell that Mark delivered.

Mark had wrestled with his conscience. He should have left well alone but this was Kirsten's father and a man he respected. He had got to know Antony over the preceding months and he believed in him. They were going to be close family members. If he acted fast, maybe he could deflect some of the shit that was going to come his way.

Now that arrests had been made, Mark felt able to highlight a possible position for Antony. The investigations had gone deep. It had to in order to build the case and many people would be drawn into the mire. Antony had been prominent and would certainly face interrogation if not by the police then the media. He had worked for Corneille. He was an accountant. How far had he helped Corneille cover up his illegal dealings? Antony was a clever accountant. Much could be laid at his door.

The shock for Antony was seismic. He had left the Corneille Company fifteen years before and had enjoyed a quiet, happy period of personal expansion. He had a network of friends and clients. These were people who trusted him. It would be useless to say his hands were clean if they had even touched the filthy pot. He would be sixty before much longer. He had become content and satisfied. Since Kirsten had joined the firm he had had a new burst of energy. His inner panic did not allow him to process his thoughts.

Diana had thrust open the door to the study and said breezily, "Hey boys are you coming for tea?"

Antony turned quickly, "Get out. Don't come in here." It was fierce and Diana in surprise closed the door dutifully.

"What's to be done?" Antony spoke to no-one in particular and then to Mark. "I understand now why you left, Mark. Of course, I could not expect you to remain with this family in the circumstances. I suppose you want me to break it to Kirsten. I'm sorry about you two. I thought you were right for each other. I can quite see why you must break off the engagement."

"No, that's not it at all. Kirsten and I are solid. It's a mess but I thought I might be able to steer things in a better direction. I should not be doing this at all and I might get the sack but I have not been enamoured by the job for some time so I will cross that bridge when it comes to it. I suppose I'm thinking maybe we should look at things and see what might come up from your point of view. I don't know if they have anything on you. That has not been my side of the investigation but we could think what might happen and be more prepared."

Antony had always ploughed his own furrow and to look at the earnest face of his future son-in-law, a young man who could help take the strain was overwhelming.

"I have never to my knowledge done anything wrong. I want you to know that." Antony removed his spectacles as his eyes watered. He spent a few moments concentrating on cleaning them.

"It's murky waters," Mark replied, "so let's see if we can make sense of things." Antony knew he would never be able to face it without someone to guide him and in doing so give him comfort. He was not a physically strong man who would be able to face prison. At that moment in time he knew it would be inevitable.

Antony had gone to work for Corneille after he had married Diana. He had a beautiful wife to keep and she had made no secret of her ambitions. He recalled how lost he had felt in the South of France when Diana had scooped him up in that possessive way she had. He had been happy working for the industrialist, a fair affable man who had been a good employer, although he had always wanted his pound of flesh.

Antony had enjoyed the acclaim from that deal that had taken him to the Cote D'Azur and Diana. It had been straightforward as far as Antony had been concerned. He had merely tracked events. His meticulous approach had enabled him to pinpoint the opportune moment to make the killing and the industrialist had done exactly that. Antony enjoyed a good monetary bonus that year as well as acquiring the bonus of a wife and it had been that financial coup that had brought him to the attention of Clive Corneille. He had been singled out and flattered.

Diana had convinced him the time was right to make his impact on the city and go with Corneille. She did not understand how fast he had had to race to keep up. The rewards were great such as the house in the country but he had always been under threat and to him it had been a relief when his time was up.

To him it had all been a sham. Now that era of his life was ready to destroy his present happiness and, not just him, it would reach like a virus into the lives of those he held dear.

Mark took his time questioning Antony. It was difficult prying into the past life of a man who was to be his father-in-law. He knew it was a delicate balance in how to win his trust and maintain his self-respect as well as find out the nub of his dealings in the company. Clive Corneille had been a smart operator but to carry out the misappropriation of funds he would need willing accomplices with the expertise of someone like Antony. He feared the worst.

Antony had never really known why he had fallen out of favour. He had seen it happen to others and accepted it as an inevitable consequence of city life. He had always been a figures man and did not look beyond his spreadsheets.

"I've remembered something that might help," Antony ventured. "When I left the organisation of course, I had to walk out without anything. However, I do have things." Mark looked curious.

"I will be honest Mark it was a big demanding job and it kept me awake at night. I dealt with the taxman you see. I had to make sure there were no cock-ups. It worried me a lot you know so I brought copies home to check, to make sure, and I used to work on them at night or at the weekends. I knew I would be in a lot of trouble if I used them in any way so I packed them all up. I think I still have them."

Mark could not believe what he was hearing. These papers could condemn Antony.

"Where are they?"

"In the loft, I think, unless Diana has thrown them away. When we moved, we put lots in store and then when we bought this house we put anything we were not sure about in the loft. We thought we would sort it out later. That never happened of course, so I think the box is probably still there."

"We had better look then, hadn't we?" Mark was more frightened for Antony. Maybe, he should advise him to burn it but burning the box of papers would not erase the fact of them having existed. Between them inevitably forevermore there would be the bitter taste of the ash that was left. Against his better judgement Mark agreed they should open the box.

It took them a while to locate the box. It had been pushed to the far corner behind the forgotten toys. It needed the strength of the two of them to yank it out and out of the hatch. It was covered in dust and cobwebs which made them splutter and sneeze. Diana came to investigate the commotion and predictably was horrified at the mess on her usually pristine landing. Antony had no time to mollify her so left her ranting about the inconsiderate men in her life.

Thus began an examination of the contents, that in due time would yield interesting contents. They were engrossed in this when Kirsten arrived home.

Once they began to unravel the workings they began to hope that there was in fact enough to exonerate Antony and more particularly show the lengths Corneille had gone in order to achieve the efficacy of his deceit. As each layer of subterfuge was peeled away it was like discovering a masterpiece under layers of deceptive grime and questionable restoration. They had gradually left the personal quest behind as they became absorbed in the adventure of hunting down their prey.

Antony had kept memos of instruction written in Clive Corneille's hand as well as others. Clearly Antony had been efficient in including every detail as conveyed to him by his company superiors. His only crime was in not challenging anything that he had been fed. At times Antony had felt foolish for accepting information without question but this was a small price to pay if he could prove his innocence. As the evening wore on his spirits lifted. At midnight they decided to call it a night and resume in the morning.

While Mark crept into Kirsten's bed reaching her warm body and feeling the comfort of her closeness Antony discovered an empty cold bed. Diana angered by the insult to her position had debunked to Samantha in London. Two could play at that game she thought. Antony cursed his wife. He looked in the other rooms and then noticed her wash things had been removed from their en-suite. There was no note of explanation. He was exhausted and fell into bed, although sleep evaded him. Diana had taken the inevitable decision. She had chosen to go. It was obvious to him that she had known he would be tainted by Clive Corneille and she had been decisive and left him. Self-preservation was fundamental to her. He thought it had always been inevitable. He could never satisfy Diana and he had been lucky they had lasted that long.

Chapter 20
Loss of Face

Whether in the bringing of the flowers or of the food
She offers plenty, and is part of plenty,
And whether I see her stooping, or leaning with the flowers,
What she does is ages old, and she is not simply,
No, but lovely in that way.

Part of Plenty: Bernard Spencer

2007: Diana: Steve: Alex: Gillian

Diana arrived late at Samantha's flat. She had been too furious to telephone and to warn her daughter and rang the doorbell with impatience. Samantha clicked the intercom expecting a drunken ex to have found his way to her door.

Diana's emotions were still bubbling. "Let me in!" She barked.

Settled in the cosy flat, a gin and tonic in hand, Diana explained. "I had to get out and knew you would understand. They will not tell me a thing. I know it's serious, but what good is it in keeping it from me? It's like a conspiracy."

"Who won't tell you about what?" Samantha paid little heed to her mother's indignation.

Diana was impatient, "If I knew what, I wouldn't have come, would I? It's your dad, Kirsten and Mark. They're all accountants together as though I am too dim to understand. I won't be patronised."

She took a slow swallow of her drink. "This is nice gin, Samantha."

"How long are you staying?" Samantha sighed, resigned to mopping up her mother's hysteria.

"As long as it takes. I won't be any trouble. It's about time I had some 'me' time. I will take a rain check at the weekend and see if they've bucked their ideas up." Samantha accepted the situation was temporary. She knew her mother too well.

Samantha's flatmate was in New York for a week which was convenient. Her mother in this sort of mood was not someone to be paraded in front of her London friends. She sorted out a bed for Diana. They could talk tomorrow.

Thursday dawned. Samantha having taken Diana a cup of tea in bed left for work arranging to meet after work to eat at a local restaurant. She would ring Kirsten during the day.

The newspaper headline caught her attention but did not worry her unduly. At work there was gossip, especially about the sex parties and which of their clients might have been involved. It was only when she managed to get hold of Kirsten that she found out the importance for the family. Kirsten was relieved to find that her mother had made it to her sister's and promised to let her dad know. The girls thought it best to keep Diana away until the weekend and then return for a family pow-wow. It was hoped that their position would be much clearer then.

Meanwhile, Samantha bought every newspaper she could think of and read the reports between appointments. It seemed that the frauds had been going on for many years, there was evidence of bribery and corruption, the football club had been mentioned in relation to Clive Corneille and there were allegations that he had had his hand in the pension pot to shoulder failing businesses. The scandal had awakened the roaring lions of the journalists who would hunt down their quarry without mercy. The jungle drums of Fleet Street were beating hard and fast.

It was surprising what a girl could learn in a beauty parlour and Samantha listened to conversations that ebbed and flowed from clients during the day. It seemed that now that arrests had been made it was fair game to tittle-tattle and many of the wealthier women knew how to dish the dirt.

It seemed that there had been a network of business men linked with government officials including one or two senior police who had been consistently feathering their own nests. Contracts had been given for personal gain. Assets of individuals were mentioned, mansions, yachts and hideaways in exotic foreign places.

Clients had witnessed the extravagance. The racket had taken the shape of a pyramid with base players taking their cut too, while at the top men like Clive Corneille had stood proud and untouchable. There were whispers of drug dealings and then there were the more seedy and salacious parties. These men were power driven and used their positions to exploit others including young girls.

There were one or two photographs in the newspaper over which the beauticians poured. Samantha had nothing but contempt for the men involved. They had evaded the law by clever manipulation and the criminal clubs of which they were involved, outwardly respectable inwardly corrupt. They were learning that no-one was untouchable.

Samantha with her practical grasp of things and noting the timescale of events, understood that it was possible for her father to be implicated. The decision then was whether to tell her mother before the weekend or keep her in the dark until then. She decided to play it by ear.

The restaurant was a smart modern over-priced eatery where they could relax. Diana had been buoyed up by her shopping excursion. The shop assistants had fawned over her, raising her spirits and allowing her to play the part of a stylish wife of a successful man. She had spent rather more than she should have done but the expense was justified and the clothes would certainly make Antony sit up and take notice. She was not about to play the part of a dismissed wife.

They sat at a solid square table adorned with deep red napkins, heavy white wine and water glasses and contemporary cutlery. The modest centrepiece was a creation of sea shells on a driftwood base. Diana liked going to new places. Her life had become predictable and she thought mundane. They would dine out regularly and, although she loved Benedicto's, their favoured place, it had become routine as did their life.

Although they still enjoyed sex, that too had become predictable and familiar. Diana appreciated the calm of her life but she had always relished prominence and popularity. She came alive before an audience and wilted when she was left unattended. Periodically, she needed glamour. The last few days had been the final straw. She had been a supportive and loving wife and yet she was feeling side lined and unappreciated. She needed to assert her authority and had left the house to send a warning shot across their bows.

She had no reason to believe that she would not be welcomed home and they might even beg her return and then she would once more feel the security of her position. Diana needed to be included in any enterprise. It fed her ego.

Samantha decided that her mother would not be pleased if all and sundry knew about Clive Corneille and she did not. She broached the topic. "Have you seen the news, Mum?"

Diana and Samantha did not usually discuss current affairs. "Not especially. Should I?"

"Clive Corneille has been arrested," Samantha spoke in a serious manner and waited for the effect but her mother treated it like gossip.

"Really! You've made my day. Nasty man! What's he been up to, not fiddling the books? He won't like paying a fine. A mean selfish horrible man," and she smiled with satisfaction.

"It's a lot more serious than that. He will probably go to jail," Samantha spelt it out.

Diana's eyes opened wide. She still had not caught any implication. "Even better," was her retort, "A celebration then?"

Samantha studied her mother. She saw a woman of mature years and yet someone who looked younger. Samantha knew her mother had a strict skin regime and tried to be active, although her figure had thickened demonstrating self-indulgence in food and drink. She was not fat but more endowed which actually gave her an imposing air. Her mother had not lost any of her fashion sense which extended to a slick hair-cut that flattered a strong face with a firm jaw line, generous wide smile with even white teeth supporting a neat nose and deep blue eyes. It had been her mother who had inspired Samantha to embark on a career in beauty.

Samantha, more than any of them, knew the effort that Diana put into her appearance and indeed, life. It was not just in the outward show but the mental inner strength too. She had been the one to test her mother on numerous occasions. She remembered with affection the time she had cut Georgina's hair at school. The girl had a mass of curls which cascaded down her back.

Bored one evening in the dormitory, they thought a make-over would be entertaining. Samantha let Georgina cut her hair first, although she wore her hair in a bob so truthfully there had not been much to cut but when it was her turn Samantha attacked the curls with a fury. Chop, chop, chop went the scissors until the curls were gone, scattered over the floor and Georgina emerged shorn as a sheep in summer.

Samantha was in big trouble. Her parents were summoned and Diana, alone because Antony had been caught up in the city, swept into the school to confront the headmistress. Miss MacIntyre greeted Diana at her door. She explained that it was not just this incident that had tried her patience but Samantha's general disregard for rules and what she termed etiquette of the school. The calamity of

Georgina's missing hair was having repercussions as Georgina's parents were up in arms and making threats regarding removing their daughter and making it generally known why.

Apologies did not answer, especially as Georgina was to be bridesmaid to a titled cousin and the bride had particularly wanted the hair of her bridesmaids dressed to fall graciously down their backs to compliment the style of the dress. Diana handled the situation with complete aplomb. She contacted the irate parents and sweet talked them into letting her take Georgina to an acclaimed London hair stylist who was able to salvage the cut hair so that Georgina looked chic and fashionable.

When the bride saw the result and how the new look framed Georgina's face to flatter and not overwhelm it – as the long hair had previously done, she did a complete turnabout and suggested the other bridesmaids follow suit. The society wedding was featured in Vogue and special mention was given to Georgina. Samantha could not help wonder if her mother had engineered that special attention.

It was Diana that had spelt out the facts of life and insisted she take precautions not only against an unwanted pregnancy but any disease from casual sex. Diana was not judgemental at all, only practical and Samantha, especially had appreciated this in her mother. Diana could be forthright if she thought any one of her children was acting improperly but she was also a realist and rarely shocked by any of their antics. It was not a trouble free upbringing but there was security.

"Did you and Dad know Clive Corneille well?" Samantha needed to prod her mother.

"As well as anyone can know a man like that. He had your dad at his beck and call and thought nothing of calling him away at a weekend if he wanted some figures or to support him in a deal. He owed a lot to your father and then suddenly cast him aside because his face did not fit." Diana sipped her wine.

"So Dad was a trusted employee?" Samantha was surprised that her mother who was usually so shrewd was missing the implication.

"Of course, Corneille depended on him." Diana was thinking of Antony rather than Clive Corneille. She was proud of Antony who was clever in a way she admired.

Samantha felt she would have to prompt her mother to make a connection. Diana seemed oblivious to any consequence. Diana had always had absolute trust in Antony, that was one of the reasons she had known he was good husband material. He had neither the imagination nor the courage to cheat on her. His work ethic was sound and this retiring reliability had provided Diana with the perfect backdrop to shine in society and be a prima donna in the marital home without serious repercussions.

Samantha had known it was all an act. Diana naturally had to take centre stage. She knew how to perform and nowhere did Diana perform more than for her own mother. The trouble for Diana was in the way she confused her two selves, the sweet, sensitive human being subsumed beneath the outward show.

Samantha had very little memory of her grandmother, Diana's mother who, unlike Antony's mother who had been warm and caring, was a cruel insensitive woman. Samantha hated those visits. She had often squirmed at her grandmother's cutting comments. There was no cheer in the woman.

Diana took on an edge in her mother's presence that in turn would set the whole family on edge. Visits had been disagreeable and always left a disquieting mark. Her mother was a complex character and Samantha appreciated her attributes as well as realising her weaknesses.

"Dad might be in a bit of trouble." Samantha had at last gained Diana's proper attention.

Diana's antennae were alerted. "What do you mean?"

"He worked as an accountant for Clive Corneille who is now facing serious fraud charges ranging over many years to the time Dad worked for him. Do you understand?" Samantha spoke directly seeing no point in pussy footing around the subject.

"Oh my god," was all Diana could reply.

For Diana it was like hitting a brick wall at optimum speed. They had not thought she was dim, they were protecting her. "No, no way, your dad is the most honest man I know. He would not be involved in anything crooked. He can be stupid in some ways but you must never doubt his integrity."

"We don't, but others might. He's getting prepared, you know, in case."

Suddenly, the restaurant had seemed tacky and the atmosphere cold. Diana had no more appetite. She wanted to get out and quickly.

They travelled home on Friday as soon as Samantha could get away from the salon.

They found Antony, Kirsten and Mark in the kitchen. Antony gave Diana a slow intense look and nodded before leaving the room expecting her to follow for the inevitable confrontation.

"I will not stand in your way, Diana."

"Tony, do you think I want to leave you?" Diana saw a defeated man before her and took a small step towards him but he raised his hand signalling halt and she obeyed.

"It would probably be a sensible thing to do. You would get a worthwhile sum and I will move out so you can have the house. It might be best if you went away for a nice holiday. You can use Charles as solicitor, I will get someone else. It really should not take long. I won't fight you Diana."

To Diana standing in their lounge the whole thing sounded ridiculous and despite the seriousness of the situation she was consumed with a sudden burst of mirth.

"So I am not worth fighting for then?" Was her quick retort.

Antony was slow to appreciate the inference having spent the last few days desperately trying to defend his honour. He had quickly come to terms with the fact that his marriage was over. He would not expect any woman let alone Diana to stand by him.

"Well, Tony, are you so unhappy with our marriage that you want to chuck it away after all these years?" She was confident that all would be smoothed over.

Antony had rehearsed his earlier speech in his head and could not find any energy to offer any counter. He felt his life was in ruins. Whatever the outcome he knew mud would stick. He was scared and wanted to run away so to him he would give that opportunity to the woman he loved.

"It's for the best, Diana," and he turned round and left the room. She heard the front door bang.

Diana re-joined the younger members of the family in the kitchen. The girls had expected a full scale row and the silence had been unnerving. Diana assessed their glances and waded in.

"I think I need to know everything so I suggest we sit round the table and decide what's to be done."

Diana took her position as chairwoman. She took a notebook and quizzed Mark and Kirsten about the situation. Mark was able to offer some hope. He said that the evidence he had seen from Antony had done more to persuade that Antony had followed instructions. There were memos in support of any amendments and the accounts generally stood up. In fact, he was hopeful that Antony might avoid prosecution but he probably could not avoid the publicity and general speculation about his role.

With Antony's agreement all the documents had been passed over to the Fraud Squad and they would have to wait for their assessment. Diana asked him to monitor the situation and if possible urge his contacts to conclude their investigations as soon as possible. They all knew this might drag on indefinitely which would damage Antony's reputation.

Diana was more worried that a lengthy inquiry would result in a detrimental effect on Antony's health. She could see he was already floundering and the family needed to pull together to shoulder him up. She had no conscience about her departure on Wednesday night. She had rarely looked back on her actions with any regret.

Diana turned to Kirsten and questioned her regarding the accountancy. She thought they should look carefully at the workload for Antony but more particularly shield him from any potentially tricky situations.

They all agreed that Antony needed the diversion of work but did not need any confrontation. Kirsten would look at the client list and divert some of the more contentious accounts to her and try to enable Antony to deal with his more supportive and amenable clients.

Diana knew that shutting Antony away could be seen as an admission of guilt. All four of them knew there was a fine line between managing to negotiate a business that could be outwardly seen as operating normally and protecting the chief operator.

The family meeting discussed Alex with mixed feelings. Diana had no time for him. Kirsten argued that he had been caught in an intolerable situation. Mark and Samantha did not know Alex so could only see the advantage of keeping him at a distance. Kirsten felt she was abandoning Alex, after all Alex did not have a family to rally round as they clearly were doing for Antony. Diana knew Steve would offer some support but kept that view to herself. For the moment, they would deal with the situation at home rather than allow contact with Alex. Kirsten felt guilty.

The next issue to discuss was the home front and how to deal with any unwanted publicity. Should they also engage a specialist lawyer at this point in time? Mark thought that was not necessary and might indeed be construed as guilt in some quarters but he did have one or two names if the occasion arose.

They all agreed there had to be a united front and somehow, to conduct their lives in a dignified way. There was one light hearted moment at this point when Samantha was told that she could not allow her attraction for the opposite sex and her party life to continue for a while.

"I'll need a support group to give it all up like AA."

"That's us," said Kirsten, "and it will do you good. It will be a detox of a different kind."

They agreed that they should continue about their business but have a meeting every weekend. All of them felt that they were capable of riding the storm.

Diana slipped into her coat and went to find Antony. She had a good idea where Antony would be. There was a riverside bar where a man could blend into the furnishings and quietly get drunk. She would have to retrieve him. He was there as she expected, propped up at the bar with a scotch in his hand.

"I'll have one of those too," she murmured in his ear. He signalled the bartender who dealt with the order. Diana sat close on the next stool willing him to lift his head and notice her resolve. Gradually, they began to feel at ease, sharing the single malt, and Diana slipped her hand into his and held it tight.

"Let's go for a walk," she suggested.

They walked and talked honestly and carefully. Diana explained how the family were to support him and more importantly that none of them had any doubts about his innocence. They would rally round.

"I don't deserve you," Antony said.

"It's me that does not deserve you," was her answer.

The weeks slipped by. At first, there was tension but after a few weeks they had learnt a new pattern of behaviour. They had been lucky there had been no intrusive newspaper reports probably because there were bigger fish to fry. Alex had not been so lucky.

Alex had been discharged from the hospital a week after the arrests. His mother was back at the house and he was unwilling to face her. She had made a brief visit during the week but it had been fraught with concern about being accosted by reporters and in true Abigail style she had played the 'poor me' card with hardly a thought for what her son was going through. Steve and Gillian took him in to their home.

The presence of Alex in their house was a challenge. Gillian had been so used to having her empire as she had done at school, harbouring treasured possessions in every room and so she felt exposed. To her it was an invasion by an enemy, an opportunity for Alex to see into her private life and then at a future date ridicule her. She was on guard. She was thankful to be at home, no longer working, so that she could keep a watchful eye. Steve needed to work. It was fortunate that the kind of jobs he did were largely alone. It would mean that Gillian had Alex for company.

The reporters would gather at the gates. Gillian thought they were baying for blood like prowling wolves and from an upstairs window would study them from behind the window blinds. She stayed in as much as possible fearing any repercussions from leaving Alex alone or being accosted in the street. Steve went to collect Alex's things.

Abigail had been expecting him and opened the door slightly ushering Steve through so she would not be exposed to the small crowd outside.

"How are you?" He asked her.

"How do you expect?" Steve gave her a meaningful smile and told her to take heart. He tried to reassure her by saying it was all a nine days wonder but both of them knew the truth.

Abigail had put Alex's things together. It had given her something to do.

"Stay a bit," she pleaded. Steve had not the heart to leave her on her own. After half an hour he tried to go once more marvelling that not once had she asked after Alex. It had been a litany of complaint, from how they had been treated by the police to the quality of tea at the police station and the rude reporters who had jostled her as she left the station to take a taxi home as well as how she could not eat and sleep. There had been no support from anyone.

Like rats, they had all abandoned a sinking ship. She had expected the executive of the football club to support the wife of the chairman but she said they were all selfish and cruel. She moaned about the timing of the arrest. They were about to leave the country only that morning. It had been absolutely rotten timing. She could have been sunbathing by the pool with a cocktail and not having to fend off the rabble outside. Steve genuinely felt sorry for her and hesitated as he stood in front of the window waiting for her tirade to come to an end.

Tears were flowing as she became more emotional and then she was there embracing him and sobbing on his chest. He momentarily comforted her before pushing her away but not before the photographer had clicked his shutter. A picture could paint a thousand words and this one certainly would.

Steve managed to leave just when the London defence lawyers arrived. Abigail had not been left completely alone then he thought.

Gillian needed to keep busy. She made a farmhouse fruit cake and some lemon biscuits. She enjoyed baking. There was something satisfying about mixing all the ingredients, happy to let her mind wander in the physical activity. She used the rubbed in method dipping her fingers into the dry ingredients and gently rubbing them into ultra-fine breadcrumbs before adding the fruit and eggs. She had read somewhere that if you want to sell a house the smell of baking bread or cake could entice any viewer to see the property as a home.

It was this way for Alex. He put his head around the door and asked if he could come in. Gillian surprised and at first a bit irritated could not refuse and organised a chair where he might be comfortable with his leg in its cast.

"That smells good." A delicious aroma was permeating the kitchen.

"It won't be ready for a while I am afraid, but I have a bit of chocolate cake left that I made the other day. You are welcome to try some." It was a natural thing for Gillian to say and Alex absorbed the solicitude as a tonic.

Alex affirmed he would like some and quietly accepted a slice without comment. The cake was delicious and transported him away from his present misery. There was no heaviness to the cake, it was light and smooth and crumbled in his mouth. The flavour of the rich chocolate made him think of good days when he had been given treats as his dad had often done to encourage and reward him.

"You made this?" He was in awe.

"It's a very simple recipe but quite unusual," she replied, "I use mayonnaise instead of eggs. It really works don't you think? I will show you if you like." Again, Gillian adopted the style of an encouraging teacher. It was a safe option in the circumstances.

"Mum hated cooking and never made cakes," Alex made the observation without malice. He had begun to reassess a lot in his life.

"I enjoy it and find it satisfying and therapeutic if I'm a bit low which is quite often the case so your dad gets a lot of cakes as a result. It's not really very good for his waistline or cholesterol but he works hard so a treat now and then does not hurt."

It seemed strange to Alex to have someone talk about his dad like that. His mother had only ever seemed to carp about him and certainly never baked. The kitchen was homely. As Gillian had been baking there were ingredients ranged on the table, sprinklings of flour lay like dustings of snow and on the windowsill was a planter of herbs. Heavy saucepans rested on a shelf over another narrow shelf of spice jars. There was a shelf too of cookery books in far from pristine condition having stained untidy covers. It was a well-used kitchen and Gillian was the capable cook in control.

Gillian had been married to Steve for eleven years and in that time had hardly ever met Alex. To her he had been the stupid boy who had tried to spoil their wedding. She had allowed Steve the freedom to connect with him even though it inevitably meant seeing his ex-wife. At times she had hated it and allowed her resentment to dominate her mood becoming recalcitrant and awkward like some of the teenagers she used to teach. She remembered the Millennium with bitterness.

Somehow, she could not help it and the sour feelings remained heavy in her stomach like a giant fallen boulder blocking her breath. She had spent most of her life feeling inadequate and put upon. She studied Steve's son and thought that the man Alex had become eight years later did not resemble her earlier view.

"I think a cup of tea and then I will start dinner. I thought shepherd's pie. What do you think?"

Alex had never joined a domestic scene in this way. Of course, he had used the kitchen but often for ready meals in the microwave or with his dad who might try and put together a simple curry or Bolognese or omelette when he got home from work because nothing else had been prepared. His mother had portrayed kitchen work as a burden. She called anything domestic a chore, and did as little as possible.

Gillian on the other hand had boiled the kettle and made the tea and while doing so had deftly wiped the kitchen surfaces ready for the next operation. He was impressed with her efficiency and naturalness. It all seemed normal. He had been used to his mother swinging from overzealous exaggerated hospitality for any visitors to a more slovenly all too much trouble attitude when they were alone.

There was little conversation while they drank their tea. It was no good talking about the current situation and they had no known common ground because of previous distance. They were both being polite. It was in their best interests.

When Gillian returned to her cooking, checking the cake which she estimated would need another half hour and reaching for the ingredients from the vegetable basket and fridge he found himself saying, "Is there anything I can do to help?" It was an utterly stupid thing to say and he regretted it immediately. He had no culinary skills whatsoever. It had just seemed the right thing to say.

Gillian on the other hand, used to sharing with Steve when he was home had, no compunction.

"That would be nice. Would you peel the potatoes or chop the onion? I can bring the chopping board to the table where you can be comfortable." There was a practical no-nonsense assumption in her manner. It would be easier for her if he was doing something rather than watching her. She did not guess he would struggle with the simple task.

The die was cast. Alex did make a valiant attempt but his woeful skills became exposed within the first minute. His defence mechanisms surfaced, although he could hardly throw down his tools and march out. He felt stupid whatever he did.

"Not done a lot?" Gillian asked. "Never mind, I'll help."

There was no criticism in her voice and as the good teacher she had always been she joined him at the table so that together they prepared the vegetables in a relaxed harmony. Alex who initially had expected recrimination and derision began to enjoy the activity. His hands employed in the unfamiliar activity somehow gave his mind a rest from the torment of the past week. It was indeed as Gillian had said earlier, therapeutic.

Steve had had a number of errands so came home much later to find his wife and son in a sort of conspiracy of cooking in the kitchen. As they had warmed to the challenge, the student Alex and the teacher Gillian had laughed at spillages and errors. Gillian had a level of tolerance that Alex had not met before. Steve had been expecting a strained atmosphere on his return but he was welcomed by the appetising smells of the shepherd's pie and the homely inviting atmosphere in the kitchen. He could not have been more delighted and visibly relaxed.

Alex took an interest in the cooking using Gillian as a kind of cookery expert. It was to him surprising how he could be released in the mundane activities and with perseverance he managed to contribute more successfully. Gillian knew how to be patient. She allowed him to make mistakes and feel his way into his kitchen confidence. Over the next few days, they shared the experience concentrating on the cuisine rather than any other concerns in their lives. The cookery books were explored and Alex suggested testing some of the more unusual recipes. The little knot of reporters had left and some sort of calm normality resumed.

The photograph did not appear until the end of the following week. The accused had been released on bail and other news was pushing them off the front pages. There had been some stilted phone conversations between Alex, his mother and Clive.

Alex could not acknowledge Clive as his father and wanted more than anything to keep it under wraps. He wanted Steve to be his father and, almost because he knew he was not his biological dad, he cherished spending time with him more. He had taken Steve for granted and taken his lead from his mother but now he valued having Steve in his life and did not want to lose him.

The photograph was with an article about the effects on the families on one of the inside pages in the weekend edition. It was designed to dig deeper into the wider implications of the scandal. There were other photographs of other wives at social events in their past lives or in front of substantial houses and on holidays but the one of Steve and Abigail struck a different note.

It portrayed a couple close and personal in a private moment suggesting that Clive Corneille's recent wife had an ex-husband to comfort her, insinuating intimacy on a level that was evidence of a continuing affair.

It was Anthea who saw the photograph first and showed Bill. They debated and Anthea rang Gillian. Anthea was not a woman to shy away from a difficult situation. Gillian decided she should collect the newspaper with her shopping.

Although Anthea had warned her that there was a photograph of Steve and Abigail and how the article had made ridiculous suppositions and, although Gillian as an English teacher knew the false twists and turns of the press as well as the high-handed exaggeration they invariably brought to an article, she was still unprepared for what she saw. She was dumbfounded and then furious. She was like a wounded animal, desperate and hurt.

Steve and Alex were watching the racing in the lounge. Gillian strode into the room and flung the newspaper at Steve. "You probably need the paper to get a winner." She yelled. "What are the odds Steve, hedging your bets as usual?"

The men had their comfortable afternoon shattered. Alex had not seen Gillian in a passion which was reflected on his shocked face. He picked up the newspaper that had fallen haphazardly on the floor and set to straightening the pages when his attention was drawn to the page with the photographs. He stared at it feeling bile surface to his mouth before snarling at Steve.

"How could you, Dad?" He left to seek out Gillian.

Gingerly Steve picked up the offending newspaper. There was the photograph, large and prominent, and he felt sick.

Alex tried to reassure Gillian. He said his dad was weak and kind and his mum was manipulative and clingy. Alex did not want the pleasantness of the current arrangement to be spoilt. That seemed a vain hope.

Steve and Gillian gathered themselves but their relationship was bruised. No explanation could make Gillian's pain of humiliation disappear and no apology could restore her trust. It was like Millennium all over again.

Chapter 21
Take Your Pleasure Where You Find It

There is a haunting phantom called Regret
A shadowy creature robed somewhat like Woe
But fairer in the face, whom all men know
By her sad mien, and eyes forever wet.
No heart would seek her; but once having met,
All take her by the hand, and to and fro
They wander through those paths of long ago—
Those hallowed ways 'twere wiser to forget.

Regret: Ella Wheeler Wilcox

2008: Alex: Steve: Gillian

Families can be strange structures. Outwardly they may comply with the conventions of the time but inwardly they ebb and flow according to the needs and desires of individuals within it. Often those needs and desires come from independent hopes and beliefs. Then it becomes a power struggle with the strongest will dominating the outcome. That power can be determined by strong emotion like love and hate or by ambition when the individual has calculated the path that he or she must force others to take.

Sometimes, within the dynamics, one member protects the status quo at all costs while another will yank and yank the fibres of attachment to breaking point. Happy are the families that can bring together those separate and distinct voices to find a new harmony different and unique that becomes their signature tune as each choir member is confident that their own voice will resonant and their own song will not go unnoticed. Unhappy are the families where voices will jangle and clash or worse never be heard above the din.

The Carstairs had their own beat of a drum call. It was loud and insistent and regular like a call to prayer and each member answered. Diana had taken her role of choirmaster and for this performance the others followed. Each of them could strike out on their own and within the repertoire make solo contributions but instinctively each would rejoice in the harmony of the whole.

So it was that they weathered the storm that had come their way, not one of them did not answer the call. They met every weekend with Phillip joining them when his duties at the hospital permitted and they spoke of developments and possibilities as if in rehearsal for some grand concert. At first, Antony had been tentative with his part but encouraged by the strong voices of the others he came to find his true self again. He had been interviewed several times and computers had been taken for analysis. With his family behind him he had been able to stand firm, in the spotlight his voice was pure and unwavering. At the end of January 2008, he was told there would be no prosecution. The authorities had been convinced of his non-involvement and they thanked him for his co-operation. He was a citizen again. There was a collective sigh of relief in the Carstairs family unit.

Steve and Gillian and Alex did not have the benefit of that collective voice. After the publication of the photograph the household had splintered. Alex incredibly felt more comfortable with Gillian. She taught him to make bread and various pastries as well as casseroles and pies. It became their space away from the confusions of the outside world. Steve took off to his carpentry and his work with Simon. They all were resentful and defensive.

Steve had been caught out in an act he did not commit. He hated the accusation and the ensuing presumption of guilt. He had no defence and yet there had been no crime. The world had derided him and that derision had invaded his home. He could only seek sanctuary with Simon and his family which incurred even more resentment that his own home had been violated. He could not apologise for something he had not done. He would not grovel.

Steve had given his all and had no more to give. As a young man he had been light hearted and willing. He had run with the boys and hunted the girls. He had been no different to other males of his generation. He had no concept beyond the immediate which allowed the surprise of the snare which tightened and held him fast in a vicelike grip more devastating.

Abigail had been waiting in the bushes and Steve had not recognised the danger. She had waylaid him and lured him with the tit bits she had scattered in his path until he had fallen into her clutches. He had been pulled into her sphere and he had willingly succumbed to her bidding. He knew now that the attraction had been skin deep. The birth of Alex had sealed his fate.

Divorce would be out of the question. He had found something in his soul that he had ignored. He worshipped his son. He wanted to smooth his path in life, to protect him, to encourage him, to guide him and when Abigail withdrew from him the boy became more important and vital, the central pivot of his world, that is until he met Gillian but by then Alex had grown.

Gillian had spent her life seeking perfection. At school, her handwriting had been symbolic of a girl anxious to please and delight. It was painstaking, the fine italic print was even and exact and it was difficult to find a personality beneath the artistry. Practice was her mantra. She would never put herself forward without being sure that she could deliver. The part in the school play was not for her, where there was every possibility of being exposed as the imposter she felt. She had developed the knack of concealment when still in plain view. During her teaching career no-one could ever guess she was hiding as she directed her classroom. She had been thorough in setting up her cover.

Her true self had been camouflaged and she felt secure with her books and her work sheets until she had been forced to take stock by the new guard like Rebekah with a k. Her home life reflected this attitude. As an only child she could spend many hours playing on her own inventing imaginary stories in support of her play and it was probably this solitary nature of her early childhood that had led her into the realms of literature. All was a good fit and there was nothing to spur her into any action to disturb the status quo until her mother had suddenly died.

Gillian had been marking scripts, a typical activity on Sunday afternoons. Her father was washing his car and her mother was in the middle of clearing the dinner dishes in the kitchen. The background clattering noise of her mother's clearing suddenly stopped and then in the silence she caught a soft gasp followed by a thud. She found her mother on the floor clutching the edge of her apron.

Gillian knew with a certainty that she could not explain that her mother was dead. Time slowed to a standstill as she shouted her father and telephoned for an ambulance. Both her father and Gillian faced the future staunchly. Her mother was absent but she had not left their lives. There was a shift in responsibilities within the household but only so as they could continue as before.

Gillian had no regret about her seductive invitation to Steve. The memory caused her to wonder at her own audacity. It was the only time in her life when she had allowed her emotion to dominate. It was her 'Carpe diem.' She had never been a girl to 'gather ye rosebuds while ye may' and had not really understood the relevance for her own life of Marvell's 'Had we but world enough and time.' Indeed her 'coyness' had been a crime. After the event with Steve she had reverted to type even though she now had physical love in her life. She still languished in the existing certainty of her life. After her father's death it was not a question of her being free to marry it was more that she needed to marry. She needed the substance of marriage in which to continue as she was. Without it her isolation would be complete.

Gillian had not understood that relationships need to be tested. At times the combat can be brutal and risk destruction but the partners that challenge each other build mutual respect. Marriage was a plant that needed to grow. A strong plant will flourish even in extremes of weather and will take on a new burst of growth after pruning, emerging stronger and more beautiful.

Gillian's marriage had been another restraint. Steve had emerged from his previous marriage with old scars caused by neglect and frustration. He found in Gillian a reliability that encouraged complacency although it was more her general withdrawal from life itself that damaged the relationship. He had too often been left guessing and like many men had withdrawn into his own interests. Neither of them knew how to handle the fall-out from the photograph. In the same way they had papered over the cracks after Millennium.

The household steadied but the spectre of Abigail haunted each of them.

Alex now knew of his mother's sin and he despised his mother for depriving him of Steve's blood. He felt he was a usurper. He wanted the secret buried so deep it would never be discovered but even if that happened, he knew the truth and knowing that truth left him bereft and alone. His co-operation with the investigation also shook any foundations to his life.

Unwittingly he had betrayed his own father willingly and happily. He felt tainted by the whole experience. He had been unmasked. His arrogance had been his disguise but he was merely a passenger who had been shipwrecked in a wild sea and he clung to the flotsam and jetsam he had found floating in that angry water. He wished he could talk with Kirsten who might give him a beacon of hope. Meanwhile, he became absorbed in learning how to cook with Gillian. It also allowed Gillian the excuse to mark time.

Steve had been pretty impressed with Simon's news. To have a substantial plot of land to develop was like winning the lottery, although Steve was conscious of the responsibility. Steve had sought to implant something of himself on the world. It was why he had shunned any academic career and sought the skills that would enable him to branch out on his own, carving quite literally and metaphorically his own destiny. He had watched Gillian become a slave to systems and had quietly congratulated himself that he had been free. He knew he had vision and drive but he did not know that even he had been subject to the whims of fate. He was genuinely pleased for Simon even though he thought it would mean a parting of the ways.

Anthea had given Steve a piece of her mind about his stupidity regarding the photograph but once done he was a welcome visitor to the nursery again. Gillian allowed the friendship to slide. At first, Anthea thought she was licking her wounds but as the weeks passed she thought the indulgence was selfish.

Alex left them after Christmas.

"I'm off to London," he told them one evening. "I've got a job. All fixed."

"Don't feel you have to leave," said Gillian while Steve added, "I can find you something here."

"No. It's all down to you, Gillian. You've introduced me to the pleasures of cooking and it made me think. I'm going to learn a trade. I'm going to join a restaurant. It's what I want to do. One day, I want my own place."

His resolution was clear. He had been busy making contacts. For Steve it was the first time he had seen his son with an independent purpose and a sense of optimism. For Gillian she could only feel her kitchen would be empty.

Alex would need to clear it with Inspector Wilkes. Tom had kept his liaison with Alex, although he could not shield him from cross-examination by other able specialist police as well as HMRC and he had been warned that there were likely to be charges of some description.

Alex had shrugged his shoulders, as usual seeming not to care. He laughed with Gillian that it would be just his luck to be banged up with Clive. He said he hoped they would not share a cell. Gillian had tried to keep things light and wondered how best to help him. Once upon a time she would have stood back and thought he deserved his medicine. His stay with them had opened her eyes.

Before leaving Gillian made a suggestion, "I think you might need a solicitor," Alex had been resigned to his fate, "There is someone I could contact on your behalf. He works in London anyway so if he agreed to look after you then you could see him there."

"London lawyers are far too expensive." Alex in his general malaise had decided to let fate take its course. He had refused any representation from Clive's army of lawyers.

"They are, I know, and it might be that I cannot afford him but I would like to try. He's an ex-student of mine and we have loosely kept in touch. He seems to think I helped him get the grades for Oxford, not true of course, but he is meant to be very good and I think he would be honest. What do you think? Shall I call him? I will pay initially anyway and then we can take it from there."

"I can't believe you would do this for me," Alex felt moved.

"Why ever not? You are family." It was again that natural easy manner that impressed him. She was the most genuine person he knew.

Alex had journeyed far in the previous year and Gillian's suggestion underlined the distance when she used the word 'family.' It made him feel he had come home. It was a good feeling and he would be eternally grateful. He would not disappoint her.

True to her word, Gillian spoke to Richard. He had no involvement with any other parties in the case and he had followed the reports with interest. He said he was always looking for new challenges and offered to talk with Alex without obligation on either side. Alex would make an appointment when he arrived in London.

At last, Alex managed to speak to Kirsten. She was glad to hear he was well after the accident and explained that it had been wise to keep apart. Kirsten found she was speaking to a man who was upbeat and conciliatory. He explained his plans and hoped she would come to the restaurant and maybe bring Mark. She told him that her sister worked in London so there was every reason she might take him up on his suggestion and would of course, want special treatment. Kirsten ended the call a relieved woman ready to enjoy her summer wedding.

Her father, Antony had relinquished much of his work at the office and was ready to join a project. Released from the possibility of prosecution and after a month or so of realising his luck he wanted something to pursue outside the norm and Simon offered him that chance. He had been tested by events and his marriage had survived. In his work as an accountant he had seen other marriages crumble from a gentle wind but his had withstood onslaughts that he would not have believed possible when he had first caught Diana's eye.

He had thought she was an exotic rare plant to be nurtured but he had discovered that underneath her bloom was a hardy perennial that could thrive in any soil, although sometimes her abundant growth could suffocate the surrounding plants. Simon had been grateful to have Antony on board because he liked and respected the man and knew financially he would have proper guidance. He would not leave Steve out of the equation either. Simon felt it would be a formidable combination and waited for all the endless paperwork to be completed before he revealed his intentions.

Antony decided he would take Diana to meet Simon one clear day in May at the nursery at Rainwick. It would be a welcome day out to travel to Marketborough and he valued Diana's shrewd assessment. He hoped Steve and his wife would be there too. The nursery was busy when Antony and Diana arrived to meet Simon.

This was their first visit to the place as there were perfectly good garden centres nearer home. Diana appraised the operation. The buildings seemed rather dilapidated and insubstantial but it was a beautiful location and the early summer plants were in full bloom filling the raised beds with colour.

Diana gathered flame coloured begonias and rich claret coloured geraniums as well as several trays of Busy Lizzies and Pansies in her trolley. She loved the idea of creating an eye-catching display around the patio area. Antony had to hold her back from the roses saying their small town house garden did not have the room. Disappointed she engaged in discussion with the young gardener while Antony found Simon and Steve. Gillian had not made the journey. Bill and Anthea were helping customers.

"Business seems good," Antony observed.

"Yes, it's been a big help having Jake," and Simon nodded in the direction of Diana and Jake. "He's got some ideas too. He's trying to get Dad to offer refreshments. Dad says people will come for a coffee or ice cream and the like and not buy and the whole point of a nursery is to sell plants. I let them get on with it. Actually, I think Jake has a point and Dad just does not like change."

"So what are your plans then?" Antony was eager to know.

"I've been giving it a lot of thought and you may be surprised. The land extends to just over four acres. The narrower piece leads to a really large field at the back. Jim has been telling me about the way his wife's family used to grow vegetables and fruit to sell at the town market. That was fifty years ago but Jim said the ground is good and the family made a decent living."

"Don't tell us you're going to set up some kind of market garden." Steve mocked.

"No, that's not my style. I appreciate the nursery more than I did but it's not for me. I know, Dad said no refreshments for the punters but I will get us some tea and we can talk. I would value your opinion." Simon had been feeling some hesitancy in declaring his hand as he wanted and indeed, needed their full support. To make things work he would need their expertise.

Simon brought out three steaming mugs of tea even though the day was warm. "What about your wife?" He asked Antony.

"She seems fine talking over there." Diana was indeed still in conversation with Jake.

Simon cleared his throat and began, "Actually, I have been talking to Jake too. He tells me that the kids of the area used to go to the waste ground. He played football there and from this he got to know Jim Woodhouse. Jake said that Jim and before that his wife used to watch the children. Jake really loved it and the place gave him somewhere to go, especially when his dad was at work or the pub."

Steve agreed that kids did not have the open spaces and freedoms they used to have.

Simon continued, "The council are threatening to take it over if something is not done. They say it is an eyesore and there are too many complaints."

"Houses, then?" Antony asked.

"I know, I would make a lot of money from doing that but I am getting keen to do something else. I could not afford to develop it with houses anyway so I would have to sell to some big building company who would not have the respect for the area and it would not then be my project."

"So what's your idea?" Steve's curiosity was aroused.

Simon took a deep breath. "Actually, in sort of honour of Jim I thought a place for the community. I reckon I could use the expanse at the back for a junior football pitch, a proper layout for the youngsters, and then a building for activities and meetings and maybe a café and then nearer the entrance a garden where people could sit and talk. Bit of a pipe dream but I thought it would be nice."

Both Simon and Antony had no immediate response.

"Well, don't all speak at once," said Simon.

Diana breezed over at that precise moment. "I've been finding out an awful lot about what we could do with our patio area. That young man runs a gardening business and would come and have a look at ours." Diana's enthusiasm carried her along and then realising she said, "Oh I am sorry you were having your important meeting and I've interrupted." She took a better look at the men beside her husband.

Steve sat looking intently trying to place the woman before him. Diana with a shock knew precisely who he was. Antony had only told her about meeting Simon. It had not seemed relevant to say Steve might be there and he had not thought of the associated trouble with Alex. In his polite fashion Antony introduced Diana to Simon and Steve.

Steve in his complete innocence said, "We've met before I think, but I am afraid I cannot place you."

"Maybe, you've seen me at Antony's office. I go there occasionally." Diana was flustered and did her best to hide it by seeming distant and dismissive. It had been an awful year when she had confessed to Antony the birth of Louise without having now to declare the father had become a friend.

"No. I am sure it was not there. Well, not to worry it's nice to meet you now and I'll probably remember," Diana heaved a temporary sigh of relief.

Later when customers dwindled at the end of the afternoon Bill and Anthea joined the group. Diana unusually had remained quiet, not wanting to draw attention, preferring to chat with Jake who seemed rather overwhelmed with all the proposals. However, that afternoon an initial plan was put together for the project.

Antony had some council connections so he agreed to seek their opinion and try to ascertain what funding might be available. Steve would think about designs and Simon would contact local businesses to see if there was any appetite for such a development. He planned to contact the football club too, although he knew they were under financial pressure from the fall-out of their director's arrest.

Bill with Jake's help, would plan the garden and landscaping. For the moment, they all agreed to say nothing to Jim in case the project did not materialise. The group though were determined to make it happen and to encourage their endeavour set a time period for completion in a year.

Diana watched Steve. To her he had hardly changed. His hair was lighter and thinner but he still had the handsome face that had set the girls' hearts racing. The frown and laughter lines and heavier darker skin to her showed a life lived without restraint. He had known heartache she thought but as he talked the relaxed mobility of his mouth conveyed a cheerful disposition. His look in repose still had that cynical air, lips loose with the hint of a sardonic smile which had been so attractive to the teenage Diana and soft eyes depicting humour.

He was a man who had no guile and no vanity, dressed as he was in casual jeans and tee shirt which could not disguise hardened muscles from a life time of manual work. Diana felt her heart flutter and was unsure whether that was because of his attraction or her nerves from the knowledge of their joint history. It was sixteen years since Jackie had been to the old house and that also had been the last time she had seen Clive Corneille. Strange how things worked out she thought.

Steve was sitting there oblivious of the existence of a daughter. She knew he had a son recalling her visit to Alex's mother but he had apparently been a nightmare and recently had disappeared to London. Maybe, Steve would not remember her. She thought she had changed a lot in the intervening years and it was only a 'one night stand' of which there were many back in the day.

She knew that Steve had had his fair share so it had been just accidental that he thought he might know her. People often did think this, but soon with absorption into present day relationships they would let it go. As usual, Diana asserted her own mantra. She would ignore it until she was forced to confront it which was in her opinion very unlikely.

Anthea decided to chase Gillian up. In her opinion the milk had been spilt and it was no use crying over it. She thought that too often Gillian had been cutting her nose to spite her face. Anthea liked to work with sayings and proverbs as her guide.

Steve was a good man, if a bit dense as far as the female of the species was concerned. She knew he would plod on, accepting the default position when he could stir the pot and push for a reaction.

Anthea had not been to Gillian's house often, certainly not for a visit as she had been tied to the nursery and it was her habit to be hospitable there. Steve who was with Simon that day had told her Gillian would be on her own and so she took the land rover and drove to the house. She was pleased that the garden looked tidy and noted the rose, Fragrant Cloud, in the front square. Gillian was surprised to see her visitor.

Anthea never one to hold back, "I thought I had better come over seeing you have sent us to Coventry." Her voice was sharp and strong. Gillian could not evade the accusation and before she could reach for her usual self-control she found herself sobbing. Rarely had this happened before and she squirmed with embarrassment at her weakness. It took a couple of minutes for the tears to subside and for Gillian to regain some composure.

Anthea did not make comment. She was not going to foster any 'poor-me' sentimentality. In her opinion this girl needed to buck her ideas up and start looking at the good.

"Sorry," Gillian muttered.

"So you should be, a grown woman like yourself. Tears indeed. I could understand a shout and a rant to get it out of your system but it seems you are letting a wound fester and nothing will heal from that."

It was so good to have Anthea giving her a lecture. Taken aback and ashamed it was the shock Gillian needed.

"I'll make tea."

"And if you've got any home-made cake I'll have that too. It looks like I will have my work cut out here."

They talked. Gillian had never yielded before and spoke of many things. It was a hotchpotch of hurts and slights that Gillian had carefully nursed and kept storing them in the drawer of her life. One by one each was examined and either discarded or kept for closer examination. Anthea helped Gillian to declutter, taking each one examining it and then dismissing it as unworthy and unreasonable or putting it on separate pile for perusal later.

The pile of unwarranted hurts grew rapidly. Gillian was being made aware of how she had built her own misery and she must let go. There was a small pile of genuine grievances and these were collected for further analysis and joint resolve.

Anthea gradually showed Gillian that she had not been strong and resilient hiding her feelings, rather it had been a weakness in not confronting and accepting them. There had been many buried wrongs, from her reticence as a teenager to her pride as a teacher and her inability to leave her parents, plus her childlessness and the complete belief that Steve had made a mistake in marrying her.

There was guilt and remorse, there was jealousy and anger, there was regret and despair, there was fear and grief but most of all there was loneliness. Gillian herself had denied the joy of companionship. Her protective attitude had been her isolation and her undoing.

"Secrets are one thing," Anthea said. "Everyone has something to hide but it's usually something they feel ashamed about or it would hurt someone else but you have kept everything bottled up. You feel angry and with every right to be angry but you don't say. You push it one side and cover it with a carpet of daily life. What did you say to Steve about the photograph? I bet you said nothing. Sometimes, a good row can clear the air. Not always, I admit, so it's a question of knowing when to hold your tongue."

"I'm sorry."

"That's another thing. Stop saying you are sorry. What have you got to be sorry for? You have not done anything wrong. In fact, it would be better if you had. You try to be too perfect. Let your hair down. I've said to you before, have some fun." Anthea was determined that Gillian should realise she had created her own prison.

Gillian automatically felt guilty.

"How many people come and visit you Gillian?" Anthea's voice softened. She wanted to help and knew the whole conversation was painful.

Gillian had no answer.

"Hiding yourself away is not good you know. You need to get a sample of other people's lives and then realise how good your own is. Now there's Mr and Mrs Carstairs for example. They do not live far from you. He's getting involved with Simon and his development plans and she seems very social. You could do worse than getting involved with things too. I know you help Steve with the books and things but maybe a bit of hands on participation would be good and get to know new people. Diana's about your age too. It would be a start."

Gillian remembered another Diana from school and prompted by the intimacy of the discussions contributed a comment. "I used to know a Diana at school. She had a big secret. I resented her."

"Did she now? Well, are you going to tell me? It's a long time ago so perhaps it does not matter anymore and I don't know her so if it's something else to get off your chest go ahead."

Gillian told Anthea about Diana. She had never told anyone else before and she found she relived every moment. She even told her about the letter and how she thought of the girl every year on her birthday. She did not think Diana would ever think of the baby again. Gillian could not tell Anthea about the examination student because of her ingrained professional code of conduct and a sneaking feeling of a connection with the boy because of it.

"You know, Gillian, you have this romantic notion that all babies are born out of love. It's not always the case. Love is an ideal and we have to choose it and work at it. I knew too many girls who got pregnant in my day and there was no love involved, even some of the married women. Life has choices and compromises. This little girl probably had a happy childhood and that is what you must believe. It is not your problem."

"But the letter is?" Even to Gillian it sounded feeble probably more because she wanted it to count.

"Oh I don't suppose it mattered so much. If she was given it, the girl would have got comfort from it. Honestly, you fret too much. You need to let things go. Get on with your life and do not worry so much about other people."

The dismissive attitude of Anthea gave Gillian reassurance. She had a way of lifting spirits.

When Steve returned home that evening, Gillian was waiting for him.

"I've booked us a few days away. I've waited years to go to Venice. I don't want to wait any longer. We go tomorrow."

"That's a bit sudden. I'm not sure I can get away. Perhaps we can go in a couple of months. You haven't paid anything have you?" Steve stuttered, taken aback by his wife's tone of voice as much as the announcement.

"No Steve. I have booked it and paid for it. I am certainly going and it is up to you if you want to come with me or not. It's your choice."

Steve had never known Gillian be so assertive. She gave him a meaningful look and he cowered before her gaze.

"Taxi will be here at noon tomorrow. I will pack for you to give you a bit of time. Supper will be ready in half an hour." With that Gillian left the room.

The holiday in Venice was wonderful. As soon as they arrived they were immersed in the magic and culture of the network of canals and walkways leading from the teeming Rialto Bridge area. Their hotel edged the Grand Canal and in the evening twilight they drank champagne on the waters' edge watching the gondolas. Gillian was wearing her emerald dress as she leaned on the balustrade watching life flow below and she felt her husband's arm encircle her waist. It had been a defining moment.

Chapter 22
Long Lost Friends

If thou must love me, let it be for nought
Except for love's sake only

If Thou Must Love Me: Elizabeth Browning

2008: Alex: Samantha

It was true that Alex had to call in one or two favours from his previous position with Corneille Enterprises to get his position at Fitzroys. It had been one of the many investments that Clive had made. The management at the restaurant had been worried about the impact of the trial on the business but they also recognised that to survive they could not alienate their main benefactor completely. It was thought that Alex would not last a month or even a week in the heat of the kitchen and so Guy accepted him as an apprentice allowing him use of a small bed sit at the top of the building. Alex had been lucky and he knew it. He had used Corneille's influence to get him the start but he knew he wanted to show them he was nothing like his biological father.

He lasted the week, not happily at all, with his efforts ridiculed and discarded more often than not, but then he went on to last a month, learning to soak up the expletives thrown in his direction and realising that this was the norm and he was not being, especially targeted. He also relished the growing success he was having. Praise by Andre, the chef was hard won. It was fleeting too. A sauce had gained approval one minute and the next Alex would be castigated for a vegetable that was overcooked. Alex began to understand that none of this was personal. It was unlike his onslaughts into the football teams as a lad when indiscriminate comments of hostility were hurled at him from the touch-line. The chastisements from his kitchen superiors were exactly that, he had not delivered to the standard required and he was told bluntly and impatiently and when he met the standard he was acknowledged for his success. It was the same for all members of the kitchen team even those in more senior positions. Respect here had to be earned. Furthermore, Gillian had been an excellent teacher and taught him the basics well. Alex had found a niche in the bustling kitchen. After two months he felt able to make suggestions to the chef and on quieter days would put these into practice. For the first time in his life he was making his own way and reaping the psychological benefit.

Fitzroy's was a smart restaurant to which diners of all ages gravitated. It was on the pricey side so tended to attract those wishing to celebrate an occasion or those with ample funds to eat there more regularly. People liked the modern interior with the solid square tables placed at distances to ensure privacy in conversations which is why it had been favoured by Corneille and his ilk. Ladies would lunch there secure in the knowledge they could tittle tattle over their Salad Nicoise. Business leaders secured deals over rich puddings and celebrities might be seen but not heard in any publicity campaign. Diana had enjoyed the experience when she had dined there with Samantha, that was until she discovered the potential disgrace for Antony from his work with Corneille.

Guy began to invite Alex to assist front of house when they were short staffed. Alex had struggled at university. He was of good intelligence but had not the capability of Kirsten and Mark as far as numbers were concerned but he did have good organisational skills and appreciated the workings of the restaurant overall, especially after his experience at the football club. Alex was becoming a more valuable member of the team, not because of his connection with Clive Corneille but because he had found his own feet and was planting them firmly on the path to his future.

He was on duty front of house when the little group of girls gathered for a party. Six fashionable and excitable females demanded his attention. He checked the booking and found the name S Carstairs from an exclusive beauty salon nearby. They were not regular customers. He directed them to a corner table hoping they would not become too rowdy. It was not really the style of Fitzroys.

"What can I get you?" He asked in his professional polite manner.

"Ooh that would be telling. What can I do for you?" Was the pert answer from the dark haired girl. "I'm sure you can get me something special." She fluttered her false eyelashes at him in an exaggerated and meaningful way.

"Leave him alone, Laura. We'll have a couple of bottles of Prosecco to start please." The blonde in the corner seat took control.

"Come on, don't be a spoilsport. He is gorgeous and I have not had fun for so long." Laura pouted.

Alex heard the comment as he directed the waiter to bring their drinks. After a few minutes he sauntered over to take their order.

Laura was still in the flirtatious mood. "My word," she said, "you must work out. You look so strong and muscular under that jacket of yours." She was already slurring her words.

"Forgive my friend," the blonde appealed, "she's quite harmless, so no need to panic." Alex could feel he was getting warm.

The evening continued in much the same vein. Alex kept a weather eye on proceedings occasionally noting the discomfort of the waiting staff, although the banter was generally amenable if risqué. Takings were good that evening and Alex checked them at the till as well as preparing bills. He was tired and it had been a long day but the table in the corner lingered. He thought he had better hasten their departure.

"Would you like any more coffee or maybe a nightcap," he purred.

"I thought you'd never ask," Laura gave him a look of sweet appraisal. Alex smiled adopting an innocent expression which hardly matched his dark brooding look. "I apologise for keeping you waiting. I hope the meal was to your satisfaction."

The blonde girl interposed, "I think it is time for the bill."

Alex presented the bill to the blonde who he assumed was S Carstairs. She offered to come to the desk to deal with it. "I'm sorry if my friends have been a bit loud and troublesome," she said. "Laura will be devastated tomorrow and it is not often we get out as a group. They had had a few before coming I'm afraid."

"But not you it seems." Alex was impressed with the style of the girl. She had an easy charm and confidence, obviously not riled by the others in the group or embarrassed. Her apology had been simple and effective arising out of courtesy rather than responsibility.

"No. only because I had to work late and then seeing the state of them I thought I had better stay on the sober side. I did not want a rumpus." She had a naturally commanding presence.

Alex gave the credit card back to her, "Thank you. Miss Carstairs," and he could not help look deeply into her blue eyes.

"Thank you," and she looked at his name badge, "Alex." Then she let out an exclamation. "You are not by any chance, Alex Mason, are you?" She said hesitantly. "Sorry I just thought you might have known my sister but it is unlikely of course. I just know he was working at a restaurant."

"Kirsten," he replied. "You are Kirsten's sister." They stood for a moment taking in the knowledge.

Alex took the initiative. "I am off duty in about half an hour. You're probably going out somewhere, but if not perhaps you would have a drink with me." He felt bold, something he had not felt for a very long time.

Samantha did not have to hesitate. Her companions looked to be in a sorry state. Laura could hardly stand, Natalie looked nauseous and the others clearly were impatient to get off. "That would be nice," she answered. Samantha also relished the idea of spending time with this handsome man, especially after Laura's antics.

"There's a quiet small table that's free over by the window there. I can arrange a glass of wine or whatever and join you when I have handed over to Guy."

Samantha had picked up bits and pieces about Alex. She knew there would be disapproval from her parents, and maybe Kirsten, but she reasoned it was not a date and it would be good to have news to take home. Her dad was not in the firing line now so she thought there was no harm. She had not enjoyed male company for so long. Everyone seemed to be hitched in some way or another.

After his surge of spirit Alex began to feel diffident. This was very unlike him. He had not been in the dating game for a good while and felt rusty. There had been no time to devote to the opposite sex and in the past he had not attracted the type of girl with whom he could talk. Samantha was stunning and he knew it was just fortune that had delivered her to him that evening. All too soon she would be bored and go on her merry way. He recognised class in a woman.

They did not talk much that night. After the opening gambits they toyed visually with the other. Samantha felt a curiosity about the real Alex and she searched his face for clues while Alex savoured her presence. Before long their fingers had linked under the table and there had been the birth of comprehension.

Samantha kept the liaison from her family. She did not quite know why except it was precious and she did not want it to be tainted. Alex too was wary. He might yet be facing prosecution and at the very least he would be called as a witness in the trial, although Richard had been reassuring and had guided him through the procedures. It was a constant shadow but with the trial scheduled for September, he would know his fate before much longer. To him it was ironic that just as he was getting his life straight and he was enjoying his job and found a woman to cherish he should be blighted by his past. Samantha having supported her father kept determined and optimistic. She was after all her mother's daughter.

The wedding was occupying her mother so there was little point in Samantha potentially spoiling the party. Marcus was a regular visitor and Antony released from suspicion and fully occupied with Simon and his plans had become unruffled about the expense. Diana could fully indulge her inclination. Kirsten was hard pressed to control her mother, but became resigned, eased by the reassurance of Marcus who appreciated her concerns.

The wedding was planned for the end of June. Her dress was an exquisite creation. The concept was simple but the execution was intricate. The white satin had been cut on the bias and the boat neckline was edged with Nottingham lace that was reflected on the three-quarter sleeves and the sweeping train. Her veil was to be held in place by a tiara of tiny rosebuds and pearls.

Samantha, as chief bridesmaid, was to wear a dress in primrose yellow that flattered her pale skin and blonde hair. The bodice was sculpted to her body and the skirt swirled from her hips with a layer of fine soft gauze. Diana would be making an entrance in a dramatic navy blue and white dress and coat.

The guest list was extensive. Margaret and Michael would make the journey from Shropshire and there was hope that Diana's brothers might be able to make it. Antony invited Simon and his family and then added Steve and his wife. It was time for Antony to worry about his speech.

Samantha had become distracted. She and Alex met when they could but their hours of work precluded spending much time together. Alex needed a career. She understood he had something to prove but she wanted more from him and indeed, more from life. Her job which had once been so satisfying had become tedious. Her clients seemed boring. She had had enough of pampering the privileged.

Kirsten noticed her melancholy on one of her weekends at home. She knew her sister could swing like a pendulum but this was a general malaise that was completely out of keeping with her personality. It was just four weeks to the wedding and everyone was jittery.

"What's the matter?" Kirsten did not see the point of beating about the bush.

"Nothing. I'm fine." Samantha was lying prostrate on the settee.

"Why don't you bring this new boyfriend to the wedding?" She had been curious and the question obviously ruffled Samantha which was even more curious. Samantha had never been reticent about relationships.

"What new boyfriend?" Samantha sounded petulant.

"Come on. I know you. Why are you keeping him under wraps?" Kirsten happily looking forward to her nuptials was eager for the confidence. As sisters they had always been close.

"I'm not. We hardly see each other. It's not been long." Samantha was being unusually dismissive and vague.

"But you obviously have a thing for him? There's nothing wrong with him is there? He's not a bank robber or murderer is he? Come on I'm your big sister you can tell me. Look at all the scrapes I've got you out of in the past."

"I don't think anyone will approve." Samantha stole a look at her sister before sliding her eyes away.

"Why not? Oh gosh he does have a criminal record, doesn't he?"

Samantha gave her sister a cool and calculated look. "Not yet and honestly he's done nothing wrong. He did not know anyway."

"Ignorance might be bliss Sis, but it's no defence in the law."

Samantha slid back onto the sofa and Kirsten stepped across and perched beside her. "You know we are here for you. We want you to be happy and if he is the one, he should make you happy."

"I am happy, that is when I am with him, and then I know, you all will disapprove and try and talk me out of it." Samantha did sound pitiful and genuinely upset.

"We know him? Well, maybe you should tell and get it over with and then it may not be as bad as you think." Kirsten cared and after her own experiences over the last year knew how easily things could turn.

"It's Alex, Alex Mason."

Kirsten was indeed taken aback. "But when and how did you hook up with him?"

Kirsten could see the current difficulties. Her dad had the worry of prosecution for weeks and Alex was in that very boat. There was his personality too. Kirsten had changed her opinion over the last few months but could he be trusted? She did not want anyone to hurt her sister and could only see disaster.

"I know what you are thinking. It's written all over your face. I really like him." There was a pause. "I think it's more."

Kirsten put her arms round her sister. "Look why don't you invite him to the wedding? His parents will be there so if he came with them you could see him and do your bridesmaid duties and we can gently introduce him to Mum and Dad. We don't have to say that you're an item. We can take it step by step."

"Mum would not like it at all."

"I don't think she would, not at first but you know, Mum, she's a pragmatist and if he really has changed his life around and the feelings between you are that strong she will come round. You can expect a lot of huffing and puffing but it will be alright. This is your big sister talking. Nothing we Carstairs can't handle." The girls hugged, although each harboured darker thoughts.

Kirsten contacted Marcus about the extra guest. It was not a good idea to say anything to Diana.

The week of the wedding was full of anticipation. Diana became a whirlwind of activity. Marcus needed all his charm and experience to combat any destruction from the turbulence. Mark's family were mainly arriving on Friday. On Thursday evening Diana double checked the guest list and seating plan. It was only then that one name grabbed her attention.

Marcus was used to receiving calls late in the evening, especially from frantic mother of brides. He told her that Kirsten had added the name. Diana sighed. It was so typical of the girl she thought, Kirsten had a kind heart. Even though Alex had been so brutal to her years ago she was ready to forgive him.

Diana was proud of her daughter, although she also thought she was rather weak. Diana really did not like it at all but she wasn't prepared to upset Kirsten on the eve of her wedding so she could live with it. He would be sitting well away from the top table so he could be largely ignored. Weddings did not come along without some complications.

Kirsten quite naturally was a beautiful bride. Her quiet composure and serene outlook as she gave her vows gave her an ethereal look that transported the familiar words of the ceremony to an almost mystical level of incantation. The spell was only broken at the church door with the cascade of confetti. Amongst the clamour for photographs Alex stood to the side entranced by only one woman.

Diana mingled with guests in between the photographs for which she was in demand. The two mothers resplendent in their wind defying hats stood in tacit good humoured rivalry.

Gillian held on to Steve for balance, her heels sinking into the turf and she was preoccupied with holding on to her hat in the light breeze. At last on firmer ground, she studied the bridal party that she had been unable to see properly in the packed church. It was one of those weddings you might read about in a romantic novel, although Gillian with her penchant for literature expected some sort of commotion to prove it was all a façade, but there was no cloud on this horizon. It was clearly a love match with family approval. Jane Austin would be pleased. Now she cast her eye over the parents. She knew Antony a little. He seemed more at ease than usual in conversing with the guests, a genial host. His wife in her striking attire demanded attention. Gillian had strained to see her from the back of the church but all she noted was the sensational hat and now Diana was in full view. Gillian felt sick. Her body shook.

"What's the matter? Are you alright?" Steve glanced at her.

"Yes, but I wish I could go home. Antony's wife, I knew her at school, that is, when I was a pupil."

"That's great." Steve enthused with his usual easy manner.

"Maybe not. It did not end well." Gillian looked terrified and slunk behind his shoulder.

"But that's forty years ago. Don't worry. Diana is the type to forget it all and I'm with you." He squeezed her hand and pulled her forward. In recent weeks he had benefitted from a new more forthright Gillian and he did not want her slipping back into being the timid mouse.

"I doubt if she has forgotten but she may pretend she has."

There was a formal greeting line. Gillian hoped to evade the introduction but Steve insisted and she shuffled along the line. Gillian watched and, as she got nearer, listened to Diana greeting her guests. Diana was a consummate performer. Gracious, charming, elegant. Diana to Gillian was completely at odds with her own awkward unsophistication.

Steve ushered her forward, "Hello, Diana. Thank you for inviting us. It is a beautiful wedding."

Diana knew instantly. "Gillian. How wonderful. You two are not together?" There was a brief nod from Steve. Diana stood frozen. "Oh goodness, all this time and you were right here under my very nose. I can hardly believe it. I am so sorry we lost touch. It was entirely my fault. It was careless of me. You look well and you are Steve's wife. It is so good to see you." Diana beamed at the two of them.

Steve was transfixed. For something that had not ended well this was a revelation. The queue was backing up slightly and Diana grasped Gillian's hand. "I'm going to have my hands full today but we must try to catch up later. I can't believe you're here. Please don't disappear again."

Gillian wanted to say it was not her that had disappeared but the relief made her overlook the detail.

Steve, Gillian and Alex were seated with Bill and Anthea and Simon on the edge of proceedings. Jake had been left to mind the nursery aided by Simon's two sisters. Anthea had rarely been able to attend occasions such as this, especially with Bill as one of them would have to look after the nursery. It only closed for vital family events. It had been a distinct advantage having Jake and conversation flowed to plans for the waste ground by Jim.

"There seems an appetite from businesses in the area. I want to try to have a word with the guy who's the wedding planner. He's got a sizeable events company." Simon nodded in the direction of Marcus.

Alex following his gaze saw Samantha in the centre of a group of male guests. He felt the bubble of jealousy rise in his stomach. Sharing was not in his character.

Alex listened with interest to talk about the enterprise and Steve was delighted that his son seemed involved. It became clear to Alex that this little group of enthusiastic amateurs needed a business plan.

Steve told them all that Gillian and Diana had been good friends at school but Gillian said that that was a flagrant exaggeration. He whispered that obviously she had exaggerated the problem at school which resulted in a small tiff.

Gillian thought a baby was hardly a small problem but true to her word all those years ago she kept the secret and had to concede that it was too long ago to matter now. Gillian and Steve had been refreshed by their break in Venice and it was clear to Anthea there had been a shift in dynamics. Alex and Simon as the single males fielded the taunts of the others, prodding their sentiment for marriage and pointing out possible eligible girls. The wine and conversation flowed in equal measure.

The dancing began under the twinkling lights. Samantha danced with the best man and her brother plus a succession of ushers who seemed to pounce as soon as a new song was played. Alex's senses were affronted as he witnessed the attention given to Samantha while he sat impotently on the side lines. He tried to quell the old feelings of hostility but his good humour was fast evaporating. He left the party.

The walled garden sheltered couples in the shadowy corners. Alex passed through the archway to the path that led to the lake beyond. In the twilight he sought refuge under an oak which was where Samantha found him some half an hour later. There was no prelude, she locked her arms around his neck and kissed him passionately allowing her body to cleave to his beneath the sheer fabric of her gown and immediately she was rewarded with the sensation of his interest. He buried his head into her hair, breathing its scent and felt for her breasts which were imprisoned by the boned bodice of her dress. He sought an opening, his fingers pawing at the folds of her skirt but the gown would not be breeched. Alex cursed.

"Dresses like this are romantic but not practical," Samantha laughed.

"I want you. You've driven me mad. Did you invite me to make a fool of me?" His voice was husky with desire.

"I want you too," she answered softly. Looking at him she realised his passion. "Don't tell me you mind about me dancing." She studied him. "You did, didn't you?"

Alex looked sheepish but said, "I don't want to share you. I want to know you're mine and mine alone."

Samantha saw the insecure boy beneath. "Alex," and she reached out and touched the trunk of the oak. "Look at this tree. It is strong and sturdy. It stands tall and will keep growing. It's been here probably for hundreds of years. That represents real love Alex. Birds will flutter in and out of its branches, some will visit before leaving for a better tree and some will build nests having decided that this tree and the shelter it provides is the best, the most secure, the place from which to sing their song, mate and lay eggs. Our love can be strong like this oak. It can be tall and proud. It can be safe. It can be a place from which we can fly but it will always enfold us in its branches. We might fly away briefly but we will never leave its orbit, its influence, because it is our love and it is strong."

Alex studied her in awe. "Marry me," he said, "Be my wife. Samantha darling, I love you." As if he realised the enormity of the proposal he sank on one knee to the damp grass. "I love you forever. Don't make me live without you. Marry me."

"Yes, oh yes, oh yes."

Their sweet talk was private and promises were made. There was no pen knife to carve their initials in the tree but initials had been carved in each other's heart.

Much later, when the moon was high in the sky they returned to dance as a proclamation of their love. They would save their future plans for a later date.

It was late and the music was slow and sensuous. Alex and Samantha were oblivious to all except each other, holding each other in the middle of the throng on the dance floor.

Anthea's sharp eyes saw and commented, "Looks like another wedding in the offing." Steve and Gillian saw and squeezed each other's hand.

From her position on the other side of the room Diana peered at the dancers. She could not help seeing the connection. To her it was unthinkable.

It was midnight before Diana and Gillian could talk. Over a bottle of champagne Diana riding on the success of the day spoke of her regret at losing touch. She spoke of the baby too. Antony had been told but not the children and she had been searching for her. There was more to tell of course, for both women, but for now they would leave it for another day. Gillian spoke of Alex and how she had shunned him only to find that he had been misjudged and deeply hurt.

Diana knew what she meant and described her meeting with Abigail, something that brought some satisfaction to Gillian. Gillian urged Diana to give Alex a chance with her daughter but Diana was adamant. She warned Gillian it could never be and she would fight it. This was the only flaw in their reunion.

Of course, Diana thought, she could not support a relationship between Alex and Samantha, and not because of Alex's past misdemeanours or even his association with Clive Corneille. It was a reason more fundamental and powerful. She reasoned in her mind. The two were almost brother and sister. Alex was Steve's son, and therefore half-brother to the daughter she and Steve shared. Jackie was a half-sister too, to her children with Antony. This meant, and it was here she became confused, that they were all step-brothers and step-sisters. She was sure there would be rules about this sort of relationship and she was convinced that it would only bring heartache. She could not allow it. What had she done? She could never reveal that Steve was the central pivot in the whole sorry mess.

Chapter 23
Losing the Plot

His was a master hand at stealing grain,
He felt it with his thumb and thus he knew
Its quality and took three times his due-
A thumb of gold, by God, to gauge an oat!

The Miller: Geoffrey Chaucer

2008: Gillian: Diana: Alex

Gillian could not help being impressed with Diana's house. Her own house seemed provincial in comparison and yet she knew she would never have the personality to fill these spacious rooms so that if she lived here the house would reduce and squash what little spirit she had. Again, she felt that she would be providing the audience for Diana's Oscar winning performance. She had tried this summer to shed the reticence she habitually felt and had certainly made changes with Steve but this was in fits and starts.

There was no magic cure when suddenly she would be confident and outgoing and gather the world at her feet. In essence, she was still the retiring schoolgirl, bashful in new company and modest in achievements. Steve told her she was a harsh judge but the years of relentless self-criticism could not be undone so easily. Anthea had taken her to one side and congratulated her on her new demeanour after Venice. Anthea had been the tonic she needed. To have her approval had somehow allowed her to venture out of her comfort zone. Venice had been wonderful.

Diana brought Gillian into the kitchen. It was less formal but still impressive and on this warm day the glass doors were open and they could drift on to the patio.

"You have a lovely home." Gillian began politely.

"Yes, we are lucky here. It is a happy home not like my Cotswold monstrosity. When we moved here, we had one of the flats in Bridge Street. It was small but great location for us and so we decided to stay in the town. This came up and we scraped the money to buy. We've had some work done but these houses have a sense of history and security and family. It sort of adopted us and made us welcome. The children love coming back here too so it can be a busy house and it sort of sweeps everyone up. Then it is handy for town. Steve mentioned you like Benedicto's. We go there a lot so it's amazing we have not run into each other before."

Gillian did not admit that their visits to Benedicto's were few and far between.

"What about you Gillian? Tell me all about you."

They sat on the cushioned patio chairs the years seeping away as they uncovered new aspects of each other. Gillian felt she had so little to say as her life had been insubstantial and ordinary but Diana gently picked away and Gillian began to feel empowered. Diana had the knack of lifting spirits just as easily as she could reduce them. Gillian had envied this quality as well as the sheer self-possession that gave Diana the right to dominate at school.

Diana seemed to admire her teaching career and examination marking, commenting in a casual way that Gillian had always been clever and how admired she was at school. Gillian knew that was not possible but she liked the fable and here was Diana one of the school's leading ladies pronouncing it.

"You must tell me how you met Steve?" Diana felt she was playing with fire but she could not resist.

Gillian was hesitant so kept it simple. "He fitted a new kitchen," was her opening gambit.

"My word," Diana retorted, "I've had lots of new kitchens in my lifetime but never one that came with those perks!"

They both laughed.

"It was not quite that straightforward but that was how we met. Of course, he was still married to Abigail."

Diana raised an eyebrow that was more inquisitive and conspiratorial than condemning but Gillian quickly added, "They were separated. I did not mean anything else. I would not you know. We didn't." Again, she felt she had to explain, to justify. She felt as though she had been caught out but Diana immediately put her at her ease.

"I can remember when we all used to swoon over him. We'd walk past the building site to get a look. And you were the lucky girl to get him." Diana felt she had so much to make up for with Gillian that she was ready to be generous.

"Not at first I wasn't. I'm a second wife." Gillian was losing her esteem. In Gillian's position Diana would never have admitted this and was eager to promote her friend.

"You only have to look to see how he dotes on you. He adores you. He can't take his eyes of you. When you were dancing at the wedding, his eyes followed you and there was no mistaking the lust in his eye. Then when you're not there he says lovely things about you. What a lucky woman you are? Then I always knew you would marry well."

"Does he?" Gillian had been completely taken aback. Here was Diana, sleek sophisticated Diana, Diana with the beautiful house and children and the clever successful husband telling her that the husband she had thought had been getting tired of her and impatient with her and taking her for granted actually saw her as an attractive desirable woman.

In Venice, it had been exactly that. It had been only the second time in her life that she had seized an initiative and she had been unconvinced that he would come with her and further to that frightened that she would have to carry out her threat and go alone, but he had come and they had loved and they had broken a taboo of restriction. Venice, with its little pathways along canals choked with gondolas and boat traffic and corridors between tall Gothic buildings opening out onto gracious piazzas had been an inspiration for them both.

Days were leisurely spent sight-seeing, eating, drinking and resting, with pauses for love, evenings were imbued with delight whether quietly watching the world from a pavement café or sharing a seafood risotto or taking an early night and nights were a contentment of love and the common denominator that they had been together, united in a cause and metamorphosing into a new and different whole. They had been bound together in every respect. It had been a belated honeymoon.

It had been a time for sharing and commitment. It had been a time when Gillian had absorbed her husband's frailty, as well as her own, and grown stronger as a result. Steve had revealed to her his demons and for once they had talked about Abigail and Alex without constraint. She had thought the days of uncertainty were at an end but within days of their return she had begun to fade into her former fears. Diana's comment had inadvertently touched the nerve that determined her perspective and given her hope.

Diana chatted affably, "I met Antony in the South of France. I know, it sounds romantic but I was working as an au pair believe it or not. Antony was completely out of his depth with the heat and social situation and I sort of rescued him from the embarrassment. Antony is very shy you know. I think he was grateful and so we went out when I got back to London and we married soon after. I was lucky as I don't think he would ever have gone for a girl like me. He's had to put up with a lot but we're happy and I would not have anyone else. Some people used to think we were an odd pair but I always knew I was the fortunate one."

"I think the same about Steve and me. I was lucky and I don't know where I would be without him."

"That's good. Who would have thought we would both find true love. Not many people do end up so well." Diana felt content.

They were making progress. They sat in the sunshine, two middle aged women recapturing a lost time and forging a new connection.

"Let's have something stronger," Diana suggested. Gillian allowed her mind to relax. Diana was good company if nothing else. For Gillian it was a rare opportunity to step outside her humdrum life.

The wine was a good vintage, not that Gillian had any kind of experience but she did appreciate the quality as it slipped coolly down her throat.

"Tell me about your children," Gillian asked. Diana was only too happy to oblige. She had no qualms about giving false praise so enthused about them. It took her a while to appreciate that Gillian had no-one of whom to boast and had the good grace to want to turn the conversation and used the opportunity to open a thorny issue.

"I know you wrote a letter to Louise." She ventured. Gillian, relaxed from the wine did not panic but was perturbed.

"It was wrong of me." Gillian unconsciously lifted her hand to twist her hair.

"No it wasn't. It was a lovely letter. It was something I should have done but I was selfish. All I wanted to do was to escape the whole business." This frank admission heartened Gillian and she relaxed,

"I thought you were so very brave and strong and I was also jealous. You had the world at your feet."

Diana ignored the compliment and tried to reassure, "She came to see me once. She brought the letter. It was important to her."

"Really!" Gillian was astonished. "So you are in touch? How wonderful!"

"Sadly no. I was still selfish and it was a bad moment so I sent her away. I regret that very much and I have been trying to find her but without luck. I recognised your writing and the sentiment, well what can I say, you were always good with words. Antony did not know at the time but he knows now. It was a bit sticky but we got through it and he supports me. The children do not know or anyone else. I do not see the point if she can't be found."

Gillian was being given an insight into another marriage. Nothing was ever perfect.

"Have you no clues? I would like to help." Gillian thought of the exam boy.

"Her name was Jackie Lewis when she came to the house and she said she had a little boy. She must have been very young when she had him, like me when I had her but she had kept the little boy. I smile sometimes because I am a grandmother and somewhere out there, is my grandson."

"Oh Diana! I don't know what to say," and she reached out and touched her arm with compassion.

It was time to pour another glass of wine.

"I always wanted children," It was Gillian's turn.

"They are a blessing, although a worry at times." Neither of them wanted to discuss Alex and Samantha. Both wanted to rebuild a friendship. There would be plenty of time to deal with that later thought Diana. She was still raw from an emotional explosive argument with Samantha on the subject of Alex. Samantha had bluntly told her mother the relationship was none of her business and she was in love before flouncing out of the house and back to London.

Steve was to collect Gillian so she had no qualms about the alcohol. The bottle was dispatched and just as they were opening a second bottle Steve arrived sober and serious. Gillian's inhibitions had been blunted and with Diana's endorsement ringing in her ears she openly devoured him with her eyes. He shuffled conscious of the invitation and caught a look from Diana standing to one side.

Then in an instant it was blindingly obvious, the memory flashed into his brain; the party, the come-on, the taking of the fruit. She had been an early conquest. He had little experience then and thought he had fumbled his way through, pretending to be a smooth operator expecting a rebuff but when none came he had not backed away.

Afterwards, like the coward that he was, he avoided her, and, then, he hid his inadequacy by seeking other conquests, most notably Abigail to prove himself. It was Diana that had set him on that path of self-destruction. He stood in her kitchen confused and awkward. Gillian would never forgive him. He felt sure Diana had known and he cursed her friendship with Gillian.

They left after a suitable interval, Gillian unsteady on her feet and cross that such a pleasant afternoon had been spoilt by a sulking husband when all she wanted was a happy seduction. She challenged him in the car as he drove out of the town centre but all he did was to sneer and say she was drunk. She knew she was merry but that was nice and why was he being so miserable? The afternoon had made her feel good, great even and then she was being forced back into the box.

On reaching home she made for the sitting room and switched on the television trying to drown out her sorrow with the sound and as she tried to focus she heard his mobile ring and knew instinctively from his response which was guarded and humble that it was Abigail laying claim to her man. She heard a raised voice, Steve's voice was arguing about the house, shouting he would damn well put it on the market if he wanted, and she curled on the cushions desperately trying to block out her fear.

The trial was looming and Abigail's self-preservation had kicked in. She needed her own base and Steve had always been her saviour.

The call had left Abigail flattened because it was out of character as usually Steve was amenable, not obstructive. She needed to keep the house. That was a certainty. It was her sanctuary if Clive had to go away, although she believed that all would be well and he would walk out of court a free man. Meanwhile, as far as Steve was concerned, as usual, she would play her master card and so she rang Alex.

Richard had prepared Alex for his role in the trial. It was not clear whether he would in fact be called as a prosecution witness and Richard tried to suggest that it might be counter-productive. A family member turned sour would not convince the jury he argued and the Crown Prosecution Service was considering the implications. After all, they had the information that Alex had provided which had been verified. Meanwhile, Alex was left in limbo, not that he worried unduly as he had made great strides at the restaurant earning promotion and he had Samantha at his back. He could deal with anything. He was feeling strong.

On the other hand, Louise had been struggling. Tom Wilkes had visited her on several occasions gently urging her co-operation. She had no belief that Clive would be incarcerated as he had evaded the law over a long period of time, men like that could always shift the blame, so fear dominated her mind set. She had lived with fear for years.

Tom knew that psychologically she was fragile but he also knew she would have to give evidence, which left her open to a whole lot of misery. He encouraged her to go through all she knew with him to be more prepared for the ordeal because he knew Clive's barrister was a mean interrogator and would question her without mercy, destroying not only her evidence but her reputation. Louise would be fully exposed and as a key witness would likely be dragged through the press with her name in tatters. She would be annihilated by the system. He did not know how far he might be able to go to protect her from the ordeal but he had to try. Men like Clive Corneille fed off the vulnerability of women like Louise.

Tom met with Louise and the solicitor Marcus had arranged in support.

"I've told you all I can," Louise opened defensively.

"I think you have Louise or rather I think you have told me what you could not avoid telling me but I know, there is more. This is your chance Louise. Clive Corneille is a marked man and he will face punishment, but we have to be sure, and we have to know he will face the full force of the law. Clive Corneille and his like have to be brought to justice."

Louise thought back to the time. She had been an innocent bystander and yet she had been punished so much. She had lost her son because of it all and that sacrifice had been made. She felt she had no more to give and gave Tom Wilkes a level look. He recognised her resolve even though he did not understand it. It was her composed demeanour that convinced him that she had more to tell, but how was he to unlock her secrets. He began by taking her through the story of Pauline giving her the film and notebook for safe keeping.

"How well did you know Pauline?"

"Not well. Our paths crossed and she helped me out when I needed a place to stay."

"Why would she trust you?"

"Who else was she to trust? I suppose I was someone uninvolved."

"Uninvolved with what, Louise?"

Louise had made her first error. "Whatever it was," she countered.

Tom studied her for a minute. He admired the woman. She was smart in appearance and ability and to her credit she had made a success of her life since leaving Ken Lewis.

"Why did you leave Ken at the beginning of 1993?" He tried to be gentle as well as probing.

"Why does anyone leave a marriage?"

"You are saying he was cruel to you? Did he abuse you Louise? Is that what you cannot tell me? I can issue a warrant right now for his arrest." Tom needed all his skills as an interviewer. Time was getting short and the trial was looming.

"He was a kind and gentle man." Louise challenged Tom with her quiet, sincere manner.

"Then why go, Louise? Why did you leave a good man, a kind and gentle man, and why did you leave your little boy?"

Louise remained silent and after a minute, Tom reached into the folder. "This is the boy you left isn't it Louise? This is the little boy you walked away from? This is the child you, his mother abandoned," and he placed Jake's photograph as a little boy in front of her. She tried to look away but was drawn to the image as he knew she would be so he added another photograph this time happy in the park, a toddler exploring the world around him with podgy legs and outstretched short arms as though appealing to be picked up by his mother.

Tom continued the parade of photographs deliberately and carefully charting Jake's progress over the years and as each one was placed on the table towards Louise Tom gave a little summary of his age and circumstance. There were school photographs showing his early years with a cheeky gap toothed smile and holding a certificate of achievement and when he was older in the sports teams and in his football kit holding a trophy. Ken was pictured as the proud father alongside his son.

"Where were you Louise? Why weren't you applauding your son?"

Louise reached out a finger and tentatively touched the image for a moment forgetting and gently tracing the boy's face.

Tom continued. He showed her more photographs and copies of certificates. Tom had been meticulous in gathering the exhibits, and he dug into his briefcase and brought out a cap, "This is the cap he got when he played for the county at junior level but his mother was not there to see it."

Tom hated the method but it was paying dividends. Although Louise continued to say nothing the tears were running freely now and he knew she would soon be broken as did the solicitor who suggested a break. Tom did not want to lose advantage so quickly interposed, "I know, you loved Jake with all your heart, Louise. So why on earth would you deprive yourself of him and deprive your little boy of his mother?"

"I do love him. I wanted him to be safe and I could not guarantee that so I had to leave. It was the hardest thing I have ever done." Louise trembled.

"Trust me, Louise. It's a long time ago now and you can be free of the pain because it is painful for you, I know, you have suffered through this so let's try to rebuild." It was time for Tom to encourage.

Louise, having schooled herself to subdue her feelings grappled with the risk of confession. She did not know what consequence might occur but for sixteen years she had lived away from society and now she wondered if she could emerge from the dark.

"I saw what happened to Pauline. I know how she died. He said, if I said anything he would hunt me and anyone I loved down. The threat was real." It was out, the fear of reprisal.

Having made the admission she slumped with her face on the table amongst Jake's photographs. It had been a heavy burden to carry and she was ready to put down the load.

Pauline had died in a road traffic accident. The reports had said she had stepped out from the pavement without looking straight into the path of an articulated lorry. She had been killed instantly. It was noted that the pavements were busy and there was a cluster of people waiting to cross and Pauline was near the front. Everyone had said she must have thought the lights had changed mistaking a traffic light for another lane of traffic for her own. Louise had seen Clive Corneille behind Pauline and seen his hand at her back. She could not prove the push but she saw him judder from the force as Pauline was catapulted forward.

"Why didn't you say something at the time?" Tom's voice was soft. He genuinely felt for the woman.

"I started to and then he got my arm and pretended he was taking care of me. She was my friend and I was upset. He took me to one side and threatened me and I knew from Pauline that there were police officers in his pay so what could I do so I ran. Clive Corneille was a powerful man and I was a mere nobody. I began a new life with Ken and then he popped up again and I did not want him to know I had a son. I talked it over with Ida and she said she would look after Jake if I went away for a bit until he left the town and I could be safe again but Ida died and he didn't leave the town."

Tom now thought a break was warranted and desirable for them all.

There had been a lot of publicity and speculation so security was tight for the trial. It was scheduled to begin on the 9th September.

Some people had a mild interest in events, people like Bill and Anthea, and from them there was a sliding scale of interest depending on position in relation to Corneille. Jim was determined to read every newspaper he could lay his hands on. It was a vindication for his suspicions, although he felt some sympathy for Alex whom he had found agreeable more recently and from Steve he had heard he was doing well in London working in some fancy restaurant. He hoped the club would get full recompense from the outcome of the trial. There was no doubt in his mind that the man was guilty.

Steve had had a difficult time fending off Abigail. He had tried to be patient and listened to Alex's plea about the house. He had no idea what would be the best outcome for his family. He loathed Clive Corneille but if he went down then it would be Steve who would be expected to pick up the pieces and yet Steve wanted justice. The man was a crook. He knew that and waited with trepidation.

Gillian had reverted to her shell which had the benefit for Steve of not meeting up with Diana. The actions of his youth seemed to haunt him and to determine his adult life. Although he had no shame about his liaisons he recognised that there had been something sordid in his behaviour and he wanted Gillian to remain innocent. Diana had already made an impact on his wife and selfishly he was anxious that Gillian should be kept in the dark about his 'jack the lad' past.

The Carstairs family had a varied interest in the trial. Mark had his professional interest and after the honeymoon he was completely back into the fray, working long hard hours in support of the case for the prosecution. It all had to be watertight. Antony and Kirsten had mixed interests in that they would track the financial effects and relate it to their clients and then there was the personal interest because of Antony's early connection with Corneille. Kirsten was aware of Alex and had long harrowing phone calls with her sister exploring every possible avenue and outcome. Diana wanted Alex removed from her daughter's life so hoped the trial would provide a solution. She had no compassion for Alex as far as her own family were concerned.

The first few days of the trial were spent with administrative matters including the swearing in of the jury. Clive was livid with the procedures and complained vocally about his lack of faith in the system. His lawyers held him back as far as they could but he was a force of nature that had been holed up for almost a year and his nerves and temper were ready to explode. He was volatile and slammed doors after ranting at the incompetence of the staff around him. Abigail made further demands on him and he tried to avoid her whining.

The London flat heaved with the strain. Clive had been drinking steadily. He had always imbibed but since his restrictions on bail he had allowed it to escalate. While operating his business his intake had been fine wines and high end spirits. He would use the labels to signal his superiority of palette to impress.

The long wait for the trial had been a limitation that a gregarious man could not stomach. He had spent his days as an influencer and depended on an audience of sycophants and now the only audience he had were his legal team and Abigail. He drank late into the night and began before lunch tossing down the single malt as medicine. When Alex refused to visit, he was incandescent with rage.

Abigail would escape to the bathroom and lock the door. A week before the trial Clive Corneille received a dire warning from his doctor which predictably, as a man used to following his own diktat, he ignored. Clive exercised tyranny over anyone with whom he came in contact. The journalists gathered full of the expectancy of drama. In the end, Clive did not disappoint.

The news at the beginning of the following week emerging overnight on the 15th September caused a disturbance that swelled to disbelief. The bank of Lehman Brothers had filed for bankruptcy. Clive Corneille took the telephone call before court and began calculating the repercussions. Caught in the dock he was unable to follow the markets and see his stock fall without any remedial measures. There were no blue chip stocks to fall back on and his share values plummeted.

Occasional messages were passed to him but in his position as the accused he was impotent. The day edged forward and as it did his mind wandered and he found it increasingly difficult to focus. He sat hands on his knees, a corpulent figure with iron grey hair and blank expression, taciturn and morose, powerless in his own destiny. He found his sight blurred and his head became muzzy. He heard voices from afar and little beads of sweat gathered on his forehead. His limbs felt heavy and there were weights around his torso stretching tight against his Saville Row tailoring. He felt the pains as he had felt the pains of the beatings from his father. They were sharp and severe, cutting deep under his skin. Squeezing his eyes shut he was transported to the blind fury in his father's face and instinctively he ran his left thumb over the groove in the back of his right hand left from the vicious bite of his father's dogs into that soft flesh, as the boy Clive had fended off another attack from the disappointed father. There was no mercy and no hiding from the wrath. In the end, Clive had destroyed the old man. Pathetic and degraded he had come to Clive, a pitiful figure broken before him, and begged for help and Clive had refused. The man had been humbled. Clive had proved himself and he would do so again. He tried to speak but no sound emerged. The strait jacket tightened until he could feel it no more.

The death of Clive Corneille was dramatic and deserved front page attention if it had not been eclipsed by the bank collapse. Even in death, Clive Corneille had not measured up.

Abigail escaped to the house, not where she had lived with Clive but instinctively to her refuge from where she would summon Steve.

Guy spoke with Alex, a difficult conversation, but Alex knew he would have to leave. The restaurant could not take the fall-out. Alex collected his things which were few. As a boy he had innumerable possessions but he had been a rolling stone for the last ten years so like a snake in the grass he had regularly shed his skin. He had learnt much in the last nine months and knew he wanted to shape his own destiny. Guy had said to take time out and return but Alex knew he would not be fettered by the constraints of employment and shook Guy's hand with warmth and gratitude.

The lovers lay in bed each lost in their own thoughts and desires, gazing at the ceiling. Samantha at last spoke, "You are free, Alex, you can do whatever you like."

"I don't think we are ever free." Alex was inured to any more hurt. He was calm and strong.

"That man can't touch you now. He doesn't own you anymore. You can walk away," Samantha seemed to feel the disturbance more than Alex but he had had more practice and was resigned to his fate.

"I think, he owns me more than ever. I will have to deal with things. I can't escape."

"It's not your problem. Leave it," and as if to enforce her words she turned and snuggled into him.

"I'm his son Samantha. I have to face it." Alex had ducked many things in his life. He felt the start of a new life and that meant facing up to things.

"A stepson and only for a brief time, no-one expects you to be involved." Samantha wanted to shield them both.

"I'm his son, Samantha. They told me the night of the accident. It is the truth. I have Clive Corneille's genes."

Samantha lifted herself up and could see his look. "You will never, never be like that man, Alex. Don't even think it. He was cruel and selfish. You are not."

"Then I must prove it. I must stand up and be counted. I have to go home and deal with it and then maybe I will deserve you." Alex was adamant and looking at her knew he had something worth fighting for. It would be hard but he had resolution.

"Who knows?" She asked, meaning his parentage.

"Only you now but I think it may come out. That night, I hated them both. They were leaving the country, a plane had been arranged and they wanted me to go too, feeding off his ill-gotten gains. It was me that told the police. He might have got away if not. What kind of person am I to blow the whistle on my own father?"

He turned towards her and felt the moisture gather in his eyes as though he were a young boy after a playground hurt, "I want my dad, not Corneille, I want my real dad, the dad I've known, the dad that was there for me. I cannot look him in the face. I'm tainted." Alex could be calculated and dispassionate about Clive Corneille and even circumspect about his mother but he dissolved completely when he thought of Steve because he loved him.

Samantha smoothed his forehead with her fingers. Her expert hands massaged his temples and travelled over his face finding the tension points, slowly releasing and relaxing. She caressed his skin lightly and expertly finding his shoulders and pinpointing with her thumbs the places of stress and hurt and then she said, "Whatever happens in the future Alex you are not alone. I am beside you, I am with you, I will support you. You have not lost your dad, your real dad, the one you know and love. He will not desert you. He loves you too. I've seen it."

They held each other close preparing for their own trials ahead.

Chapter 24
Losing Balance

Oh the gladness of a woman when she's glad
And oh the sadness of a woman when she's sad
But the gladness of her gladness
And the sadness of her sadness
Are nothing to the badness when she's bad

Bad Woman: Anon

2008-2009: Alex

The legacy of Clive Corneille was lamentable. His empire tumbled like a tower of playing cards or collapsed like a row of domino soldiers because as each company folded another would be brought to grief and then another and then another. The receivers were appointed by the courts so all Alex had to do was face the flak which was considerable. Some meetings were stormy, with creditors venting their anger and others for smaller offshoot companies had sparse attendance when proposals were rubber stamped. Alex had a steep learning curve with the experience, although after a while it became the norm so he was able to disengage from personal responsibility. Coincidentally, the publicity surrounding the Corneille Group began to dwindle.

The dissolution was complex and dragged on through the winter. Assets were sold and rescue packages were brokered but more often than not the liquidation meant closures without due recompense. This was the public face of the corporation. It was a sign of times to come as global recession began to bite. The Corneille businesses would become far from unique.

Alex had no hesitation in selling the accumulated property portfolio and stood firm before his mother's exasperated tears. Any money he accrued he privately distributed to those Alex had deemed had been unfairly treated by the collapse. It was a risk inviting investigation but he needed to make reparation and become distanced from the debacle. Pension funds were replenished as far as possible and small businesses which would have been wiped out without more assistance than the meagre pay-outs from the liquidator were given a helping hand. His magnanimity began to be heralded if not generally and publicly by national newspapers certainly in private homes and in local press.

To some he became a saviour and while Clive Corneille's name was reviled Alex was building a name for honesty, integrity and charitable endeavour. It was an aphrodisiac to his soul. Things were bumpy and it would take years before all financial matters could be resolved and he could completely shake off the stink of the ordeal. He wanted to sever any connection as far as he was able. The effects on him as a person would remain with him for the rest of his life.

The will of Clive Corneille made provision for Abigail but the bulk was in Alex's hands. He resisted acknowledging the reason, even to himself. It took months to resolve private funds but by the spring of 2009, he was able to access the majority of hidden treasures squirrelled by Clive into the bank accounts in chosen tax havens. He was ready to begin to make investments of his own.

Samantha was there in the background urging his efforts and applauding his successes. They were discreet and met at quiet country hotels for stolen nights of intimacy. Only Kirsten was aware of the meetings and she urged caution by her sister. Diana after some initial arguments with Samantha about any relationship with Alex had generally remained in ignorance of the growing romance, believing in her daughter's good sense that a fling had been possible in the feverish period of the wedding but a full blown relationship was out of the question, and so watched the news from afar thankful that none of the Carstairs family had any involvement in proceedings.

There was an uneasy truce between Alex and Abigail living together again in the old home but the dynamics became different. No longer was Alex a son without purpose or ambition. He was the controlling force. He was away from the house much of the time if not dealing with business he would be seeing Samantha for a brief interlude. When home, his new skills and confidence from the restaurant meant another kind of domination for he could manage the household and provide nutritious meals for them both.

Abigail though was fading. Her solitary confinement sent her spiralling down. The acquaintances she had been surrounded by had abandoned her and she did not have the wit to forge new ones. Clive had always been in her orbit. She had depended on him even throughout her marriage to Steve. He was there in the background with his life rubbing off on hers and she had held the ace card with Alex.

Now Clive had given her more than Alex, he had given her his name. She had relished the position it afforded her on marriage but now the name was toxic and while Clive had escaped, she was paying the price. The only sympathy that came her way was her own and she exercised self-pity to an art form. Inevitably, she began to create a web and like a black widow spider she invited Steve in. He had always been the unsuspecting fly.

Initially Alex had little time to see Steve and Gillian and even more he felt the difficulties of meeting Steve without support, conscious of the betrayal and raw from the revelation. Alex knew he could not hide his angst and as often the case he would resort to his surly character creating a greater rift to divide them so he would tend to meet Steve publicly, maybe joining him and Simon, and he found the nursery a good place with its timeless quality.

As the winter wrapped the earth in winter chills it was less amenable and he saw less of Steve. He missed Gillian too and was tempted to call in but he was ever mindful of the spectre of Clive Corneille. He could not shake the image of Clive's claim of parentage. It was a burden he could not share with the one person from whom he needed reassurance. He had become involved in Simon's plans from listening to discussion and helped to pull in the support of the football club and that with the commitment of the council made the whole idea feasible.

Steve had made designs which had been placed with a local architect and planning permission was expected. Funds were in place and Alex had been instrumental in drawing up a business plan. It was all systems go. He liked the idea of looking forward. He knew Steve was pleased and relished that fact.

Encouraged by Anthea and feeding from the headstrong Diana, Gillian was making plans. Buoyed up with the Venice trip, she made a list of all the places she wanted to visit and began her research. It gave her many happy hours through the winter which she discussed with her two friends. Diana was a mine of information. It became fun meeting for coffee or lunch and listening to her stories, mainly her escapades.

For once as far as she was concerned, Steve stood on the side-lines and he in his realisation of who Diana had been, sought to avoid any direct meeting with the woman. He was not embarrassed by it but there was a concern that if his wife got wind of it they would both suffer.

Abigail's antennae detected a weakness. There was no obvious sign but she had always had an unerring instinct. It was in her survival kit.

"The kitchen sink is blocked. Alex is away again. Can you sort it, Steve?" She would implore. "The lock on the back door is sticking. I'm on my own here." She would appeal to his better nature.

"The light in the hallway keeps flickering. What shall I do? Is it dangerous?" She would ask.

Steve was well aware that Alex had his hands full and anyway he thought Alex had few practical skills. Steve had always been the man to fix things. It was the natural order of things. He would do that for anyone who asked and saw no reason not to respond for his ex-wife and son. Winter days were short for his renovation work so he had time to spare plus Simon was immersed in his schemes and Gillian was forging future plans. Self-conscious about his sexual fling with Diana he preferred to avoid any discomfort in her presence so he was happy to oblige his ex-wife. In his view he was being kind, Abigail saw it as much more.

December, over two months after the death of her husband Clive at his trial, brought the matter to a head. He had brought round a tree as had been his custom when they were together and she had said she needed the cheer of a real fir in this time of misery. She had cried as she made her request. Steve could not refuse. It was a simple thing to do.

Abigail certainly looked gaunt. Her hair hung lank which added to the pallor of her skin to give her the appearance of a waif in need of sustenance. Steve pitied her and followed her instructions as she directed him in the reorganisation of the room to take the tree.

It was damp outside, so to avoid bringing dirt in with the tree, he had taken off his boots. It was a comfortable scene, a muscular male installing the five foot tree in the alcove while the female of the species admired and encouraged. The decorations had been stored in the loft so it was logical for Steve to retrieve the box.

"Take care, won't you?" Abigail fussed from the bottom of the ladder on the landing. She had already opened her bedroom door wide having earlier spent a pleasant hour giving it the boudoir effect. Lingerie was draped on the bed and chair. Steve tried to avert his eyes.

"Remember when you slipped and twisted your ankle. I got a cold compress and had to help you. You were laid up for days and I looked after you. It was nice having you at home and we all played card games." In truth Steve remembered her impatience and general annoyance at the imposition and it was Steve and Alex who had played cards. He said nothing and allowed her the fantasy.

The cardboard box was retrieved and brought down to the living room where it was opened to reveal so many memories. Abigail delved into the tinsel and baubles and brought out the little Christmas figures that reminded Steve of Alex as a little boy mesmerised by the giant tree and anxious to be lifted by his father to place the ornaments in its folds. For a moment Steve held the little boy in his arms but turning to Abigail shook off the sensation.

"Well, I will leave you to it," he said withdrawing from her space, "Enjoy," he added.

"But you must help me decorate the tree. I can't reach the top and you always had the knack of making it look wonderful. It will be a real tonic for Alex when he gets back. He has been working very hard putting it all right. He worries about me I know, but I've told him to sell everything, I don't mind. I try to support him as I always have. When you worked all those long hours when he was a child, he depended on me. It was a pity you were not around more." She was pushing buttons.

Steve metaphorically shrugged his shoulders. Strange the slant others put on things. He did care about Alex so set to unravelling the fairy lights. While he worked on the tree Abigail floated around occasionally bumping his arm as she reached across. She held the bright baubles one by one in her hand to pass over to Steve, stroking the smooth surfaces and occasionally placing a swift kiss on a favoured ornament and dangled the tinsel provocatively around her neck as though she was a lady of the night beckoning a punter. There was no disguising the electricity that she exuded and momentarily Steve had a frisson of interest.

The tree done, they both stepped back to admire. Abigail made sure her vantage point was shoulder to shoulder with Steve and heaved her bosom deliberately in ecstatic joy.

"It's wonderful," she exuded, "Thank you so much. You are a very special man Steve Mason, in fact a magical man. You can transform anything." There was little disguise in her look. Steve thought he was immune.

"Steve moved away but she intervened, "A photo, we must have a photograph. You will take one for me won't you Steve?"

What could he do but oblige? She found the camera in the cupboard and gave it to him. "I hope the batteries are ok?" She said. "I'm sure I have more somewhere if not. What happy times this camera has recorded Steve, when we were together as a family? It's old now and a bit heavy but you are holding the means of cherished memories in your hand."

Steve, impatient to be gone having spent an uncomfortable hour took the shot. "Oh you must take me with the tree, like we used to," Abigail purred.

"Fine, stand over by it."

"Goodness I can't have my photograph taken looking like this. You've cheered me up so much. I won't be long. I will go and change. Help yourself to a drink if you like. There's some beer in the fridge." Her congenial manner was underlined with an invitation which produced sexual tension.

Steve had no intention of drinking a beer. He was driving and did not want to delay his return home. He was getting impatient and his guard was up.

Abigail was an age. There was a rush of awkward memories in this room, like the telling photograph or the Millennium when he and Alex had been defeated by her ploys. His phone pinged. It was Gillian. "Where on earth are you? Had you forgotten I'm going to that lecture on the Roman Empire?"

It had completely slipped his mind. "Sorry I will be back soon."

"Well, I was hoping you would take me. Diana's agreed to come too and it would be nice to have a drink afterwards." Steve had so wanted Gillian to make friends but it irked him for the friend to be Diana. "Where are you, exactly?"

Steve could not lie. "I'm at Abigail's."

"Why?" Gillian had gone cold.

"She wanted a Christmas tree. I have brought her one."

"And I suppose you helped her put it up and even decorate it?" She said sarcastically. She did not believe it was possible. Steve's inability to answer told her all she needed to know.

For once all composure left her. "You lying, cheating bastard. You've spent all afternoon with her no doubt reminiscing about old times and what else have you been doing Steve? Gosh I bet you've loved having her attention. Has she come on to you Steve? Don't tell me you couldn't resist. Oh yes, you've played me for a fool and a fool I'll be no longer. I'm your wife Steve, not her, not that simpering selfish bitch, me, me, me!" She was shouting now.

On gathering her breath she said in a cool even tone, "Don't come home Steve. Stay there if she wants you so much because I don't want you anymore."

She was gone leaving Steve angered and bewildered. Gillian never behaved like this. Gillian always understood. Once again, Abigail had invaded his life. He had to leave.

Abigail was on the bottom step of the stairs when he bolted for the door and she stepped out to bar his departure. "I'm so sorry I was a long time. I couldn't decide what to wear."

Steve was left in no doubt of the look she wanted to achieve. She had fixed her hair and make-up and the black dress was provocative in the low cut neckline in which an uplift bra had urged her breasts to swell immodestly. Abigail was shameless. The tight fit and short skirt were titillating in a steamy and vulgar fashion. It was meant to be sensuous and erotic but Steve could only feel disgust.

"What the hell are you trying to do?" He pushed past her and retrieved his boots.

"I need you Steve. Stay here." Abigail in her fifties had no allure. It was pathetic and Steve realised what a fool he had always been. He was angry in an absolute sense.

"You must be out of your mind." He flung the words in her face like a slap.

"When we first met, you liked to screw me then, didn't you? Couldn't get enough of me then, could you?"

Abigail was a woman spurned and worse she had seen the revulsion in his face. "Yes, well you needn't be so smug. I had men when we were married. I had lots of men. I was bored with you. You thought you were a stud but let me tell you, you were pathetic, a sorry excuse for a man, and I'll tell you something else you couldn't even get a child, not up to the job."

Steve's hesitation gave Abigail the opportunity for the final blow. "You don't think Alex is really your child, do you, Steve? He's Clive's. He's his son. He's not yours and never will be."

Abigail exhausted sank on to the stairs. Steve dumbfounded reached out with his hands towards her.

Alex opened the door to the scene, his mother to him scantily dressed, his father standing over her and menace in the air.

Steve retreated and Abigail screeched, "Tell him, tell him Alex. Tell him he's not your dad. That's why you've been sorting out Clive's estate. He's your real dad. Tell him."

Alex gave the merest nod to the question before his father staggered through the door, beaten and annihilated. His anger had dissipated and all that remained was an empty shell of a man. Abigail's words echoed in his ears and as he left she was crying to Alex, "He was going to kill me, Alex, I swear."

Alex caught between the two followed Steve and tried to apprehend him. Alex appealed, "Dad," but Steve shoved him roughly to one side and ran to his truck.

Gillian did not go to the lecture and made her excuses to Diana. She waited at home but Steve did not come. An hour later, her anger had deserted her and the thought came that he may not return at all. Two hours later she had become more convinced and three hours later she had lost faith. She rang his phone but there was no connection. She sent a text but it was not delivered. All her life she had felt lonely but the feeling of rejection she had that evening was complete.

Steve had nowhere to go. He drove automatically out of town trying to put distance between him and his persecutors. Alex his treasured son was not his. He was a cuckold. He had been duped. Not only this but for an instant, for a nanosecond he had been out of control. What would have happened if Alex had not returned at that very moment? He could not answer. He did not feel guilt. How could he when he still felt murderous when he thought of Abigail? When he thought of Gillian, he felt despair.

The truck seemed to guide him towards the nursery maybe because he was not concentrating and it was a well-known route. A late December afternoon dusk merged the landscape so he became cocooned in the familiar cab with the paraphernalia of his life in its pockets, a workman's life, one without subtlety and guile, a grafter, a creator with tools and wood and craft, an artisan who had been blind to the world outside his own. He had been the fool. He reached the nursery but conscious of the lights he turned away and left Rainwick for the anonymous lights of the town.

Joining the rush hour traffic he edged towards the ring road, passing the football stadium where Clive Corneille had wielded his power and angered again he abruptly steered off the main thoroughfare and came to the suburb of Stonebrook, once the small hamlet where little Ida Brindell had been born and Jim lived and Simon would build. Steve felt small and inconsequential. He pulled his truck on to the waste ground and turned off the engine and lights. Here he could lean back and try to forget. He turned off his phone.

Jim found winter a difficult season. Days were short and nights were long and his bones ached in the cold. He missed Ida's warming stews. He was loath to draw the curtains against the world outside until fully dark. When Ida had been there, he had been content to shut it out and be in their small world but that was in another life. He would sit in the dark room looking out before the evening would close on him completely and often stand by the window watching for any passer-by, a contact with civilisation.

That night he caught sight of the truck pulling over and was curious. The pick-up had parked in the shadow blending with the wall and scrub so he could not be certain but as it had passed the street light he was convinced he recognised it as Simon's mate Steve. He wondered why he would be there at that time in the near dark.

After half an hour Jim made up his mind. He would go and see. He knew Jake and Ken would be mad at him, especially after what had happened at the beginning of the previous year, but his instinct told him that something was amiss. He had never been someone who held back when there was something to be done. Steve was lying back, eyes closed, covered by his old donkey jacket to ward off the cold when Jim tapped on his window. He peered into the dark and determined a face.

"Is everything alright?" Were Jim's opening words.

"Needed a bit of space," Steve muttered.

"Why don't you come over and have a cup of tea? It's mighty cold out here." Steve hesitated but it was true; it was cold, even in his boots his toes were feeling numb and the end of his nose was ice.

Jim bustled into the house and put on the kettle. "How about a cup of tea and I've got a nice tin of chunky vegetable soup, too much for me on my own but I'm sure you could help me out."

Steve watched Jim deliberately put the soup in the pan and take down two bowls. There was some crusty bread too. He suddenly felt like a king.

They talked of the development. Jim had been told of the ideas which had been the surprise that had given him a new lease of life. It was all exciting to the old man and he could not be more interested. He recognised in Steve someone who took pride in what they did and would not cut corners. Steve was not a seeker of profit in the pecuniary sense. He had met his wife too. She seemed a decent sort.

"So what were you running away from?" Jim judged the moment.

"That obvious," said Steve.

"Well, you can rest up here for a bit. You don't have to say anything. It's not my business but sometimes an ear can help." Jim had plenty of time.

"You didn't have children did you?" Steve ventured.

"No, we were never that lucky. We had each other and we made that work. Jake has become a sort of adopted grandson. Not that I say that to him but he sort of stole into my life. I am very lucky."

"I learnt today that my son is not mine." Steve was glad to let it out.

"Knocked you for six, did it?"

"I suppose I thought we weren't the same somehow but I relished that really. He was a bit different to me but it didn't make any difference to how I felt." It was good to talk. Steve's sociability had never extended to personal comments and there had been a lot in the last couple of years to upset him.

Jim knew only too well the delicacy of the situation.

"He's a good lad Alex. He hides it a bit though. I had a chat with him the day of his accident you know." Jim had often thought about that day. Alex had been kind and it had not been false.

Steve was alert, so Jim continued. "It was at the football club. He invited me up to the directors' suite, very plush. I'd never been there before so it was a nice treat. We talked a bit about this and that. He was getting a handle on things at the club and I got the impression he wanted to sort a few things out. There was a lot of cost cutting and waste. I suppose he had been learning about Clive Corneille and his influence. Nothing was said but I knew he was uneasy. He treated me very well. I had tea and sandwiches, very tasty. He was a gentleman that day. Then Inspector Wilkes came. I knew him from my burglary and he wanted to talk with your boy. Of course, I left but I did tell him to trust the Inspector and I believe he did."

Steve was processing what he knew. "You mean he would have informed on Corneille."

"I'm convinced of it. I felt he was troubled and the only way to deal with it was to let it go. I was shocked about his accident but things developed fast after that. That Clive Corneille was a nasty piece of work. I know, he's dead and you should not say anything like that but it's my honest opinion." Jim took a gulp of his tea.

Steve took a deep breath. "Clive Corneille is Alex's father."

Jim gave him a steady look and then with a clear firm voice he said, "You are his father."

There was intensity in the message that Steve could not ignore.

Jim continued emphatically, "You have been the man in his life. You have been his father. You have formed him. He is your son and his actions have proved that. This last year he has been a credit to you. It is your influence that has given him the decency that he has shown, the strength of character and the compassion for people. Clive Corneille has nothing in him. Your son, your son has rejected that evil and turned to the good because of you. Don't desert him now when he most needs you. Don't let him think you don't care. Be the father you have always been. Show him it makes no difference to you."

There was complete darkness outside that room but inside it a lamp had been lit. The mote from Steve's eyes had gone. He had a new vision, a different vision. He had been shaken to the core. He did not need to hide.

"Your wife will no doubt be waiting for you. She will be worried," Jim could see Steve's need.

Steve was already home in his mind when the doorbell rang. "Well, another visitor. I am blessed tonight."

Jim opened the door to find a lady standing there. It was dark and the street lights were behind her.

"Hello Mr Woodhouse. May I come in?"

Steve exchanged his place in the confessional to the woman. "Thank you," he uttered and he shook Jim's hand firmly. It would take him almost an hour to get home and he was eager to be there but the time would allow him plenty of time for reflection.

Louise stood before Jim who was assessing her carefully. "I'm sorry if it's a shock."

"I knew you'd come back one day."

Louise followed him into the front room, recently vacated by Steve. Her eyes were drawn to the photographs on the mantelpiece and she absorbed the familiarity of the room. There were no real changes. The furniture seemed the same and the coffee table on which Jake had tried his toddler puzzles was still there. The bookcase under the window was still stuffed with books, many of them on plants and football. She had missed this haven. She had missed Ida.

Both of them sat without knowing what to say. So many memories and such heartache were present in the room. Jim whose usual way to overcome a situation was to offer a 'cuppa' was too shaken.

"It's good to see you. I'm sorry about Ida. She was a wonderful, special lady."

"Yes," was all Jim could say.

"Tell me to go if you want. I will understand. I hoped we could talk." Louise looked intently at Jim Woodhouse.

"No Jackie, I'm not letting you disappear again."

"I call myself Louise now, Jim. It is my birth name."

There was so much he did not know or understand about this woman but Ida did and that was enough recommendation.

"Why now?" He wanted to know.

"Clive Corneille has gone. He can't hurt me or Jake now." Even for Jim this was a shock, especially after his conversation with Steve. How many more people had been scarred by that man he thought? It had already been a tiring evening. Jim wondered at the extent of the man's reach.

"You'd better tell me," and she did.

"Does Ken know you're here?" He asked eventually.

"No. I wanted to see you first. It's difficult. I don't want to barge in. I never thought I would be away so long." Louise was gracious in what she said, although Jim thought there was pain underneath.

"I'm sure he would want to see you, but he has moved on." He felt it was his duty to warn her as well as protect Ken and Jake.

"He has someone else?"

"That's something between you and him. What about you?" There was much that he wanted to know not least because of Ida.

"No I am single. I needed to keep a low profile. A friend helped me and I have done well. I have a good life but an empty one." Louise had a measured honesty in her response.

"Tell me about Jake," She added.

Jim did not know what to say. His experience gave him no preparation for this. His instinct was to protect Jake who was happy at the nursery and running his gardening business and Jim was nervous of distress. He could not help be scared of being the one to lose Jake. Louise as she was now called would claim him and he would be the loser for it. What had he just been telling Steve? It was not really the truth was it? Louise would claim him even though Jake's upbringing was not down to her. He felt bereft.

"He's a good boy, doing well," was all he could say.

"I wondered if you might speak to Ken for me so we could meet. I know, it's difficult but if Ken wants to move on with someone else I can at least make it easy."

Jim could see no objection, although he felt the foundations of his world shudder. Perhaps it was because he was old and feared change.

Chapter 25
Finding Answers

*'Tis all a Chequer-board of nights and days
Where Destiny with men for Pieces plays:
Hither and thither moves, and mates, and slays,
And one by one back in the closet lays.*

Omar Khayyam

2008-2009: Community

Alex had to restrain his mother. She was adamant that the police should be called but he said he would not support her. He could not leave her until he was sure that the crisis was over. She had bathed and took a sleeping tablet and retired to bed. It was early, only eight o'clock but he was exhausted. This could not go on.

His mobile beeped with a text. It was Gillian. "Is your dad with you?"

Alarm bells rang. He had not gone home. Alex rang her.

Alex could not tell her about the scene. It would reveal too much but he did say there had been an argument. Steve had left almost three hours before. Gillian told him she had said some unforgivable things. She was worried. His phone was not responding.

"He's just cooling off, probably with Simon somewhere," Alex offered. "I'll chase him down."

He began ringing round everyone he could think off before taking a tour of the area to try to spot his dad's pick-up. The last year had tested everything for Alex. The turbulence had flung him from his former existence of self-seeking churlish behaviour to someone who had empathy. He had lost that previous life in his battle to survive.

He had risen to the challenges and found hidden depths within his character, ironically by being self-assertive and self-reliant he had emerged appreciating weaknesses in others, not to be used for personal exploitation but for an understanding of their condition, a revelation that strengthened him and allowed him to make relationships on an equal footing.

He saw his dad as vulnerable, a man who had feet of clay and someone who had persevered with stoic acceptance of his lot, resilient but quelled by fortune. In a strange way he felt the potency of Clive Corneille flow through his own veins and knew he had the inner grit that was absent from Steve who led life with an idealised view.

As a child, it had been easy to wind his parents up with a tantrum or crocodile tears. His father had been too trusting and open, ready to indulge while his mother had a devious streak swinging from roles of victim to puppet-master. There were obvious cracks in the partnership which even as a little boy Alex could exploit. Alex had been cunning in his actions. His mother was self-obsessed and his father was an innocent. His mother had to be removed from the equation while his father needed a strong arm on which to lean. Alex hoped that his father had not been pushed over the edge.

He arrived at Primrose Crescent at about eight-thirty noting an empty space where Steve usually parked. It was an ominous sign and Gillian's face completed the picture.

"Anything?"

"Nothing," was her retort.

Their natural space had become the kitchen where she made coffee and thanked him for coming. It had been hell waiting on her own and she was grateful.

"I was angry with him for being at yours this afternoon. I lost my temper and told him not to bother coming back. It's really all my fault." She confessed. "Where is he, Alex?" Gillian too, was an innocent. Alex thought.

"He'll be fine. He was angry when he left so he's gone somewhere to cool off. He's maybe had a drink or two and will have to walk home. I'll wait with you."

"I wish I hadn't upset him. I should not have said what I did." She twisted a strand of hair.

Alex wanted to reassure her but he could not tell her the real reason for the anger. That was something that Steve had to tell, so meanwhile, he just said that his mother was being a pain. It was all he could manage. Both were clock watching while Alex made small talk to try to ease the tension. He would have liked to get Gillian's view about his plans for a new restaurant but this was not the time. Alex indeed was a reformed character.

At nine o'clock, a key sounded in the lock. Steve was back. There were no words and Gillian was swept into his arms, a moment later Alex too joined the group hug. It was a turning point from which each could learn.

"I'm off, but I will ring you tomorrow, Dad. Get a good night's sleep." Steve was no longer hollow inside and he patted Alex on the back, a familiar gesture of love and respect.

"Thanks Alex."

"You can't get rid of me that easily, Dad," he tried to emphasise the word 'dad' to reassure both of them. "Tell Gillian. She needs to know."

The next day while Steve was coming to terms with the admission, Louise was meeting Ken which Jim had brokered. It was a wary encounter on each side. Louise, with her unfamiliar name was also unfamiliar in appearance. She was immaculately groomed. Her hair was stylishly cut eradicating the soft curls that had once framed her face, make-up had been expertly applied to disguise not only flaws in complexion but inner nerves and clothes were chic and cut to mould to her figure and she wore elegant shoes and carried a matching handbag, all a far cry from when they had been together. She could have stepped out from the pages of a glossy magazine. Ken in his casual polo shirt and jeans found her intimidating.

She began by explaining what she had been doing and how Marcus had helped her find work.

Ken listened his heart quickening and blood pressure rising. "What of us, Jackie?" He could not call her Louise yet, "what about me and Jake?"

Louise did not know how to answer. With hindsight she realised she should have fought for what she had had. Ken's accusation was showing what she had squandered.

"Forgive me, Ken. I thought it was right at the time." She could see his temper rising and wished Jim was there.

"We were married. No secrets in marriage. You should have told me." Ken let out the bitterness.

"I know, I know. It was wrong of me. I thought I would be away for six months max and then I would explain and it would all be fine. I was frightened Ken. I was scared witless."

She could not convey what it had been like for her. She had not the capability or resources to deal with it all. She had no parents to turn to, she had seen her friend killed, she had understood something of the power of the organisation and at Diana's party had seen the look on Clive Corneille's face and she had been indebted to her husband on whom she did not want to bring trouble and then at all costs she wanted to protect Jake. Maybe, she had not behaved as she should have done but she was young and frightened and, once she had left, it became more and more difficult to return even if she had thought it was safe.

"So you saved your own skin?" Ken had accumulated years of resentment.

"I wanted to protect you and Jake too."

Ken was not ready to listen. His pride was hurt and this stranger was unknown.

"I thought Clive Corneille would leave here. He always had before so I didn't expect him to stay round here. He had threatened me and my family. Ida knew. It seemed the best plan to disappear for a while."

"That's one thing, but no word in all these years?"

"I sent money, every year on his birthday and Christmas."

"Yes, and I kept it. I never spent a penny. It's in a building society account. Couldn't be sure where it came from." He looked at her fiercely not seeing his wife, only a stranger who had cast him aside and tried to pay him off.

"I thought it would help. At first, I couldn't send much but then I did better. I owe you a lot Ken." Louise had known it would be a hard conversation. She had been taken aback by his hostility and hung her head.

"You don't owe me a damn thing except an apology so you can stuff your money. We don't need it and well, you only have to look at you to see you preferred banknotes to us. Coming here dressed to the nines and looking down your nose. Don't think you can squirm back into our lives. We're happy. Jake's doing well so do not spoil it for him. Do you hear me?" Ken was shouting.

"I hear you, Ken. There is so much to say and I know, you are cross and hurt." Louise suffered. She remembered Ken's kindness and here was a man incensed. She did not know how to make it better but she would have to try.

"That's an understatement," he spat the words venomously.

"I was to be a witness in the trial Ken, the trial of Clive Corneille. I had seen him kill my friend." It was the ultimate confession.

Suddenly, Ken's vitriol had been discharged. Subdued he said, "Tell me now. Everything."

It was a sorry tale of a young girl, unhappy at home and briefly enticed into a world of corruption and vice. She had felt suffocated at home. She told him honestly about the party she had attended with Pauline and what she had seen there. She was a young teenager and she had avoided participation which Ken privately acknowledged had shown tremendous strength of character.

She told him how the young soldier had offered her protection for a few days when she had felt vulnerable and she had taken it with the result that when he had gone she found she was expecting Jake. She told him more about her adopted parents and their lifestyle and her guilt that she had to acknowledge on a daily basis while her mum claimed the little boy. She tried to convey her feelings of jealousy and the fear that she was losing Jake gradually and inevitably to her mother.

She had felt the suffocation from Meredith until she felt she had to extricate her and Jake. She reconnected with Pauline, the former friend who had taken her to the party hosted by Clive Corneille. In the time that had elapsed Pauline had gathered evidence to condemn Clive Corneille. It had been a sort of insurance policy. Pauline had been involved in things that Louise could not begin to understand. It had been a coincidence that Pauline had passed the box to Louise just before she had died. It had been straight after that, that Ken had found her at the pub where she had hoped to find a job.

Louise took a pause and could see that Ken, absorbed in the story, had lost the anger. He caught her eye with an expression of sympathy.

She told him about going to see Diana who had rejected her and how Clive Corneille had been an honoured guest and how he had sent someone to follow her explaining how Marcus helped her to escape. It was no wonder that his presence at the football club had brought panic. She knew of his power. She had been threatened. She had run before he could hurt her or Ken or Jake. She believed in Ida who would be her guide.

"Why did you leave the box with me?"

"I thought it would be safe and I would be back. I also thought if they found my body that maybe they would look at my things and an honest copper would put two and two together. I am so sorry Ken. I really am."

It was a world that Ken only really knew about in films. He'd known ruffians and petty criminals but he had little conception of the dirty operators in a world where power was absolute. Girls like Louise were there for the picking and it sickened him. By then, he had read much in the newspapers. He also had begun to see through the armour she wore to the defenceless woman he had known before. She had after all not changed that much.

"What about going back to your parents? Couldn't you have kept low there for a while?" He needed to know everything.

"I never told the police Ken I couldn't. My mum was difficult and hard to live with but I could never go back there. Dad worked at the depot in the offices booking in the lorry loads. One day, after school I didn't go straight home. Ken I saw him, Dad, my dad, taking an envelope from Clive Corneille. It was a back hander. There were scams everywhere and Dad was one of the cogs in the wheel."

Ken could understand how at eighteen or so she had felt trapped. She had limited options and he was glad that she had had Ida and that this guy had helped her. He wished he had been included but realised why not. He shuddered to think what might have happened to her if Marcus had not been there.

They had met in Jim's sitting room to be private and Jim had joined Jake at the Swan. Jake had assumed that Ken was out with Kathy but she was there behind the bar as usual which puzzled him. Jim was not anxious to return home which also puzzled him.

"So where do we go from here?" Ken asked.

"Obviously, I would like to meet Jake if you don't mind," Louise crossed her fingers.

"I cannot stop you. He's a man now." It was a non-committal answer and while his tone was more conciliatory she was not convinced of his blessing and that was important.

"I would not go against you, Ken but I hope and pray you will not stand in my way."

"No I won't stand in your way. He needs to meet his mother." He gave her a long, steady look.

Louise sighed with relief.

"Jim tells me you've made a new life, Ken. Tell me about you. Tell me about Jake. Please."

Ken found she knew all about Jake's job at the nursery and his gardening business. It seemed she had been keeping tabs but he was able to tell her the little things, his likes and dislikes, the way he cleared up after him, his wry sense of humour and the way he dated girls but there was no-one serious or so he thought. Louise assured him that she was not about to make trouble and when Ken touched on having a girlfriend she assured him a divorce would be straightforward.

After an unpromising start, the two had regained some of their old affinity so when Jim finally returned having been escorted to his gate by Jake there was an amiable truce. Ken would choose his moment to broach Jake about his mother and take it from there. The wheels were in motion.

Other wheels had been turning that winter. While Steve was licking his wounds Alex had removed his mother to the Spanish villa on the pretext that it would be a good place for Christmas. Abigail had always adored the villa, loving the sunshine and clear blue skies as well as the lifestyle. It had the party vibes she so adored. He was able to deposit her there with some confidence.

Removed from the house, Alex gave Steve the go ahead to put it on the market. It was not really his call but he was learning a thing or two about getting his own way so was confident that he could iron over any difficulties with Abigail. He was imposing his will.

He would be losing his base too which spurred him to carry other plans forward. He wanted no further delay to being with Samantha so it was time to come out of the shadows. He planned carefully. He was a man of moderate means and he had ambition. He met Samantha in London and even though they already had an understanding from Kirsten and Mark's wedding he surprised her with a night at the Savoy in a junior suite that boasted a little balcony where wrapped in thick coats and blankets and wrapped in love, drinking from a bottle of Veuve Clicquot, he proposed formally dropping on one knee as the dark Thames below flowed steadily to the sea and the twinkling city Christmas lights could not match the sparkle of Samantha's eyes or the diamond on the ring from Boodles. Even at that late hour Samantha rang her mother in her bubble of elation.

"Hi, Mum. I'm engaged." She giggled.

"Congratulations," Diana quipped. "Who's the lucky man?" Diana had been half asleep.

"Alex, Mum, there's never been anyone else. We're at the Savoy. It's been wonderful." Samantha was giddy with excitement. "I just had to ring you, Mum. I have the most divine ring. I am so happy. I've got to go, speak tomorrow," and Diana was cut off which considering what she wanted to say was a good thing.

Diana went back to bed to toss and turn. Antony was still deep in sleep and the news was not something she wanted to relay and moreover to explain her reason for the objection so she let him sleep.

Samantha was a wilful independent child and Diana knew she would dig her heels in if she did not handle the situation carefully. She would not go in all guns blazing as she might with other members of her family but she would find a way. She was good at negotiating out of disaster.

Near the end of January she invited Gillian over having thought with Gillian's track record she could persuade her to intervene. Gillian was malleable, she could not help it, it was just her nature, and she would see the sense of it as well as keep the secret. It would be difficult telling her about Steve but they were grown women not in the first flush of youth so these things could be accepted. It was part of a different past. Diana had put much of her life in a box when it did not suit.

Alex had been wonderfully attentive to Steve over the last month which had steadied the ship. Moreover the house was on the market. It would be gone and Gillian was feeling a release from its claim. There would be extra funds in the household to use for travel if she could persuade Steve, but it was much more than this, she felt she could wipe the woman from her marriage.

Steve on the other hand had been cast asunder. For the first time he knew Gillian's perennial pain of not having a child of her own. Alex had been the most testing of all children but he was Steve's and that bond had permeated his life. In fact, Alex had determined his life. He wondered if he had known the truth would it have been easier to leave Abigail.

He did not know because Alex had stolen into his heart even though he was a cuckoo and Steve was not the man to quit responsibilities. He did think that the whole relationship might have been different and he might have felt justified in divorcing Abigail years earlier while still providing and caring for Alex. He might even have had custody which was a sobering thought.

Lately, he had seen the world differently and the idealism he carried on his shoulder did not help him to stand tall but was in fact the burden that had kept him bowed to the needs of others. The relationship with Abigail had been flawed from the very beginning and Alex had been the glue that had stuck them haphazardly together.

Steve saw Jim often and Jim with his non-judgemental common sense helped him to see the greater good. Steve realised the selfishness of men. It was their birth right to have progeny and once delivered they could sit back. It was the frailty of leaving no human mark on the world that hurt him. There would be no-one to research him as their ancestor. His family tree ended with him. It was true he had nephews and nieces but there would be no direct line. Clive Corneille had taken the one thing he had cared about the most.

Jake called on Diana the very morning when she was to confront Gillian about Alex. It could not be helped and indeed, Jake cheered her up enormously. He wanted to prune some of the bushes in the back corner and set to in the cold, whistling as he cut and chopped. He had been transforming the little garden since she had engaged him as a gardener. He was good company too. They seemed to have the same sense of humour and she often made him a coffee and he would linger chatting before moving to his next job. Gillian's presence made this more difficult but perhaps it might be a distraction after her frank confession about Steve. Diana was not one to dwell on difficulties.

"This marriage between Samantha and Alex, it can't happen you know." Diana got straight to the point employing a force of will.

"Why not?" Gillian was surprised. "I thought you would be pleased." It was clear to Gillian that Diana was a snob. She had thought the years had taught her to be better than that but clearly not. Gillian was affronted as her younger self would never have been.

"I think it is time I came clean." Diana gathered herself, "They are related."

Gillian had no idea what she meant. "I know, there is no blood actually but they are step-brother and sister. I don't think it would be right."

Gillian's brain tried to reason the statement and gingerly she asked, "How?"

"Louise is Alex's half-sister." There it was, it was said, all out into the open. There was no hiding anymore.

Jake knocked on the patio door. His grin deflected the repercussions. Diana hurried to inspect the work leaving Gillian momentarily stunned.

Jake was particularly 'chipper' and could not wait to share his news with all and sundry. It was the most fantastic story. Jake had a sunny not sullen disposition so there were no recriminations for his mother, only awe for what she had endured and a joy to have her back in his life. He had taken her to the nursery and she had been introduced to Bill and Anthea. She had met Steve too when he was picking up a load of fencing in his truck but she had not met Simon who had been grinding out the post holes on site.

Jake could hardly wait to introduce her to everyone he knew and proclaim 'This is my mum and what a beautiful mum she is.' He was a bit more bashful than that though.

Diana bustled about to get him his customary coffee with Jake having removed his boots leaving them on the patio and Gillian quietly processing information. It was a strange combination, a young man bursting with his news and Gillian trying to absorb hers.

Jake produced his new phone. It had been an expense but he argued it was good business sense to have the technology and he found the photograph of his mother. He looked at it several times a day hardly daring to believe.

"Want to see a picture of my mum?" He curled his tongue around the word and smiled at the effect.

Diana was glad to be diverted and took the phone. The familiar face stared back at her.

"This is your mum?" She stared at the image.

"Yes, she turned up out of the blue. She'd been in hiding. I can't tell you why but everything is fine now and she found me. I can't believe it. I've got more photos," and he slid his finger to bring further images to her attention. All Diana could think was that she had found her missing daughter after forty years. She studied the image with reverence and then focussed her eyes on Jake. What would this mean to them all? Involuntarily her hand shook as she handed back the phone to Jake, her grandson.

"Show Gillian the photos, Jake, while I pop upstairs. Diana already in an emotional state had been overcome and needed to compose herself. When she returned, Gillian and Jake were happily discussing the event. Jake found Gillian an easy companion unlike the prickly Diana even though he felt a connection with Mrs Carstairs. Gillian was only too glad to take her mind away from the previous topic of conversation.

"We must meet her Jake," Diana proposed and added, "Yes, bring her here and we can get to know her." Jake was surprised but gratified. This was more than he could have expected.

"When shall we say? What about next week? Gillian, which day is best for you? What do you say Jake?" Diana was forcing the issue. She was leaving no room for refusal.

Jake took his leave promising to get back to her and thinking what a hospitable woman Mrs Carstairs was.

Gillian was also anxious to go, although did need to clarify one thing. "You mean Clive Corneille is Louise's father?"

Diana looked blankly at Gillian. Her mind was still occupied by Jake.

"You said about them being step brother and sister. I had no idea you would have known a man like that all those years ago but then Abigail did, although she wasn't at school with us and no-one mentioned Clive, I'm sure."

"I didn't know Clive Corneille. I've hardly met the man and quite frankly I would be much more discerning." Diana dismissed the allegation which she could not understand.

"So he is not Louise's father, then who is?" The penny dropped.

"Oh my god! It is Steve isn't it?"

Diana had the good grace to hang her head in shame. "It was a long time ago and it was different then."

"Why didn't you tell me before?" She had gone cold. Would she ever be free of the past?

"What would it have achieved?"

"But now," Gillian assessed Diana and she laughed. She could not help the chuckle. Life was so unpredictable she thought, no matter how hard you tried to harness it there would always be twists and turns and lessons to be learnt.

"And that is your only objection to Alex marrying Samantha?" She emphasised.

"Yes. I have reservations about Alex, I won't lie, but Samantha is a handful. You understand, don't you?" Diana, in the circumstances, thought she was being reasonable.

"But Alex is not Steve's son so that's alright, isn't it? He's Clive Corneille's son. Steve is heartbroken, not that you would understand. Everything turns out well for you as usual Diana. I'm going. Thank you for the coffee."

"Gillian, don't leave. I'm sorry. I really am. If I could turn back the clock, I would. It meant nothing, it really didn't. I can hardly remember it." For the first time in her life, Diana cried for another person.

"Insult to injury. You take the biscuit." Gillian had found her voice which was at last being heard.

"I made a terrible mistake like many young girls. Gillian. I need you. I do." Gillian looked scathingly at Diana.

"It's not the mistake as you put it Diana, it is your complete lack of integrity. You have no honour."

"Jake's mother is Louise, Gillian. She's my daughter," Diana sank to the chair exposing a fragility that Gillian could not ignore. Gillian's natural compassion had always been her Achille's heel.

They talked as they had never talked before, as equals. Gillian was able to censor Diana and Diana felt humbled by the friend she had neglected. Their histories were intertwined. It was impossible to disentangle the strands that had become enmeshed to the extent that in places the fusion was solid and dependable. They knew and understood the core of the other. Louise was the nucleus of their relationship.

They agreed to meet Louise together. Gillian thought Steve too should be there but Diana felt that would be too overwhelming and pleaded with her friend to wait. It was for once a meeting of minds.

Louise had recognised the name so was prepared and keen to see what had happened to her mother in the intervening years. She was not ready to forget but for Jake's sake she might forgive.

There was no mistaking the kinship between Louise and Diana and Gillian looked for evidence of Steve which she found in the gentleness of manner and the slight twist of her mouth. Diana sent Jake into the garden on the pretext of measuring for a new pergola she had seen.

"I know, you must despise me and I know I do not deserve forgiveness. It was a bad time and I was in a bad place and I treated you despicably." Diana was ready to eat humble pie.

Louise glanced at Gillian wondering why she was there. Diana interposed, "It was my friend Gillian who wrote the letter. She was there for me when you were born. I did not know she had written it. Gillian is a much nicer person than me."

Louise thought for a moment. "I see. When I came that day and met you, I could not understand the woman I saw and the sentiment of the letter which made it hard to take." Louise had been through difficult interviews, so was compassionate.

"I had no right to send the letter," Gillian said. "I wanted you to be loved and be happy."

"Perhaps not but you gave me years of hope and fantasy about a loving mother who cared and that made me a better person so I suppose it did more good than harm." Louise conceded.

"You are very kind," Gillian responded.

"It seems I have found two mothers and I didn't think I had one." Louise liked the women and if they were genuine she would not want to waste time. She would tread carefully but that did not mean she could not get to know them.

"I know, I have no right to ask but I do want you in my family, Gillian too. We both want you," and united they studied Louise.

When Jake returned with measurements, there was a relaxed air and the three women had opened a bottle of Prosecco. It seemed to be a celebration.

Gillian told Steve that evening. She was full of enthusiasm and love. Steve cried.

Jake had been a solitary young man and now he was overrun with family. Mrs Carstairs, Diana she insisted he call her, was a very glamorous grandmother, and on her side there were two aunts and an uncle, plus a cousin to be born later in the year and he had known his grandfather all along, someone he liked and respected, and another grandmother in Gillian plus an uncle Alex who was soon to be married to an aunt named Samantha.

It took a bit of getting used to but he gave it his best shot, although relished the comfort of returning to Ken and Kathy who had recently moved in together. When anything got too much, he found Mr Woodhouse. Whatever new family members had come his way he felt he belonged to Mr Woodhouse. Jim would forever be his icon.

Simon had driven hard and with the help of his friends the waste ground had been transformed. Steve had provided imaginative and practical ideas for a centre to support a youth football club with changing rooms and storage on one side and then connected to it through a glass corridor a complex that included a large place for meetings and bazaars and entertainments, a café area which opened on to comfortable lounge area; both surrounded by a patio for summer use, an indoor games area and toddler room separated again by another glass corridor so that participants did not disturb the quiet relaxation of the lounge and there were general rooms for office use, a technology room and small meeting rooms for hire.

The project had snowballed and, once the influence of the football club had become known, local businesses were eager to get on board. It was innovative and modern and yet timeless in appeal. Of all the things he had done Steve felt this was his finest and thus a legacy of which he could be proud. Steve's grandson Jake, Steve could not get used to the thrill of this word, and Bill worked on the landscape and garden area. It was open enough to ensure security but with sufficient private seating for discreet conversation or quiet contemplation. They installed fountains to calm troubled minds. Both would have liked to include pool areas but health and safety issues made the risk too great. It was all a labour of love. Jim would mosey over and give his views. By the end of April 2009 when spring would burst forth in vibrant colours it would be ready to open.

The opening took place one Saturday at the end of April when amongst threats of rain circulating round the country, in Stonebrook, a suburb of Marketborough, the air was clear and bright which matched the buoyant mood of the participants. Simon, Steve and Jake made an early start checking and rechecking. Louise had discreetly got involved at the request of Ken and organised catering.

Alex had unearthed a couple of lucrative charity trust funds that could be used to maintain the centre, although Simon hoped that the place could be self-sufficient. It did mean that they could go ahead with confidence and appoint a caretaker. Ken gave up his job at the factory to take the position and Kathy left the pub to take over the café. Jim's only regret was that Ida was missing.

There was one union still to be made, long delayed but fitting for that day. Simon surveyed the scene as well as his life. His army life had given him satisfaction of being with a team and relying absolutely on that team but this group of people were diverse in age and outlook and circumstance and yet they had come together like a team working towards a common goal. They were not professional soldiers highly trained automatically slipping into a role. They were together through good will and belief and decency. They did not fight under orders—they came voluntarily for a common good. He watched people moving hither and thither laughing and chatting, urgent to have all ready for the two o'clock start. He saw Steve with an arm briefly reaching protectively around Jake's shoulders as they both shared a joke with Alex and Samantha. Kirsten a child swelling her belly was with her mother and Gillian while Antony and Mark had heads together no doubt wrestling with some knotty financial conundrum. Ken was perambulating, greeting everyone as a genial host and he knew Kathy was in the kitchen sorting things with the caterer. She would start work the following week. Phillip, who had been on duty at the hospital, had just arrived and Simon watched as he made his way to his family. He was glad he had made all of this possible. Bill and Anthea were sitting on a bench with Jim. Seeing the three of them made Simon's heart swell and he blinked his eyes losing focus for an instant. When his sight was clear, a woman stood still and silent before him like an apparition from inside his memory.

"Hello Simon."

She was there, a real live breathing person, someone never forgotten.

"Jackie." He stood.

"It's Louise now Simon, my birth name."

She was serene and soft yet there was a composure that he had not known before.

"I wrote." He said, "I wrote several times but you never answered."

"I did not get the letters, Simon. I thought you did not care."

"I cared. I've always cared." He looked at her, drinking her in with shimmering eyes.

Somehow, their feelings bled into each other.

Then Louise delivered the best gift of all. Together they looked at Jake, their son, their united future.

At two o'clock, a crowd gathered for the unveiling of the name plaque at the entrance by Jim. Amongst them were Tom Wilkes and his wife. He was off-duty, although never quite leaving the law behind as he picked out Carl with his young family in the crowd. It looked as if Liz was giving him an ear-bashing as the toddlers tried to escape her clutches. Carl, now flaccid in appearance, had joined the ranks of the ill trodden.

Carl saw Tom and he called over, "Hey Inspector. I used to play football here. It was me that coached them all. If it hadn't been for me getting the team going, we'd never have got this place."

Tom exchanged a knowing look with his wife.

Jim stood in his best suit as upright as he could manage and shaking slightly with emotion drew the cloth away. He needed his stick to secure his balance as he read the words inscribed.

"The Jim and Ida Woodhouse Centre

Opened on 25 April 2009."

Simon and Jake reached him together. "You made this possible." The photographer from the local newspaper took the picture that would appear the following day.

That evening the group congregated to assess the day and bask in the glory of it. There was even more news as Alex and Jake with Bill's approval had signed a deal. Alex and Samantha were going to develop the old sheds at the bottom end of the nursery as a fine dining restaurant and later a beauty salon. Steve had a new design project for his attention. Immediately ideas flowed and everyone wanted their slice of involvement.

Jim made the comment that summed so much up.

"I am nearly at the end of my life but it is like a new beginning," and Gillian remembering a verse from her schooldays when students had actually learnt great swathes of text quoted a verse from Rudyard Kipling.

Cities and Thrones and Powers
Stand in Time's eye,
Almost as long as flowers,
Which daily die:
But, as new buds put forth
To glad new men
Out of the spent and unconsidered Earth,
The Cities rise again

Cities and Thrones and Powers   Rudyard Kipling

There was general mild applause with Steve touching her hand in awe and looking into her eyes saying with some feeling, "Plenty of new beginnings here."

Samantha never one to hold back, "A summer baby," and she grinned at Kirsten who modestly dropped her gaze before Diana leapt in with, "And another wedding to organise," as she smiled at her second daughter, "and I will have Gillian's help this time." The friends had found harmony once again.

"Funny how weddings crop up in pairs," mused Antony. "No-one thinks of a father's pocket."

"Or threes," Ken could not resist adding while Simon said, "And maybe more," nudging Louise.

Before there was any comment Alex butted in, "Actually, I am convinced there will be a Spanish wedding before too long as well." The group looked to him for elucidation.

"Mum has this expat in tow, who seems besotted," and at this his eyes rolled, "his name is Gordon and guess what, he was in insurance as a risk-assessor. I don't think he could have been very good at his job. He has not assessed the risk of a relationship with Mum very well." There were various chuckles and knowing looks.

"Well, Mr Woodhouse," said Jake in a serious voice, "it looks as if we're the only two bachelors left here so we'll have to get cracking." He winked. "I think you'll beat me to it though, judging by all those ladies who would not leave you alone today."

The glasses were replenished and toasts were made to anything and everything in the euphoria.

They had come together as though they were grains of sand in an egg-timer, packed tightly at the narrow neck before fate and fortune may take their toll as they tumble onwards.

In later years, no-one would be able to recapture this time and this place except in memory. They would find new and different challenges to overcome but whatever they were, this group had been indelibly united in their past and that would live with them forever.

Printed in Great Britain
by Amazon